Down Town

MERCER
UNIVERSITY PRESS

Endowed by
TOM WATSON BROWN
and
THE WATSON-BROWN FOUNDATION, INC.

Down Town

The Journal of

James Aloysius Holcombe, Jr.

for Ephraim Holcombe Mookinfoos

Ferrol Sams

Mercer University Press
Macon, Georgia

Published by Mercer University Press
1400 Coleman Avenue
Macon, Georgia 31207
All rights reserved

First Printing, May 2007
Second Printing, July 2007
Third Printing, January 2008

This is a work of fiction. All the people and events are
either fictitious or used fictitiously.

Books published by Mercer University Press are printed on acid free
paper that meets the requirements of American National Standard for
Information Sciences—Permanence of Paper for Printed Library
Materials.

Library of Congress Cataloging-in-Publication Data

Sams, Ferrol, 1922-
Down town : the journal of James Aloysius Holcombe, Jr. for
Ephraim Holcombe
Mookinfoos / Ferrol
Sams. -- 1st ed.
p. cm.
ISBN-13: 978-0-88146-072-8 (alk. paper)
ISBN-10: 0-88146-072-9 (alk. paper)
1. Georgia--Social life and customs—Fiction.
2. Georgia—History—Fiction. 3. City and town life—Fiction.
I. Title.
PS3569.A46656D69 2007
813'.54—dc22
2007012030

To Helen (of course)

Chapter 1

Whenever Richard Cory went down town,
We people on the pavement looked at him:
He was a gentleman from head to crown,
Clean favored, and imperially slim.

Whenever Major Cofield went down town, believe you me, folks around here sure looked at him. He was different.

Where he had come from before the war was never clear in anybody's mind, but he had first appeared in our section of Georgia a few months ahead of the Battle of Kennesaw Mountain and just after the gallant J. B. Hood of Texas played hell in Tennessee. Old man Higham Thompson let him and his platoon of Rebel soldiers camp in his pastures and use his barns for their horses. The Major and Mr. Thompson got to be friends, and he was always in the Big House when he and his men weren't scouting around for supplies for Joe Johnston's troops.

They all had to leave to fight at Kennesaw, it was said, and nobody heard a word from any of them until after Appomattox. In the meantime, Sherman had damned well ruined all of Georgia. Our town was out of his beaten path, but the old folks said you could see the smoke rising when he burned Atlanta. Old man Thompson died and left his wife, who everybody said was a heap younger than he, with a little baby girl and a thousand or so acres of land out east of town almost to the county line. Things quickly went from bad to worse for the widow Thompson.

Everybody in my generation has heard the horrors of Reconstruction, and we tried to match those legends with our own memories of the Great Depression, but in reality Reconstruction was worse. It was hard-scrabble existence rather than living, what with no labor for the farms, no salt, sugar, or coffee; everybody had to raise what they ate or else do without. The few men who did make it back after the war pretty well had their pick of women or young girls to marry, since most of the able-bodied young men had been killed; the Confederate cemeteries all over the South attest to that.

Well, soon as the fighting ended, here came old Major Cofield riding into town on as fine-a-looking horse as anybody had seen in many a year. He rode directly out to the Thompson plantation and within one week had married his friend's widow. There was a heap of widow women around, but unless they also had a heap of land, they didn't stand a chance against the pretty young virgins.

Major Cofield set tongues to wagging when he married Widow Thompson, and there were those who said he had got her big with that baby girl before he ever left for Kennesaw, since Higham Thompson had been married to his young bride for five years and never got her pregnant. Lo and behold, within ten years there were four little Cofield boys running around, and folks quit saying the Thompson plantation and started calling it the Cofield place.

Hundred-and-forty-year-old gossip may not jerk your neck, but it meant a lot to folks back then. About all they had to hang on to was inherited gentility and the love of Jesus Christ, and most of the time it wasn't even a dead heat between the two. Gentility always came out ahead, and it was supposed to be fostered, nurtured, and propagated by the womenfolk.

The names the Major hung on those boys have been a point of some interest to the more sophisticated Cofield watchers. Nobody ever assumed that Mrs. Cofield had a blamed thing to do with naming them or anything else, for that matter. Everybody assumed that the Major's creed was "Big I and Little U." The oldest boy was named Percy Putnam Cofield, and his brothers were John Deschamps, Edward Schofield, and Betsill Marmaduke Cofield. They all grew up being called by their first names, except for the youngest who was known by his initials, and in those days nobody thought anything about it.

Percy, the eldest, died of membranous croup when he was eight years old; there wasn't anything the doctor could do to save him. The Cofields were Methodists, and the Major had given the congregation three acres to build a church on one end of his farm where the land was too poor to grow cotton. He also gave them the lumber to build it. The Cofields didn't have kith nor kin, and the Major let it be known through church members that they didn't want any condolence calls when their boy died, and furthermore it was to be a funeral by invitation only.

Well, sir, there weren't any invitations. They only had the preacher and themselves, and the rest of the county felt shut out. Some were hurt and some were mad, but from that day on the Cofields have been prime targets for community interest, speculation, and gossip. There is still a marble angel with Percy Cofield's name on it out in the woods near the county line.

Mrs. Cofield lived on for about five more years, but folks say she just gave up and dwindled away. The youngest boy by then was one year old and the little girl was twelve and beginning to blossom. The Major figured he could raise the three boys by himself with some live-in help, but he sent the little girl, who was supposed to be a Thompson, to live with her mother's sister.

Turned out Mrs. Cofield was from Tennessee or some place like that, and how old man Higham Thompson met up with her in the first place is a big gap in the local folklore. There's no sense in asking any of the descendants at this late date, for by now everybody has discovered the new industry of genealogy, and it turns out nearly everybody in Georgia came down from nobility some place back there.

Through Virginia, of course; I sure haven't yet heard anybody bragging about landing here with Oglethorpe.

The three boys were sent to the little neighborhood school Miss Emma Cottongim had started up in one of her family's outbuildings. Miss Cottongim did not tolerate foolishness or mediocrity in her students. She was a spinster, the last survivor of a proud clan, and she was a gifted teacher and an impartial disciplinarian. There were no public schools in that era and hers was acknowledged as the very best. If a student misbehaved, she spanked him. If a student was lazy and would not apply himself, she dismissed the student, harnessed her horse to her buggy, took the student home to his parents, and refunded their money; always with the admonition that the parents should concentrate on teaching him manual skills, for he sure and certain would never make a living with his brain. If the child was brain-impaired, she still refunded the money but was much gentler in her advice.

Two of the Cofield boys finished Miss Cottongim's school at the seventh-grade level, which was as far as she took students. The youngest got a buggy ride from Miss Cottongim at the end of the fifth year; she didn't refund any money, but she gave her regular little talk to the Major. Gently. That woke up the other two, for they had a pretty graphic picture of how the Major interpreted manual skills. They all learned to read, write, and do arithmetic. They were especially good in addition, subtraction, fractions, and long division. They loved multiplication. That was genetic.

The only real anecdote I heard on the boys was about Johnnie, the middle one. When I knew him he was bald as an onion, but they told it on him that when he was young he had a real crop of red hair that grew every which way on account of so many cowlicks. One January morning he decided he was going to get it tamed and slicked down before he went to school. So he slipped in the kitchen after breakfast and got his hair all wet down good with ham gravy. He could comb it and even part it like his brothers, and he felt pretty good about himself. It was the middle of January with ice all over the ground, and by the time the boys had walked to school, the ham gravy had set up and congealed all over his head so that it looked like pink lard.

Miss Cottingim took pity on him, threatening to whip anybody who laughed, and she let him sit up close to the stove so his head could thaw. It did just that in a pretty big way, and his hair sprang up like a rabbit getting out of a trap. Everything would have been all right except that the melted gravy ran down his neck into his shirt and he smelled like breakfast for the rest of the day. He was grown and bald before he could laugh about it, but his brothers had fun with it.

The Major was as stern a teacher at home as Miss Cottongim was at school. Despite his standing as the most prosperous man in our county after the war, he saw to it that his boys became good farmers, and they worked in the fields, tended to livestock, slopped and killed hogs, milked cows, and cut stove wood just like everybody else.

From an early age he passed on to them his hard driving ambition and his commitment to making money. He also taught them the importance of sticking together. I guess that was from his army days. It is reported that he drilled into all three of them, "You don't fight one Cofield; you fight all of them." As an illustration, he took a piece of string and told each boy to break it, which they did. Then he took the three pieces of string, plaited them together and invited each boy to try and break that. It must have been a good object lesson because the longest day they lived nobody ever heard of a single instance of disagreement between those three brothers, not even after they were grown, married, and had children.

Now, that's saying something.

Furthermore, when they came to town, we people on the pavement stopped and looked at them and talked about them and speculated, just as our parents had done to their father. I don't care what anybody says about them; they were leaders.

Some folks loved them and some folks hated them, and I guess that's a pretty good definition of leadership.

When they were all in their early twenties, the Major up and died on them. They finished out that year's crop and were somewhat disappointed at the financial rewards for all their labor. Halfway through the next year's crop, they sat around by the kitchen lamp and got to figuring and speculating.

When they got all the figures added up, it turned out that they had paid out a heap of money to other folks for the dubious privilege of busting their asses in hard labor and all kinds of weather on their ancestral land.

"What we need is a bank," said Mr. Johnnie.

"Yeah, and a seed and fertilizer store," said Mr. Ed.

"What about selling them newfangled automobiles?" contributed Mr. B. M.

Well, no seed ever planted in rich, honest Georgia soil sprouted more quickly than the ideas of that night.

"We need cash," said Mr. Johnnie.

"How much?" said Mr. Ed.

"A heap."

"How we going to get it?" said Mr. B. M.

"Hmmm," said Mr. Johnnie. "Let's study on it a while."

So they did.

Mr. Johnnie and Mr. Ed spent a lot of time in town, easing around, talking to lawyers and checking out business requirements and such. Mr. B. M. stayed on the farm to supervise the hands and the sharecroppers, although the latter didn't need much supervising. They knew they had to work from sunup to sundown to pay out of debt to the Cofields in the fall, and how they managed to have as many children as they did has always seemed like a physiological marvel to me.

First thing the boys did was to plait themselves together for their lifetime by forming a company or corporation or whatever they called it back then under the title of "Cofield Brothers."

The very next thing they did was put Mr. B. M. on the train to Chattanooga to buy out their sister's (or half-sister's—your pick) share of the family land. She had married and had a baby, and Mr. B. M. struck such a sweet deal with her that in later years she refused to speak to him.

Then they did an unheard-of thing for that era, since everybody was still remembering too vividly how so many folks had lost their land after the war because of unpaid taxes, and that's how the white sharecroppers had got started.

They mortgaged the homeplace.

"Johnnie, are you out of your mind?" said Mr. Ed.

"How else you think we going to get started if we don't have some capital?"

"What you got in mind, Johnnie?"

"I've got in mind buying up land around the courthouse square and building a store, maybe selling some of them new Ford automobiles everybody's talking about, and starting a bank and also a lumber mill."

"Hmmm. Good God, Johnnie, you're thinking big. You think it's safe?"

"You want to spend your life working like slaves and giving the biggest part of what you make to merchants and bankers?"

"Let's do it."

"Don't want no mortgage on homeplace," said B. M., tersely.

"Just set back and take things easy, B. M. Me and Johnnie gonna look after you."

"All right, I guess. Don't like Bud Bazemore get a handle on us. Done swallowed up heap farms around here."

"Don't you worry, B. M. We ain't got the first intention of borrowing from old man Bazemore's bank. We paid him off last month; we're going to Newnan and get our mortgage. Hell, I aim to run old man Bazemore out of business!"

And so they did.

They bought a brick building on the courthouse square from one of the Perdues, David, I think. His daddy had given every one of his boys a store building on the courthouse square and a thousand acres of land when they got married, but this one had got used to having slaves wait on him all the time. Also he had been sent off somewhere up north to college. At any rate, he had no stomach for farming or working with his hands, and Mr. B. M. bought the building, which the Cofield brothers turned into a bank. Also some land. Cheap. Mr. Perdue moved off up to New York, they say, and got real rich speculating in land and such up there. Things were rough in the South, but I've always heard things were booming up North after the war.

The Cofields bought up one whole side of the courthouse square next to the Griggs House, which was the hotel in town and sat on the street that ran down to the railroad. This made it easy for the drummers to find, and Mrs. Griggs was a real lady and set a good table. Kept a henhouse out back, so fried chicken was available quick. The Cofields built a store right across the alley from the hotel and put the building for their automobile dealership right next to that.

In fact, Mr. Johnnie stayed in the Griggs House while all this building was going on, and he fell in love with one of Mrs. Griggs's daughters, Miss Beauty was her name, and after a short courtship up and married her about a year after they built the store.

Well, sir, those Cofield brothers had sure come to town. You can bet all the folks stood and looked at them. It seemed like almost before you could say Jack Robinson they had a bank, a general store, and our first car dealership going. In addition to that, they saw the need for it and put in an icehouse and a lumberyard. Everything they did set the whole town to talking, but the brothers played like they never noticed it, kept business matters tightly confidential between themselves, and toted their heads. The Major would have been proud of them.

Mr. Ed Cofield was the next one to move to town. He built a big two-story brick house diagonally across the square from Mr. Johnnie, which left nothing but the courthouse between them, and it turned out they had designs on it. However, slow and steady wins the race and Rome wasn't built in a day and everybody learns as they go along.

The town was pretty well split between the Baptists and the Methodists. They were all true Christians, for they were as jealous of each other as the disciples of Jesus had been. Oh, they joked about it and even had joint services in alternating churches on fifth Sunday evenings. I always thought this was at the behest of the respective ministers, who had some tom-fool notion that Christian cooperation would contribute to peace in the land. The two churches would get together on fifth Sundays and sing hymns and visit with each other, but they never opened the doors of the church for new members on those Sundays, and it was sort of like a truce between the armies of the Lord. Underneath, there was a well spring of jealousy.

Mr. Bud Bazemore was a Baptist and the Cofield brothers were Methodists. It didn't take Mr. Johnnie long to size up this situation and use it to his advantage. His favorite scripture verse was, "Where a man's treasure is, there is his heart also"; Mr. Ed, incidentally, liked "Render unto Caesar the things that are Caesar's." And I can still imagine him in a toga.

A good many of the more prosperous Methodists had chafed for years under the thumb of old man Bazemore and were tickled pink to open accounts in the Farmers and Merchants Bank, a name which Mr. Johnnie shrewdly thought had more universal appeal than Bazemore Bank. Then Mr. Johnnie hired Hershell Cranford as teller, cashier, and general manager at the bank. Mr. Cranford was a Baptist deacon and had twelve brothers and sisters, and Mr. Ed started him off at a salary that was considerably higher than anything the Baptists had ever paid anybody. Plus, Mr. Ed had married a sister of Mr. Cranford's wife who had as big a family as her husband. Talk about guile and sedition. Those Cofield brothers may not have gone any further than the seventh grade under Miss Cottongim, but somebody in that bunch must have read *The Iliad*. It's a wonder they didn't change the name of our town to Troy.

That bank took off like a skyrocket and the store was showing a big profit. Mr. Johnnie had hired a member of another outsized clan in the county to run the store, plus they stocked everything from groceries to clothes and ready-made coffins. They kept the coffins stored in an upstairs room separate from the rest of the merchandise and rented two rooms at the head of the stairs to old Doctor Morris. Cheap. He had the biggest practice of any doctor in the county, and consequently had more folks who needed coffins. It wasn't that he wasn't as good as the other doctors, but all they had to treat folks with back then was calomel, purges, poultices, and laudanum.

Most folks died "in spite of all the doctor could do." That was in the days when people died because of God's will and not medical malpractice. Doctor Morris would go and sit up all night at the bedside of a pneumonia patient or a woman with a baby that wouldn't come, and nobody ever had anything but respect for him. My daddy said that one cold, wintry, and wet night, Doctor Morris had sat up all night long at a baby's crib in a sharecropper's shack about six miles out from town. Those folks didn't even have a kerosene lamp, just candles. Doctor Morris did everything he could think of to bring the baby's fever down and had even told the mother that the fever would break of its own after the turn of the night. It was getting on toward daylight and the baby kept getting worse and the fever going higher. And old Doctor Morris turned to the mama who had been hovering at his elbow all night, fetching cold rags and whatever he wanted.

"Shutie, have you by any chance got a bacon rind in the kitchen?"

"Why, yes, Doctor, I believe I do."

"Well, bring it to me, please ma'am."

"Whatcha goan do with it, Doc?"

"I'm going to grease this baby's butt with it."

"Oh, Doctor, will that help?"

"I don't know, but it sure as hell can't hurt anything."

My daddy told that for the truth, but I never found it fully credible.

Mr. B. M. sold Dr. Morris the first T-model Ford in the county. Cheap.

Mr. B. M. was the least loquacious of the brothers. He was good at figures, so good that he hardly even had to put any of them down on paper. This talent had sprung surprisingly from his brain long after Miss Cottongim had pronounced it dead. He disapproved of Mr. Johnnie paying the high salaries they did for folks to run the bank, the store, the lumber mill, and the ice house. Sometimes he grumbled, but never in public.

"Johnnie, no sense paying Cranford that much. He'd work for considerable less."

"B. M., stop and think how many kinfolks and Baptists use our bank just on account of Cranford."

"Yep. Still say you could get him for less."

"B. M., I intend to keep Hershell Cranford tied so tight to us that he'll feel like he's one of the family."

"Still too much."

When World War I came along, Mr. Johnnie asked Mr. Hugh Peppers to step across from the courthouse to the Ford place. Mr. Peppers was an elected county official, ordinary or clerk of the court, something like that, I'm not sure just which. Anyway, he was in charge of the draft in our county. He had married one of the Cunningham girls, who were such established members of gentility that they could step high, say anything they pleased, even cuss a little if you will and still be respected as ladies just because they were Cunninghams. Their mama even smoked cigarettes when they first came out and drank liquor, too.

She told Mr. Peppers, "Hugh Peppers, you're not marrying one of my girls and settling her down in that little three-room house in my backyard. Since you've got her pregnant, you're sure as hell going to marry her, but I'll give you just two years, and if you haven't built her a house suitable for a Cunningham, I'll horse-whip you till you're raw meat and then maybe shoot your sorry ass."

Mr. Johnnie told him, "Mr. Peppers, that's a fine house you've built up there on the hill the other side of your mother-in-law's house. Yes, sir. Fine house. I hear tell your wife's got it furnished nice, too."

"Thank you, Mr. Cofield. Thank you very much. And thanks to Mr. Ed at the bank or I couldn't have done it."

"Yes, Peppers, I know that. As you know, we've got this draft snatching men up from all over the county. My brothers and I are on the back end of that age group, but I understand they're not drafting anybody with a family. Is that correct?"

"Yes, Mr. Cofield. Not unless we have to go into a second or third list."

"Well, you know I've got two daughters and Brother Ed has a son. But Brother B. M. doesn't have any children yet. I would appreciate it very much if you'd see to it that he doesn't get called up. Yes, sir, we all would appreciate it very much."

"Well, Mr. Cofield, I can't guarantee anything. Especially about Mr. B. M. He's highly eligible, you know. You and Mr. Ed should be safe. For a while, at least."

Mr. Johnnie had already learned how to narrow his eyes when he was discussing business. In addition, he could do it without frowning or wrinkling his forehead. His hair had already left him all over the top of his head, but it still looked fierce and red on the sides, and there were pretty sizable tufts growing out of his ears. He leaned back in his chair and said, "I know you got three boys, Peppers, all of them single and right in the middle of the draft age. Is that right? And none of them has been called. Ain't that right, too?"

"Why, yes, Mr. Cofield, not yet anyway."

"Well, sir, I ain't real sure how you managed that, but I expect you to manage the same thing for me and Ed and B. M. Think you can do that?"

"Well, I'm not at all sure I can, Mr. Cofield. Regulations are pretty strict and I get inspected pretty often."

"I don't know about all that and I don't care, Peppers. All I'm telling you is I want the three Cofield brothers treated the same as the three Peppers brothers. You know, old man Harris already has six boys in training camp."

"Mr. Cofield, three of them volunteered."

"Mr. Peppers," and his eyes opened wide. They were blue. "How would you like it if we called your long overdue note at our bank? Reckon the Bazemores would cover it for you?"

"N-n-no, Mr. Cofield, I suspect they wouldn't. Everybody knows there's bad blood between the Bazemores and the Cofields. Mr. Bud Bazemore hasn't spoken to me since he found out I went to your bank."

"That's a pity, Peppers. In fact, it's a dirty, rotten shame for folks to feel like that."

He paused and chewed his cigar butt. "Maybe you could go to Mrs. Cunningham and see if she can help you."

Mr. Peppers stood up rather precipitously. "Mr. Cofield, on second thought, I'm pretty sure I can arrange to have your wishes accommodated. I have to get back to my office, if you'll excuse me, sir."

"Fine, Peppers, fine. Appreciate you coming over. Nothing like a nice chat with friends. Drop by anytime."

The next day Mr. B. M. sought out Mr. Johnnie. "Brother, I'm concerned about this draft. Picking off boys and men right and left. Afraid I might be next any day now. Don't want to go."

"And we don't want you to go, B. M. Why don't you get married and settle down?"

"Think that'd help?"

"Couldn't hurt. My wife's youngest sister would be a good catch for you."

"I know 'bout her. Ain'tcha wife got another sister?"

"Yes. But she has more prospects than the youngest and is probably not available."

"Middle sister's better looking. I'll study on it."

Mr. Johnnie seemed more like his daddy than the other two, and there was no doubt the Major had done his job well. The Cofield brothers were definitely plaited.

Mr. B. M. had opinions as terse and inflexible as his speech patterns. In his later years, when he was the only surviving brother, he told me about getting married. I knew that he had married a short-legged, duck-butted woman from Griffin, but I'd never heard how he met her. She also had buckteeth.

"Ed and Johnnie married and settled down. I decided it was time for me to do same. Johnnie's wife was Beauty Griggs. Had two sisters. One was my age. Sweet girl. Other one was younger. Skinny, too. Sharp tongue in her head. I called on the older one. Pretty good looking. Soft-spoken woman. Told her I was ready to get married and if she was interested I'd come a-courting. Thanked me but said she didn't believe she was interested. Got my hat and went home.

"Somebody told me Judge Samuels over in Griffin had a daughter 'bout twenty-five years old or so. Found her house and called on her one afternoon. Middle of July. Hot as blazes. Setting on the porch in the swing, fanning like crazy. Introduced myself. She invited me to set. Told her I was ready to get married. Heard she might be same frame of mind. Would she be interested. Said she'd heard of the Cofield family and yes, believed she would.

"Got married two weeks later. She was Baptist. Told her I was Methodist. Couldn't take on any closer ties to Baptists than already had. Said it didn't matter to her. So it was a done deed. Methodist preacher married us. Been church folks ever since. Raised our three children Methodist. Two girls looked like my side of the family. Boy spit image of his mama."

By a convoluted process, Mr. B. M., I reckon, had what might be called an arranged marriage. But he had set his head and arranged it himself. There are just some things you can't leave to a brother, no matter how smart he is. On rare occasions, stubbornness can be a fair substitute for intelligence.

At any rate, none of the Cofield boys went in the army and none of the Peppers boys did either. They all stayed in the county and learned to be men on a civilian basis. So far as I know, not a one of them ever got shot at, either.

Chapter 2

It didn't take long for the Cofields to shut down the Bazemore Bank. They burrowed in and just sort of slipped up on the blind side of the Bazemores, who had become as complacent over the years about financial standing as they had about their social status. Sort of like the Romans not paying much attention to the Visigoths until it was too late and they were swarming over the Aurelian Wall.

The Bazemores were town folk, well-to-do but not what you'd call filthy rich. They mostly ran their bank and, of course, as a result of unpaid loans and foreclosures, had accumulated a considerable amount of farmland out in the county. They were aristocrats and Baptists and hobnobbed with the Lewises, the Robertses, the Masks, and what was left of the Perdue clan. Most of those were female Perdues who had chosen mates judiciously and settled down in the land of their fathers. All those Perdue boys saw Atlanta or even New York City as the promised land and had hauled out of town as soon as they could arrange it.

Included in this group of local elite were the Melroses. They were the only Methodists in the upper stratum of Bazemore-dominated society. They were newcomers, so to speak, having moved in only after the Federal troops had been pulled out of Georgia. Where Mr. Melrose had come from was a little unclear, but he was the weaker side of that marriage. He was a little bitty man, so pencil-necked that his shirt collars were always too big for him and he looked like a long-stemmed dahlia stuck down in a bud vase that was too big, except he had only a smidgen of chin which made his Adam's apple a marvel to behold when he was talking or eating. His wife was the one who attracted attention.

She was about four inches taller than he, with the aquiline features of a French countess, including the pinched nose, down which she could look most tolerantly. She carried her shoulders squared and had an ample bosom assuring her femininity. She was regal in bearing, and when she walked, she did not glide, wiggle, or sway. That lady marched. Usually about one or two steps ahead of her husband. She had inherited considerable wealth and when, because of her noted frugality in dealing with local merchants, I questioned this, my daddy assured me that she was "rich as six inches up a bull's ass." The irreverent metaphor never quite fit with my vision of this extremely Victorian lady. She had married her one and only suitor who had read law with an elder lawyer in Covington and passed his bar exam. They moved into our town, bought a lot right next to Mr. Bud Bazemore's house, and built a fine Victorian house with curved mahogany stair railings and such furniture as was rarely seen. Most of it was uncomfortable.

She used a combination of ladylike and financial charms on Mr. Bazemore by inviting his wife to tea and depositing a considerable amount of money in his bank. In no time Mr. Melrose was appointed justice of the peace, and his wife bought a two-story brick building on one corner of the Bazemore side of the courthouse square, furnished him a downstairs office with hard, wooden chairs and an impressive law library, and rented out the upstairs to various tenants. She referred to her husband ever after as Judge Melrose. I still do not know his first name. She confided once to Mrs. Cunningham that Judge Melrose had never seen her feet without stockings on, and it was disgraceful the way these young women were wearing sandals in public and showing their bare toes. I relayed this information in some disbelief to my father, who was a friend of Judge Melrose. Daddy replied laconically, "Son, did you ever fuck a checkbook?" The Melroses had one child.

Everybody in town looked up to Mrs. Melrose, one way or another, and she looked down her nose at everyone in town, one way or another, sometimes kindly, sometimes disapprovingly, but always stately. You had to make your own way there.

Well, everything in our town had been pretty stable under the Bazemores for a decade or so, but anybody who crows long enough on top of the dunghill is bound to stir up some envy in the ones below. You season this with a little greed and eventually there's going to be some conflict. Usually interesting.

Well, bless Pat if Mr. Ed Cofield didn't build his house right next to the Melrose house so that Mrs. Melrose was situated between the Bazemores and the Cofields. She kept an eye on both of them. And enjoyed it. She had a special swing on her front porch which, I thought, must have been designed by none other than Mrs. Melrose herself. It was standard wicker and it was white, but it was a two seater. Half of it faced east toward Mr. Bazemore's house; the other half faced west toward Mr. Cofield's house. Mrs. Melrose usually sat facing west. She did needlepoint. Carlotta, her daughter, did fancy embroidery. Both of them had long necks but Carlotta had inherited her father's chin, or rather his lack of one. Between them they had the comings and goings of the neighborhood pretty well covered. Every time I saw that swing I thought of Millay's line:

> ...and you and the long necks
> Of neighbors sitting where their mothers sat
> Are well aware of shadowy this and that
> In me that's neither noble nor complex.

Mrs. Melrose and her daughter did relish a little scandalous titillation—and were not above sharing bits of information. With a select few, of course.

One of the high points of their lives together was the afternoon Mr. Ed Cofield took his shotgun after Mr. Bud Bazemore.

Before the Cofield boys hit town, the Bazemores pretty well controlled it. They owned the bank, lots of land, the livery stable, the telephone exchange, the cotton gin, and the newspaper. Mr. Bud's boy was mayor and had prospered mightily and had also been elected to the state House of Representatives. There he prospered even more mightily.

He had a wife who apparently was not easily pleased, for he had built three different houses for her, each one grander than the previous one. He had several notes outstanding at the bank, but what was to worry about that? It was Father's bank.

Mr. Bud had three children and they all called him Father. He was a tall man, portly, with a head of thick white hair. He wore white linen suits with a black shoestring tie and a white Panama hat. He had heavy jowls and eyelids and his face always looked on the verge of melting downward. He usually had a long brown cigar clamped in his lips. I never saw it lit, but it did displace his wrinkles to leeward. He was a physically vigorous man even in his dotage. Still filled, I assumed, like Moses, with his natural juices. He was a figure of unassailable dignity, and his children calling him Father seemed appropriate.

Anyway, the Cofields came to town and Mr. Bud's world crumbled around him. First, the T-model Fords put the livery stable out of business. Then Mr. Ed Cofield ran against his boy for mayor and won. Then Mr. Johnnie ran for state representative and won. Then, to top it off, the bank failed. All notes on Mr. Bud's boy got called and that boy sold every lickspittle thing he owned and moved off to Atlanta. Last I heard of his wife, she was still not happy.

Mr. B. M. Cofield bought the last house the boy had built and moved into it. It was two-story brick and faced across two streets squarely in view through a pecan grove of the Melrose front porch.

The one thing the Cofields had overlooked was the newspaper. Mr. Bud was the owner, publisher, and editor. He was a well-educated, literate man; practiced law on the side. He wrote all the editorials in the paper, and various ladies from different communities around the county contributed columns of local interest. It was a weekly paper and was called *The Enterprise*, the title printed boldly in large Old English script across the top of the front page. Being the only paper in the county, it was anticipated and conscientiously read every Wednesday afternoon.

Mr. Bud had lost his wife; his son and one daughter had moved way on off; and he was reduced to living in that great big house with his other daughter who was a widow woman. She had some means of her own but she revered Father and devoted herself to caring for him in his later years. In addition to that, "those damn Cofields" had moved him off the top of the dunghill to the backside of the barnyard, where he scratched and pecked and clucked around but didn't do much crowing. The Bazemores still had the cotton gin and warehouse in town, and had plenty of money coming in. Their coterie of friends was still politically loyal, but it was obviously much smaller since the people in our town had elected "that damn Ed Cofield" as their mayor.

It was politics that really stuck in Mr. Bud's craw. He had been mayor for years, and after him his boy. Nowadays we would have called his son Bud Lite, but back then his nickname was BB, which stood for Bazemore Boy. After Mr. Ed Cofield beat BB for mayor and the bank busted and BB sold all his houses and moved his wife to Atlanta to make her happy, Mr. Bud kind of dwindled for awhile. His daughter was a true lady, a Baptist who actually believed in forgiveness and was even pleasant to all the Cofield children who had pretty much gone to school with her and couldn't help what their parents had done. She counseled and consoled Mr. Bud and saw to it that he went to his law office and the paper every morning all spic and span and with a fresh cigar. In other words, as they said back in those days, she kept sand under his feet.

Mr. Bud in public seemed as jovial as ever and got to where he'd say "good morning" to Mr. Ed when he walked past his house on the way to town. He never, the longest day he lived, however, did anything but grunt and roll his cigar to the other side of his mouth when he ran into Mr. Johnnie and Mr. B. M. Of course, he tipped his hat and bowed if their wives were with them, which was not very often. Mr. Bud had his principles, but he was also a gentleman. We people on the pavement looked at him. And the Cofields. And waited.

So did Mr. Bud. Wait, that is.

Now, in our town politics gets to be a very personal matter. I know that public service in a democracy is supposed to be a noble calling and its participants are supposed to be devoted to a particular agendum and put service before self. Julian Bond has been quoted as saying a little defiantly, "Watch that baby shake that thing; we can't all be Martin Luther King."

Well, local politicians can't all be George Washington either. That maxim may well hold true on a state and national level also. Seems like once you get elected to office around here, it gets to be a matter of prestige, power, and popularity, and sooner or later the more you manifest the first two the quicker you lose the third. Hereabouts the first thing that pops into an elected official's mind when somebody requests a favor is, "Did this sumbitch vote for me or not?"

In our town you pretty well knew, because people will talk and kinfolks usually stick together. We're still pretty tribal around here. Also they had poll watchers from both sides in those days who sat jam up close to the ballot box with a list of voters on a clipboard. Ostensibly they were there just to tick off who had voted, but they also wanted to put the eye on everybody whose vote had been bought and to be sure they voted right. If somebody hadn't shown up by three o'clock, a confederate was tipped off and sent to haul the miscreant to the polls. Elections have not been nearly so much fun since they passed all those laws, did away with the poll tax, and put in voting machines.

Mr. Bud had taken a severe blow to his vanity when the Bazemore name went under to Cofield in the mayor's race and then his candidate for representative got beat by Mr. Johnnie. He acted normal enough, but underneath he simmered. And plotted. He was not nearly as good a Baptist as his daughter.

And he still had *The Enterprise*.

On the pavement, we watched. And kept on waiting.

Mr. Ed Cofield had prospered. He had two children, a boy and a girl. The girl was the apple of his eye. The boy was not overly industrious; some folks said he was lazy, but he felt friendly most of the time. After Mr. Ed beat BB and had been mayor for about two years he made the mistake of buying his daughter a grand piano for her high school graduation. Everybody talked about it. Nobody else had ever even seen one.

Mr. Bud Bazemore wrote an editorial about it. It listed the price of that make of piano, the salary of the mayor, which was twenty-five dollars per month, the amount of debt the city had listed, and proclaimed that public officials should be as surely above suspicion as Caesar's wife; inferring unmistakably that there was some hanky-panky going on and that perhaps that piano had been purchased with tax money.

When Mr. Bud got right in front of the Melrose swing the afternoon *The Enterprise* hit the street, Mr. Ed Cofield stepped out from his front door with a double-barreled shotgun and hollered for him to stop. Mrs. Melrose and Carlotta stopped swinging. They enjoyed recounting the incident.

After calling Mr. Bud what he was in Mr. Ed's opinion, editing his remarks as much as he could because of the presence of ladies, but still alluding to Bud's ancestry, his physical appearance, and his sexual proclivities, he pointed his gun at Mr. Bud's belly and said, "I've a good notion to blow your g.d. guts all over this sidewalk."

Mr. Bud, unarmed, vulnerable, and also conscious of ladies, could not bring himself to run. He removed his cigar completely from his mouth and kept sputtering between each phrase of Mr. Ed's diatribe, "Now, Ed, you old buzzard you, don't do anything foolish, you old buzzard you."

Finally Mr. Ed said, "You're so g.d. sorry (I quote Carlotta) you ain't worth shooting." With that he raised his gun and fired both barrels into the air.

"*Blam! Blam!* it went," said Carlotta.

"It was more *Boom! Boom!*" said Mrs. Melrose. "It blew a limb out of our pecan tree."

"We jumped so that I dropped my thimble and didn't find it for two days, and Mother pricked her middle finger so deep it bled on her needlepoint."

"It was my index finger, Carlotta, but I soaked my work in a little cold water and saved it."

"Mr. Ed Cofield turned around and marched home. He slammed the front door so hard when he went in that I jumped again," said Carlotta.

"Mr. Bazemore, who knows quite well we've always voted for him and his side, tipped his hat to us, put his cigar back in his mouth, and went home. I wouldn't say he ran, but he did pick up his pace considerably. His back was straight as an arrow but I'm here to tell you he was stepping high. Of course we've never mentioned the incident between us and the Bazemores," said Mrs. Melrose.

"Of course not," echoed her daughter. "We wouldn't dream of it."

Now, that is a pretty good example of gentility in our town. Breeding will tell, they say.

And it sure does. Sooner or later.

Everything it knows.

Chapter 3

The Cofields became our leading family, not just in town but in the whole county. All of that was not due solely to their drive and financial and political success. A considerable part of it came from their marrying ladies. There's an old saying that if you want a girl to be a lady, start with her grandmother. From what I've seen, there's a lot of truth in that. Although occasionally I've thought maybe you should get on back to great-grandmothers or even beyond. Money sure won't do it.

All three of those Cofield boys had married women from good families and it showed in all their daughters. The old saying about boys in our town was "shirtsleeves to shirtsleeves in three generations," and that didn't hold with the two Cofield boys, but we'll come to that later.

Mr. Johnnie had four daughters and no sons; Mr. Ed had one of each; Mr. B. M. had two daughters and one son. All seven of those girls went off to college and graduated; both boys went off to college and didn't.

The first real bad thing that happened to the Cofields was that Mr. Johnnie's wife, who had been a Griggs, died about two years after her youngest daughter was born. The whole town was shocked and grieved; even Mr. Bud Bazemore and BB sent flowers. Separately, too.

Mr. Johnnie was a changed man. He looked after those girls and provided for them and loved them the longest day he lived. He never married again, either, although that was the customary thing for a man in that position to do. It wasn't for lack of opportunity. A lot of widows and spinsters set their caps for him for the next forty years. I never heard one breath of suspicion that he ever even had a girlfriend after Miss Beauty passed.

He had a spinster cousin about ten years older than he who was sort of genteelly destitute, you might say, and she moved into his big house and looked after his girls when he was out of town on business. She had snow-white hair, a full head of it, always restrained by a matching white hair net. She was so heavily corseted that she moved like an ocean liner. Her name was Miss Cynthia Gayflowers and she was a Baptist. This didn't stop her from getting the Cofield girls to the Methodist church, right after which she walked across to the Baptist church and played the piano for the BYPU. She taught piano lessons for extra money and the three youngest learned to play; the oldest one chose not to be bothered. She had a good business head on her, though.

All four of those girls grew up to be well thought of in the community. Had good reputations, too, although we watched the third one a little closer than the others. Mr. Johnnie doted on them and in all his political and financial shenanigans his daughters were sacrosanct. They did not go to the polls and hand out cards on Election Day; they stayed home and practiced on the piano.

Of course, on election night no females went to town. The deacons and stewards stayed home with their womenfolk, behind locked doors with a shotgun handy. The town went wild, and the men who weren't already drunk got that way after sundown while the votes were counted by hand, sometimes over and over. There were lots of gunshots, for everybody in those days carried a gun and the few who didn't carried knives which they were prepared to use on very short notice for functions other than cutting off a cud of chewing tobacco.

It was rare that anyone got killed. Dr. Morris had a good reputation for treating trauma as well as pneumonia. He lost more patients to the latter than he did the former.

The Cofields didn't drink. For one thing, they were all three on the Board of Stewards in the Methodist Church and faithfully went down to the altar every year on Temperance Sunday and signed the pledge that for the next year no alcohol would cross their lips. Also, Mr. Johnnie personally disapproved of it. He said that it clouded men's thinking both during and after drinking that stuff, and he had money in the bank from a lot of them to prove it. Men used very poor judgment about business matters and loans when they were intoxicated, even a little bit, Mr. Johnnie told his brothers. Where a man's treasure is, there is his heart also.

Things might have been a whole lot different if the next generation had listened to him.

After World War One when the soldiers came home, they organized the American Legion and the American Legion Auxiliary. The whole South was electrified and proud about winning that war. We were due one.

The Cofields and Peppers were not eligible, and their wives had to stick with the United Daughters of the Confederacy. The Auxiliary ladies had more to tolerate by way of marital alcohol than did the UDC. Those American Legion conventions could might near shut down Atlanta. The UDC was a serious and somber group; they saw to it that the schoolchildren all over the county marched to the cemeteries on Confederate Memorial Day and put flowers on the soldiers' graves.

The American Legion Auxiliary was made up of a much younger group of women by and large, although there was some crossover of women who qualified for both. The UDC may have had Memorial Day, but the Auxiliary had Armistice Day. They sold red paper poppies to raise money and held ebullient barbecues every November. The children enjoyed the trek to the cemetery in May because it was a welcome jaunt into springtime and usually came during geography class. That never quite measured up, however, to the excitement of roaming the streets to sell poppies and then gathering over barbecued pork and Brunswick stew after a ragtag parade through town.

Mr. Johnnie served two years in the legislature after beating BB, and then he ran for state senate and beat out Mr. Bud. He threw his support for state representative to his lawyer friend, Mr. Highsmith, and be blessed if he didn't win, too. For the next twenty-five to thirty years there they sat in the state capitol in Atlanta, getting more power and seniority every time they got reelected. They sure knew how to use it, too.

Georgia had the county unit system back then, and a voter in our county could cancel out six or seven hundred votes in Atlanta. There are one hundred and fifty-nine counties in Georgia, and go figure: the rural folks ruled the roost.

One progressive and forward lady in our town collared Mr. Johnnie one day on the street and told him that with all the power he had accumulated in state government, it did look like he could get one road paved somewhere in our county so we could get to Atlanta easier.

By then Gene Talmadge had come to power and Mr. Johnnie had taken to wearing suspenders, although his weren't red. He hooked both thumbs in his suspender straps, reared back, and said, "Lady, we don't want any paved road in this county. We might could get out easier, but you couldn't ever tell what might come in on one."

The lady fumed, but she had it coming. She belonged to the American Legion Auxiliary, her husband was a Bazemore supporter, and they were Baptists to boot. Mr. Johnnie wasn't about to spend any political capital at the suggestion of anybody who didn't vote for him, and on top of that kept all her money in an out-of-town bank. This may sound a little cold-blooded, but sometimes nowadays I look around our county and marvel at how wise Mr. Johnnie Cofield was.

Life sort of settled down for a while in the county and things hummed along. Here came woman's suffrage, and soon as they got the vote the ladies abandoned their long dresses, bustles, and high-buttoned shoes and diked themselves out in low-cut, long-waisted, bob-tailed dresses the like of which Mrs. Melrose had never dreamed. They even wore silk stockings that exposed their legs to public view, sometimes all the way up to their knees, and their slippers had such high heels that a lot of the ladies had to learn how to walk again. Dr. Morris for awhile got to be real expert in treating sprained ankles.

They commenced to rouging their cheeks and painting their lips and plucking their eyebrows and, hard as it is to believe, shaving their legs. The bolder ones gave up long hair in a hurry and quit cutting grapevines to get the sap for rinsing it after the weekly washing so the hair would shine. Some had what they called a "bob" and others a "shingle" and then here came the "permanent wave," and all of a sudden there was a new cottage industry of "beauticians" in our town. Mrs. Melrose finally unbent enough to get her hair bobbed—it was getting noticeably thin anyhow—but she never the longest day she lived had a dress that showed her knees.

Some of us in town think that she and Carlotta got together with the Bazemore girls after the short skirts came out and formulated the rule that ladies never cross their legs except at the ankles. When this rule was violated, the cruder males in town could boast that they had had their pictures taken.

With all this freedom and liberation, it wasn't too long before Mr. Johnnie's kingdom got challenged. It all came about, really, because of the American Legion and the county unit vote. You find a man who can capitalize on sympathy and is also shrewd enough to play on the envy and resentment poor dirt farmers have repressed for years toward what they regard as rich city folk, and you get a ready-made political base that's as hard to resist as the storming of the Bastille.

Not that I'm comparing our town and county to the French Revolution; no heads were chopped off or anything like that, but a heap of cussing got started that hasn't let up to this day. There wasn't any tidal wave that swept Mr. Johnnie off the top of his mountain; it was more a gradual erosion and an indication of things to come. Don't think he wasn't smart enough to see what was happening and sagacious enough to do something about it.

I will compare the political situation in our town and county to the city of New Orleans, built below sea level and potentially subject to destruction by storms or flooding from the Mississippi River. Levees and dikes are the answer.

Mr. Johnnie shored up his political base the best anybody could. By the mid-twenties he controlled every elected office in the county, one way or another, filling them with either kin or enthusiastic sycophants. There were occasional weak spots in the levees; some disgruntled free-thinkers might challenge one of his candidates, but the only votes they usually got were their kin, some neighbors, and of course the bitter hardcore of Bazemore supporters.

I mean, he had a satrapy as strong as Sulieman the Magnificent and all he had to do was put down occasional uprisings in his outposts. Most of them were inspired by the Bazemores and were overcome with ease. Mr. Johnnie rather enjoyed them; they kept his leaders in trim and made Mr. Bud hold his head a little higher, stomp a little harder, wear out a cigar a little quicker, and growl instead of grunt when he met a Cofield on the street.

Then, all of a sudden and unexpectedly, there was friction in the Cofield clan. The bank came up on hard times. There were rumors that it was about to fail. Enough customers began withdrawing their funds to weaken the bank's line of credit, and the whole river would have come crashing in on their heads if Mr. Ed Cofield hadn't up and died on them. It was pneumonia that got him, in spite of all Dr. Morris and the other local doctors could do. They even called in a specialist all the way from Atlanta, but Mr. Ed, the oldest and most dignified of the brothers, couldn't be saved when the crisis struck. Everybody was shocked. Most were truly grieved.

Mr. Bud Bazemore did not send flowers. His daughter did. Mr. Bud actually went into a decline for awhile and his daughter had a time working him through Mr. Ed's death. It's a real blow to a man when his most detested enemy up and dies on him. It creates a vacuum that's hard to fill; it's never as much fun again to cuss somebody else, and you've lost the person you could blame for everything.

Of course, Mr. Johnnie and Mr. B. M. were terribly grieved by Mr. Ed's death. I was too young to remember this, but later the gossip was that Mr. Johnnie's grief was somewhat assuaged by Mr. Ed's life insurance policy. It was a very considerable amount, and since the corporation had paid for it, Mr. Johnnie explained to the widow that it was not to be paid to her personally although she had been named beneficiary.

That money, they say, saved the bank. Mr. Johnnie had promised Mr. Ed that he would look after his wife if he didn't get through the pneumonia crisis, and he sure did. Mrs. Cofield wore black for the next twenty years and hardly ever left her house, even to go to church.

The bank rebounded and prospered greatly, and Cofield Brothers just kept on expanding, Mr. Johnnie's heart and treasure right along with it.

To placate Mr. Ed's widow and keep her from raising sand about the insurance money, Mr. Johnnie and Mr. B. M. had to take on the nurturing of Mr. Ed's son. This was a sometimes onerous chore for Mr. Johnnie, who had those four bright and beautiful daughters and was accustomed to commendable performance from Cofield progeny. Mr. B. M. was not so judgmental. He had two bright and beautiful daughters, but his own son did not leave him much room for concern about brother Ed's boy.

Mr. Ed's boy had been named Huntington Holsonbeck Cofield and don't ask me why. When his daddy died, he had a thing or two to say to his uncles about the insurance money, and they felt duty bound to placate him and find something he could do that would justify the Cofield Brothers paying him enough money to live on. He was a grown man, had already flunked out of two colleges, and had lived through two automobile wrecks, although the last one had banged him up pretty bad. He had several broken bones and a torn-up jaw that had to be wired together, and he spent more than a month in a big hospital with specialists of all sorts. Dr. Morris said it was a wonder he lived.

He was a changed man when those specialists and Mr. Johnnie got done with him. He gave away his raccoon coat and quit drinking white liquor. He started dating a pretty flapper from a good family in Atlanta, and they never drank anything but bottled in bond, no matter what it cost. Nobody ever called him by anything but his nickname, which was "Sport." After he married, his wife called him "Hunt," except on occasions when he was particularly obtuse she strung it out to "Huntington Holsonbeck Cofield, you-listen-to-me."

They ran him for mayor and he won by a landslide. After all, his daddy had just died and the sympathy vote is hard to beat in a small community. We had three little bitty dwarf sisters who lived on a farm with their normal-sized brother, and we elected one of them county tax assessor, which paid enough of a salary that they could live on it, and she held the office till the day she died, and nobody ever even thought about running against her. Nobody ran against Sport Cofield either, at least for some twenty to thirty years.

After he married and settled in the big house with his mama and his bride, Mr. Johnnie put him in charge of the Cofield Ford place. Then Mr. B. M. thought it would be a good idea for them to get in the funeral business, all of which was going out of the county, and they bought Sport a hearse and tried to get him to learn the art of embalming. Sport's mama put her foot down about having dead people embalmed in her house, and besides our town only had an open creek for sewage disposal, and on a still hot day it got pretty fiercely fragrant, you might say, and Mrs. Cofield didn't want dead people's blood added to it, at least not from her house.

You can imagine the name we gave the creek.

It didn't take Sport long to strike a deal with a big mortuary in Atlanta. He would deliver the properly shrouded deceased ceremoniously to Atlanta, wait for them to do the embalming, and then bring all the trappings and the real profit back to our town. Cofield Brothers sold some pretty fancy coffins in those years, and Sport got the profit from them.

He was slow-spoken, affable, indolent, and usually loyal to his friends. He raised two children to adulthood; so everybody loved him and his family. After all, he was a native-born son of our town. As long as Mr. Johnnie and Mr. B. M. lived, however, he walked in their shadow. They saw to that.

After they died, he walked in his wife's shadow. She saw to that. Or he just sort of ambled, I guess you could call it. He missed his uncles sorely.

The Cofield brothers were so occupied with Mr. Ed's death, getting his insurance straightened out and saving the bank, that Mr.

Johnnie failed to notice the rising political waters until they were lapping at his back door. Looking back, I wonder if Mr. Johnnie ever regretted getting Mr. Peppers to save the Cofields from the draft, for it was the American Legion that hit our county at the polls somewhat like a Class IV hurricane, or III at least.

Three of those WWI veterans got together and almost cleaned out the courthouse. They were from three separate sections of the county and each was a member of a sprawling clan of kinfolks, some of them heretofore loyal Cofield supporters when the only option they had was to vote for some weak-kneed Bazemore candidate. Those three would never have even known each other if they hadn't met at American Legion meetings, let alone joined up politically.

They needed jobs. Cotton had succumbed to the boll weevil and dropped to about ten cents a pound. Public service paid more than farming, and what's more the check came every month. If you once got elected, it was hard as the devil to unseat you; the Cofields had proved that.

The one who lost by the biggest margin was judge of the ordinary court. There wasn't a relative of any veteran in the county who didn't enjoy voting against Mr. Peppers, and he retired with what dignity he could muster to his big house on the hill, where his wife was getting more like her mother every day. He just kind of dried up and dwindled and his face got as white as his mustache. The only time he appeared in public after that was on Sundays, when he taught a class and sang in the choir. Methodist. As for his boys, we waited and watched. They got married and had families, but watch as we would they never amounted to much. Some of them didn't even have children. "If you won't fight..." may have some truth to it as well as the opposite.

Clerk of the court was pretty much of a pushover also. It went to a former second lieutenant who was tall and spare and sort of gray all over, from clothes to hair. His name was Mr. Wallace Watson and he was as much of a permanent presence around the courthouse for most of my lifetime as the clock in the tower. He blinked his eyes a lot and chewed tobacco, but he never raised his voice. He had a habit of looking over your head or shoulder when he talked to you, but he always seemed very sincere.

He never brought himself to the marriage bed. Or, for that matter, to any other that was ever discovered. He looked after his widowed mother until the day she died and was kin to half the western part of the county. He never had opposition at the polls after that first election. Even the Cofields supported him. He led what the ladies in town called a blameless life.

The third county office the Cofields lost was that of county school superintendent. It was the challenged position that Mr. Johnnie defended most vigorously and of which he took the defeat most personally. The county was divided into school districts, and Mr. Johnnie was chairman of the board of our town district. It had the only high school in the county and Mr. Johnnie saw to it that his district got the lion's share of tax money. He had installed a college-educated sycophant as a schoolteacher and later ran him for county school superintendent and, lo and behold, had himself another little mini-fiefdom in place. No one ever accused Mr. Johnnie of lacking ambition.

Chapter 4

Down in the lower end of the county, where no town boy ever showed up after dark if he had a lick of sense, no matter how sweet a little girl lived there, dwelled a whole clan of fierce and proud folks who fought among themselves occasionally but always turned a united front to outsiders that was as impregnable as a phalanx of Caesar's soldiers with their shields and spears and swords. They would *fight* you.

In the middle and then in the forefront of that clan a young man named Christopher Columbus Summerfield stepped forth. He was a veteran and a Legionnaire who had been wounded twice in France. He was discharged as a major in the infantry and never seemed to mind in later years if people called him "Major." On top of that, he had UDC credentials on both sides of his family. He was one of the few men in our county who had been to college, and after the war he got a law degree.

In college he had played football when they wore little leather helmets but had no padded uniforms. That was in the days before football became a business empire. It was a sport back then and a young man could vent anger and hostility, get his brains knocked out, and prove to the world and all the girls that he was not a wimp. The same attitude prevailed when Christopher Columbus Summerfield enlisted in the army and killed Germans. Apparently he never lost the willingness and readiness to fight. Or the opposite.

Mama said Mr. C. C. Summerfield was a charmer and had brought a lovely wife to the county. Mama said that was a blessing because he was kin to nearly everybody in his part of the county, and some of them had already taken to marrying first or second cousins. A lot of them were cross-eyed, Mama said, and some of them were just not right. Two or three of the women, she said, had nails that would split.

Mr. Summerfield had a host of nicknames. Lots of his kin called him Lum, a few of the ladies called him Christopher, nearly everybody else called him C. C. or Mr. Summerfield. Mr. Johnnie called him a heap worse on occasion but never where Mr. C. C. could hear him.

Mr. Summerfield campaigned on Tom Watson's coattails. Mr. Summerfield, like his mentor, became a "man of the people" who proclaimed that tax money for schools should be distributed equally and not hogged up by the elite of our town. Every school in the county should have qualified teachers and no little child in our county should ever again grow up illiterate. A lot of his dirt farmer supporters had not the faintest idea what illiterate meant, but it sounded dirty and low-down and they sure didn't want their kids to be one. On top of that, he got all the sympathy vote because of his wounds in the recent fight of our noble country against the Krauts or, as he occasionally called them, "the vicious Boche."

Of course, he accumulated the votes of everybody who had ever even thought of supporting the Bazemores, and Mr. Bud even got out and campaigned for him. The newspaper, needless to say, endorsed him as "that valiant and gallant young soldier who has returned to his homeland to protect it from internal enemies." Mr. Ed was safely dead and Sport didn't have any idea what had become of his shotgun.

Mr. Bud was wise not to worry about any other personal affront to his dignity or his person. Sport made the mistake of approaching Mr. C. C. in the drugstore while Mr. C. C. was smiling and shaking hands and handing out his election cards. I guess he thought he was going to look good to his uncles.

In front of a whole crowd of Saturday afternoon farmers and a few mill workers, he said, "Lum, you're wasting your time. Ain't no way a sorry Summerfield from out in the sticks can hope to whip our candidate. You have to look up to the Cofields for all they've done in this town."

With that Mr. C. C., quick as a cat, grabbed old Sport by the throat and lifted him plumb off the floor.

"You sniveling, snot-nosed little flunky, this is the only position in which a Summerfield will ever look up to a Cofield! You understand me? And, goddam your soul to eternal hell, if you didn't already have a broken jaw and it wired shut, I'd break it for you right now. And you can tell that onion-headed, cigar-smoking uncle of yours what I said."

Then he set him back on his feet.

Sport sort of looked around out of the side of his eyes, straightened his tie, and mumbled to Mr. C. C., who was still as red in the face as a turkey gobbler with his blue eyes all sparking wild, "Hell, Lum, I wasn't trying to insult your family. I apologize."

With that Mr. C. C. smiled, clapped Sport on the shoulder, and said, "Fine, young Cofield, apology accepted. Come on over and let me buy you a dope. When I'm elected, I'm going to look after all the children in this county, including yours."

Mr. C. C. got quite a number of votes that afternoon. A few folks even dug in their pockets and gave him a little cash to help with his election expenses. Sport did not tell Mr. Johnnie about this encounter, but someone did, and Mr. Johnnie summoned Sport to the Ford Place and upbraided him.

"You tell that pencil-legged, whore-hopping drink of muddy water that we'll meet him at the polls. And tell him what I called him."

Sport wisely chose not to be the messenger.

It was a tight election. Mr. Johnnie was not accustomed to paying more than two dollars and a drink of white liquor to the part of the electorate that was susceptible to such inducements. Mr. C. C. found out about it and upped the ante to five dollars and two swallows. On top of that, he not only charmed the female electorate but gave selected country women the promise of a permanent wave. The Bible says, "Vanity of vanities, saith the preacher, all is vanity." Mr. C. C. knew a thing or two about human nature.

Also, he had most of the UDC and all of the American Legion Auxiliary behind him, plus he was a Mason and had the Eastern Star as an almost solid block. They even had the Rainbow Girls giving out his cards.

He won. The vote was close, but positive. Count as they would, the Cofields had to admit defeat by almost a hundred votes. There was a lot of whooping and hollering and a lot of pistols fired that night when everybody got drunk, but nobody got shot. Dr. Morris did have to get out to sew up a couple of knifings and set the arm of a man who got so drunk he tripped over our little Confederate monument.

Our town loved an election. We didn't have movies or television back then, but we did have a good number of telephones with party lines, so communication was faster than you might think. Nothing could beat a murder or rape trial for entertainment except a red-hot election, and you could actually talk about the elections a lot longer. Like I said earlier, politics is a popularity contest.

I will say this for Mr. C. C., although my family and I have always been loyal to the Cofields: he did go to work on the county schools, even built a few new ones and got them out of the first floor of the Masonic buildings scattered around the county. *The Enterprise* made it a point to print a picture of the dedication every time with a complimentary editorial by Mr. Bud Bazemore, who loved to see a defeated Cofield and was not above rubbing a little salt into fresh wounds; it kept them open and smarting, you know.

Mr. Johnnie was busy in the State Senate and had been elected president of it; so he had become a figure of prominence throughout the state. Consequently, he wasn't able to spend too much time on the local level and his levee leaked a little more each year. Next election, be blessed if the Summerfields and Bazemores didn't run a candidate for sheriff.

Mr. Porter Griffin was a well-respected merchant out in one of the little towns in the south of the county. He had served time in prison for making liquor, but it was in the federal prison in Atlanta and not on our local chain gang. Folks in our county still didn't think much of the federal government, and his sentence gave Mr. Griffin a certain aura of martyrdom for the noble cause. Prohibition could have deprived our citizens of one of the staples of Southern living, but instead it stimulated the rise of the bootlegging industry. Either way, it was the fault of the federal government, and nobody in our county personally knew any federal employees except Mr. Ed Mixon and nobody could stand him. He was born and raised among us but had become a federal Revenuer and thought he was high and mighty.

Also, it was common knowledge locally that Mr. Porter Griffin wasn't really guilty of making the liquor. One of his boys had turned out wild and it was his still that Ed Mixon had raided. It happened to be on one of Mr. Griffin's farms, though. It was said, and widely believed, that Mr. Griffin went to court and pled guilty just so his boy wouldn't be sent to jail and made even wilder. He was sentenced to two years in the Atlanta penitentiary but got six months off for good behavior, and ran for sheriff.

Mr. Griffin proclaimed himself to have extensive knowledge of law enforcement: From the inside out, he said. In addition he was Baptist, a Mason, had UDC credentials through his women folk, had two brothers who were Legionnaires, and don't forget the support of every bootlegger in the county. He won by a landslide. Mr. Johnnie fumed, Mr. Bud beamed, and Mr. C. C. grinned. Mr. Griffin's boy got wilder, even without having gone to the pen.

Mr. Johnnie took this new defeat very calmly, at least on the outside. Dealing with all those politicians from all over the state had given him more self-control than he had been used to and also made him less outspoken in public. When his local satrapy cussed and raised hell on election night, Mr. Johnnie leaned back in his chair at the Ford place, took his cigar out of his mouth, and very judiciously calmed them all down. "Well, boys, they won it," he said. "Now let's see what they can do with it."

I always admired Mr. Johnnie Cofield, and soon as I was old enough I voted for him every time he ran and for whomever he sponsored when he wasn't running. His four daughters were the best company you could imagine and I always liked to stay as close to them as they would let me. One of them would let me a lot closer than all three of the others put together. Miss Gayflowers was usually hanging around pretty close, though, and she had a sharp and virginal eye, dedicated to preservation of feminine purity. Nobody messed with Mr. Johnnie Cofield's daughters long as Miss Cynthia Gayflowers was in charge, but a lot of boys had aspirations.

Chapter 5

All this time I've been leaving Mr. B. M. sort of in the background, but that doesn't mean he wasn't important in our town. Mr. Johnnie took over the political side of the corporation, Mr. Ed had the bank until he died, but Mr. B. M. had prospered also.

Soon as Mr. Johnnie got ensconced as president of the State Senate and made powerful connections all over the state, be blessed if Mr. B. M. didn't go into the asphalt business; had himself an office in Atlanta and went there five days a week in his Cadillac. This fellow in Scotland had invented a substance named macadam after himself, and it turned out to be a cheaper way to pave roads than concrete, brick, or stone. Our state called it asphalt. God knows why; it has only one S in it and no Fs.

Anyway, every state commenced to paving roads every which way. Turned out Mr. B. M. was a broker and his office consisted of one chair and a telephone. When a road contractor got a bid, he called Mr. B. M., who called an asphalt company with an order, and Mr. B. M. collected fees from both. He prospered mightily.

Also, he pretty well took over the Cofield position in the Methodist church, which always gave Mrs. Melrose fits and snits, and she would occasionally even break out in hives. With dignity, of course, and always with a degree of asperity and hauteur. Nobody else liked to tangle with Mrs. Melrose, but it didn't bother Mr. B. M. one bit. He was impervious to feminine disapproval, since that was all he had ever experienced at home and he assumed that just went along with being a woman. It never interfered with him making money or having a hot breakfast, so it was inconsequential.

It never occurred to him that somebody didn't like him. He dismissed any opposition to his church policies or positions abruptly as "They just against all Cofields. Otherwise, all right."

Mrs. Melrose was always very cordial to the wives of the preachers and, by inclusion, the preachers themselves. Mr. B. M. sat in church every Sunday and voiced his opinions to the preacher during board meetings, but he cottoned up to the bishop. He learned early that preachers in the Methodist church come and preachers go, but bishops go on forever. He knew which reins to grab to guide a horse and which side of ecclesiastical bread to butter. He smoked cigars as long as Mr. Bud Bazemore's and a lot longer than Mr. Johnnie's. Except for that and the Cadillacs, he was personally pretty frugal. His favorite saying was "Ain't worth a dollar"; he applied it to people as well as things.

As I have pointed out, his was what you might call an arranged marriage, and Miss Pansy turned out to be a bossy woman. Since he had arranged it himself, he more or less had to go along with the bed he had made and do the best he could. He was so tall and skinny that when we had to read "Legend of Sleepy Hollow" in the fifth grade, I thought of Mr. B. M. Maybe he didn't get much at home but the hot breakfast.

He and Miss Pansy had two daughters within two years of getting married, and Miss Pansy set in to raise them, as only a Southern lady with plenty of money and time on her hands could do. After those girls came, though, she apparently put her foot down, or maybe both of them, for all I know, and even then crossed at the ankles, for it was ten years before they had another baby.

It was a boy. Miss Pansy said, "Mr. Cofield, you can raise this one. I don't know the first thing about boys and care less, and my hands are full with these two lovely young girls. This boy is all yours. You understand me, Mr. Cofield?"

"Yep," he answered.

Miss Pansy never called Mr. B. M. anything but "Mr. Cofield." She told my mama once at a UDC meeting that there wasn't any way she could call her husband Betsill or Marmaduke, and that she certainly wouldn't stoop to using those horrid initials. "Why, Miss Roberta, you know what those letters stand for and my husband doesn't have one of those but twice a week anyhow, and I can't bear to refer to them." Everybody has to have somebody to confide in, I guess.

Anyhow, when the baby boy came along and she gave him to her husband to raise, she said, "What do you propose to name him, Mr. Cofield?"

"How 'bout 'Junior'?"

"And have him called 'B. M.', 'Junior,' or, even worse, 'Little B. M.'? Over my dead body; think again."

"Pa named me after some his kin. Don't see nothing wrong with it."

"Change one of the names so the initials are different."

After some little time spent hemming and hawing, they came up with Strathmore as the middle name.

"That's fine, Mr. Cofield. That was my mother's maiden name. Now the initials are fine. 'B. S. Cofield' sounds so much better than B. M. Cofield, don't you think?"

Mr. B. M. replied, "If you say so."

"And you can call him 'Strath' if you want a nickname."

Mr. B. M. put his foot down along with his cigar, which he wasn't allowed to light in the house anyhow. "Call him what you like. I'ma call him 'Son.'"

When he got old enough to socialize, we all called him Little Turd until he was in the fifth grade and a new guy moved in from Atlanta and labeled him "Turdelet." Then when a real Frenchwoman moved in and asked for a roster of all our names on the first day of school, one of the boys sneaked in Turdelet's paper as Strathmore Turdelet Cofield and she pronounced it "Toordulay" and from that day on he was called "Toor." Even in polite society. Like they say in the Bible, he was in our world but not of our world. Like all the other Cofields, we watched him. Most of the time it made us feel better about ourselves.

Both of Mr. B. M.'s girls had inherited his long legs and some of their mother's face; they were real lookers and grew up cultured out the wazoo. Miss Pansy saw to that. She even insisted on one of them taking voice lessons. Their neighbors could attest to that. The girl learned how to quaver and when she would be practicing, Mrs. Tobias who lived two doors down would have to shut all her windows, no matter how hot it was. It wasn't just the bad notes, she said, but it set all the dogs in town to howling and that upset her cat and got him to growling and scratching. One time the cat even peed on her sofa and she couldn't have company for over a week.

Mrs. Tobias said she could always tell when Marie Cofield was going to sing in church, because she practiced on Saturday the live-long afternoon and that gave Mrs. Tobias an excuse to skip church the next morning because of a sick headache or some such. Also, the cat would be nervous for at least twenty-four hours. Mrs. Tobias did love that cat; said she always knew where Tabby was at night, which was more than she could say for her husband. When Tabby died at age fifteen, Mrs. Tobias had him stuffed and kept him on top of the piano next to the picture of her husband as a young man.

I digress, but I am from the South; I can't help it.

Toor inherited his daddy's head and face; his fixtures too, I guess; I never personally saw either of them. From his neck down, however, he was Miss Pansy made over, except for the fixtures, of course. He had the shortest legs in town except for the little tax assessor woman and the widest hips and biggest buttocks you ever saw. His mama was just duck-butted; Toor was built like a bowling pin. His arms were as short as his legs and he sort of wallowed when he walked. It wasn't that he was fat; he was just built funny. Couldn't play ball because he couldn't ever run fast enough to make first base and he couldn't swing the bat far enough across his stomach to make a hit.

When Miss Pansy weaned him, she turned him over to Mr. B. M. to raise, although she gave him the same privileges she accorded his daddy, which amounted to hot meals and clean laundry. Toor slept in the bed with Mr. B. M. until he grew up and left home. By that time, Miss Pansy was too old to get pregnant.

Mr. B. M. wasn't much on reading books or playing games, but he was an expert in arithmetic and making money. He taught Toor the value of a dollar and how to count to twenty before he even went to school, and that without using his fingers and toes. Toor could always figure in his head and sometimes the rest of us thought that was all he could do up there.

When Toor first ran home crying because the mean boys made fun of him, Mr. B. M. straightened him out in short order.

"Shut up. Wipe nose. Their pas ain't got two dimes to rub together. Who cares if you can't play ball? I'ma teach you how to make money, Son, and that's all that matters in life. Plus you haveta go to church every Sunday. Even if don't listen, be there. Looks good. Helps to have money, though."

When he was twelve, Toor Cofield took a logging truck, although he could barely reach the pedals, and got some of the hands to load it with puncheons discarded at the Cofield lumberyard and drove all over colored town selling firewood to the tenants. They had to unload it and chop it up, but Toor drove that truck all winter and opened his own account at the Cofield bank. At recess, when somebody asked him what grade he had made on a test, he would tell them how much money he had in the bank. He never would have passed geography and English if it hadn't been for Edna Mae Chancey who sat in the desk in front of him and would slip him a note with the answers. Her mama was a widow woman with six children to raise, and Miss Pansy was good to give outgrown clothes to the Methodist Church. Mrs. Chancey had told Edna Mae to be nice to little B. S. Cofield. He learned a firm sense of values at an early age.

When each one of Mrs. Chancey's daughters finished the seventh grade, she was deemed old enough to get a job in Atlanta or Griffin in the mills or somewhere. After Edna Mae had to leave school, Toor brought home report cards with a good many F's and D's but an A in math. Mr. B. M. put up with that for two months and decided something had to be done. The Cofields didn't control the schools anymore and Mr. B. M. wasn't about to approach Mr. C. C. Summerfield for special favors. Especially since Mr. C. C. had a pencil-necked geek of a son who couldn't play ball either but was making straight A's in school.

He consulted Miss Pansy.

"What reckon oughta do, Pansy?"

"I'm not responsible, Mr. Cofield. I told you I was raising the girls and Strath was up to you."

"Done good job the girls, Pansy. Both grown and finished college. One already married. Reckon oughta send Son off to school?"

"Whatever. It might be nice not to have him underfoot."

That's how Toor got sent off to boarding school at a very prestigious military academy where everybody called him either "Cofield" or "Strathmore," and Mr. B. M.'s extracurricular donations precluded any thought of academic failure. He even made officer his senior year, and Miss Pansy consented to attend his graduation with Mr. B. M. so long as he did not light his cigar in the car.

Chapter 6

The town was pretty stable and slumbered along through the Hoover days and the Great Depression without any significant change in the fabric of our society. Mr. Ed's boy had grown up, Miss Gayflowers's little Cofield chicks grew to maturity without any scandal, although one of them was very beautiful and dashing and had more than her share of opportunities. All four of them got sent off to college and married well. So did their husbands, come to think of it, although none of them was from around here.

Mr. C. C. Summerfield and Mr. Johnnie Cofield were confirmed political rivals and both had strong, opinionated support; so elections were always hotly contested and exciting. One of the Harrisons had broken ranks and supported Mr. C. C. in an election and Mr. Johnnie had fumed and cussed. Each side hated to lose even one vote. The next year the Harrison man returned to the Cofield fold; he had fallen out with Mr. C. C. because he didn't hire one of his brothers-in-law, who everybody knew was sorry, as a bus driver. Mr. Johnnie beamed upon him in the Ford place and had all manner of good things to say to him. When Harrison left, one of the Cofield stalwarts challenged the welcome.

"Mr. Johnnie, you're treating him today like he was your best friend and last year you were calling him a sonofabitch."

Mr. Johnnie wiped the top of his head and replied, "That's right, Hulett, but this year he's our sonofabitch." Mr. Johnnie had not got where he was without acquiring more than his share of wisdom.

Mr. C. C. had about become as entertaining to watch as the Cofields. Mr. Bud Bazemore by now had advanced to a ripe old age, and I do mean ripe. He had pretty well given up on politics and had directed all his supporters into the Summerfield fold. People in our town have very long memories, however, and some of them are not overly prone to forgive past transgressions. Mr. Bud was no exception. He got real sick and his daughter had to call a cousin's hearse from a neighboring town to carry Father to the hospital in Atlanta. Piedmont, it was, before the doctors there had got real ritzy and moved to affluent Buckhead, which was as far as they could get from Capitol Avenue.

Mr. Bud didn't want to go to the hospital in the first place, and when the hearse/ambulance finally came, he insisted on sitting in the front seat with his hat on and his daughter had to lie on the litter in the back. When they got about two miles out of town, they stopped and changed places. Mr. Bud had explained his position clearly.

"I'm not going to give those goddam Cofields the pleasure of seeing me hauled out of town lying head down or feet first."

They were his last words. He hemorrhaged to death before they got to the hospital. It was several years before his daughter could laugh about it. Mr. Bud had his privileges and was recognized as a fine man. His daughter was a most forgiving lady. The whole town enjoyed watching the Bazemores.

We enjoyed watching Mr. C. C. too, although there were some who thought it the better part of valor to do it from a safe distance, and it wasn't just Sport Cofield, either. Mr. C. C. had consolidated several of the small schools in the county and upgraded our high school in town to a county school. Turned out he was a good businessman, thrifty with public funds and always conscious of the value of a dollar. When our schoolhouse in town, which had been an antebellum boarding academy, burned down, lo and behold, Mr. C. C. had had the foresight to insure it and was able to build a new high school with the insurance money plus some funds he had saved and hoarded.

The plans even called for an auditorium, which would be the first one we'd ever had. That was evermore big business in those days. When it came time to order the seats, he sent out specifications to several different companies, interviewed salesmen, and presented their bids to the Board of Education. Then he notified the company they had chosen and their salesman came down with a contract.

The county school superintendent's office consisted of one room and one employee. Mr. C. C.'s desk had the telephone and his secretary's desk had the typewriter. His secretary had one of the longest drawls in the county and it took her a while to tell you anything. *Bad* and *had* were both two-syllable words, and she was never in a hurry to pronounce them.

It didn't take her long, however, to tell about the salesman from the Union Seating Company bringing the contract to Mr. C. C.

"He came in the office dressed up like a sore thumb. You could tell he had his shirts done at a laundry and his hair had a heap of Vitalis on it. He and Mr. Lum shook hands and then he pulled out the contract and Mr. Lum made him go over it in every little detail. After about twenty minutes or even more, I would guess, it seemed like forever, Mr. Lum pulled out his fountain pen, the big black one his wife had given him for Christmas. A Parker, I think, and signed the contract in three different places.

"The man, his name was Mr. Bruce Tollison, put the contract in his coat pocket, the inside breast pocket on the left, and then took out an envelope and handed it to Mr. Lum.

"Mr. Lum looked at it and said, 'What is this, young man?'"

And Mr. Tollison said, 'It's a little token of my appreciation to you for getting me this bid.'

Turned out it was a gift certificate for one thousand, not hundred, one thousand dollars to the George Muse clothing store. I squinched tight as I could in my chair and got ready to run or git up under my desk, but Mr. Lum just as calm as he could be, he didn't even change color, said, 'I see.'

Then, while I held my breath, you better believe, he paused awhile and rubbed his chin and said, 'You know, I think I signed that contract in one place on the wrong line. Let me see it again, please.'

"And when Mr. Tollison handed him the contract back, Mr. Lum tore it and the gift certificate together into about five or six, it may have even been ten or twelve, little pieces and threw them on the floor. It was then his face turned plumb brick red, and I commenced rolling my chair backwards, you can well believe. I was glad his pistol was in his desk drawer, the which he always toted a gun but when he was in the office he put it in his bottom desk drawer, for he usually carried it in his hip pocket but it was uncomfortable to set on.

"I'll never forget the longest day I live, even if it's a hundred, what Mr. Lum said then. 'You crook,' but he used the Lord's name in vain before *crook*, 'you get out of my sight and my office and don't you ever enter either one of them again.'

"Mr. Tollison commenced to stammering and apologizing, I guess he was used to doing business with folks who were a lot different from Mr. Lum, but when Mr. Lum started toward him and I had rolled my chair slap back in the corner, he had the sense to head for the door.

"That's when Mr. Lum said what I'll never forget. 'You're nothing but pusillanimous scum and a discredit to the mother who bore you and the father who sired you.'

"That's the fanciest cussing I ever heard without using no naughty words, although I had to go look up *pusillanimous* before I was real convinced about it.

"Then Mr. Lum drew back his foot, he has extra long legs anyway but they looked even longer then, and kicked Mr. Tolliver so hard right in the seat of his britches, I mean so hard I thought it was going to snap his neck.

"Then he came back in and sat down in his chair and said, 'Forgive me, Miss Opal, for that outburst. Would you mind to get me a glass of water?'

"And I said, 'Just as soon as I collect myself and quit fanning.' And then we both busted out laughing. I tell you it's an experience working for Mr. Lum Summerfield. He is a man of very strong principles even if some folks, I won't call they names, might say he has too vigorous a way of enforcing them, and I hope he stays in office the longest day he lives."

Mr. Johnnie Cofield never overlooked an opportunity to deride Mr. C. C. When Mr. C. C. took off a day or two every court week to defend a client who had hired him as a lawyer, everybody who could took the opportunity to attend court for that case. We didn't have

TV back then and radio was not all that entertaining unless it was broadcasting an Atlanta Crackers baseball game. Mr. C. C. was always theatrical, especially in his closing arguments to the jury, and we all enjoyed listening to him, even if we were against his particular client. We learned a lot of new words that way, too.

Once he was defending Mance Tarpley for disorderly conduct, disturbing the peace, and public nuisance. The solicitor had told the jury that whenever Mance Tarpley came to town, honest god-fearing men cleared the streets, left their businesses, and went home where they locked all the doors, and their women and children cowered under the beds and in the closets until they were sure that the villainous bully and tyrant had left town.

Mr. C. C. rose up for his closing argument and said, "Gentlemen of the jury, the prosecution has labeled my client as a threatening menace to society and a scurrilous man of violence with not one witness to testify to that characterization. While I have the deepest professional respect for my fellow member of the Bar, I submit to you that he does not personally know Mance Tarpley. Gentlemen of the jury, I do. I have known him since childhood. He was raised across the creek from me, and I have seen him under many different circumstances and on many different occasions.

"I know him well, and," pointing his finger at Mance, he thundered, "I am telling you, gentlemen of the jury, that this man you see sitting before you in the docket this morning is a craven coward. Why, I could take a corncob and a chicken feather and run him off the steep side of Stone Mountain!"

With this, Mance Tarpley jumped to his feet, balled up his fist at Mr. C. C., and yelled, "That's a goddam lie!"

The jury found him guilty after thirty minutes of deliberation, during which an occasional burst of laughter could be heard through the closed doors of the jury room. They say that Mr. Johnnie laughed for thirty minutes himself, and said, "I reckon that damn well proves old C. C.'s not as good a lawyer as he thinks he is."

Another trial that tickled Mr. Johnnie was when one of his sons-in-law and Mr. C. C. represented opposing clients in a civil suit.

Spade Waddell and Wade Cantrell were neighbors on the south side of town. Cantrell was bad to drink and Spade was bad to eat. Every now and then you saw Cantrell sober; he had a deep bass voice and about twice a year could be coaxed into singing in the Methodist choir. Spade Waddell, however, was forevermore and always gargantuan fat. He wheezed when he talked and he chain-smoked cigarettes. He had never been seen in a church, even when his mother died. His mother had been what everybody in town called a mean woman. She was butt-headed stubborn and took no sass off anybody. She was even reported to beat her husband with a broom.

Mr. Barney, her husband, once had a bad case of piles during court week, when the town square was crowded with folks. He took his pants and drawers off and asked Miss Lou to pour peroxide on his piles. By mistake, she got the Absorbine, Jr., and dosed his behind generously with it. His screams drew a good crowd before he finally burst out the door and ran around the house yelling at the top of his lungs. Miss Lou stood on the side stoop, waving her apron and ordering him to get back in the house and quit making a fool of himself.

Before the gathered assemblage, Mr. Barney asserted himself for the only time in his marriage. He dashed up to Miss Lou, turned his bare tail up to her, spread his cheeks, and yelled, "Blow on it, Lou, goddamit, blow on it."

Spade inherited his mother's stubbornness and in addition had very fixed opinions. Once he made up his mind, hell and high water couldn't change it. He was one of only three Republicans in the whole county.

Once he was asked to umpire a baseball game and called one of the pitches a ball. The catcher and a dozen other folks hollered, "Spade, you can't call that pitch a ball; he swung at it. Hard!"

Spade stood his ground and wheezed out, "Well, by God, he shouldn't have. Play ball!"

Spade Waddell and Wade Cantrell had never gotten along.

Spade built a huge chicken house right slap on the line between him and Wade Cantrell and commenced raising hens and selling eggs. Cantrell sobered up long enough while the henhouse was being built to tell Spade he thought it was over the line and on his property a little.

"I know where the goddam property line is, Cantrell. Get your sorry ass to the house and take another drink."

Which he did. Spade was by far the biggest of the two, although Cantrell did have a beer belly that was impressive. Spade was right, though; Cantrell didn't have any ass at all. He had to walk sway-backed to keep that belly from pulling him over on his face.

One word led to another between the two over the next couple of years, the words becoming ever sharper and more venomous. Finally one day after a heavy rain, Cantrell had sobered up enough to realize that what he had been smelling was not his upper lip or his bad teeth but the aroma from the Waddell chicken house. He got his shotgun and blasted the chicken house door off its hinges, and when Spade came home from peddling eggs, there were white leghorn hens all over that end of town, as nervous and squawking and flapping as a bunch of old maids who had stumbled into a Masonic meeting. It took a week to catch all of them.

Spade filed suit. Trespassing and destruction of property.

Cantrell counter-sued. Maintaining a nuisance and a health hazard.

Spade hired a son-in-law of Mr. Johnnie's who had opened an office in our town because he was tired of getting up every morning and driving all the way into Atlanta. He had married the beautiful feisty Cofield girl and needed to spend more time at home, so he would take any case he could get. Locally.

Cantrell hired Mr. C. C. Summerfield, who took the case because Wade Cantrell, drunk or sober, had never voted for a Cofield.

When trial day came, the courthouse was packed. Everybody had been watching and waiting to see how those two lawyers would come out. Well, sir, I'm here to tell you it was a hoot. They went at it hammer and tongs, all polite to each other and legal of course, but leaving no simile neglected or any metaphor unmangled. I got the

impression that both of those lawyers were having too much fun not
to be laughing inside, but on the surface they were serious as Judge
McGee, who was only about half as fat as Spade Waddell and never
once let a smile cross his face.

The trial lasted a whole day and a half. Waddell and Cantrell
both vented their feelings in public and under oath, and witnesses for
both sides had testified. A few neighbors who lived way on the far
side of Cantrell's house testified, again under oath, that they had
never detected any unpleasant odor emanating from the henhouse;
three ladies from the Methodist choir swore that they had never seen
Mr. Cantrell drunk.

The ladies were not committing perjury.

The jury was out for an hour and returned to tell the judge they
were hopelessly divided. Judge McGee pulled out his watch, declared
a mistrial, and trundled off to Miss Love Perry's tearoom for lunch.

Mr. Johnnie, who had not been in court, laughed so hard his
head started sweating and he had to wipe it again. "I guess we learned
that we've got two sorry lawyers in town, even if one of them is my
son-in-law. Boys, your tax money was spent on that judge and jury
for two days to prove just two things."

"What's that, Mr. Johnnie?"

"First, Cantrell don't drink, and second, chicken shit don't
stink."

That became a saying in our town for years, at least 'til the
chicken house fell in and a lot of people moved in that had never
heard of Spade or Cantrell.

With all that inadvertent rhyming, Wade, Spade, Waddell,
Cantrell, stink and drink, I'm surprised somebody hasn't written a
country song about it. I've for sure and certain heard worse on the
radio lately.

Chapter 7

Do not think that all our entertainment was centered on the Cofields and the Summerfields; it was just that their political feud was ongoing and neither side ever let it rest, even between elections. Everybody enjoyed a funeral, too, except for the grieving family, of course. We gathered around and comforted the loved ones as best we could but then we would get away from the family and bring up all the interesting things we had heard about the deceased.

Dr. Morris is a case in point. I found out when he died how he had felt about Miss Lutie Ivey and her family. She married Mr. Archibald Ivey when she was fourteen and they called Dr. Morris out to their farmhouse when she went into labor. When I knew Miss Lutie, she was an old lady who wore a black straw hat to church and prayed the sweetest prayers you ever heard. Hers were always a lot shorter than Mr. Fife's, and every Sunday we Methodists hoped the preacher would call on Miss Lutie for the morning prayer.

Seems that Miss Lutie started having her babies at age fourteen and she had a passel of them. Dr. Morris delivered every one of them since, poor as Mr. Archibald Ivey was, he didn't want a granny woman fooling with his wife and was willing to pay the extra that a real doctor charged. There were about ten or twelve of those children and they all grew up sort of harum-scarum together but under pretty strict tutelage of Mr. Archibald in the field and Miss Lutie in the house. At least the best they could. At any rate, they were all sent to school when it was too wet to plow and carried to church on Sunday even if it was raining. They had principles.

It came out at Dr. Morris's funeral that Miss Lutie had about driven Dr. Morris crazy having all those babies; always telling him what to do, how to do it, and when to do it, and usually in the middle of all the previous kids raising sand in the next room. I had known two of the younger Ivey girls in school. Miss Lutie had named them Willie Mae and Render Belle, but some of the mean boys had nicknamed them "English" and "Poison," which made Render Belle swell up and pout and made Willie Mae, the one with all the freckles, cry. The teachers couldn't control everything that happened at recess, but the girls had an older brother named Son Joe who could throw a rock straighter and harder than anyone I ever saw, and he soon put a stop to all that name-calling.

The way folks used to gather outside the house when we were having what we called a "setting up" after somebody died and before the funeral has pretty well changed since we got funeral homes in our town. But I went with Mama when Dr. Morris died and stayed outside with the knots of men-folks while Mama went inside. That's when I heard a tale I'd never heard before about Dr. Morris and Son Joe Ivey.

Son Joe had been dead at least ten years; got thrown out of a runaway wagon and broke his neck. But Oscar Hosey got all the men-folks laughing out in the yard while the mourners were inside, and I was just barely old enough for him not to run me off when he told it.

"Did you fellows know how come Dr. Morris wasn't all too crazy about that Ivey family? Spite of all the business they brought him? Well, you know how dignified doctors are and how serious they try to take theyselves, especially when they in they office.

"Well, when ole Son Joe Ivey was about fifteen or sixteen years old, he had growed off pretty fast and, from some of his buddies' accounts, pretty big in certain areas. And he walked in Dr. Morris's office one afternoon before the last school bus had run, and Dr. Morris didn't have a patient at the time, and told Doc he wanted him to check his pecker.

"Doc asked him how and when did it bother him and Son Joe told him 'All the time'; so Doc told him to stand up and lay it out on the table and he went over it very careful, inch by inch, and finally said, 'Boy, there's not a thing wrong with that thing of yours,' and

Son Joe grinned and said, 'I know that, Doc, but tell me, ain't it a beaut?'

"And Doc snatched up that old ragged wire fly swatter off his desk and whacked it 'til Son Joe was bleeding and yelling. They say then ole Doc put some Sayman's Salve on Son Joe, tied him up with a rag, and throwed him out'n his office. Old man Archibald got on his mule and came to town to cuss Doc out, but Doc cussed him out and made him pay seventy-five cents for the office call and gave old man Ivey a lecture on raising a rapscallion what had no respect for his elders."

John McCollum said, "I heard that tale thirty years ago but I never believed it."

Oscar stood his ground. "You don't see a single Ivey at this setting up, do you? It's the truth."

I've always believed it myself. First off, I never caught Oscar Hosey lying, and second, I want to believe it; it gives our town a little extra flavor.

The main thing about Dr. Morris dying that has kept my attention all these years is not any of the anecdotes that were funny that came out at the time of his death, when everybody was reminiscing about him with great affection and respect, but the account several years later that Emmett Pringle told me of his consolation visit on Mrs. Morris when Doc died.

Emmett was a newcomer to our town. He had been here only about twenty years when he and I became friends. He had married one of the Ballentyne girls who lived across the street from our house, had started his own business and prospered mightily. He and his wife, Mae, were sort of trapped between generations, older than my group but younger than WWI veterans. They consorted with each generation but leaned toward us younger ones.

Emmett loved local lore. He flung a fit once when I called it gossip, but he was forever picking me about various families around town. He freely shared any of his local lore with me.

"Son, when old Dr. Morris died, Mae insisted that we had to pay a condolence call on Mrs. Morris or else we'd have to ruin Saturday afternoon by going to the funeral; so naturally I chose the condolence call.

"When we walked in, Dr. Morris was in his coffin in the front room with a few people sitting around in chairs. Mae signed the book and then asked if we could speak with Miss Lena.

"Now, son, you know as well as I do that Miss Lena has got herself sort of a reputation, you might call it, around town. I think she and Dr. Morris had long since lost interest in each other and kind of branched out, if you know what I mean. Anyway, she'd always been what some folks around here charitably call high-strung. At any rate, she could put on a good show.

"Mae and I went in the bedroom to see her. The shades were all pulled, but you could still see. Miss Lena was lying flat in the bed with a cold rag over her face. Katie Lou Posey was sitting on the right-hand side of the bed holding her hand and Mrs. Adams, who everybody said was Dr. Morris's girlfriend from Atlanta, was holding her hand on the other side.

"Miss Lena raised one corner of the washrag and moaned softly when Mae and I told her how sorry we were. Then before we could gracefully tiptoe out of the room, there was the biggest commotion you ever heard in your life at the door.

"I looked up and there stood little old dried-up Henry Bussey and his big fat nymphomaniac wife. I know you've heard about her. He had a handkerchief looked to be half as big as a bed sheet and he was crying and blubbering and yowling enough to wake the dead. You know he'd worked for years for Dr. Morris, driving him on house calls and doing odd jobs and what not.

"Miss Lena raised the corner of the washrag again, turned loose Katie Lou's hand, and started crying herself. Henry ran over to the bed and grabbed her hand and got down on his knees. 'Oh, Miss Lena, what in the world are we going to do? He was such a good man. I loved him so.' And Miss Lena patted him on the head over and over and cried some more. 'I know, Henry, and he loved you, too. Thank you for coming.'

"Henry stayed there until it got plumb uncomfortable to watch him, and then he got up and he and his wife wandered out into the hall.

"Soon as the door was shut, Miss Lena flung that washrag clean across the room. It nearly hit Mae; she had on her red silk dress and that would have been another story. Miss Lena sat straight up in the bed, pointed her finger at the door, and hollered, 'For God's sake, Katie Lou, follow them! They'll steal everything in the house.'

"After all that we decided we'd go to the funeral also, Saturday or no Saturday. Sure enough, Henry sat with the family, but his wife was nowhere to be seen."

We talk a lot about the "Great Depression," or at least my generation used to do so. Of course, there was nothing *great* about it except from the standpoint of it being *large*. Our county was made up of a few business and professional people and a very large percentage of farmers who were small landowners. Nobody jumped out of windows or anything like that; for one thing, we didn't have any buildings higher than two-story, and many an over-vigorous and overly adventurous lover could testify that such a leap was not mortal.

Everybody pretty well had enough to eat because they raised it or did without. Of course, in late winter or early spring, when the cured hog meat ran out, some families were reduced to living on fatback, corn meal, and sorghum syrup, which was known elsewhere as molasses. Sowbelly was a substitute when the fatback ran out, the main difference being that there was no streak of lean meat at all in the sowbelly. One of my black friends told me years later of going to the grocery store for a dime's worth of sowbelly, and the plea, "Miss Agnes, Maw say send her some this time without no nipples in it."

My six brothers and I were never reduced to sowbelly, but I often wondered how people managed to eat syrup mixed with hot grease rendered from the hog fat and baked corn meal called "hoe cake," all of it mixed up in the same tin plate, and then work all day. They returned at night for the same meal and nobody starved to death.

That menu was what made so many people in our county take to eating squirrels and rabbits and possums and coons. On Sundays, when you could grab a chicken and fry it, there wasn't a single piece of it that wasn't consumed with gusto. Some of the Summerfields even ate the feet and the head, said it was fun to crack the skull and eat the chicken brain. The one who told that at school quickly acquired a nickname that over time became simply C. B.

The stock market crash was not something we understood. Stock to us was what you worked or fed or milked every day. What we understood was the boll weevil and cotton sitting at ten cents a pound. It wasn't long until the county was made up of a much smaller percentage of small farmers and a much larger number of professional and business men who had become large landowners. Some of the farms were sold on the courthouse steps for back taxes and bought by opportunists for a fraction of what they were worth, even back then. Others were lost to foreclosure on loans made by the men with cash, to whom farmers turned in desperation because the bank charged interest and on top of that would not make loans on worn-out land with gullies in it. One of Mr. B. M.'s favorite sayings became "Business is business," and "Ain't worth a dollar" ratcheted down to "Ain't worth a dime" and even "Ain't worth a plugged nickel."

The farm boys at school held their heads up and pretended they liked a plain corn pone for lunch and on good days a baked sweet potato. They even made jokes. When John Pyron came to school with his arm in a sling and we asked him what happened, he said, "I broke it eating breakfast."

"How in the world did you break your arm eating breakfast?"

"I fell out of the persimmon tree."

All of us liked John.

Lester Bray topped him. "We had kinfolks come down to spend the night and when they went to bed, Pa told 'em, 'If you need anything during the night, just call me and I'll tell you how to do without it.'" Everybody liked Lester, too. He and John laughed a lot and never let anything get them down.

I heard tell that poor people were marching, but that was way off somewhere and nobody marched in our county.

To tell the truth, I don't know where they could have marched. There wasn't any pavement anywhere except on the sidewalks, and the streets around the courthouse were always too muddy or too dusty. "So on they worked, and waited for the light, and went without the meat," but I never heard of anyone cursing the bread. Occasionally I heard muted griping about turnip greens when they had been served as the main dish more than ten days in a row.

Then, what do you know, here comes Roosevelt. Herbert Hoover had received upwards of two hundred votes when he ran against Al Smith; if there was anything some of the Baptists hated worse than a Republican it was a Roman Catholic. Well, Hoover taught them a lesson, believe you me. When Franklin Delano Roosevelt ran, there were only three votes against him. One of them was Spade Waddell, and another was Miss Madelyn Pritchett who everybody called "Bill" for pretty obvious reasons; except for her bosom, she was more masculine than feminine. The third was Wyatt Porter, who was the only colored man in our county registered to vote. He was tall and thin, very light-skinned, and had a deformed foot with a great clumsy built-up shoe. He had the pressing club in town, which was what our parents called the dry-cleaning plant and what we now call the laundry. For some reason, nobody ever messed with him, not even the Klan. Mr. C. C. was even reputed to have solicited his vote when a local race got tight one year.

Anyway, everybody knew who the three Republicans were and it was a joyous day when we went solid for FDR. We stayed that way, too. Somebody coined the term "yellow-dog Democrat" and it meant that you would vote for a yellow dog provided he was a Democrat. Our county hadn't ever forgotten the Civil War; they for sure and certain remembered Hoover, and they were not going to fall into that pit again. Sometimes you had to hold your nose when you voted, but when I was old enough to look around the country, we were not the only ones electing yellow dogs.

Anyhow, FDR was the savior of mankind. At least in the South. First thing we noticed after we got over the Bank Holiday was the WPA and the CCC. Those programs gave at least subsistence to a lot of the young adult economic evacuees who had fled their farming background for jobs in the city only to return when their jobs fell out from under them; we had an uncle on the Perdue side who had come to stay at our house.

Mama took him in because he had no place else to go, and Papa was smart enough not to grumble. At least not where she could hear him. With seven boys, beds had always been tight at our house, and when Uncle Hubert moved in, he slept in the bed with the two youngest and I had a permanent pallet on the floor. I'll never forget the day he left for CCC camp off in Tennessee, and FDR has been my hero ever since. My uncle never amounted to much but at least FDR got him out from underfoot.

Then here came the WPA. It paid people to work on the roads and it built a community hall in our town. You had to have a public organization to sponsor it in order to get the government money, and be blessed if the American Legion didn't step forth. They got folks to furnish trees and rocks, and it seemed like no time before we had a log house one block over from the courthouse with electricity, running water and a kitchen, and the prettiest stone foundation you ever saw. They had to tear down the Bazemore livery stable and the Masonic hall to build it, but both of them were ramshackle eyesores anyhow, and the American Legion Hall was a welcome addition to our town.

Of course, the WPA got a bad name and a reputation for paying people to do much of nothing. For the workers on the road, they even furnished the shovels. My uncle on my daddy's side said the men needed those shovels, for they had to have something to lean on because they sure weren't working.

First news you know, the REA was formed and here came electricity all over the county. Cheap electricity. Even the tenant houses got wired and nobody needed kerosene lamps anymore. The farmers were as proud of a naked light bulb hanging from the ceiling as Mrs. Melrose was of her twelve-light dining room crystal chandelier, and they were a lot more public in bragging about it, too.

As I recollect, it was about this time that the government started giving out old-age pensions. All you had to be was over sixty-five and below a certain income level. Of course, ninety-nine and nine-tenths of our folks who were over sixty-five met the income criterion, and all of a sudden grandparents started swaggering a little and came to town on Saturday just like somebody. My granddaddy lived with one of his sons and said he'd be damned if he'd accept a handout from a Union government, but he was a rare exception. "Everybody else is doing it" was not just an excuse of teenagers. Relatives all of a sudden discovered they did have room in their houses after all for destitute aunts, uncles, and cousins, and the county poor farm emptied out faster than Capitol Avenue when the blacks moved in.

Those pension checks represented cash money once a month, which was a revolutionary concept in our county. Some folks even quit making biscuits every day and started buying loaf bread instead. The new prosperity was not enough yet, however, for anybody to start getting fat; everybody still watched their pennies.

I remember in the sixth grade the teachers asked everybody to tell what Santa Claus brought them in their stockings, and Pearlie Mae Landrum, who always walked in little fast steps with her shoulders hunched as close together in front as she could get them and was generally sort of mousy and looked whipped down, said, "A jar of mayonnaise."

Toor Cofield laughed out loud and said, "Is that all you got for Christmas?"

And Pearlie Mae turned real red and looked like she wanted to cry, but all she did was nod her head and then put it down on her desk.

I wanted to jump on Toor right then and there and beat him up, but he was a heap bigger than I, plus the teacher would have whipped both of us. But that was the last day for years and years that I even pretended to like Toor. Like I said, people in our town have long memories. Everybody knew that if it hadn't been for FDR and the

New Deal and the WPA, Pearlie Mae's daddy wouldn't have had the fifteen cents that jar of mayonnaise cost. Also, of all his daughters, she was the pet.

My daddy told a story about a schoolhouse in Tennessee. Nobody ever believed it was anything but a joke, but it sure outlined the way a lot of people thought. This fourth-grade teacher started off with, "Children, who built this new schoolhouse we're in?"

The chorus went up, "Roosevelt!"

"Who got us electricity in the schoolhouse?"

"Roosevelt!"

"Who paved the road that runs in front of our schoolhouse?"

"Roosevelt!"

"And, children, who made all of you?"

One lone little boy spoke up quickly, "God."

Whereupon another little boy jumped up and yelled, "Throw that damn Republican outta here!"

That pretty well sums up what we mean by yellow-dog Democrats.

Chapter 8

Despite all FDR could do, however, our county didn't change much as far as visible prosperity was concerned. Sure, more kids went to college than just the Cofields, but their folks had to scrimp and save to help them, and the kids themselves had to be determined. One boy went to a school in Rome called Martha Berry where you had to work your way through, milking cows and working in the fields and slopping hogs, just like he had done at home all through high school. It took him six years instead of four, but he made it; he got his degree and never came back to our county except to help bury his parents. He was the only member of his family who ever went to college. The others figured if that's all it amounted to they had already done it. They've had a heap of babies who have grown to adulthood right here and had babies of their own, most of whom have gone to college and are prominent in the community. FDR didn't live to see this, but I suspect sometimes that he envisioned it.

He sure helped with my education. Mr. Johnnie had hired my daddy to work for the Cofields right after he had moved to town, and he saw to it that Daddy had some money to send my three oldest brothers to college and he helped me out considerably. One of the brothers finished, the oldest one, and the second one almost did. The third one went two years, discovered alcohol, and said to hell with it. We four younger ones got grants from the UGA and had extra jobs off campus and got through all four years without too much help from Mr. Johnnie, but I always put him right up there with FDR and I have been a yellow dog ever since. At least in public. I never voted for any president whose last name started with a C or a K, but I keep hoping that somebody will come up on the Democrat side that's a pure-bred real yellow dog instead of just a sorry mongrel. I've got

"Blood will tell" and "Cream will rise" too firmly embedded in my credo to fall for these so-called "liberal" agenda.

College kept me too busy to pay much attention to Kate Smith's storm clouds gathering far across the sea. I was majoring in horticulture, working in the university library, bussing tables at a greasy spoon in town, and, to tell the truth, perfecting my technique for getting sex. I had been teased all my life about being a sissy because I liked to read more than play ball and liked to talk to girls more than I did boys. It didn't take me long after I reached the rutting age to discover that it wasn't just talking to girls that I preferred, and I also learned that girls were much more likely to relax around a guy who had a reputation for being effeminate than they were around the stud bulls who played football and had nothing on their minds except the quarterback sneak (whatever that is) and getting laid. Quickly and abruptly.

I soon found out that quoting Edna St. Vincent Millay and commenting in detail on girlish interests, including gossip and playing bridge, would get you past the portals of paradise a lot quicker than anything Frankie Sinkwich could do on the football field or say in the back seat of a car. I have never married, but Millay continues to serve me well. I have always been very discreet, and no one has ever suspected what I was up to with certain ladies. Including the ladies themselves until it was too late to back out.

It all got started with Pearlie Mae Landrum, of all people. When she got nubile and then blossomed into early womanhood, she had a figure like those Petty girls in *Esquire* magazine and walked with her shoulders squared and a bosom nobody could ignore. Her face wasn't much to look at because of acne scars, but she developed a happy personality. The Cofield girl who was feisty took up with her and they became best friends. Pearlie Mae's folks still were dirt poor and she would often wear clothes that we all knew came from the Cofield closet as hand-me-downs, although they looked better on Pearlie Mae than they had on Sara Belle Cofield. Sara Belle had the prettiest face, but her form was no match for Pearlie Mae's. In addition,

Pearlie Mae was a whiz in math and literature and they used to study together every afternoon.

I was in the ninth grade and they were both in the eleventh, which made them seniors in those days. Mama had insisted that I study piano since I didn't play ball, and she thought everybody should have some extracurricular interest. I took from Miss Gayflowers, of course, since we were all Cofield loyalists. I learned pretty well, too, and this only enhanced the reputation I have previously mentioned.

People in our town thought that boys who took piano were sissies, as they called them in those days. They may have been right, too, for the only other two boys in our town who played sure fit the legend. One of them swished when he walked and the other one pranced. Swisher grew up and made a career out of music, married, and had two children. Prancer blew his brains out in basic training. I have never swished nor have I ever had the slightest inclination to prance. My older brothers would have beat the living shit out of me if I had.

Anyway, I went for my Wednesday afternoon lesson with Miss Gayflowers at the Cofield house and got there a little early. Sara Belle was a little late for hers and had just got started. Pearlie Mae was sitting in a rocker on the front porch.

She gave me a bright smile and said, "Pull up a rocker. I'm waiting for Sara Belle to finish and she's just got started. It'll be at least a half hour."

Naturally, at that age, I was considerably in awe of older girls, so I sat down and couldn't think of anything to say except, "That's a pretty sweater you're wearing, Pearlie Mae; it looks real good on you."

Perhaps I put a little too much emphasis on *you*, for she quit smiling and looked at me real steady for a long time; I could feel my face turning red.

Finally she said, "It'll be a while before Miss Gayflowers gets through with Sara Belle; she hasn't been practicing her scales. Come with me. And be quiet."

She started down the hall and so did I. I had never seen her tiptoeing before. Up close and behind like I was, it was such a marvel to behold that I still remember.

We went in the back bedroom where Mr. Johnnie slept when he was home. She shut the door and quick as a wink pulled that sweater over her head, sat down on Mr. Johnnie's bed, and said, "Come here. I've been watching you grow up. You're a nice boy and I think it's time you learned something from someone who cares what happens to you."

Well, sir, she sure had a willing pupil. It was a very short session but I knew I was going to study this subject for the rest of my life. We got back in the rocking chairs ten minutes before Miss Gayflowers was ready for me, and the only words Pearlie Mae spoke were, "I'll come in the back of Bazemore's barn on Monday at recess and you come in the front. We'll meet in the middle."

I was so overcome and tongue-tied I could only nod my head.

Miss Gayflowers complimented me on my lesson that afternoon and said it was a pleasure to have a pupil who was serious about music and dedicated. I remember telling her that I wasn't just dedicated, I was inspired. Whenever I played "Flight of the Bumblebee," even ten years later, I still got a hard-on.

Pearlie Mae and I had a good thing going, but after a couple of sessions in Bazemore's barn when we were nearly late getting to class after recess, she suggested that we meet at lunch. "You're really getting the knack of this," she said.

I am the one who blew that relationship out of the water, so to speak. After about a month I made bold to tell her that she was my Aggie de Castrer. I'll never forget the way her eyes narrowed.

"You've been reading Kipling, haven't you?"

"Yeah," and I sort of swaggered when I said it.

"You ever read any Edna St. Vincent Millay?"

"Naw," I replied.

"Well, if you think Kipling knew anything about women, you'd better start on Millay. The only thing about 'The Ladies' that will

serve you well is the line, 'What did the Colonel's Lady think? /
Nobody never knew.' Remember that, nobody ever needs to know."

She took a deep breath, put her hand under my chin, and said,
"You've been fun, Buster, but listen close:

> …think not because of this, the treason
> Of my stout blood against my staggering brain
> That I shall remember you with love or season
> Scorn with pity. Let me make it plain:
> I find this momentary frenzy insufficient reason
> For conversation, should we meet again.

And Pearlie Mae was gone. I was glad when the WPA tore down
Bazemore's barn, and I was glad years later when her husband asked
me to play "Amazing Grace" at her funeral. Pearlie Mae was full of
grace and some of it spilled over onto me. And "nobody never knew."

Well, enough of all that. To get back to FDR…. He foresaw the
storm clouds coming far across the sea and all of a sudden we had the
draft. And they lowered the draft age to eighteen. Up until that time,
people regarded soldiers in the regular army as dangerous bozos who
drank liquor and brawled all the time, and nobody would ever think
about picking up one who was hitchhiking any more than you would
have anything to do with a tramp or a hobo who was hiding on a
freight train or the gypsies who came through town in their wagons.

All of a sudden it turned out to be our neighbors and cousins
who were in uniform, and everybody got real friendly with the
soldiers and it was unpatriotic not to pick up one who was
hitchhiking. Also, folks felt guilty if they didn't buy war bonds.

One farm family in our county had thirteen boys. Eleven of
them had either been drafted or volunteered and they were all
sending allotment checks home to their mama. They got only
twenty-one dollars a day once a month, as the song went, but it was
more cash money than Mrs. Kerlin had ever seen. She even bought
herself a pair of silk stockings. When the next to the youngest boy
turned eighteen, she encouraged him to quit school and enlist.

He loved his mama, as who didn't back in those days, but when he went for his physical they turned him down for medical reasons. Mrs. Kerlin put on her hat and I guess her silk stockings and went to town to confront the draft board and demand why they had turned this boy down and had taken the other eleven. She was so intimidating that the board member she was addressing backed down and told her, "Mrs. Kerlin, your son has only one testicle and does not meet requirements."

"Say what?" said Mrs. Kerlin.

When it was repeated, she stood in amazement for a moment and then thundered, "I thought you was training 'em to fight! If I'd knowed this was what you wanted, I'da sent they Paw." And flounced out.

I never believed that tale, but it made the rounds and one boy who knew a little Spanish labeled the boy "Uno Kerlin." Six months later he graduated from high school and enlisted in the navy. He later married a yankee, which came from getting his basic training at Great Lakes, and settled in Chicago.

He has never come back to our county, even when his mama died. He has about a hundred or so nephews and nieces running around, and they say they never hear from him anymore, although one of his brothers went to see him about five or six years after the war was over. He reported that Uno had four little girls, was happy as a hog in the sunshine, and had his name changed officially to Uno Kwatro Kerlin. He was running a pawn shop in Chicago called "You Know Kwatro," U. K. Kerlin, Proprietor, and had a house the likes of which Mr. Johnnie and Mr. B. M. put together had never seen, the brother said.

I've always wished I had known Uno Kwatro Kerlin; he must have been a man of considerable principle. I have occasionally wondered if he ever read Millay. I doubt it.

When Alf Landon ran against Roosevelt, he might as well have stayed in Kansas, which he primarily did; I don't think he ever left the state to campaign much. He sure didn't come through Georgia. FDR carried every state in the Union except Maine and Vermont, and in our town nobody thought they amounted to much anyway. Landon got only one vote in our county and everyone said that was Spade Waddell. Mr. Johnnie Cofield lived next door to Spade's mama and said that he'd watched Spade all his life and that he was as butt-headed and contrary as a team of unbroken mules.

The rest of the county was jubilant; it had turned out the whole nation felt the same way we did, and we started being nice even to the yankee soldiers who were hitchhiking. All that victory went to FDR's head, however, and first news you know he tried to stack the Supreme Court; wanted to add three new members to make twelve and get his way on some sort of decision about which he was hot to trot. Most of us didn't quite understand it but Mr. Johnnie set us straight.

"You don't want anybody to mess with the Supreme Court," he said. "It ain't that I approve of everything they do, but look where the whole South would be if it hadn't of been for the Dred Scott decision."

Then, be blessed if FDR didn't have a falling out with Senator Walter George from our state because of his leadership in the U.S. Senate and defeat of one of FDR's bills. He came to Georgia, wheelchair and all, and made a powerful speech urging all of us to vote for Senator George's opponent, who was a man from a county next to us and might have done all right if he had picked somebody else to run against. All of a sudden people remembered that, after all, FDR was a New York yankee, and be damned if any yankee was going to come to our state and tell us how to vote. Mr. Johnnie and Mr. C. C. and Mr. Bud all campaigned for silver-haired Walter George, and we sent him back to the Senate with the largest majority he had ever garnered.

I heard a lot of Daddy's generation grumbling about what the Democratic Party was coming to, but we young folks didn't pay much attention to all that; they were the same folks who kept saying that my generation was hell bent for leather and going over Fool's Hill in a buggy.

Wendell Willkie ran against FDR next time on a "one world" platform, of all things. I was in college and might have voted for him, maybe just to show my independence from Daddy and Mr. Johnnie, but they hadn't lowered the voting age to eighteen by then. We were old enough to fight but not to vote.

FDR had altered prohibition enough, however, so that 3.2 beer was legal and Willkie never said a word about that. The college boys learned how to drink beer and most of them smoked cigarettes. Hardly any of the girls liked beer, but a good many of them took up smoking, although all of them hid the fact from their parents. We thought we were pretty wild. I never smoked or drank while I was in college, which added to my reputation.

FDR had chosen Henry Wallace as his vice president and that scared the bejabbers out of everybody on campus except the few people who said they were Communists and fellow travelers. We all prayed for FDR's health.

Pearl Harbor changed everything. In the whole world, I guess, but most certainly in the United States and our county. FDR was our hero again, and we were one hundred percent behind him for interning the Japanese and also a great many Germans. We were the only part of the country that had ever been invaded and occupied by a hostile military force and we all knew that it *could* happen here, improbable as it might seem that Sinclair Lewis knew what he was talking about. As I have said before, people in our town have long memories.

One of my uncles on my daddy's side was head of the draft board, and believe you me, he was a far cry from Mr. Peppers. Talk about a model of probity! He drafted his own three boys and all seven of us, picked us off one by one.

He did exempt one of my cousins, but it was because my aunt was a widow woman with no income except from her farm, and there was nobody to run it except my cousin. I always thought being exempt from the draft affected him, but he managed to overcome it. It sure beat getting torpedoed or shot at, and there was a slogan of "let's feed our troops"; so it mollified him somewhat to put in a few acres of wheat instead of planting the whole farm in cotton. That helped him hold his head up when he went to church. A good many young blacks were exempt, some of them for illiteracy, but most of them for the same reason my cousin was. The entire county was behind the war effort after Pearl Harbor.

We pretty well drained the county of eligible males. If you were in college and making your grades, which I was, you were granted a deferment until graduation and then it was "You're in the Army, Mr. Jones; No private booths or telephones," and everybody was singing about bluebirds over Dover and even resurrected "We're coming over." Lots of guys got their parents to sign for them and enlisted as soon as they finished high school, since we had only eleven grades back then and most everybody finished when they were seventeen.

Toor Cofield got drafted. Turned out he hadn't done as well in his fancy military school as the family had believed. They say it was because he had fallen in love and quit studying. That was his story and he sticks to it 'til this day, but in spite of old Mr. B. M.'s efforts, my impartial uncle popped Toor's butt in the infantry. He didn't even finish basic training before he got sent home with what his mama said was a medical discharge.

"Something to do with his nerves, he doesn't sleep well," she told my mama—I've always suspected it was a Section Eight, but we won the war without him, so who cares?

Long about that time, Georgia got Gene Talmadge as governor; you talk about somebody having a huge following of yellow dogs. He was from someplace close to McRae, Georgia, called Sugar Creek and the folks he attracted were called the Wool Hat Boys. They always wore white shirts under their overalls when they came to town and also put on wide-brimmed, black wool hats. Talmadge was smart as a whip and college educated, but you'd never know it to hear him talk. He would even lapse into saying, "hit don't" and "have went" if he had the appropriate audience. He was quite an orator and connected, marrow and bone, with the farmers who supported him.

And support him they did. He'd been elected commissioner of agriculture and had spoken up for the little man, the small farmer, the Wool Hat Boys. They had even seen some tangible results; he got funds approved for improvement of their farms and advocated a "fish pond for every farm," to be paid for at government expense. About the time he ran for governor, somebody discovered ten or twenty thousand dollars, I forget which, but in those days it was a formidable amount of money, missing, and his opponents just plain came out and accused him of stealing it.

Gene had already coined the phrase "them lying Atlanta newspapers," one which contained at least a modicum of veracity and which still holds today, if you will notice. The newspapers rankled under the county unit system and, of course, rural Georgia reveled under it. Gene never failed to seize a good opportunity and neither did Mr. Johnnie Cofield, who from his position as president of the Georgia Senate supported Talmadge at least one hundred percent. Crowds would appear at whatever courthouse lawn "Ole Gene" was visiting, and Mr. Johnnie would always see that some ardent supporter would be stationed high in a tree, safely remote from fractious and abusive supporters.

"Ole Gene" would always start his orations with "My fellow Georgians!" and there would be a roar from the crowd. Then he would attack them lying Atlanta newspapers, them city slickers in town who never plowed a furrow or slopped a hog, them far-off bankers on Wall Street who wouldn't think of eating corn pone and turnip greens, but "them's the people who are trying to run your lives and the government of Georgia! Well, I'm here to tell you, my fellow Georgians, they'll never do it if you elect me governor!"

"Yea, Gene!" the chorus would swell.

"You tell 'em, Gene!"

About then Mr. Johnnie's prompter would yell out above the crowd, "What about all that money you stole, Gene?"

Then he would snatch off his coat, snap his red suspenders, raise his fist, and thunder, "You've been reading them lying Atlanta newspapers, I can tell! Well, let me tell you something, my fellow Georgians: yes, you mighty right I stole that money! You know why I stole it? I stole it for *you*! For *you*, you hear me? The poor farmer and all the other poor people in Georgia! That's why I stole that money!"

In the frenzied acclaim that followed, the planted stooge was always able to shinny down the tree and mingle in the chorus, "You tell 'em, Gene."

He swept the state, with the exception of Atlanta and a few of the larger cities. From Rabun Gap to Tybee Light, Georgia was Talmadge country. If you think yellow-dog Democrats are opinionated and fanatical, you've never run into one who was also a Wool Hat Boy.

Mr. Johnnie strutted and Mr. B. M. brokered a lot of asphalt. We learned earlier than most about trickle-down economics.

Gene's boy, Herman, who later became governor and then senator, was president of the fraternity to which one of my older brothers belonged. I never joined, because frankly I just didn't like being around all that many males all that much. Herman had himself a reputation in college, and when one of my poetry enthusiasts missed two periods, I went to him in what I don't mind telling you was somewhat of a panic. He gave me the secret name of a retired nurse way out in the country and even lent me the seventy-five dollars she charged. He was the soul of discretion and "nobody never knew."

I will always love Mr. Johnnie Cofield and Herman Talmadge. One of them made it possible for me to go to college and the other one made it possible for me to stay there. And stay single.

Chapter 9

The week after I got my degree in horticulture, and why I chose that I have forgotten after all these years, I was in the navy. I shook hands with Daddy, made a few very encoded telephone calls to select girls, kissed Mama, and shipped out to Great Lakes Training Station.

At first they tried to make a cook out of me, but when they found out I could type, I got transferred real quick. Typing came easy to me after all those sessions with Miss Gayflowers, and after "Flight of the Bumblebee" it was no problem to type dictation even as it was spoken. When the ensigns found out how close-mouthed I was, it wasn't long before I was typing classified material and kept getting moved up. And out. I wound up moving from one misbegotten island in the South Pacific to another and finally ended up in New Guinea as we progressed. I even got to spend some time with Admiral Halsey.

He was brilliant, but his gift was not grammar; he was bad to say "between you and I," for instance. When dictating, he would sometimes get confused about numerical balance between subject and predicate, but I would type it correctly as we went along. Neither of us ever mentioned it but he was sure to have noticed it. Each time he read a report, he'd cut his eyes at me and grunt. He was responsible for me getting two promotions sooner than I expected them, and he absolutely refused to let me be replaced by a WAVE. I've always wished I could have eyebrows like Admiral Bull Halsey or John L. Lewis or even John Nance Garner, but then as far as I know, none of them could play the piano. You can't have everything.

I doubt if they could recite much poetry either. In New Guinea I didn't recite any at all. I memorized a lot, because I'd rather stay in quarters and read than go to the USO or consort with the natives. In the first place, the native women would not have understood a word of it, and in the second place I was lucky enough to be shipped home before they started looking good to me. I kept to myself and memorized nearly everything in Untermeyer's *Collection of Modern American and British Poetry*, which Mrs. Jimmie Kate Cole, my high school English teacher, had given me when I came home on leave before being sent to the Pacific jungles.

Mrs. Cole was a saint if there ever was one, and she's right up there with Herman Talmadge and Mr. Johnnie Cofield on the list of people who have affected my life for the better. Of course, when Herman came home from the war and settled down, so to speak, he gave all us veterans free driver's licenses for life, and Mr. Johnnie Cofield had very privately sent me off to college as well as a whole lot of other boys and girls who were hard-up financially, but Mrs. Cole got me ready to go off to college and fanned the embers in my soul to flame up for poetry; she made the roll of my list of saints. I never ever quoted any Millay to her daughter, although it was a temptation on occasion. Mrs. Cole was perceptive and she would have known right off what I was up to. In fact, she was very, very perceptive and I wouldn't have risked being cast out of her favor for all the twat at Agnes Scott. So to speak. It is safer to run with the bulls at Pamplona than it is to get between a widow and her virginal daughter.

Enough has been written about the horrors of war without me adding to that type of cathartic literature. Nothing of consequence has ever been written about our town, however, and it is to that purpose I address myself in these early morning hours of my declining years. Probably my favorite recollection of military service is how my name was used.

Mama named me James Aloysius Holcombe, Jr.; after Daddy, of course. She couldn't call me James because everybody called Daddy that, or risked having a fight on their hands. I therefore had been burdened with *Aloysius* in class and around town. When I was in the third grade, my two younger brothers and one of my older brothers engaged in a puerile contest one evening after a supper of dried butterbeans, sweet potatoes, and buttermilk. It was no real contest. I won. Hands down, or even up, it made no difference. The older brother made a pasteboard crown with "# 1 Fart Buster" on it, and I was proclaimed champion.

Mama heard us laughing and we had to tear up the crown real quick before she came in the room, but from then on all my brothers have called me "Buster" and the name has spread to all my friends, although few know its origin. The teachers and Sunday school teachers and old maid aunts and such always called me Aloysius, but I've been more widely known as Buster.

The military always went by a person's first name with middle initial, and for those years I was James A. Holcombe, Jr., which gave me a different identity and for a while a different life; none of which I intend to reveal since it has no bearing on our town. I was a wee bit sympathetic about John Kerry refusing to release all of his military records, although I'd have chopped off a leg before I voted for him. I have always suspected that he had a dishonorable discharge that was expunged by Jimmy Carter when he pardoned all the draft dodgers who had fled to Canada.

Oscar Hosey said, "That Jimmy Carter won't do. I ain't never seen no other president get out of office and mouth off as much in my life. He got his ass whupped fair and square by the American public and needs to live with it. He ought to stick to Habitat and Guinea worm, whatever the hell that is, and keep his political opinions to hisself. Personally, however, I ain't never believed those rumors about his wife and the state patrol."

Dr. Hentz said, "I don't ever trust somebody who brags in public about being born again. I've delivered enough babies in my time to know you have to be very careful about a retained placenta; if you don't get it all out, you're in deep poo-poo. If Nicodemus had been an obstetrician instead of a rabbi, he'd have sure and certain asked about that, and that whole encounter might have left us a different quotation. And a different theology, come to think of it."

Be that as it may, but along the same lines, I had to come to terms with my feelings about FDR when I found out he had betrayed Churchill and sided with Stalin at Potsdam. I thought he was a better judge of character than that, but he's still my hero. Any of us will get senile if we live long enough; I even feel it creeping up on me now and then.

Anyhow, FDR should be forgiven almost any sin for giving us Harry Truman, if he was going to go and have a stroke at Warm Springs with his girlfriend and die on the spot; and wouldn't the press have a heyday with that nowadays? Thank God for Harry Truman. Henry Wallace would never have dropped the bomb and I would have rotted to death in the Pacific. I'll trade Germany and Eastern Europe and all the Japanese in the world for that Missouri haberdasher any day. That's just my personal feeling, but you better believe the first time I ever voted it was for Truman against Dewey, who was from New York and had a little French mustache. I think everybody else in our town voted that way except Spade Waddell and Bill Pritchett.

Well, sir, it seemed the Depression was finally over. A lot of our black families had moved north just before and during the war; the tractor did away with the need for field hands and cotton wasn't really worth raising anymore; the federal government even started paying farmers to plow it under. The blacks who stayed had no trouble finding jobs. The men either learned how to run a tractor or got jobs at the Ford plant or Conley and the women had no trouble at all finding housework, because by then a large number of white women had found jobs outside the home.

There were exceptions, of course. I was appalled to discover that Barbara Mitchell, who had been valedictorian at my high school graduation and whose family was well-off by prewar standards, had married Tommy Kendrick, had three children, and was living behind the family home in a chicken house with nothing but a dirt floor. Barbara swept it out once a week, but I always thought her daddy should have let them live with them in the big house and forgiven her for marrying Tommy. Mr. Mitchell said he came from sorry folks, was sorry himself, and would never amount to much. Turned out he was right, but Barbara always had a hangdog look about her. And it wouldn't have hurt her daddy too much to put up with sorry. Lots of folks did.

By and large, however, we all of a sudden had a considerable number of two-income families and nearly every one of them had a car. Some didn't, of course, and there was a great deal of carpooling to jobs in Atlanta with anywhere from six to seven people in each car traveling back and forth together to Atlanta. This made the transmission of local information and gossip, no matter what Emmett Pringle called it, more rapid and universal than at any time before or since. People worked harder and harder for more and more money to buy more and more things, and I heard dozens of my former classmates come out with the creed of the fifties: "I had things rough when I was growing up and I want things better for my children." I am an old bachelor and, to the best of my knowledge, childless, but that seems like one of the most self-defeating manifestoes I ever heard, and it led to the hippies and the flower children and "If it feels good, do it." That's only my opinion but it is very true.

All veterans with an honorable discharge were eligible under the GI Bill for small business loans or college. I chose the latter and went three years to law school, passed the bar first time around, and settled back in our town for life. One of the indications that the Depression was over was that we now had several lawyers in town and all of them were prospering. Even Mr. Hubert Lawson.

I had known Mr. Hubert all my life. He had a speech habit of using the word *yes* instead of commas. It was tedious to listen to him if you wanted information and not just entertainment. He was bald on top and parted his hair about two inches above his left ear; so he was always smoothing the few long hairs he had with his right hand. Sometimes that was synchronous with all the *yesses*. He always wore little black bow ties and a white shirt. He was a lawyer, all right.

He was married to Miss Clyde who played the piano, sang to her own accompaniment, and had cataract surgery on both eyes. This was before they discovered how to implant lenses, so she wore thick glasses that magnified her irregular pupils and made them shimmer and dance, but she could see better than she looked. She was so stout she walked spraddle-legged and sway-backed, which made her corset creak. She always had her elbows spread out like she was explaining something and a pocketbook swaying from her left wrist. You could hear her coming down the aisle at church before you ever saw her.

She had come from a family of more affluence than Mr. Hubert had been able to provide her, but she put on airs with what she did have, and everybody in town sort of understood and pretended to accept Miss Clyde for what she thought she was. I had her in Sunday school for a couple of years and liked her very well, except that her voice was too high and sort of brassy and it didn't fit right with "Jesus loves me, this I know." I would much rather listen to Mr. Hubert. And to look at him, too, come to think of it.

Back in the real hard times of the Depression, they heated the courthouse with coal, and convicts built fires in the grates of each office every weekday morning. They maintained a coal pile on the lawn of the courthouse right next to the back steps. The coal pile kept dwindling down faster than the clerk of the court thought it should, and he alerted the town marshal to keep an eye out and see if somebody was stealing public property. Well, bless Pat if one dark night about twelve o'clock the marshal didn't catch Mr. Hubert Lawson, bow tie and all, filling his scuttle from home with county-owned coal. The older lawyer in town, who was Mr. Johnnie Cofield's lawyer and the district attorney to boot, decided not to prosecute and they tried to hush up the matter. Everybody knew that Hubert Lawson always voted for the Cofields and sometimes he was even able to persuade Miss Clyde to also. Still, it was a scandal that went around town in whispers, which made it even more delicious.

Turned out Mr. Hubert already had a reputation for being light-fingered about courthouse documents that were supposed to be public, and lots of times other lawyers had to go to his house to research titles and such. For a fee, of course. Mr. Johnnie Cofield told the district attorney, "I've always thought that if Hubert Lawson had ever developed even one vice, like smoking or drinking liquor or even, God forbid, running around on Miss Clyde, he wouldn't have took up stealing."

I've thought about that a lot through the years and wondered if Mr. Johnnie was trying to say that every man needs a mote in his own eye. He was a forgiving man. And very wise.

Anyway, when I got back to our town to live, the Depression was over, and one of the most confirming signs was that Mr. Hubert Lawson had accumulated enough clients to buy himself a brand-new automobile. Legitimately, too; the clients, I mean. He bought the car from the Cofields for a cut-rate price and the promise of Miss Clyde's vote in perpetuity. It was progress. But the whispers lingered around him like musty air. Long memories, you know. As far as I could tell, the town forgave him the purloined documents, yes, but one scuttle of coal, yes, hung around his neck like a millstone. Yes.

Chapter 10

The town didn't grow like toadstools bursting out of the ground overnight after a rain; that came later for the whole county. We did have enough new people who moved in to give us more folks to watch, and for the first time since '32 native sons were returning because we had jobs. It became fairly common to have a new house being built here and there, and it was accepted Sunday afternoon entertainment to check the construction and wander through it. And comment on it, of course.

One of the Mayfield boys set out to build his mama and daddy a new house because they had raised about eight younguns through hard times and had never owned a home of their own. It was what we nowadays would call a modest bungalow, but to Mrs. Ella Mae Mayfield it was as grand as Buckingham Palace. She was a devout Christian and one of the most literal and fundamental Baptists you can imagine; she was even known to call up individuals and pray over the telephone, for either their illnesses or their sins or, more often, for something she wanted them to do; and she on a party line.

When Mrs. Melrose came calling to inspect the new house after the walls were all up, Mrs. Mayfield was on the premises and proudly showed her around. The aristocratic Methodist lady with the straight spine and square shoulders said, "Why, Mrs. Mayfield, you don't have a single closet in this house."

To which the indomitable new homeowner replied, "That's right, Mrs. Melrose; I ain't got a thing in this world to hide! How many closets you got? I ain't never seen inside your house." Then she bowed her head and said, "Let us pray." Mrs. Melrose departed with what dignity she could still maintain, but not before she had been thoroughly exposed to the Lord. She wrote a bigger check than usual to the Methodist church the next Sunday and invited her preacher's wife to tea.

By the time I finished law school, there had been almost a mini building boom in the town. Toor Cofield had managed to get himself married to a girl from Chattanooga who was distantly related to the Lynch family up there; said he met her at a dance at his school, and she was only fourteen years old but looked like she was seventeen or eighteen. He always bragged that he was the only boy Beatrice Schultz had ever dated and proclaimed that he gave her a diamond ring when she was fifteen years old to keep other boys away from her and made her promise to wait for him. All of us always felt like she was the only girl he had ever dated and that Toor had to catch himself one before she was old enough to have good sense or to be able to separate the price of diamonds from the value of intelligence.

Anyway, by the time I got back and hung out my shingle, Toor and Beatrice had bought a lot next door to Emmett Pringle, built a big red brick house which Beatrice insisted on painting white, and spawned five children. The youngest one was stillborn, but that hadn't slowed them down. The town had a whole new generation to watch.

Then next door to him, the new doctor in town had bought and built. I say new doctor for he hadn't been among us but about twenty years. He had come into the upper part of the county right after the First World War; he had been a doctor in the army and had ambition. Why our county and ambition were in any way compatible in those days I have never been able to ascertain, but his family was supposed to be from Alabama; so I guess, come to think of it, that it was a step up for him.

He didn't stay in the upper county very long. In fact, it was said that he nearly starved to death the first year he was in practice. At any rate, he moved to the county seat and rented an office above Judge Melrose's law office.

He had married an army nurse who had been raised in an orphanage in California, of all places, and she worked in the office with him. He was always very dignified and distant, which made him seem more constantly professional than good old, down-home Dr. Morris or any of the other hometown doctors. He and his wife were formal with each other in public and most of us suspected also in private. She always called him "Doctor," except when he wasn't present and then she referred to him as "The Doctor." That may have been because she might get confused about his last name, which the rank and file of the populace surely did. His name was T. Jefferson Grizzelle on his shingle, and of course everybody in our town would say "Grizle." He would very politely but coldly correct us, "It is Grizzelle, please," putting the accent on the last syllable, "not Grizle. There are lots of Grizles in Alabama, but only a few Grizzelles, and there is a considerable difference in the two families."

We could identify with this, for we had all grown up with two different pioneer families named Betsill. It was said that one family made nearly all the liquor in the county and the other set tried to drink all of it. The consumers usually turned out better than the producers.

At any rate, the Grizzelles settled in and joined the American Legion and the Methodist church, although Mrs. Grizzelle was reported to have been raised a Catholic in that California orphanage. She was a marvel to behold. She had a sharp little beak of a nose and two chins, the upper one of which was only slightly bigger than the lower. She never cut her hair but wore it in a bun on the top of her head toward the back. She also had thick rimless glasses that glittered and twinkled with every motion and made her eyes seem extra small. Her head was small in proportion to her body, which was square with rounded corners, so that I was always reminded of a cockatoo perched on a small bale of cotton. It was as much fun to listen to her as to watch her. Her voice was even deeper than Bill Pritchett's; she sang alto in the church choir but could have sung bass right along with Wade Cantrell.

She did all right with her consonants when she spoke, but her vowels always came floating out like echoes from some subterranean cavern. I can still see her now with that white cap on top of her head, striding out into her husband's waiting room, coming to a full stop until she was sure she had everyone's attention, fixing her gaze on the next patient, and then intoning as solemnly as though she were announcing royalty, "The Doctor will see you now."

She also made interesting noises when she walked. Her corsets creaked as loudly as Miss Clyde's, but there was never one built that could harness Mrs. Grizzelle's thighs, and you could hear them whispering one to the other, tightly bound flesh, silk against silk, whenever she passed. In one of her very rare efforts at camaraderie, she confided to Miss Mae Harp at an Auxiliary meeting after she bent one of the folding chairs, "The first year we were in practice, The Doctor got paid in nothing but sweet potatoes. I got fat on them and have been fat ever since." You had to like her.

When the Grizzelles cleared the lot next to Toor Cofield and built their house, they used cream-colored brick and even built a guesthouse out back of the same material. I've always suspected that was the reason Beatrice Cofield made Toor paint their red brick white. At any rate, with the Pringles, Cofields, and Grizzelles all lined up side by side, we now had what we less materially fortunate citizens called "Millionaires' Row." Whenever anyone used the term in front of the Melroses, Carlotta and her mama would snort and say, "Hah!" in perfect unison.

The Grizzelles had a bunch of daughters and finally a son. All of them bragged a lot at school about what they had and we didn't have, and that set them apart from us as quick as nobody knowing their grandparents, knowledge of which reduced all us locals to a common denominator when it came to bragging. There's nothing like moving to a new state that empowers you to invent a whole new set of ancestors, and "nobody never knew."

Those Grizzelle girls even bragged about their baby brother who was naturally destined to be spoiled rotten and set apart even more than his sisters. Among other things, they bragged that he was "a forceps baby," and lots of the girls in school had become so accustomed to degrading comparisons from the Grizzelles that they thought that gave little Timothy extra powers or something. It took Pearlie Mae Landrum to set us all straight. "Maybe the forceps are the reason his head is lopsided and he's still saying 'ta-ta' for 'thank you' after he's nine years old!"

We were pretty much in a state of flux about then, although when you're fluxing you don't pay much attention until it's all over and too late to change anything. You're too involved in your own day-to-day scrabble to do the best you can for yourself, especially if you see some guys out in the county progressing mightily and pulling ahead of you when you know they don't have a bit more sense than you. And not nearly as much in some instances.

First off, there was a big paving boom. The two main highways in the county crossed each other right by the courthouse, and before Eisenhower could get inaugurated, Mr. Johnnie Cofield yielded to local pressure and got both of them paved all the way to neighboring towns. We were wide open to the outside world and didn't even realize it. Progress became synonymous with bulldozers and red clay, and old landmarks came down by the dozen. Mr. Johnnie was dead on it when he said you couldn't ever tell what might come in on a paved road.

Mr. B. M. kept quiet and sold more asphalt than he had ever dreamed of.

Along about then Mr. Johnnie Cofield up and died on us, suddenly and unexpectedly. Just like Mr. Bud Bazemore felt when Mr. Ed Cofield died, Mr. C. C. Summerfield was devastated; he, too, had lost his favorite enemy. He no longer had a single nemesis upon whom he could blame everything that went wrong in the universe. He went into a decline, lost weight and his fiery temperament, and even quit wearing his teeth when he came to town. Six months later, before any of us had really recovered from Mr. Johnnie's death, Mr. C. C. took the Luger he had captured from a German officer in WWI, went down to his barn, and blew his brains out.

No wonder the rest of us didn't realize anything else was happening.

If you think that left a political vacuum in our town and county, you don't know anything yet. The next one to fall locally was Sport Cofield. He had been mayor for at least twenty-five years, and most of the time he had been unopposed for reelection. The five-man city council was always packed with Cofield sycophants and the town had just drifted along with the tide of events. Well, all of a sudden we had spending money, a Republican president, and a fair number of new folks in the town. First thing you know, Eisenhower had appointed Bill Pritchett as postmistress, which didn't surprise any of us too much. We had previously had a lady postmistress for FDR's first term, who was also an old maid, but she was the ultra-feminine, fluttery type who never finished sentences, had always voted for the Bazemores, and was Baptist. Mr. Johnnie put up with that for one term but then used his influence to have Miss Flutter Lady replaced with his brother-in-law, who was Methodist, had five children, and had trouble holding a job.

His name was Mobley Whitaker and he was famous for being absent-minded. Once when he had a job in Atlanta, he drove his car in to the city, worked all day, and then came home on the bus because he had forgotten he had driven the car. He lived on a lot too small for a pasture, and for the twenty years he was postmaster he always carried his cow to some vacant lot in town for her to graze all day.

His nephew was a friend of mine, and he told me, "Daddy gets aggravated twice a day, morning and evening, when he sees Uncle Mobley taking his cow for a walk like she was a pet dog or something."

Mr. Mobley never smoked nor drank liquor and raised his children the same way. In later years his daughter got in an argument with her cousin, my friend, about the evils of alcohol, and finally proclaimed, "I'd rather commit adultery than take a drink of whiskey!"

To which he replied, "Hell, who wouldn't?"

She didn't give up. "And the same goes for beer and wine, Smarty."

My friend returned the volley, "When you get to Heaven, you can straighten Jesus out."

That not only ended the conversation but also their family reunions. The cousin joined the Baptist church and had to be baptized as an adult, but she was safe with grape juice and crackers.

When Bill was sworn in as postmistress, she didn't make any changes. She chain-smoked but didn't bother with putting ashtrays in the post office; her bosom took care of the ashes and she threw her butts on the floor and stepped on them. She did the same thing when she was invited to the Cofield's housewarming and was never invited back.

Weight-wise, she could hold her own with Miss Clyde or Mrs. Grizzelle, but the difference was that she didn't wear corsets, not even a girdle; she just let her fat drift around free and natural. When she walked, if she had been real feminine, she would have waddled, but she was slew-footed and moved with determined force and lumbered along with her feet making clumping sounds. Anybody who got in front of her when she was walking did so at his own peril.

Whenever I got to a cocktail party late, Bill would be sunk in the corner of a low sofa, with a cigarette in one hand and a glass of whiskey in the other, her knees spread so far apart that she was taking everybody's picture who came within focus, whether they knew it or not. I can testify that she always wore stockings rolled just below the knee and panties that were not quite as white as the rolls of fat hanging in swags along her thighs. She was a most unselfconscious individual and you couldn't help liking her, but I was never tempted to introduce her to Millay. Some opportunities in life are better left unexplored.

We had two levels of society in our town, people who drank at parties and people who didn't. One's attitude toward liquor determined where you'd get invited. In those early days after the war, when prohibition was a thing of the past, nobody ever served cocktails. Each person or couple brought their own bottle, discreetly encased in a brown paper bag as though it was still against the law. The host furnished glasses and water. Nobody drank anything but bourbon or Scotch, and the majority leaned toward the former. We were still a pretty thrifty lot and Four Roses was a favorite.

All my brothers except the youngest, who didn't like parties of any kind and had married a girl who felt the same way, belonged to the drinking crowd, and I could sashay back and forth between the two groups; although whenever there was a conflict, I couldn't help but choose the drinking crowd. *In vino veritas*, or as Miss Bunch Brown said, "What's in there sober comes out drunk," and it was always more illuminating as well as entertaining to set my bottle on the kitchen counter with everybody else's than go somewhere prissy and sip tea or fruit punch.

Once at a party at John Hale's house, somebody commented that they were glad to see me there instead of at Mrs. Clyde Lawson's musicale, and one of the new-comer jackasses said to me, "Yeah, Buster, it sounds like you can swing both ways." I took a long sip of my bourbon, got right in his face, and said, "So what, asshole? You got a problem with that?"

He never came back to another party, and I won't call his name because a few years later it turned out he did. He asked his company for a transfer and he and his family moved off. I never did like him but I've always felt a little sorry for him.

The drinking crowd consisted of about eight couples on a regular basis, plus four or five others if it was going to be a big shindig. Most of the time, however, about once a month the core group would meet at whosever house was hosting the group. Three of my brothers and their wives qualified, as did Sara Belle Cofield and her husband, Calhoun Hipp, Sport Cofield and his wife, Emily, the county agent and his wife who had been born and raised somewhere else and came in trying to drink vodka with fruit juice until they got teased out of it.

Pearlie Mae Landrum had married Ace Turner from Calhoun, Georgia, who had come into town and started a very profitable hardware store. Pearlie Mae began buying all her clothes brand new at Frohsin's or Regenstein's or J. P. Allen's or every now and then the Regency Shop at Rich's, size eight and under; but she and Sara Belle were still buddies. Mary Lou McElroy was old county family and at least distantly kin to almost everybody else born in our town.

She had brought in Tim McElroy from Florida as new seed; she didn't want to risk having kids who were cross-eyed and had split nails. She was bad to get thick-tongued after two drinks, but our crowd would forgive any one of us almost anything provided it didn't happen when you were cold sober.

Bill Pritchett and I pretty well rounded out the core group. We were the only two singles included, and nobody ever suggested that we come together. It was a pretty perceptive bunch of people who almost always knew when to mention something out loud and when to keep their mouths shut. Whatever happened at one of our parties stayed there and was never told to non-drinkers.

The party that caused several couples to drop out of the circle was at my brother Harold's house. Harold was what we today would describe as a functioning alcoholic; back then everybody just said he was "bad to drink." He had a job as rural letter carrier and he never missed a day at work, although any driver meeting him way out in the country was always careful to give him a right smart more than half of the road. He got caught on an occasional cold or rainy day cutting his workday short by saying to hell with it and throwing what undelivered mail he had in a deep ditch and hurrying back home to bed. He would probably have been fired, except our family had very strong Cofield connections; so he only got a reprimand and that a mild one.

Mr. Mobley Whitaker was postmaster at the time Brother Harold got caught, and he didn't like confrontation of any sort, let alone with Brother Harold, who was known for his sharp tongue and his belligerent banty-rooster attitude. His wife could hold her liquor better than Brother Harold, and she could bless him out to a fare-thee-well when she took a notion, which was frequent. They had no children of their own and were not overly popular with the nieces and nephews.

Brother Harold had what I would call a titty fetish, and where it came from I never could figure; not one of the rest of us boys was like that. The men and women in our group always hugged and air-kissed and thought nothing of it; even Bill Pritchett. However, if Brother

Harold had had more than two drinks, which he usually had, he took it one or maybe two or three steps further than a conventional hug. He'd drape an arm over a woman's shoulder, slip the other one under the opposite shoulder and try to cop himself a feel. Left or right, made no difference. The girls who had grown up here had long since learned to hold their drink in both hands up under their chins with elbows guarding their breasts.

Since I never took more than one drink, I enjoyed watching female newcomers the first two or three times they got greeted by Brother Harold. It didn't take long for them to learn what I privately called the HHDP—the Harold Holcombe Defense Position. His wife watched even closer than I did but always out of the corner of her eye. I was usually a little embarrassed for the newcomer, but Sister Lula would swell up like a frog and I would know that later there would be an accounting and hell to pay. I had long since learned that it was not within my purview to reprimand Brother Harold; he could quote Cain quicker than anybody I ever heard.

And most often appropriately.

I sometimes wondered why some husband didn't slap the living shit out of my brother, but it was whispered that Sister Lula always took care of that, in private. Social decorum could not be disturbed beyond certain limits, regardless of how much liquor was consumed. Not even at the party I'm talking about. The only reason I'm telling it now is that it never made the rounds and it needs to be recorded or lost forever. It's another one of those things that makes our town just a little different from most.

Spade Waddell might be said to have been the root cause of the turmoil that night, although he had never been invited to a respectable house in our town for any reason and was not likely to be. When Mr. Johnnie died, Spade reared his Republican head and took out after Sport Cofield. Mr. B. M. never messed with politics; didn't think he needed to.

Spade put out a privately financed weekly paper for about six weeks before Sport was to run for mayor again. It was mimeographed. He brought out the fact that the city books, including all the financial records, were kept in the private home of the city clerk, who was Sport's next-door neighbor and wouldn't let an ordinary citizen see them. He pointed out that the city had run a special water line to the Cofield lumberyard for which the taxpayers had never been repaid. He told that there was not even a meter on that water line and when they had a fire and set off the sprinklers, untold thousands of gallons of taxpayers' water had been squandered free of charge. Then he took off on the city councilmen, all five of them, outlining how closely they were tied to the Cofield Clique, as he called it. They had secret meetings; they kept poor records; they passed ordinances without a quorum; they profited off work for the city with no bids ever being submitted.

He laid all this blame at Sport Cofield's doorstep and challenged the voters to sweep out the city council chambers as clean as that Greek fellow had done to a horse barn hundreds of years ago. I mean, he reamed old Sport a new one.

What was Sport to do? Mr. Johnnie was dead, Mr. B. M. was busy consolidating control of the bank along with Toor and was pretty abrupt about not being interested. Sport consulted Mr. Johnnie's lawyer, who was also father of one of the councilmen, the one Spade had referred to in his paper as "Old Fish-eye." He was tersely advised to pay no attention to the letters. "Just get out the vote. Don't get in a pissing contest with a skunk," was the way he phrased it.

There was by then a bunch of newcomers in town and they all swarmed in and registered to vote. One of the town's own sons, only child of a widowed mother, had been educated at Mr. Johnnie's expense but felt he owed nothing to Sport. His name was Eustace Pilcher and he had left Georgia soon as he finished Georgia Tech. He got himself a job with Coca-Cola and went to New York where he flew higher and higher, according to periodic reports from his mama. After the Depression, he apparently flew so high in New York that alcohol melted the wax on his wings and he was reduced to bringing his family back home, where, of course, we all watched him.

Well, bless Pat if old Eustace didn't qualify for mayor and persuade five malcontents to run for council. City hall, of which at that time we did not have one, was swept by the River Styx—I mean, plumb spank clean.

We were stunned. Nobody could talk about anything else for days, and Miss Georgia McCollum's bowels were not even mentioned at the UDC meeting, although everyone usually inquired of her daughter about them during the social hour.

Three weeks later Brother Harold and Sister Lula had the group for supper. The town had pretty well simmered down and accepted the fact that Eustace Pilcher was our mayor and a new day was dawning and we had a new focus of watching.

Not Emily Cofield. When she married Sport, she thought she had popped her butt in a tub of butter, as the saying went. She had swept into town all vivacious and charming and gracious and with pretty lips that stayed little girlish and pouty until the day she died. It had taken a while to dawn on her that Uncle Johnnie and Uncle B. M. had a condescending attitude toward Sport, and furthermore she didn't think he was getting a fair shake financially when the corporation dissolved.

While she praised and bragged on Sport when he wasn't around, he very soon discovered that those beautiful lips of hers could put a flamethrower to shame when she took him to task, which was on a fairly regular basis. Why any woman thinks she can change a man after he has reached middle age is beyond my comprehension, but I have sure and certain observed a lot of determined energy wasted in that direction.

Anyhow, at Sister Lula's everybody slowly and pleasantly reduced their level of sobriety until inhibitions were lowered to the point that we'd better eat supper. Our group was so sophisticated and practiced about Four Roses that dinner was rarely announced before eleven p.m.

Brother Harold was about two sheets in the wind before the party started, his philosophy being that a host should take a little nip all through the afternoon as he was helping prepare for guests. John and Roberta Ingram were relative newcomers to our town; they'd been running with our group about a year. John was a great big tall guy, affable and slow-spoken, sort of like a cross between John Wayne and Randolph Scott. He had been brought in as general manager of the first real industry we had attracted to our county. His wife was a real pretty woman with what you call a stunning figure, and that's about as far as she went. I always thought she had a displeased look on her face and when she talked she wrinkled her nose just a little, like she smelled cabbage cooking. They had come to the party a little late but a good half-hour before Sara Belle and Calhoun Hipp, who were always the last to come.

John settled Roberta on the sofa next to Bill Pritchett, got his picture taken without noticing it, and went off to fix her a drink, howdying and shaking hands on the way. Brother Harold plopped himself down right beside Roberta and hugged her up tight and be blessed if he didn't cop a feel with both hands. Roberta gave him a sharp look and an even sharper elbow and moved to an overstuffed chair after very politely saying, "Excuse me," to Bill Pritchett. Brother Harold promptly went over and sat on the arm of her chair and here came the arm and hand again. About this time Sister Lula took note of what was going on and said, "Harold, I need you in the kitchen."

At precisely the same moment John Ingram came back with their drinks, set them down on the end table, towered over Harold, and rumbled, "Buddy-boy, you've got a problem and all of us know it. I am your guest or I'd mop up this floor with you right now. My advice to you is that you are a sick man and you need to go and get some treatment. Get up, Roberta, we're going home."

And they did. The whole room got quiet and Roberta turned to Sister Lula and said, "Good night, Lula, we had a wonderful time." I didn't even notice the cabbage cooking. Roberta Ingram was what you might call a true lady.

With that, Sister Lula said, "Dinner is served. We won't wait for Sara Belle and Calhoun."

Of course, none of us was going to be crass enough to talk about Harold and Roberta, at least not then and there; so Emily lit in on the election again. I had to help pull Bill Pritchett up out of the sofa and nearly got a hernia in the process, but it fell to Brother Harold to escort Emily Cofield to the table. I had noticed, as had we all, that Emily was drinking a little faster than usual that night, and that with every drink her voice became louder and shriller. She was among friends who had all supported Sport at the polls, and she had been letting off steam in a continuous and repetitive panegyric about Sport and the calumny and worthlessness of Eustace Pilcher. Her tongue did not get thicker with liquor but it sure got sharper.

On the way to the table I overheard her once more belaboring the catastrophic fate that had befallen Sport. "How anybody in this town could have the stupidity and the audacity to put a sorry creature like Eustace Pilcher in as mayor of our town over a man of Sport Cofield's character and standing is just more than I understand. Why, Eustace's mama took in washing and dipped snuff 'til the day she died, and that sorry Eustace never sent her a dime to live on while he was great big Mr. Big Shot in New York City.

"He didn't even put running water in the house, and the poor old soul had to draw all her water from the well. Uncle Johnnie paid for his education and this is the way he shows his gratitude. He never could have gotten a job teaching math here if old man Lum Summerfield hadn't took pity on him."

"And that mealy-mouthed wife of his! Would you believe the way she keeps house for him and those four teenagers? Cooks supper about four o'clock in the afternoon and leaves everything on the stove and whoever comes in feeds themselves at whatever time they show up. They don't ever sit down at the table like real folks and have a blessing like I'm sure they were raised to do. I'll never, never understand why the people in this town didn't stand behind a fine man like Sport Cofield, especially after all that his Daddy and Uncle Johnnie and even Uncle B. M., in his own way, have done for this town and county. It's just a disgrace."

Brother Harold, still smarting from his dressing down from John Ingram, said, as he pulled out her chair and seated her, "Emily, you might as well face the fact that the day has long passed when a Cofield can get elected to any office in this county."

With that, he pulled out his own chair and sat down.

Emily glared at him. "Well!" she exclaimed. "That is an ansult." (When Emily drank she substituted a short *a* for a short *i*, which made her speech pattern impressive, albeit inaccurate.) "I have never been so ansulted in my life. I just wish you'd repeat that statement. I just wish you'd say it one more time. I dare you to repeat it."

Brother Harold, durn his drunken time, obliged her.

I had barely got Bill hitched up to her place at the table when he stood up, tapped on his glass, and said, "I have just told Emily that the day is long gone when a Cofield can be elected to public office in this county."

Emily threw down her napkin, pushed her chair back, and stood over him, staring down at his bald spot which had turned red as a beet. "Well!" she said. "That does beat anything I have ever heard in my whole entire life! That is the supreme ansult of all time and I am completely ansulted! *But*, I am a perfect lady and I am a guest in your home and therefore, while I am a guest in your home, I will not tell you what I think of you!"

She drew a deep breath; I thought her bosom might pop. "But let me tell you one thing, you goddam beady-eyed little shit-ass: you come over to my house some time and I'll clean your clock!"

With that, she sat down and began eating.

I guess somebody somewhere in that group would probably have thought of some way to break the silence that followed, but Calhoun and Sara Belle came in right then, gushing, and howdying, and air-kissing, and giving about a dozen excuses why they were late. We didn't believe a one of them since we'd heard them all before, but it was a familiar routine that restored a level of comfort to the room.

We went through the motions of dessert and helping Lula clean up the dishes, but by the time we all left everybody was cold sober except Brother Harold, Sister Lula, and Emily Cofield, who had developed a loud case of hiccups and swollen eyelids.

The only comment I ever heard about the incident came from Bill Pritchett, who was talking to herself as she got in her car. "Be damned if that don't beat a hawg flying sideways." And that sums it up about as well as anything.

At 1:30 my telephone rang. It was Sister Lula. Brother Harold had fallen down the kitchen steps on his way to the garbage can and cut his head pretty bad. Would I come and take them to the doctor?

As soon as I could dress, I went over. He was at the foot of the kitchen steps all right, bleeding like a fountain and yelling that he couldn't see. "I'm blind," he hollered. "I hope you're satisfied!"

I ran in and got a towel out of their bathroom to wrap around his head and I couldn't help but notice there was blood on the bedroom floor and one of Sister Lula's shoes she had worn to the party had blood and what looked like a little piece of flesh on the spike heel. Also there was a trail of blood all the way through the kitchen and on out and down the steps.

I wrapped Harold's head up 'til he looked like a Swami or something. The reason he couldn't see was that his left eyebrow was lying down almost to his lip and there was blood coming into his right eye from a cut across his forehead. I called the young doctor who had come to our town about five years earlier and about put Dr. Grizzelle out of business. Dr. Hentz had five small children and didn't mind working night or day.

He did a marvelous job on Harold; stopped the bleeding and started sewing; didn't even have to use Novocaine, Harold was so anesthetized. He did, however, have to listen to Sister Lula explain the whole time he was working how the accident happened. It took so long to sew him up and Sister Lula kept chattering and repeating herself so much that there were some pretty obvious contradictions in her recital. The odor of alcohol was heavy in the air and it didn't all come from Brother Harold.

Dr. Hentz and I avoided exchanging glances the whole time she talked. *In vino veritas*. Right. But not always.

When I got them home about sunup, I quoted the only line of poetry to Sister Lula that I ever ventured. First I said, "You'd better clean off your shoe real good when you get in, Lula."

Then I gave her a little peck on the cheek and thought briefly of Ace Turner's wife.

What did the Colonel's Lady think?
Nobody never knew.
Somebody asked the Sergeant's wife
And she told 'em true.

Sister Lula said, "Say which?" And her a third-grade teacher, too. I never tried any more poetry on her; pearls before swine, like they say.

Brother Harold healed up real good. In spite of all Dr. Hentz could do, however, he was left with a pucker to his left eyebrow which made him look like he was leering. That didn't help his reputation a bit, but he managed to live long enough to retire from the post office with a pension, which kept him comfortably in Four Roses 'til the day he died. We were all relieved to see him go, but every now and then I miss him.

Sister Lula got them to name a women's circle in the church Roberta Ingram Circle, and everybody in town wound up admiring Roberta. She took her church work seriously and set out for all the ladies in the church to get their husbands down to the altar rail with pledge cards on Temperance Sunday. Her husband got promoted and they had to move to Alabama before she found out how miserably she had failed. I was watching that Sunday morning and only two women from her circle put cards on the altar. And none of the husbands. Roberta had, however, without ever saying a word, cured Brother Harold of hugging. She was a true lady.

That was not the last party, by any means, but it was the last of the really wild ones, and the group kept gradually getting smaller. At one of them, Ace Turner was out of town and Pearlie Mae had come by herself. She had on a dark blue velvet sheath of a dress that screamed Frohsin's. It was the exact color of her eyes. On top of that she smelled like Chanel No. 5 or Toujours Moi, and I was tempted for old times' sake to murmur a little Millay to her. Didn't hurt to test the waters, you know. She looked like a million dollars.

I handed her the drink I had fixed for her out of my bottle, looked at her cleavage, and said,

> I, too, beneath thy moon, almighty sex,
> Go forth at nightfall crying like a cat....

She took a little sip, stirred her drink real daintily with her little finger, then licked the finger lightly, looked at me over the edge of the glass, and said,

> And if I loved you Wednesday,
> Well, what is that to you?
> I do not love you Thursday—
> So much is true.
> And why you come complaining
> Is more than I can see.
> I loved you Wednesday,—yes—but what
> Is that to me?

"Let me tell you something, Buster Holcombe, when I married Ace Turner I took some vows, and if you've got a problem with that, just work with it. Thanks for the drink." And she walked off.

The next time the group had a party, I accepted a dinner invitation from Carlotta Melrose instead. She served fruit punch before dinner, and we had chicken casserole, green beans, and Stouffer's macaroni and cheese. She discussed the latest rumors in town about the sex life of the black preacher and, of course, how awful the Cofields were. Then we had plain vanilla ice cream and I got home early.

Pearlie Mae was always nice to me when we met after that, and I couldn't help crying when I played "Amazing Grace" at her funeral. I sang in my head, "And nobody never knew." It was a sweet and dignified service. Sara Belle Hipp sat with the family, what was left of it.

Chapter 11

Progress had hit our town. Eustace Pilcher was pretty ineffectual as a mayor and as a math teacher, too, truth to tell. He couldn't maintain even the semblance of discipline in his classroom, and one spring afternoon in second-year algebra, Jim Jackson and three of his cronies jumped up, hollered, "Surf's up," and started shifting and sliding around on top of their desks like they were in Hawaii. It created such a commotion that the principal himself had to come in and quiet it down. He didn't renew Eustace's contract for the next year. We've always had good schools in our county, mostly because there are some things we just will not put up with.

Eustace talked the new council into hiring his wife as city clerk, and they even made us a city hall by boarding up the old tool shed that had stood behind the calaboose before it fell in. Eustace managed to get him a job as substitute teacher one county over, where they will put up with anything.

The new council woke up, started working together, and convinced Eustace that he should be a one-term mayor. This happened after the government of France had started some sort of celebration and publicity program. A lot of small towns all over the United States were singled out to be honored and their mayors were invited to Paris for a week, all expenses paid. They even invited the mayor of LaGrange, which had been named after Lafayette's barn.

Our town was singled out and old Eustace got an invitation exactly one week after he was sworn in as mayor. Emily Cofield was indignant. She went so far as to call on Eustace and plead for him to send Sport, since he had been mayor for twenty-five years and Eustace was just barely sworn in.

Eustace turned her down cold, which caused a relapse of her hiccups at the next party, the one I missed because of Carlotta

Melrose's chicken casserole. Eustace took off to Paris all by himself, leaving his wife to work at her new job and cook stove supper for the kids. Everybody in town was either proud or jealous, and that pretty well lines out customary reactions about anything hereabouts.

Proud and jealous soon turned into outrage or glee. Life magazine ran a whole spread of pictures and a story about the celebration in Paris, and right in the middle of the page was a picture of our very own Eustace Pilcher, complete with identifying caption for the whole world to see. He was sitting in a bathtub as naked as a jaybird, cross-eyed, grinning like a possum, and obviously drunk as a coot. His glasses were on crooked and he was holding up a bottle of champagne like it was a basketball trophy. I had never known before that he had hair on his chest, and certainly not on his shoulders. In fact, he was so hairy he didn't look all that naked to me, but it scandalized every woman in the WMS.

Mobley Whitaker was hard put to get all the copies of Life in the appropriate boxes before our post office was stormed. Those who had subscriptions couldn't wait to get their hands on the magazine, and those who didn't subscribe were crowding in to look over their shoulders. The whole town was buzzing.

The Baptist Board of Deacons met and voted to reconsider his nomination as a deacon, and the council met very secretly and began discussing political options. There was no way they could back Eustace for a second term. Far as I know, nobody ever came out and confronted Eustace about it. I guess I came as close as anybody. I ran into him in the post office one morning and he said, "It's little Aloysius Holcombe, isn't it? All grown up but I recognized you right away. The family resemblance is strong."

This sort of got under my skin. I looked him in the eye and said, "Good morning yourself, Icarus."

He said, "It's Eustace, Aloysius, Eustace."

It had gone right over his head. I said, "Whatever," ordered a roll of stamps from Mobley Whitaker, and left. I was reaffirmed in my vote for Sport Cofield. So was Emily. She didn't get hiccups at the next party but said, "I *told* y'all" so many times that we wished she would get them.

Eustace got himself a herd of goats to pull a little covered wagon he lived in, quit shaving, bathing, or getting a haircut, and took to the road—Florida in the wintertime, north Alabama and Tennessee in the summertime, all by back roads. Last I heard, he was still going strong, but he never came through our town. Folks said you could smell him and the goats before you ever saw them. His children, without exception, turned out well, however. I don't think any of them ever drank. There is a God.

It turned out that apparently God was behind the new city council, too. Or vice versa; often it's hard to tell the difference.

First they put a meter on everybody's water line, including the planing mill, and started collecting past due water bills on a business-like basis. They even collected all the back taxes, balanced the books, and first thing you know the city was out of debt and had a little cash on hand.

Before they hired Susan Pilcher as city clerk, we had only one paid city employee. He was a failed farmer named Gundy Mitchell who was marshal, garbage collector, and water superintendent. He was a slow-talking, proud man who had fallen on hard times and needed cash to support his family or he never would have taken on such a job, where you pretty well have to get along with everybody you meet every day of your life, no matter what sort of temper they might be in.

Because he had to pick up garbage and dump it into his truck and also had to get down on his knees pretty often to read water meters, his clothes were usually not very clean but pretty fragrant after about ten or eleven o'clock in the morning. In addition to this, he didn't shave but twice a week on account of a skin condition, and if his gums happened to be aching, he didn't wear his teeth. He did, however, always wear his policeman's cap and badge which said "City Marshall." He was a comfortable figure in town and we all respected him.

One summer day about middle of the afternoon he was put to the test. A lady driving a pink Lincoln automobile came flying into town on the paved part of the highway, hit the dirt road at the courthouse, raised a big cloud of dust, and very nearly ran over Miss Lora Holt who had parked her A-model on the square and was crossing the road to Rosenbloom's store. Gundy had a load of garbage, but he also had on his cap; he took off after the Lincoln, which had to slow down because of the ruts and dust, and apprehended the driver in front of Dr. Grizzelle's house.

Even without his teeth, Gundy could handle a cud of Brown Mule, but he spit it out and tipped the bill of his cap before he spoke to the lady.

"Ma'am, you were speeding and come pretty near hitting one of our citizens who, on a good day, is very nervous and jumpy and will be a while getting over this encounter. In fact, I suspect she'll be whining about it at council meeting tonight and in Ruby's grocery store for the next six months. Lady, you don't know Miss Lora Holt. So I'm afraid I'm going to have to give you a ticket or be accused of shirking my duty."

With this, he reached in his hip pocket, pulled out his pad, licked his pencil, and prepared to write.

"Well," exclaimed the woman, "after all that, if you'll just hush I'll take the ticket but I want to tell *you* one thing: I've been guilty of speeding in nearly every state of the union, but this is the first time I've been stopped by an unshaven, toothless, tobacco-chewing son of a bitch who smells like a hog pen and is driving a garbage truck. What a hick town! Gimme the ticket."

Gundy squared his shoulders and drawled with extra politeness, "Well, ma'am, since you've explained your position so plainly, I'ma let you go with a warning this time. Don't let it happen again, though."

She batted her eyes at him and said, "You're a darling, but get a shave before you stop me again."

Gundy was not so polite at council meeting, which happened to be that very night. Miss Lora Holt had not yet arrived. He

interrupted the reading of the minutes to recount the incident with
what, for Gundy, was considerable passion and ended by his tossing
his cap and badge on the table.

"Iff'n you don't get me a proper police car, I ain't about to ever
stop another automobile in this town. I quit. Right now."

Although it was a considerable strain on the budget, the council
voted unanimously to procure a police car. In fact, one of the
councilmen sold them his own second-hand Ford that very night. It
was by unanimous vote. A couple of the councilmen thought the
price was a little high, but nobody thought they could afford losing
Gundy at that time. Taking bids was never mentioned; turned out
they had learned well by precedent. At any rate, we had our first
official police car. We do manage to hold our heads up and look after
our own.

Chapter 12

Along about this time something happened in the town that diverted attention from the new city council and mayor. Timothy Grizzelle got married. Timbo, as we called him, had overcome a lot. For one thing, he had overcome his mama, although he did look like her. We just never held a boy's mama against him since we all had to go through the same painful experience of outgrowing one. We might feel sorry for a boy whose mama made it hard for him, but we never blamed the boy. In fact, we always cheered him on.

We all put the blame for Timbo squarely at the feet of his daddy. Doctor Grizzelle was overly proud to start with, and after he outlived all the other doctors in the county and became the only doctor we had, sometimes he came across as being plumb arrogant. He remembered his sweet potato days and became what Miss Bunch Brown called "pennywise." He wouldn't go on a house call unless he saw the money first, and he was forever asking for a discount whenever he bought anything, even if it was a cantaloupe a farm boy was selling to put himself through school. He acted like being "The Doctor" was the same as being "The King." We grumbled but nobody ever confronted him; you never could tell when you might get sick and have to call him. Sam Champion said if Dr. Grizzelle got any more dignified, he was in danger of falling over backward.

Timbo was the baby of the family and had been an unexpected surprise because of Mrs. Grizzelle's age plus the sweet potatoes. His older sisters were required to defer to him in everything, and being the only boy he was, of course, the flower of the flock and the only hope of carrying on the name. We all accepted this as going without saying, but his mama and sisters persisted in saying it.

Frequently.

We watched.

Only Miss Bunch had the forthrightness to proclaim, "That boy just ain't right."

There wasn't anything for Dr. Grizzelle to do but step up to the plate and raise Timbo himself, but he kept trying to do it in his own image. The Doctor couldn't do anything about the boy's looks; Mrs. Grizzelle had tended to that. He did break him from drooling by the time he was ready for high school, but the boy was just plain mushmouthed and even after he was grown his lower lip always got suspiciously moist when he was talking. He never did master complete control of that lower lip. In repose, it sagged loose and pouch-like and his speech sounded like it was coming around hot oatmeal. Very gingerly.

What The Doctor did manage to accomplish was instilling his own attitude into his son. Timothy Grizzelle grew up thinking he was an extra-special child of fate who deserved nothing but the best, and if it even entered his head that other folks thought he was weird, he never manifested it. He was prone, however, to lie a lot, especially about his grades.

His daddy put him in Woodward Academy as a boarding student as soon as he was ready for eighth-grade work. Chronologically.

This had formerly been called Georgia Military Academy, where people who could afford it sent boys who were discipline problems and wouldn't study in the local schools. I had a cousin who got sent there and he spent most of his first year being restricted to campus on weekends, walking the bullpen with his rifle. They whipped him into shape, though, and he finally settled down like a gelded stallion and got enough education to rise a couple of levels in the Ford Motor Company later.

The academy had the reputation of being very strict on academics as well as discipline, and most of its boarding students were scions of wealthy families from South and Central America. After the war, they changed the name to Woodward Academy and began taking in more day students and lots of girls. By the time Timbo went there, it had become somewhat of a snob school, a sort of Southside Westminster if you will, but cheaper.

After Woodward, Dr. Grizzelle put pressure on some Atlanta specialists to whom he referred paying patients with problems he couldn't handle, and Timbo was admitted to Emory. At the end of the first quarter, Timbo came home. His mama told Miss Mae Harp it was because there was too much pressure at Emory and Timbo was a highly sensitive boy. His middle sister told it that Timbo's grades at Emory didn't meet Father's standards. Neither one of them was outright lying, but we got a good example of dissembling.

At any rate, Dr. Grizzelle then had to go and put what pressure he could on Mr. Johnnie Cofield, who had helped appoint every member of the State Board of Regents. Timbo went to the University of Georgia in Athens and stayed there. In fact, he stayed and stayed and stayed there, summers and all.

Right before he graduated, the bombshell hit the town. Timbo had managed to get himself engaged to be married and the wedding was to be in June. Miss Mae Harp became even more popular in the town than she had already been for all of her life. She was our pipeline of information from Mrs. Grizzelle, and Miss Mae did not mind sharing the tidbits she could glean. Miss Mae put her own twist on the knowledge she procured, but we all knew her and Mrs. Grizzelle quite well, thank you, and were able to sift the wheat from the chaff. My mama was never a gossip, but even she found some excuse to call on Miss Mae a couple of times a week beginning the middle of April. The town buzzed and suspense grew.

First off, we learned about the bride. She was a gorgeous girl who had met Timbo while they were students at Woodward and, like Beatrice Cofield, had never dated anyone else.

We all said, "That figures."

Her father was an extremely wealthy man from up north who was simply crazy about Timbo.

"Uh-huh," we opined.

His name was Stanley Sinkwich, but he was not related to the university football player. He had made a heap of money and had married an Atlanta girl from a well-connected old-money family. Miss Mae couldn't remember the name of the well-connected family but did remember that the Sinkwiches lived in a mansion in East Point and that Sylvia had gone to some fancy girls' school in New England after Woodward.

Mrs. Grizzelle told Miss Mae that Timbo and Sylvia had very similar and compatible backgrounds and enjoyed the same social standing in their respective communities. When Sara Belle Hipp repeated this tidbit to Calhoun, who had been raised on Lullwater in Atlanta but never bragged about it, he said, "Hot shit!" Sara Belle repeated this only *sotto voce*, but it got around. Calhoun's sentiment was pretty universal. In our town, anybody who put on airs was just begging for a pratfall. Like I said, everybody knew everybody else's grandparents and the truth is the light.

A month before the wedding, Miss Mae got on the phone almost out of breath and told Miss Gray Miller that Mrs. Grizzelle had just let it out that Sylvia Sinkwich was Catholic. And the wedding was to be in a Catholic church. And it would be performed by a Catholic priest. And all such as that. And, land sakes, there wasn't a Catholic anywhere in or around our county. And, "I declare, Gray, I'm just going to have to lie down and stretch out for a few minutes. I'll call you back later. I'm plumb dizzy."

As soon as she recovered, Miss Mae called Miss Gray again, although it was an hour and a half before she could get a clear line.

"I forgot to tell you, Gray, the invitations are going out tomorrow. Going to be mailed in Atlanta, so don't look for one for two or three days. Mrs. Grizzelle told me not to expect one myself because it's to be very formal and all such as that and she knew I wouldn't fool with all that and anyway, she said, I was too old and infirm to stay out late at night. I came very close to telling her I wouldn't be caught dead in a Catholic church nohow. You never know when Jesus might come back, Gray, but we both know it won't be in a Catholic church. The very idea!

"You might as well not look for an invite yourself; you're getting some age on you and I know your rheumatism gets worse at first dark. Mrs. Grizzlle said the church is small and they're having to limit the number of guests. Sylvia's mama has got the Grizzelles cut down to a hundred invitations, and the reception is to be held at the Capital City Club, whatever that is. Mrs. Grizzelle says it's very expensive and private and the Sandwiches or whatever you call them don't belong there, but Mrs. Sandwich has a brother-in-law who has reserved it for them and Mr. Sandwich will pay him back later after they see how many guests show up. The wedding is set for six o'clock and the reception at eight. Mrs. Grizzelle told me that's because the wedding will take an hour at least, what with mass and Communion and all. And my word, I think I'm getting dizzy again. If it takes Catholics that long to get married, it's no wonder they don't believe in divorce. They don't have time for it. Bye now."

The invitations came, replete with tissue paper and cards to the reception "immediately following the ceremony." It was the Capital City Club, all right, but a good many of the invitations did not have cards. The new young doctor and his wife got one, but none of his patients did. Dr. Hentz had built a large practice from Dr. Grizzelle's malcontents because he would get out at night, would make house calls, and would even let people charge until they sold their cotton. Dr. Grizzelle referred to these people very loftily as not being loyal, and not a one of them got an invitation.

Neither the new mayor nor the councilmen got invited either, but the county commissioners, the sheriff, the judge of the ordinary court, and the clerk of the court did. The little county treasurer did not; Mrs. Grizzelle was afraid she might come. All the Cofields, the Melroses, the Perdues, and the Lawsons were invited, and every single one of the Holcombes except Brother Harold; Mrs. Grizzelle knew damn well he'd show up.

We teased Brother Harold about it, but if it bothered him he never showed it. For six months after that wedding, though, Dr. Grizzelle kept complaining to Mobley Whitaker about what bills he did send out not being delivered in a timely fashion. If at all.

I wouldn't have missed that wedding for anything, and in hindsight it would not have been nearly so entertaining if it weren't for modern technology. I mention airplane travel, paved roads, and pressurized shaving cream as examples, and you'll see why later. It was on a Saturday evening and I had a very private poetry reading already arranged, but as soon as I got my invitation I called and rescheduled it, which was all right because the lady was invited, too, and had insisted that her husband who was supposed to be out of town cancel his business trip in favor of the Grizzelle wedding.

She said, "You're right, Baby, nobody with peacock brains is going to miss that wedding. I've been watching the Grizzelles longer and closer than you; we lived next door to them before they got rich and built that big house, you know, and I'm here to tell you, something will happen that you don't want to miss. I don't know what it'll be, but something will happen. Mark my words and get set. I'm psychic, you know. Even if I'm not the seventh daughter of a seventh daughter and born under a caul. On top of that the whole pack of them is snake-bit."

I rode to the church with young Dr. Hentz and his wife. We had become friends when I drew up the title for the land where he built his house. I had also recently revised Dr. Grizzelle's will. At a discount, of course. At least I professed it to be. I was considered loyal, although I still had plans not to get sick.

Dr. Hentz was invited for political reasons; it wouldn't have looked right if he had been excluded. All of the Holcombes knew, however, that the reason Brother Harold had not been invited was because he had switched over to Dr. Hentz after he sewed up his head and eyebrow and was not loyal. We didn't mention that, of course.

The Catholic church in East Point indeed was small. It was also brand-spanking new; the bricks still looked sharp and raw, and the shrubbery couldn't have been planted more than a year. We got there decently early.

First thing I saw when we walked into the foyer was Dr. Grizzelle. He was diked out to a fare-thee-well with a morning coat, striped trousers, gray gloves, and, so help me God, spats. He looked like a member of Teddy Roosevelt's cabinet. He came rushing over to us, spoke very briefly and hurriedly to Dr. Hentz, and pulled me aside.

"Aloysius, I'm glad to see you. I have a bit of a problem and I need your advice."

"Yes, sir, Doctor, how can I help you?"

"Well, Aloysius, it transpires that Timothy does not have a marriage license and the priest won't marry him without one."

"That's a state law, Doctor; don't blame the Catholic church. Tell me where he left it and I'll go get it."

"You don't understand, Aloysius; he doesn't have one. He neglected to get one. The wedding party is all here and the guests are coming in. What do you suggest that I do?"

Well, ta-ta and thank you, I thought. I looked at my watch and considered for a moment.

"Doctor, the only thing I know to do is call our county ordinary and ask him to bring a license up here. That is, if I can catch him before he leaves his office and gets drunk. It's Saturday afternoon, you know."

"Hmmm. Yes. You think that's necessary?"

Before I could answer, in walks this big-shot socialite specialist from Atlanta to whom Dr. Grizzelle had been referring patients for years. He had on a tuxedo. His wife had on long gloves. They were kin to the bride. Dr. Grizzelle rushed over to him with his coattails almost streaming out behind him and explained the situation. "Mr. Holcombe here, my attorney, thinks we should call the judge of ordinary court, who is one of my loyal patients, and ask him to bring a license up here and fill it out."

The big shot flicked a glance at me and said, "That won't be necessary, too much bother. Calm yourself, Grizzelle, and go tell the priest to go ahead and marry them and we'll get the license Monday."

"But, Doctor, Timothy and his bride are flying out for a honeymoon in South America tonight and won't be here to sign the license for two weeks."

"What's the big deal? Tell the priest you'll get it for him as soon as they get back. Quit worrying. Come on, dear, let's go be seated."

As he started walking off, he turned to Dr. Grizzelle and said, "If he balks, offer him a sizable contribution to the church. It looks like they could use it." He winked. "Money talks, Grizzelle. We both know that."

As I was thinking what a spectacle he must present at the Piedmont Driving Club, I heard Dr. Grizzelle say with a good deal of formality, "You heard what Dr. Blackford says, Aloysius. I won't be needing your services after all," and he bustled off. To the church office, I guess.

I went in and sat down in an aisle seat right next to Dr. Hentz. He nudged me. "Got a problem?" he whispered.

"No license," I whispered back.

His wife nudged him. He whispered. She nudged her neighbor and whispered. Then it was nudge, whisper, nudge, whisper 'til the news had moved at least six rows down. Then it hit Mr. B. M. Cofield, who by now was so deaf that he thought nobody else could hear.

"No license?" He thought he whispered, but the rest of the church heard it. Miss Pansy elbowed him so hard he said, "What?" I mean, quiet settled in until the organ started playing.

About this time, Joel Culpepper, who Timothy had inveigled into being one of his ushers because they had gone to first grade together, tapped me on the shoulder.

"Dr. Grizzelle wants to see you."

I was conscious that a good many necks craned to watch me walk out, but with the organ playing nice and soothing I didn't create any commotion. Dr. Grizzelle almost grabbed me with both gloves. "Aloysius, that priest was adamant. In fact, he became quite rude, especially after I offered to donate twenty dollars to his building fund. He says he'll call this whole wedding off if he doesn't have that license here before it starts. Would you be kind enough to call Comer Davis for me and see if he'll get a license up here? As quickly as possible, of course."

Comer was our judge of ordinary court, but by popular usage was called "the ordinary." Everybody liked Comer, who was so affable and nonjudgmental of his fellow men that nobody could help liking him. He was reputed to be a brilliant lawyer, but to the uninitiated observer he masked it well. He habitually smiled when listening to someone, nodding his head as though in agreement and punctuating his responses with "Yeah, yeah, yeah" and "Well, well, well." I never heard it said of him that he spoke ill of anyone. The Cofields, Bazemores, and Summerfields all liked him. We never let on to him that we all knew he had a drinking problem.

"Dr. Grizzelle," I responded, "I'll be glad to try to call Comer. Maybe I can still catch him at the office. Where is the telephone?"

"The only one besides the one in that priest's study is the pay phone here in the lobby and it would be terribly inconvenient and perhaps a little embarrassing to use the one in the office; it's crowded with people."

"It'll be long distance to call from here, Dr. Grizzelle."

"Well, if you don't have any change, I can pay for it."

I was dumbfounded. I had at least six quarters in my pocket but I was not about to consider a discount at this point in time.

"I don't have a dime," I lied. "We'd better hurry, you know."

I walked over to the little niche in the wall where the telephone was mounted, took the receiver off the hook, and looked at The Doctor. He jerked the glove off his right hand, reached into his pocket, and pulled out a coin purse. I'm not lying. It was a pendulous leather one with two compartments, and it had a heavy clasp on each one. He unsnapped it and, without bothering to count, dumped a whole pile of coins on the apron beneath the phone. I guess this is when I fully realized the urgency and emergency of the situation and the stress the doctor was under.

The phone rang and rang and rang. I looked at The Doctor who was hovering close to my side but keeping an eye out for late-arriving guests. Just as I shrugged my shoulders to indicate failure, I heard the receiver being tumbled off the hook in the ordinary's office.

"Hello." The voice was thick but not as thick as I had heard on previous occasions. *There is a merciful God*, I thought.

"Comer? Thank God I caught you at the office. This is Buster Holcombe and I've got a big favor to ask of you."

"Yeah, Buster, yeah. How you doing? Yeah. How's your mama and papa? Yeah, yeah."

"Never mind all that, Comer. I've got a real emergency situation and only you can help me."

"Yeah, yeah." I could hear a guarded tone creeping into his voice. I fancied that he thought I was about to ask him to fix a ticket or to bail me out of jail somewhere. "Whassa problem? Yeah, yeah."

"Comer, I'm in the East Point Catholic Church at the Grizzelle wedding—"

He interrupted. Very congenially. "Yeah, yeah, Bootsie and I got an invitation to that wedding but Mama and Papa aren't doing well and we didn't think we could leave town. In fact, I was about to go—"

"Comer," I interrupted in turn. "Listen. This is important. Very important. Timothy Grizzelle neglected to get a marriage license and the priest here won't marry him without one and—"

"Yeah, yeah, yeah, it's a felony against him if he does. Yeah, yeah."

"Comer, we know that. Dr. Grizzelle has waited on you and your parents for years, and he wants you to get in your car right now and bring a license up here to the Catholic church. Right now, Comer. The guests are all here and waiting."

"He forgot to get a license?"

"Yes. Absolutely. Can you hurry?"

"Did they get their blood test?"

Our state had passed a law that no one could get a marriage license without a blood test for syphilis. It was passed after a considerable debate in the House of Representatives. A lone and impassioned female member of the legislature had taken to the floor in opposition, saying that it was an insult to Southern womanhood and therefore unthinkable. Women should be excused from such a demeaning law.

An old and grizzled legislator from rural South Georgia rose in rebuttal to say, "In all due respect to the lady and her Southern womanhood, I'd like to tell my fellow legislators that I've had clap six times and I never yet caught it from a man."

He had received a considerable donation to his campaign from a clinical laboratory lobbyist, although he had no opposition.

"I don't know about that, Comer," I said hurriedly. "Hold on a minute." I turned to Dr. Grizzelle. "Did Timbo and Sylvia get their blood tests, Doctor?"

He drew himself up and in formal, even sonorous, tones said, "I don't know, but I can tell you right now that Timothy's blood is *good*."

"Never mind about the blood tests, Comer. I'm sure Dr. Grizzelle can take care of that. Can you get the license for us?"

"Yeah, yeah, yeah. I reckon I can do that for the doctor, but I don't know where that church is in East Point."

I gave him explicit directions that were really quite simple. "Can you please hurry, Comer?" It was a reasonable question. I had never seen him hurry about anything. In fact, the more he drank, the slower he drove.

"Yeah, yeah, Buster. Sure. What time does the wedding start?"

"At six o'clock, Comer."

"What time is it now, Buster?"

I looked at my watch. "It's exactly five fifty-five."

"Good godamighty!" exploded so loud over the telephone that it rang all across the lobby. Dr. Grizzelle jumped. I jumped. I don't know which one of us knocked the remaining coins off the apron, but they rolled noisily all across the tiled floor. Dr. Grizzelle immediately removed his other glove and busied himself.

"Hurry, Comer, hurry, hurry, hurry," I said and hung up. I watched for a moment, then said, "Do you need any help, Doctor?"

"No, Aloysius, I've about recovered all of them. Let me go now and try to reason again with that priest."

It obviously worked. At ten after six, when all of us were getting restless, the wedding began. Joel Culpepper brought the mother of the groom in on his arm to her seat on our side of the church. I heard the creak of corset and the soft whisper of thighs as she passed, because I was sitting right on the aisle. Mrs. Grizzelle had on a long blue dress, a large white orchid, white gloves above her elbows, but sensible shoes. As she released Joel's arm and he bowed in departure, she faced the altar, and before all of her fellow Methodists and the other steadfastly Protestant guests crossed herself, genuflected ponderously, entered her pew, and knelt briefly on the *prie-dieu* before moving back up onto her seat. There was a coordinated and audible exhalation of disbelief from our side of the church.

What an auspicious beginning.

The bride's mother went through the same ceremonial entrance, except she remained kneeling on the *prie-dieu*. Apparently she was going to pray until the bride came in. She prayed and prayed. The music had stopped. We waited and waited.

Joel Culpepper tiptoed in, went down the side of the pews to where his wife was sitting, and whispered in her ear. She removed her wedding ring, gave it to him, and he tiptoed out with it. I learned later that when the priest asked Timbo for the wedding ring, it transpired that he had packed it in his luggage, which was already checked at the airport. When Joel answered Timbo's pleas for help and presented his wife's ring as an emergency loan, the priest asked sharply, "Has this ring been blessed?"

"Whatta ya mean, blessed?" asked Protestant Joel. When told that he could not use a wedding ring that had not been ceremonially blessed prior to the service, Joel responded, "Well go ahead and bless it, Reverend; it can't hurt it."

That priest, as Dr. Grizzelle had labeled him, must have become pretty testy and impatient by that time, for I learned later a lot of maneuvering and shenanigans were going on back in the church office. Joel said there was some shoving and shouting involving Timbo, his father, Mr. Sinkwich, and the exasperated man of God, whose seminary training had apparently not prepared him for circumstances such as he now faced. The Sinkwich family was a cornerstone of his parish and heavy contributors to his church, and both Mr. Sinkwich and Dr. Grizzelle were insisting that this wedding must proceed.

Comer Davis had not yet arrived with the license, but the priest finally agreed to begin the nuptials provided that The Doctor and

Mr. Sinkwich would give him their solemn word of honor that not a living soul was to leave the sanctuary until he had the license in hand. Furthermore, he needed a wedding ring for the bride, one that had been blessed in the tradition of the one true church. He crossed his arms and that was that. It was now six thirty-four.

Here came the usher who was the bride's brother, in his tails and spats, down the center aisle to where Mrs. Sinkwich was still kneeling. He interrupted her prayers and we all saw her raise her head and mouth, "What?" with her brow wrinkled in disbelief. She then pulled and tugged and handed her wedding ring over.

Some five minutes later (it seemed an eternity), the priest and two assistants whom I took to be altar boys appeared in the pulpit, very dignified and solemn and properly robed. They went through a good deal of bowing and scraping and chanting which seemed pointless to our side of the church, and the priest stepped forward with his hands clasped in prayer before him. The organ began again, but not before Mr. B. M. had startled everyone by saying, "Who's that? The Pope?" Miss Pansy poked the hell out of him.

Timbo had his daddy for best man, and they appeared in front of the altar rail. I was surprised to see how much larger Timbo was than his father. That boy had grown up. His lower lip was sagging but he was not slobbering, and I thought briefly of heavyweight boxer Primo Carnera all tailed and gloved and spatted.

The bridesmaids and ushers all filed in appropriately, and finally Mr. Sinkwich came in with the bride. She was very beautiful and looked ethereal in her gown and veil. Mr. Sinkwich's face was so red I thought it would pop, and I couldn't help thinking that he gave his daughter's hand into Timbo's with some reluctance before he seated himself by his wife and mopped his brow.

All this while the two altar boys had been standing immobile with their hands clasped in piety. It was hot in the church and this was before air-conditioning. While the priest was busy talking and chanting, all of a sudden the smaller of the altar boys plopped over in a dead faint. His fall made a boom like a drumbeat. The priest did not even stumble in his ritual nor take any obvious notice, but in a very few seconds another white-coated figure appeared from behind the side curtain and dragged the boy off out of sight by his heels. Mrs. Grizzelle's orchid quivered, but the droning and chanting proceeded without interruption. The impression on our side was that the fainting was just another puzzling part of the ceremony. As Oscar Hosey would have said, "Them Catholics."

The only other interruption came when the priest raised the chalice over his head in the blessing of the sacraments before administering Communion. Mr. B. M. whispered, "Reckon that's real wine?" If his ribs weren't sore that night, I'm sure Miss Pansy's elbow was.

By the time all the kneeling and crossing and chanting were over, it was eight-fifteen and Mr. Sinkwich's face looked ready to burst. As Oscar Hosey phrased it to Joel Culpepper, "Boy, that gal flat married the dawg shit out of him, didn't she?"

Comer Davis had lost his way but had stopped to get directions in College Park and had phoned that he was on the way. He must have been drinking because he was driving as slow as a terrapin.

The priest was in a plumb lather by now. He laid down the law. He was a fine one to do it, for he was red-handed guilty of breaking one. The guests were instructed to go on to the Capital City Club. Immediately. After some palaver, Mr. Sinkwich was released to go with them. The Grizzelles—father, mother, son, and newly blessed bride—were held hostage and could not set foot out of the church until the priest had that marriage license safely in hand and properly signed.

It turned out to be quite a party. Dr. Hentz said he couldn't spend any more time away from his practice, but I stayed and caught a ride with Mae and Emmett Pringle. I couldn't help gigging Emmett a little when he kept asking questions and marveling as the full sequence of events appeared. "Emmett, are we indulging in gossip now or just recounting facts?"

"Son, this ain't gossip by any stretch of the imagination. This is genu-wine living history, and I wouldn't believe a word of it if I hadn't had it unroll right in front of my own eyeballs."

It was like Old Man River, it just kept rolling, right on rolling along. Mr. Sinkwich got to the club and ordered champagne to be poured constantly and copiously until the bride and groom arrived. It was a rare and determined Baptist who stood steadfast and didn't succumb to at least one glass, and "while I'm at it I might as well take another one." I enjoyed watching.

The young male relatives of the bride got pretty rowdy and Mr. Sinkwich was trying to keep an eye on them. He did not look happy. At nine-thirty the Grizzelles, all four of them, appeared, and The Doctor announced that the new couple was going to take a bow and thank everyone for coming, but they did not have time for a proper receiving line since they were going to be late for their plane if they didn't hurry. They would change into their going-away clothes here at the club. "Because of previous careful planning," he said.

So help me, God, he said that. And with much dignity and a straight face, too.

It wasn't long before they came flying down the steps and jumped in the getaway car, which Joel was supposed to pick up later at the airport. Timbo helped Sylvia in amidst enough rice falling to feed an Asian village for a week. Then he ran around and jumped in the driver's seat, all ready to scratch off.

It didn't happen. A bunch of his new cousins who had been drinking champagne straight from bottles had gone to McKesson & Roberts' Drugstore around the corner next to Davison-Paxon and bought a couple of big cans of that newly discovered shaving cream under pressure. They covered the windshield with it.

Timbo jumped out to clear off enough glass so he could see to drive. One of his new cousins grappled with him. Timbo lost his temper. He rabbit-punched the guy. The others started laughing like crazy and crowded around. It looked to be a melee covering the entire sidewalk and a good half of the street.

All of a sudden, Doctor Grizzelle strode determinedly into the fray. He stepped between Timbo and his antagonist and forcibly shoved them apart. I was standing close enough to hear his judicial tones, "Now this is enough of this disgraceful behavior, young gentlemen. Calm down and discontinue this foolishness immediately."

They minded him and pulled away from each other. The cousin was grinning, but Timbo wasn't. Dr. Grizzelle took out his handkerchief and smeared enough soap away on the driver's side to provide at least a little vision, pushed Timbo into the car, and said, "On your way, Timothy."

When he straightened up to wave farewell, two of the irrepressible but heretofore nonparticipating cousins stepped forth with spray cans poised and laughing like crazy. Before the doctor could move, he was covered in foamy shaving cream, head to toe, front to back, spats, gray gloves, and all. He jerked his glasses off so he could see, and for a minute he looked like a snowman with revolving eyeballs. Mrs. Grizzelle let out a howl and guided him back into the club. Mr. Sinkwich slammed his champagne glass on the curb and stomped on it. That man had the reddest face I ever saw, but he sure put the quietus on those cousins.

Timothy made it to the traffic light at Peachtree and had to stop. A carload of strangers saw the fix his car was in when they pulled up beside him and rolled down the window, yelling and laughing at him. Apparently Timbo thought they were some more of the wedding party trying to torment him further. In fury, he took a punch at the laughing face on his left. He forgot that his own window was up and his fist crashed through it. As I said, he did look a little like Primo Carnera. It takes a lot of force to break a car window.

The upshot of that was they had to take him to Grady Emergency Room to have a couple of significant lacerations repaired and the bleeding stopped. They missed their plane, but the luggage and wedding ring went on to South America. On account of all the careful planning. A quote from Robert Burns would be appropriate about here, but I'll forego the obvious.

Miss Mae Harp didn't wait for Mrs. Grizzelle to place her telephone call the next day. She did it herself.

"How did the wedding go, Mrs. Grizzelle?"

"All in all, it was quite a splendid affair, Miss Mae, despite some of the things you may have heard. Sylvia was a vision and the bridesmaid gowns were lovely. Mr. Sinkwich must have spent a fortune on the reception."

"Well, how is everything going this morning, Mrs. Grizzelle? I hear they missed their plane."

"Everything is much calmer, Miss Mae. And well under control. Timothy had to have a little medical attention at one of the Atlanta hospitals, and they came down here about three o'clock and spent the night in our guesthouse. Sylvia was so upset that Doctor had to give her a sedative. Timothy came up a while ago and got them some coffee and said Mr. Sinkwich had called the airline and is coming down here to check on Sylvia. They're a very close-knit family, you know. Thanks for calling."

"You're welcome. Bye."

Mr. Sinkwich did indeed come down. Furthermore, he took Sylvia home with him. He may not have believed in divorce, but he got one of the quickest annulments in history and didn't demur when Sylvia decided to go into a convent.

Timbo got a sizable inheritance when his parents died and left our town to live abroad. Last time I heard anything about him, Toor Cofield swore he spotted him in Paris all painted white and standing on a garbage can. He went and looked up at him and even called his name, but Timbo never moved a muscle or batted an eye. Toor said at first he thought it was a statue of that Italian who used to be the world champion in boxing perched up there with nothing on but a jockey strap and white paint. I can't imagine Paris, or any other place for that matter, being a more fascinating place to live than our town. Until the day he died, Oscar Hosey would wag his head, spit snuff, and say, "Them Catholics."

Chapter 13

Don't think that progress and prosperity came to our town in the twinkling of an eye. It just seems like it did when I look back down the years at it. In fact, it hit the county well before it developed in town. About three or four years before the Grizzelle wedding, a new family had swept into the county, or *erupted* might be a better word. There were only three of them but sometimes it seemed like there must have been a dozen or more, when consideration is given to the turmoil they created. The mama was a soft-spoken true Southern lady whom everybody loved. She hadn't been here for a year before Mrs. Melrose died, and she took over her Sunday school class. She persuaded the official board to incorporate acolytes and lighted candles into the worship service. I mean, she swept in. It changed our church. We were now citified.

It was her husband and their only child who erupted and got things stirred up and kept them stirred up. Mr. Buncombe Braswell had bought a sizeable tract of land from two of my old maid aunts, built a lake and a brick house on it, and set out to transform the county. He was a big-shot contractor in Atlanta who had made a fortune rebuilding after Scott Hudgens, Home Wrecker, Inc., had finished transforming Capitol Avenue. He and his partner specialized in commercial buildings, and the Braswells lived on Arden Road out in fashionable Buckhead. Why they moved has never been exactly clear to me, but I've always wondered if it was because of religion.

We all hear about fundamental Baptists, but the Braswells were fundamental Methodists. They were very rigid and outspoken about drinking, dancing, smoking, and swearing. I don't imagine they had many close friends in the Piedmont Driving Club or the Cherokee Club, and Peachtree Road Methodist Church was probably too liberal for them. Mrs. Braswell held firm to all her convictions, but it didn't take most of us too long to realize that, as far as Mr. Braswell was concerned, lying, stealing, and adultery could be overlooked if you didn't drink, smoke, or dance. The Lawsons, of all people, became their closest friends.

Their son had just graduated from Emory and he was a spectacular and eccentric character, an affectation he cultivated assiduously. Mrs. Braswell referred to her husband as Big Buncombe and her son as Baby Buncombe. The names may have originated in tenderness when the only child and heir was in his cradle, but they stuck as long as Big Bunc and Baby Bunc lived. Even their hired hands referred to them as Mr. Big Bunc and Mr. Baby Bunc. We all enjoyed watching but sometimes it was painful to listen to them. Even those in the county who professed not to like them had to admit, however, that they were interesting.

Mr. Big Buncombe Braswell had been born and raised in Buncombe County, North Carolina, and I guess that's why he got his name. He had come to Atlanta as a tile setter, moved up to marble, and by the time he came to our county he was an engineer. We all knew he was because he never let an opportunity pass to tell that he was one, and pretty often he would even make the opportunity. Nobody ever saw any diploma nor did anyone ever ask to see his license.

He could never discuss any financial project in less than six figures, and this was while Eisenhower was still president. He set out to ingratiate himself with our county commissioners and then talked them into designating him as county engineer. At no salary. He didn't need any more money than he had, he said. Then he put in to transform our county. It took him a while and several sets of commissioners, but he did it.

What he did was get zoning laws and building codes set up in our county. "As tight," Oscar Hosey said, "as a bull's ass in fly time."

People squawked, fumed, cussed, and even threatened to run the Braswells out of town on a rail. Yeoman farmers and big landowners alike asserted that nobody was going to tell them what they could and couldn't do with their land. Mr. Big Buncombe laughed like crazy whenever somebody cussed him at a public meeting, of which there were many.

He'd right out giggle, and say, "Go ahead, Brother, you don't bother me: I'm a first-class son of a bitch and got papers to prove it."

He would reprove anyone who took the Lord's name in vain. To him, sonofabitch was not cussing; therefore, he was not sinning when he said it. As far as I am concerned, all cussing is done for shock value anyhow, and he knew what he was doing.

It worked. After he had offended nearly everybody in the county one way or another, except Hubert Lawson and Miss Clyde, he worked his way through about three sets of county commissioners, each new set getting elected by promising to fire Mr. Big Buncombe Braswell as county engineer, and then after three months rehiring him. Be blessed if we didn't get that zoning that Oscar Hosey so accurately described.

First thing was there could be no trailers in the county, regardless of the family emergency, except in designated trailer parks, and therefore we had to have specific areas designated for that purpose. One of the sitting commissioners was astute enough to see the financial advantage of owning one and had about fifty acres of his property zoned for that purpose when the initial land-use plan was formally adopted. Before you could say "Jack Robinson," the place had filled up and was called a "Mobile Home Village."

Oscar Hosey gave us another memorable quote: "It's like the Jewish prostitute said, 'You got it, you rent it out, you still got it. Such a deal yet.'"

Oscar was pretty crude, but he was also pretty perceptive.

Next thing Mr. Big Bunc accomplished with his zoning was the law that no house could be built on less than one acre of land anywhere in the county except within incorporated areas. That didn't bother us in our town since we had been incorporated ever since we ran the Indians out. Furthermore, after Mr. Carter Stinchcomb had replaced Eustace Pilcher as mayor, we had central sewage. Of course, at the time Mr. Carter got it through a federal grant and it consisted of two oxidation ponds, which reminded some of us occasionally of the Cantrell-Waddell suit, but only when the wind was in the east. At least it had dried up the creek that ran slap through the middle of town and had accommodated the raw effluent of the Cofields, Culpeppers, and other early settlers. The stench from that creek hung heaviest when the air was still and was very embarrassing when we played football, since it ran right by the athletic field and was reinforced by outflow from the school itself. We locals had accepted it as a way of life and part of the eccentricities that made our town different; we even referred to it by the obvious, albeit vulgar sobriquet. We always felt like apologizing when we played football, especially if it was Woodward Academy. We didn't mind their players so much as we did their snooty parents.

At any rate, after we got our oxidation ponds out close to the city limits, we had to get a new name for the creek, so by popular acclaim it became known as Carter Stinchcomb Branch as a testimonial to our mayor. It was never officially voted on and no sign was put up and very few people are still living in our town who revere Mr. Carter for all his accomplishments.

Oscar Hosey, before he died, wagged his head and said, "Like him or not, Carter Stinchcomb sure dried up Shit Creek."

What Mr. Big Buncombe Braswell did for our county was to put it on the map with a reputation as prestigious property. Atlanta, just like he kept saying, was coming our way, and the zoning pretty well excluded poor people. A bunch of entrepreneurs, from up north of all places, bought up several thousand acres of land out west of our town while land was still cheap, paid five dollars an acre for some of it and never more than fifty. Then they hired an ambitious young graduate of Georgia Tech and had the property incorporated as Magnoliadale. They built a great big lake and put in even tighter zoning than the county. They had an industrial park, a city hall, a bank, a golf course, and so help me God a country club. They even paved golf cart paths all through the city, but they didn't have the first sign of a trailer court or mobile home village.

Magnoliadale grew so fast it made heads in our town spin and tongues wag. Sometimes accurately. You never saw the like of people who moved into that new city. Started off it was mostly airline pilots, a heap of whom were working on second marriages and were trying to make mama happy. Then, by cracky if that Tech graduate didn't commence to attracting real true industry into Magnoliadale's industrial park and here came a bigger pack of yankees than had come through with Sherman, and a good many of them from Ohio, too.

None of the newcomers had the faintest idea how and why the Huddlestons, Adamses, Stinchcombs, McElwaneys, Turnipseeds, and Dettmerings were kin to each other. This was before any of us had even heard of DNA, but there was a considerable amount of it shared in our county, although the old-timers didn't need it. We could look at somebody and know why a McElwaney nose was on a Dettmering face or a Huddleston jaw showed up on an Adams woman, no matter how many generations back it went. The newcomers acted as though it wasn't important and they could care less. Believe you me, that young Tech graduate put in and learned all about us though, which was just one of the many factors that contributed to his success.

With most of the newcomers playing golf and drinking cocktails and acting like they were colonizing Lower Patagonia or something, we locals began to feel threatened, especially when somebody started the rumor that the Tech boy wanted to move the courthouse to Magnoliadale. Personally, I would have traded it in a heartbeat for the golf course and the golf cart paths.

All this new development did to Mr. Big Bunc was to reenergize him. He worked even harder on the county zoning, and before you knew it, land prices had skyrocketed to five or even ten thousand dollars an acre, and dirt farmers were selling out. In fact, as soon as we all realized the courthouse was sacrosanct, a few of them even took their newly acquired money and moved to Magnoliadale and started playing golf. They are obliged to have known the rest of us were watching them closely, but they did it anyhow. Like that fancy doctor said at the Grizzelle wedding, "Money talks, you know."

The unspoken attitude in our town toward Magnoliadale became guarded tolerance. It was all right to be nice to those people, but don't let your daughter date one. You can't ever tell when a young person might fall in love.

Baby Buncombe Braswell was a startling experience and drew as much attention as some natural phenomenon like a thunderstorm or Halley's Comet or some such. Personally I always thought of a volcano that was rumbling and snorting and might erupt at any moment. As Oscar Hosey said, "That boy's a trip without a suitcase." Wherever he went, indoors or out, he sort of exploded onto the scene.

He did it all on purpose and for effect. Else he wouldn't come to town in his Jeep with nothing on but boots, short breeches, and a .45. People who went out to the Braswell farm reported that he drove his tractor with that pistol strapped to his waist. He could shoot it, too. Once he drove into the yard of one of their tenant houses and surprised a family loading a truck with all their furniture but without paying their rent. Becoming apprised of their intent, he said, "Well, well; you taking that dog with you?"

"Naw," the man of the house replied in surly tone.

With that, Baby Bunc whipped out his pistol and shot the dog dead in the head. Then he turned to the stunned man and said, "What about that boy? You taking him?"

"Yes, sir, Mr. Baby Buncombe Braswell, sir. Yes, sir!"

"Good," said Baby Bunc and clambered back in his Jeep.

That story got around and the number of visitors to the Braswell farm declined sharply. The number of people in the county who were leery of Baby Bunc increased even more sharply. Some of us wondered if Miss Bunch Brown weren't nearer on the mark than Oscar Hosey.

He talked wild, too. About anything and everything. He raised crazy topics in his Sunday school class and then delighted in arguing with anybody about them. Loudly and in your face. He proclaimed that he was a fascist and you even got the feeling that he considered selective genocide a virtue. As long, mind you, as you didn't drink, smoke, or curse. When accosted about his belligerent attitude toward alcohol, he boasted that he was an alcoholic although he had never had so much as a sip of even beer or wine. He knew this as an incontrovertible fact because he had an uncle who had drunk himself to death and Baby Bunc had a lot of that uncle's personality traits. The very thought of a drunk Baby Bunc loose on the town was enough to make your hair stand on end and devise shelter for all women and children in cyclone cellars.

I had done some legal work for the Braswell family about deeds and such and never regarded Baby Bunc as warily as most of my friends did. He lived to shock people and he loved doing it, but underneath he was like everybody else in that he wanted to be liked and maybe even admired. It was just that he didn't have the faintest idea where lines and boundaries were in social intercourse.

He asked me one time, "You ever see a billy goat's pecker?"

When I confessed to gross ignorance, he enlightened me.

"When it comes out of its sheath, it has a flap turned down on the very end of it. Looks like a little hand. And he can move it around just like a little hand and uses it to insert it into a nanny."

"Do tell," I responded.

He persisted. "And did you know that billy goats are always ready and don't have to wait for the female to go into heat? That's a fact. They use that little old hand apparatus to get some whenever they want it, and I'm here to tell you that billy goats are a randy lot. One billy can wear out a whole herd of nannies."

I shrugged, hoping he'd catch the hint.

He continued, "Whenever they have to ship a load of goats anywhere, they try to keep females and males separate. When they can't, guess what they do. They make a little cut right on the end of the billy's pecker so it'll be so sore he can't use it for three, four days. Else every nanny in the car would get there pregnant."

"Baby Bunc," I interrupted, "I do appreciate your sharing this knowledge with me. I would have probably died and gone to my grave blissfully unaware and unconcerned about damn goat peckers if it hadn't been for you. Do you tell many people about this?"

"Do I? Let me tell you one thing, it's a great icebreaker at a dinner party. If they'll talk about that, they'll talk about anything." He laughed heartily and roared off in his Jeep.

For the life of me, I couldn't imagine Baby Bunc being a dinner guest at one of our group's wing-dings, considering the way he felt about drinking, nor could I envision him eating chicken casserole and potato salad in the Melrose dining room. I knew that he and his wife were habitués at their Sunday school potluck suppers, thought for a minute and then grinned, musing that the Sunday school class had by now discovered that potluck referred to a lot more than just the meal.

I always liked Baby Bunc, although I occasionally got accused of being the only man in town who did. He was a real flamboyant character and it was fun to watch him, if you weren't too close, but there was a soft, even noble side to him also. He loved his dogs and always carried them to ride with him. In the hot summertime, he forsook his Jeep and rode the dogs in the car so he could leave them in air-conditioned comfort with the motor running, sometimes for an hour or longer while he transacted business.

If he discovered someone with an insurmountable problem, he was quick to jump in and help them solve it. Uninvited and free of charge. Of course, more often than not, his solution was worse than the original problem, and some folks learned pretty quickly the truth of that old saying about the road to hell being paved with good intentions.

On several occasions, through my law practice, I observed him coming to the aid of unfortunates. Poor kids. He was responsible for anonymously getting quite a few of them through college, and he for sure and certain didn't have to worry about any of them turning on him by running for public office. Big Buncombe Braswell may have been powerful enough to get our county zoned, but neither he nor Baby Bunc stood a snowball's chance in hell of getting elected to any office whatever.

I have never felt that Mr. Big Bunc was properly appreciated for his contributions to the county; we could at the very least have named a road for him. Looking back, I don't think it ever entered his head to seek out public recognition; as an engineer, he saw our county as a challenge, and he didn't give a rat's ass whether anybody liked him or not, long as they did what he said.

I wonder sometimes if Baby Bunc's main problem was that he

Baby Bunc was a different story. I think he really and truly deep down wanted people to like him. Sometimes the people who try the hardest to be liked are the ones who are liked the least. Baby Bunc just didn't have the social skills to bring it off. Whenever somebody rejected him for some outlandish conversation or action, his answer was to dish up more of the same. He was more intelligent than most of us, and I have thought in retrospect that if he hadn't been the only child his parents had, he might have been happier. First off, of course, they spoiled him rotten and he could always get anything he wanted out of them. Then there was his name. If they had called him anything else in the world besides Baby Buncombe, like "Bubba" or even "Junior," he might have fared better. He's obliged to have had a lot to live down. I cringe when I consider how I might have turned out if my brothers hadn't labeled me "Buster." Everybody needs to grow up with siblings; it helps you learn how to handle competition.

I wonder sometimes if Baby Bunc's main problem was that he wanted to outdo Mr. Big Bunc, and I've always wondered why Mr. Big Bunc let him talk him into financing some of his wild schemes. First off, it was swimming pools. Baby Bunc didn't know a thing about building one until he made himself a jerry-rigged one out on the farm. Then he took up the notion that he could build them cheaper than anybody else and that there was a big market for them all over the southeast. Before he could set up that sort of empire effectively, he convinced himself that he had to have an airplane. Before he could buy an airplane, he had to learn to fly one. His daddy grinned and wrote the checks. When somebody asked his mama how she felt about Baby Bunc flying an airplane, she smiled sweetly and said, "I have long ago turned him over to Jesus and quit worrying about him."

There were some who thought that was a pretty dirty little job for Jesus, but nobody voiced that to Mrs. Braswell. Everybody liked her, although there were a few catty observations about a lady who could come to church in a mink coat and still chew gum during the sermon, but that was about what everybody expected Bill Pritchett to say and we ignored it.

The swimming pool enterprise failed spectacularly. Mr. Big Bunc had to smile through clenched teeth but he paid off the debts incurred. Baby Bunc got to keep the airplane; like I said, he could talk his parents into anything. Along about here he could have really benefited from a couple of older brothers to get nose to nose in his face and shout, "Have you lost your fucking mind?"

It might even have helped if his daddy had done it, but his daddy didn't cuss. As Baby Bunc boasted once at a Sunday school supper, "My daddy ain't got but one bad habit: he lies." That was as close as anybody ever heard him praise his father. He seemed to think he had been born head of the Braswell household; he sure ruled it with an unyielding hand.

Next thing you know, he discovered the medical field with all its new advances and technology, and he regarded it as an untapped mother lode of riches just waiting for him to mine it. He talked Big Bunc into backing him and they built a brand-spanking-new hospital a few miles out of Atlanta. With an impressive display of brashness, he bought the land and drove an architect to drink drawing plans. Then be blessed if he didn't start the building without getting it zoned properly. I had long since learned that any effort on my part to give him a legal opinion was like spitting in the wind and had resigned myself to juggling deeds and mortgages around for him, for which, by the way, I sent a monthly bill and insisted on collecting it. I've always done a lot of free legal work for poor people, widows, and old maids, but I am not an economic fool.

When he got through paying off the fines and penalties from Fulton County, here came the federal government disclosing that he had not appeared before the North Georgia Planning Commission and had no Certificate of Need for a hospital. He had never stopped construction and was putting the roof on the third story; told me he had learned long ago that forgiveness was easier to get than permission. That may have worked with his parents, but the Feds were not impressed. Here came injunctions, warrants, threats of criminal action, you name it. I read "cease and desist" so many times that I still think of them as one word.

Mr. Big Bunc quit smiling, went to the Cofield bank, kissed up to Toor, and mortgaged every acre of land he owned. I thought his smile had become what I had read for years would be called "fixed," but I had never personally witnessed it before as an accurate description.

Baby Bunc took to the newspapers. When he got through giving his candid opinions about county, state, and federal branches of government with their legions of self-serving bureaucrats, he took off on the medical industry.

"I'm no philanthropist," he declared. "My interest is strictly financial. Hospitals are like dairy cows, and I say, 'Milk them, milk them.'"

When he was asked by the North Georgia Health Service Agency reviewing his CON how he would staff the hospital if it were approved and finished, he asserted, "Doctors are a dime a dozen and worth not quite twice that. They like money as much as I do and will be no problem."

The newspapers had not had such a field day since Lester Maddox closed the Pickrick Restaurant to blacks and used axe handles as a symbol of defiance. If Baby Buncombe Braswell overlooked any segment of society to piss off royally, it may have been the Methodist Children's Home and the Salvation Army, but I'm not sure about even them.

Well, he didn't ask permission soon enough about that hospital and he sure as hell didn't get forgiveness. It never did get finished. Stood there for three years with vines growing over it, for he had not killed all the kudzu when he was grading the site, and finally the bank was able to sell it for about twenty-five cents on the dollar to a motel chain.

Mr. Big Bunc finally got through bailing him out of that fiasco, but he had quit grinning and didn't have but five acres of land and his house that weren't mortgaged to the hilt. Baby Bunc still had his airplane and decided that if he could discover illegal liquor stills and report them to the Feds, he might recoup some of his losses as well as repair his reputation with them. Also, it would be a stroke for the Lord, since making alcohol had to be as big a sin as drinking it.

He crashed that airplane in a swamp just behind the Betsill property, and he and the plane were both burned to a crisp. I asked the sheriff later if there was a bullet hole in the plane, and he said, "Who in the hell knows? It was burned to smithereens and there wasn't any use looking." He started to walk off and then turned back. "And besides, who the hell cares?"

Our sheriff was a great big guy with a pretty short fuse. I waited 'til he was well out of earshot before I said, very softly, "I do."

Baby Bunc was totally unpredictable and as wild as a buck, and the town is a more tranquil place without him, but I still miss him. We all enjoyed watching him and some of the old-timers, of which there are very few left, still talk about him.

He was not a straw man.

Life goes out;
Not with a bang
But a whimper.

I never saw Baby Bunc whimper, but he sure banged around a lot. Even in the end.

His daddy had done his share of banging heretofore, but losing his only son took the fire out of him. The airplane wasn't insured; what life insurance Baby Bunc hadn't borrowed on went to his wife. Mr. Big Buncombe Braswell was left with a frail and sickly wife in a house that was mortgaged to the roof. Toor Cofield gave him a job as handyman at the bank and even called him "maintenance engineer," an act which partially erased my grudge toward Toor about Pearlie Mae at Christmas time.

Mr. Big Bunc kept up a good front of being a strong and resilient man, but people in the town knew he was hurting inside every waking minute, and he couldn't even get drunk every now and then like the rest of us. He held to his principles and earned more respect and warm regard in his impoverished latter years than he had ever experienced in his flaming career as county engineer. People in our town will laugh at you and eat your ass out if you're putting on airs and bragging, but they will not turn on you if you get really down and out. It's a wonderful town.

Mr. Big Bunc died peacefully and quietly in his sleep a month after his wife passed away. The sheriff discovered him early because Toor Cofield called him when Mr. Big Bunc was fifteen minutes late reporting to work and asked him to investigate.

"I ain't never been late to work," Toor said, "and he's always here when I get here. Better check on him."

I guess some folks would call that going out with a whimper, but what I heard most people say was "Peace."

All of which brings me back around to the Cofields.

Chapter 14

For generations the Cofields were the leading family in our county and our town. Only one remains and he is whiling his last years away in a prison which, considering everything, I guess is of his own making. The bars of it may be made of solid gold, but prison is prison and he is for sure and certain in it. The few of us now who know him feel sorry for him. We can't see anything but sadness surrounding him over there in his great big house all alone, and the four pillars of sadness are his children, each one of whom has turned also into solid gold. It's a cold, glittering, fascinating metal, and when it gets a hold of you it will mummify you.

You hear folks compliment someone by saying, "He has a heart of gold"; usually that's followed immediately by "but...."

All of Toor's children had taken gold into their hearts, and it had pumped gold out into every capillary in their bodies. They were all solid ingots and nothing else mattered to them, certainly not Toor. Every time I think of him, I remember the story about King Midas. It has sure come to life in Toor, although if his daughter had jumped into his lap, as heavy as they both are, they'd have crashed through into the basement. I guess those kids had never been taught about love, at least as an abstract concept. Certainly I never saw any of it manifested in their upbringing, either between their grandparents, their parents, them and their parents, and certainly not between the children themselves. It was just not an affectionate, loving family.

Oh, to be sure, they were fed, clothed, bathed, carried to the doctor and church, but you always got the feeling it was from a sense of duty, and a whole lot of that depended on how much the duty cost. First thing when Dr. Hentz arrived in town, Toor Cofield called him up and asked him how much an office call was, how much a shot of penicillin cost, and how much would it cost if all four children came to the doctor and had the shot at the same time. A little figuring showed that if all four were sick, Dr. Hentz's fees beat Dr. Grizzelle's by about a dollar apiece, and *Bingo*! Dr. Grizzelle lost all of Toor's practice, including the planing mill employees and the tenant farmers. Dr. Grizzelle was always asking for a discount but had never stooped to granting one himself. It was just a coincidence that Dr. Hentz was a good physician; all Toor was looking at was the bottom line.

He couldn't help it. He had been raised that way. Miss Pansy had turned him over to Mr. B. M. soon as she weaned him, and the only guidance he ever got from his mama consisted of indirect commands relayed through Mr. B. M.

"Mr. Cofield, tell B. S. to be sure and comb his hair before he goes to school." Or "Be sure that boy brushes his teeth and takes a bath and puts on clean clothes." Mr. Cofield was never loquacious, but daily routine got pretty tedious even for him and resulted in "Brush teeth," or "Comb hair," or "Take bath," or "Clean drawers." He just plain didn't waste words.

Toor slept with his father until he went off to military school. I've always thought it was Miss Pansy's directive effort at birth control, and I've always felt Toor missed out on some nurturing that the rest of us have taken for granted. I can't imagine Mr. B. M. in any more bedtime conversation than "Say prayers." "Go pee." "Turn out light." Talk about silent night and cold comfort.

In later years, Mr. B. M. became a little more outgoing and talkative; the older people get, the more they like to visit. "Son about twelve years old. Got his lessons, went to bed. 'Bout eleven o'clock woke me up crying. 'What's matter, boy?'

"'My stomach hurts so bad I can't sleep.'

"I turned on light. Wouldn't let me touch his stomach. Hurt too bad. Kept on crying louder and louder. 'Hush, son, done taught you not to cry. Over anything. Be quiet. Goan call doctor in Atlanta. May be appendix. Hush up now.'

"Knew Dr. Dan Elkin at Emory. Worked on me when I had car wreck. Beat up bad. Nearly died. Fixed me up fine. Limp a little but still living. Called him up. 'Bring him in, I'll meet you in the emergency room at Emory.'

"Loaded Son in car. Quit crying on way to Atlanta. Time Dr. Elkin got to him, said wasn't hurting anymore. Dr. Elkin examined him good. Got blood. Stuck finger in butt. Studied on him awhile. Said, 'B. M., this ain't his appendix; he's all right.' Told him, 'You ain't heard him yelling and hollering like I did.' Elkin said, 'Well, it's a long way up here. If you want me to I'll go ahead and take the appendix out while you've got him here; might save you a trip again in the middle of the night.'

"Studied on that a few minutes. Said, 'Take 'em out.'" He paused. "Elkin was right. Them appendix ain't never bothered him again."

After Mr. B. M. died, I asked Toor about his appendectomy. He got a real sheepish grin and said, "That's right. The only thing wrong with me was I had a final exam the next day and hadn't studied and knew I'd flunk it. I didn't want to face the ruckus that would have caused. Know what I mean?" I thought for a moment about Miss Pansy and agreed with him.

"Besides," I said, "Dr. Elkin probably needed the money."

When Mr. B. M. got real old, he got confused in addition to being deaf. Nowadays I guess we'd call it Alzheimer's, but back then it was just senility and nearly every family, sooner or later, got somebody who had it. Miss Pansy never acknowledged it. She'd get Mr. B. M. cleaned up, dressed up, and take him to walk all over town every afternoon. She always took little short steps, but she took a lot of them in a very short period of time, which, plus her low center of gravity, made her look like she was trotting. Mr. B. M., on the other hand, lurched. What he called "a little limp" following his wreck was the result of two seriously shattered legs that for the rest of his life necessitated the use of a walking stick. He had long skinny shanks which weren't all that much bigger than his cane, and it was a sight to see him gamely following Miss Pansy like he was walking on tommy-walkers, always thirty to forty feet behind her. When she turned a corner, she always looked back, waved her directive arm, and trilled, "This way, Mr. Cofield."

Nowadays they would be a traffic hazard, but back then all they had to watch out for was Lora Holt in her A-model and Miss Kate Eastin in her Chevrolet. Everybody else knew to watch out for Miss Pansy and Mr. B. M. Cofield. We also knew to watch out for Lora and Miss Kate. Miss Pansy took her husband to church on Sunday, too. He'd sit there good as could be and knew to stand up when she punched him for the hymns and the doxology.

We had a preacher back then, the Reverend Cleveland Jones, who Mae Pringle despised. After Emmett died, she continued to sit up front every Sunday morning in the third pew on the left, which she and Emmett had anchored for years. But for Wednesday night prayer meetings, Mae started sitting in the back of the church with Bill Pritchett so that Bill would go with her to the Elks Club on Thursday nights. Mae came to my house late one Wednesday night all in a dither.

"Well, Buster Boy, I can't believe what he pulled tonight! You were there; you heard him, but you were sitting up there so proud and solitary at the piano that you didn't really get challenged. I was sitting way in the back with Bill Pritchett and all of a sudden that preacher up and says, 'I want you to look beside you, behind you, and in front of you and say to each one of your neighbors in the pews, "I love you and God loves you."' Well, I could hear old Tom Watson Murphy sniffling on the bench behind me, and that fat Henry Boggs was right in front of me and had already belched twice during the service. So I turned to Bill and said, 'I'll just be goddamned if I say it.' Sheesh. The man's got a head like a hickory nut!"

Nobody could suggest anything to the Reverend Jones about improvement that he ever took to heart or put into effect. He insisted on reading every announcement in the bulletin from the pulpit, even though I personally had told him everybody in our congregation could read and would appreciate the opportunity to do so. His announcements were as long as his prayers, and his prayers were all drawn-out mini-sermons addressed to the Lord of all Mankind, as he continuously called Him. I don't know much about his sermons because I never managed to stay awake through more than one or two of them. My stomach always woke me up in time to play for the closing hymn. Sitting behind the piano had certain unrecognized benefits.

One of the most serious disruptions in our church occurred while he was minister. And although I won't say he instigated it, he sure did nothing to divert it. It was the so-called Campus Crusade for Christ—an uprising, far as I could tell, of adolescents against their parents and tradition and, of course, conventional morality and restrictions. Sort of a sanitized and pious outgrowth of the hippie movement. I guess it swept the whole Southeast, but I know for a fact that it decimated our youth Sunday school classes and the MYF; maybe even attracted a few of the Baptist kids.

Young people started meeting in organized groups and stayed up so late on Friday and Saturday nights that they professed to be too tired to come to Sunday school. Instead, they got old Cleveland Jones snookered into inviting them and visiting groups from other colleges to "share" during regular church.

I had always considered *share* a transitive verb, but they converted it overnight into an intransitive one, and I have always resented their messing with the language.

So did Mae Pringle. "What the hell are they sharing?" she snorted. "Sheesh! You know they're not staying up 'til three or four a.m. yakking about Jesus. I hear Mary Beamis has missed two periods, and God only knows who'll fall next. I want you to tell that stupid preacher to quit saying, 'We have another group of young people from LaGrange College who are here to "share" with us this morning.'"

I didn't even bother. We got off better than the Presbyterians, who by then had managed to establish a significant beachhead in the community. Their preacher became so bemused with the Campus Crusade for Christ movement that he resigned his pulpit and took up full-time Christian golf; said the golf course was a better place to "share." There were pretty well confirmed rumors that he was a young man blessed with independent means and financial support from his family.

I did eventually get Cleveland to limit the closing hymn to just two verses. It's been my observation that if somebody is going to join the church or go down for an altar call, two stanzas will get them, and if they're not so inclined, singing all four or five or sometimes even six wouldn't budge them from the gates of Hell. That's not the way I presented it to the Reverend Cleveland Jones, however; he was a real prissy young fella and took everything seriously, most of all himself. I can't for the life of me remember ever seeing him smile. Not even the time when Mr. B. M. Cofield all of a sudden at eleven-forty yelled out so even the ones in the balcony heard him, "Twelve o'clock!"

Miss Pansy punched him so hard he thought she meant for him to stand up and he started to do it. Mr. Big Bunc was in the pew right behind him and reached over and patted him on the shoulder until he settled down. Reverend Jones never interrupted his drone with even the slightest hint of a stumble. That takes first prize far as I'm concerned of a missed opportunity for the benediction.

I do think, though, that was the reason Toor Cofield didn't call the note on Mr. Big Bunc and later gave him that janitorial job at the bank. Toor wasn't at church that morning but Beatrice was and the whole community felt like that was a nice thing for Mr. Big Bunc to do. The whole sequence of events made us all feel better about Toor and about Mr. Big Buncombe Braswell. Sooner or later, even an old blind hog will stumble up on an acorn.

Another plus to the episode was that the preacher got moved—in a nice, quiet unobtrusive Methodist manner, of course, but that was the stimulus that sent Dr. Hentz calling on the bishop. Bishop Moore had been bishop for a long, long, long time, and I guess had garnered more respect than any of them since Bishop Candler. He was the one that got the property on St. Simon's Island and built Epworth-by-the-Sea as a Methodist center and retreat. Dr. Hentz was a converted Baptist. He had married a Methodist and had sense enough to join her. Somebody had appointed him layleader, and in that capacity he had gone with our preacher at the time and Mr. B. M. all the way to St. Simon's for the grand opening of Epworth-by-the-Sea. He was by no means the most reverent layleader we ever had, and he came back and told me, "Buster, I give you my word of honor, there were eleven pictures of Bishop Moore in the dining room and one of Jesus. I think maybe we've got ourselves a pope."

Mr. Lum Summerfield, although he was a Baptist and not a regular churchgoer, didn't like Cleveland Jones either. He only heard him one time and that was at Mr. Wilbur Watson's funeral. The next day Mr. Lum caught me in my office. "Buster," he said, and I always liked Mr. Lum. He was one of the few of his generation who didn't call me Aloysius. "Buster, does that preacher of yours have any Indian blood in him?"

"Why, yes, Mr. Lum; as a matter of fact, he does. I was curious about that myself because of his slick black hair and beady black eyes, and I asked him. He's half Indian but is real self-conscious about it. His mama belonged to some little tribe in Alabama that starts with a Y. I can't remember the name of it but they're not much; have about a fifteen-acre reservation somewhere out from Phoenix City."

"By God, I thought so. I went to Wilbur Watson's funeral yesterday. Wilbur and I had been friends since we were boys and he doesn't have much family left. That preacher got up and said, 'Wilbur Watson was old and weary and it was time for him to die,' and I got to thinking about the way Indians would treat old folks, leave 'em a day's supply of food and walk off and leave 'em on the side of the trail, and got to squirming in my seat. Then, be blessed if he didn't start repeating it over and over."

"Yes, sir, Mr. Lum, I know what you mean. It's a habit pattern of his."

"'Wilbur Watson was old and worn out and it was time for him to die, and he did it very gently,' and I said to myself, 'Just goddamn those Indians,' and picked up my coat and walked out of the church."

When Mr. Lum Summerfield didn't like somebody, he made no bones about it. He was a man of firm principles and held to them, even in the Methodist church.

Dr. Hentz didn't like Cleveland Jones either and when he finally got a belly full, he bypassed the district superintendent and went straight to the bishop and the next June Jones was gone. Quietly. Methodists have more taste and decorum than Baptists. I say, "share."

When I asked Dr. Hentz how he had managed the transfer, since getting moved after just two years was kind of a no-passing grade for a preacher, he looked at me real steadily and said, "All of that is supposed to be confidential, but I did point out to King Arthur that our church is right next to the courthouse with its big booming clock, and that our congregation has the reputation for extending forgiveness to our ministers for any transgression except high noon. If the benediction isn't pronounced by the last stroke of twelve, not a soul in the church is going to hear it and you might as well forget it. You're not going to believe it, but the bishop gave a little royal chuckle and said, 'I understand.'"

Then Dr. Hentz winked at me and said, "I pointed out to him the drop in membership and the decline in contributions, and all dignified he said, 'Thank you for coming,' and I recognized that as a benediction and left." That Dr. Hentz may not be very reverent, but he is a whiz at human nature.

After Bishop Moore died we got that prissy, unmarried, overeducated PhD, and he was the one that Toor and Beatrice persuaded to come and preach Mr. B. M.'s funeral. When he was electioneering, one of his friends told him he needed to get a wife if he expected to be elected bishop in the Methodist Church, and he is reputed to have replied, "A wife. Ah, yes, a wife. But, my word, Matt. Suppose I don't get elected; what in the world would I do with her?"

For my money, Oscar Hosey is as good a judge of human nature as Dr. Hentz, albeit not so educated. After Mr. B. M.'s funeral, when they had the hearse go all over town with his body and pause at the bank, the Ford place, and, so help me, even the planing mill, Oscar said to me, "Them Cofields putting on all them airs don't keep old man B. M. from being dead as anybody else, and I'll bet that old maid in britches who preached has got lace on his drawers."

Within a week after the funeral, Miss Pansy had herself moved off to Wesley Woods at Emory where she could decline in peace and not have to put up with Beatrice, Toor, or those four grandchildren. Her daughters looked in on her pretty frequently and that was plenty for Miss Pansy. I think she died happy and probably relieved.

Miss Pansy had even warmed up to Beatrice Schultz. The only thing they had in common was Toor, and it soon transpired that neither of them really liked him. This, of course, was not a bond that would ever be acknowledged, let alone discussed. I will say that they were more discreet than most daughters-in-law and mothers-in-law in our town. They didn't talk about each other.

I've always wondered why young girls moved into our town, set their caps for local boys, and then married into well-established families and didn't let the honeymoon sheets get dry and stiff before they commenced finding fault with their husbands' mamas. I've seen it over and over. It's always a losing battle for the bride. Mama is firmly entrenched locally and nobody expects her to change just because some fliberty-gibbet young woman moves into her territory and challenges her, no matter how cute and flirty and feisty the newcomer is. Mama always wins, like Walter George when FDR sponsored Lawrence Camp. Nobody from outside is going to mess with one of our local icons and get away with it.

When Mary Turner married one of Old Lady Vollenwider's boys, she got all hot in the collar at Christmas because Mrs. Vollenwider gave her son new underwear for his Christmas present. She even had the temerity to confront the old lady about it.

"He's married now, Mrs. Vollenwider, and I think it's proper for me to buy his underwear for him. After all, I am his wife, you know."

Mrs. Vollenwider never looked up. She just flung her thread over her knitting needle to begin a purling row, sighed, and very calmly said, "I know, dear, but that's what I've always given him at

Christmas; he expects it. What's the problem? His size hasn't changed since he married, has it?"

Mary had little enough sense to tell it at her circle meeting and it made the rounds, of course. When it trickled down to Oscar Hosey, he picked up his empty Coca-Cola bottle, let loose a stream of snuff into it without spattering a drop, and drawled, "What's she griping about? She controls all the pussy, don't she? That'll take new underwear outen the picture ever time. Effen she uses it right. I just jumped three of your men; crown my king." Oscar was an expert at keeping things in proper perspective, but this particular proof of his wisdom was never repeated to Mary Vollenwider.

It wasn't that Miss Pansy disliked Beatrice or vice versa. They were just two totally incompatible women. When Beatrice first came to town, she had a hard time with us about her name. "It is not "Be-*at*-truss,'" she would explain over and over, "it's pronounced '*Bee*-atrice.' Please." Then she would repeat it at least three times without any punctuation marks and give a flashing smile that was about as sincere as sunlight on polished steel. She might have made an excellent first-grade teacher or else she still was marked by her own first-grade teacher, for she never spoke to anyone about anything without so many repetitions that you were reminded of a phonograph record with the needle stuck. Then when the needle finally jumped the groove, she would usually wind up with a statement that came bursting from her subconscious and should never have made the sound waves.

"*Bee*-atrice, *Bee*-atrice, *Bee*-atrice, *Bee*-atrice." Smile. "That's all right, don't worry don't worry don't worry about it, all ignorant people say Be-*at*-truss."

When she and Toor got married, they moved into the big old house with his parents. After she missed her second period and wouldn't quit talking about it, her mother-in-law delivered an ultimatum. "Mr. Cofield, you build that girl a house and get her out of mine. And make haste about it. There's not room under our roof for two women, let alone these two. And furthermore, I want everybody to know that I have not the slightest intention of ever baby-sitting any grandchildren. You can let B. S. and that girl know I said it, too." She was never heard to refer to Beatrice as anything but "that girl."

To this day Toor Cofield's house holds the record for being the largest one built in the shortest period of time that our town has ever witnessed. If Beatrice resented Miss Pansy, she was smart enough to keep it to herself. At least she didn't have to worry about Toor getting underwear for Christmas.

Oscar Hosey dismissed the erection of the house and the motive behind it as trivial. "Hit's just female jealousy, at's all in the world hit is. That Beatruss gal's as long-legged as a three-month-old colt, and effen Miss Pansy's butt gets any closer to the ground, she's gonna need to grow web feet to get around." I miss Oscar.

Don't think for a minute that we didn't like Beatrice Cofield. She was more fun to watch than anyone we'd had in a long time, and in addition to that she was more fun to listen to. If you didn't take it personally.

She called on Carlotta Melrose. This was back in the days when all the women hadn't gotten jobs and had time to call on each other in the afternoons. She took her two oldest boys along, ages two and four, and Carlotta made it a point of receiving her on the front porch, judiciously assuming that she'd rather risk the lawn and shrubbery to the assaults of "those Cofield children" than the furniture and bric-a-brac inside the house.

"Carlotta, I love those shoes just love them just love them just love them. They're divine divine divine absolutely divine just love them. I have some just like them just like them just exactly like them." Pause. "Mine aren't the cheap kind, of course."

Carlotta gaped, swallowed, and recovered. "Thank you, Beatrice; you're very kind."

"No no no no. I really mean it really really really really mean it they do wonders for thick ankles."

When she had three children, she called on Lucille McElwaney, who also happened to be receiving on the front porch as soon as she saw Beatrice coming up the driveway. Beatrice never referred to her

husband as Toor and disdained nicknames for any of the rest of us. I
cringed every time she called me "Aloysius" but then forgave her
when I considered that she always referred to Toor as "Betsill." She
was definitely not from around here.

"Lucille, it's good to see you good to see you good to see you
been meaning to come see you for months and months and months
and months but been busy busy busy you know how it is with three
children three children three children three children can you imagine
no of course you can't I forgot you don't have any. Well anyway I
have a project for you a good project it doesn't involve spending any
money no money involved at all so just relax I'm not out soliciting or
anything like that if there is anything else like that I've never thought
of it in that light before. Anyway." Deep breath. "I've just come from
calling on the wife of the new foreman Betsill hired for the planing
mill you know I'm sure that Betsill runs the planing mill doesn't
outright own all of it just part of it but he runs it he runs it and is
responsible for it." Breathe. "As I was saying or was I of course I was
anyway this is a man named Grady White and Betsill brought him in
from Hawkinsville, Georgia, Hawkinsville Hawkinsville I don't know
whether you know where that is or not I'm not exactly clear on it
myself I know I've never been there at least I don't think I have
maybe on the way to St. Simon's but anyway it's way down in South
Georgia somewhere and they don't know a soul here not a single
living breathing soul and I found out that Mrs. White is a Baptist and
since I know you're one too a very very very active Baptist I'm told.
Don't be modest on me Lucille everybody in town even we
Methodists respect you respect you respect you for your good works
all I ever hear about you is good works good works good works."
Breathe. "While I was visiting Mrs. White it occurred to me came
over me in a flash just a flash all of a sudden just a flash like an
inspiration that's the word I was looking for all along Lucille
McElwaney would be the very person to meet Mrs. White and
become friends I don't mean real real real close friends but a friend to
a newcomer who doesn't know a soul not a living soul not one single
solitary living soul here and is obliged to be lonely, lonely, lonely."

Pause. "She's a nice person a really really nice person moved into that little house with green asbestos shingles that Betsill built down close to the planing mill you won't have any trouble finding it I know it's the only green house on the road green asbestos shingles just remember that. I think you'll really wind up enjoying her she's a very nice woman very very nice woman and you two already have a lot in common a lot in common she doesn't have any children no children at all a lot in common." Pause. "*She's* not well-educated either."

Beatrice never had any idea that she offended anyone, but the last I heard, Lucille McElwaney had never met Mrs. Grady White. She did, however, dig her diploma from GSCW out of a bottom drawer and hang it in her parlor. Just in case. She and Carlotta were good friends and enjoyed laughing together. Each of them told me about those two incidents and I didn't have to recite a single line of poetry. It's a wonderful town.

I never recited any poetry to Beatrice, either, although if she could have kept still and quiet for a minute "My Last Duchess" might have been appropriate. She was long-limbed and high-breasted, and despite her mousy hair and bug eyes, she would have been right attractive if she weren't so goddam vivacious. I tell you one thing: she sure kept the Cofields in our line of vision. She was all over town in her automobile with four kids hanging out the windows, and she chattered like a squirrel. I got the impression she sometimes even frisked her tail like one, but I left all that up to Toor. I never was the slightest bit tempted.

A lady told me once that the two times you should never ever speak were while watching a sunrise and during sex. As far as I know, Toor never saw a sunrise in his life, and I can only speculate on the latter.

Mr. B. M. had bought a great big Cadillac about the time he got a convicted trustee through the state prison system as a body servant, gardener, houseboy, chauffeur, and general handyman. He didn't have to pay him anything, just provide him shelter, food, and clothing. *Such a deal*, Mr. B. M. must have thought. The man's name was Cyrene, and he turned out to be genial, well spoken, and polite.

No one was afraid of him, although he had been in prison for killing his wife. After all, as the community thought in those days, they were both black.

Beatrice inveigled Mr. B. M. into lending her his Cadillac for an afternoon and invited her neighbor to bring her two children for a ride around town; maybe even over to Jonesboro and back. With the four Cofield children, this meant there would be nine people in the car, albeit six of them were small.

She solved the problem by sitting in the front seat herself with her oldest son, Will, wedged between her and Cyrene. The neighbor was privileged to sit in the back amidst the five younger children, the youngest of whom was named Martha Hodnett and was standing upright between her mother and the rest of the children.

About fifteen minutes into the tour, Martha Hodnett spoke loudly and clearly into the chatter, "Will has a black daddy."

All conversation stopped. After a rather embarrassed silence, Beatrice stepped into the breach. "No, Martha Hodnett, darling, this is Cyrene, Cyrene, Cyrene. He is not Will's daddy, he is Will's friend, his friend, as a matter of fact he is all our friend he works for Will's daddy but he is just a friend, a very very very dear dear friend. Isn't that right, Cyrene?"

Before the oppressed chauffeur could reply, Martha Hodnett jumped up and down on the back seat and chanted in rhythm with her leaps, "Black daddy, black daddy, black daddy."

Beatrice never used Cyrene for a chauffeur again and also never organized another neighborhood safari.

Martha Hodnett grew up, went to law school, and still enjoys the reputation of being the most effective trial lawyer in the region, especially in divorce cases. She is hard to fool.

I always dreaded going up against her. No matter how convincing the hard cold facts I laid out before the court, she could get up before a jury and convince them that black was white and that I was a bald-faced liar.

She was twenty-two years younger than I when she hung out her shingle, but I was still in my prime and became interested in deepening our relationship. I asked her one day during a recess while the judge went to pee if she was familiar with a sonnet by Millay that began with "I, too, beneath thy moon...."

She gave me a straight look and said, "Mr. Buster, how much protection do you have against a sexual harassment suit? I'm not overly fond of poetry and certainly not 'The Lay of the Last Minstrel.' Let's go get a cup of coffee."

I've always loved that girl. She had the good looks of her Hodnett grandmother and the pit-bull personality of her paternal grandfather, but she also had the insight to call me "Mr. Buster" instead of "Mr. Holcombe" or worse still "Mr. Aloysius." I've never been put in place any more adroitly, before or since. Like I said, she's hard to fool.

When the locals watched Toor's marriage and his family, ninety-nine percent said, "Poor Beatrice." Not me. I always thought, *Poor Toor*, and I never blamed him for drinking a fifth of Scotch every night. I've occasionally envisioned Toor in sodden slumber with all the lights out and Beatrice at two o'clock in the morning still talking a mile a minute with four kids stumbling around the house bumping into furniture and sleeping where they dropped.

Toor and Beatrice. Perhaps I should start saying Betsill and Beatrice, for she repeated his first name so often and so pointedly that by the time he was fifty only a handful of us old-timers still used his nickname, and far as I know most of us, and most certainly not Beatrice, had any idea of how it had got started in the first place. She set out to give the boy a little dignity in the community. His only goal was to make money and as much of it as possible. Her major objective apparently was to achieve and maintain social prestige, and to obtain that goal she needed to prize Betsill away from some of his money. She had a long row to hoe.

That boy loved money. He loved to make money. He loved to have money. I guess he had learned it at his father's knee or maybe in his bed before he had appendicitis. He always talked about money, but he hated like hell to spend it on anything that was not going to make more money for him. Talk and wheedle as much as she could,

Beatrice never got a charge card at Rich's or anywhere else. She
wound up buying secondhand clothes at Bargain Brown's.

Mr. Talmadge Brown had established a cottage industry way out
on a dirt road by buying unclaimed freight from the railroads in
Atlanta and hauling unopened trunks and boxes out to his farm and
selling the contents.

Beatrice soon discovered that a lot of those trunks were full of
clothes and she was forever hauling her kids out to plunder through
them when a new lot came in. Then she became transformed into a
counter snob and would boast, "I didn't spend but two dollars two
dollars two dollars mind you for this entire outfit the whole entire
outfit every single bit of it. Fifty cents for the skirt that's just one half
of a dollar fifty cents just fifty cents and feel the material beautiful
material gorgeous just gorgeous material and then I dug a little
deeper it was a big trunk a very very very large trunk I was almost
standing on my head before I got to the bottom of it I know I must
have looked ridiculous if anybody had come by but fortunately they
didn't and right at the bottom of the trunk I found this blouse this
very blouse I'm wearing right now and as you can see it comes very
very close to matching the skirt so close to it it takes a very careful
observer to notice it's not exactly not just exactly but close enough
the same shade of green and it's apparent to anybody just anybody at
all if she's a female males couldn't notice but any female would
recognize immediately I mean right off the bat that it's pure silk pure
one hundred percent silk just feel the material and talk as I would and
I talked very very hard and very earnestly if I do say so myself Mr.
Brown wouldn't let me have it for a dime not one thin dime less than
a dollar and a half but still and all the whole outfit came to just two
dollars except for the shoes of course which I already had and did you
know Carlotta Melrose has a pair just exactly well almost exactly like
them Betsill just grunted when I told him about this marvelous
bargain just grunted but I told him what a marvelous marvelous
marvelous buy it was and probably couldn't be most likely couldn't
be duplicated at Rich's for less than ninety-nine or even a hundred
dollars he just grunted but I think in fact I'm positive downright

positive that he was impressed." Deep sigh. "You know how husbands are."

Those kids of theirs didn't stand a chance, I guess. They learned to worship money from their daddy and they learned to squeeze a penny from their mama. They learned early, too. One day my back doorbell rang and there stood little Will Cofield in a Cub Scout uniform, of all things. He was butt-built like Toor but had the buckteeth of Beatrice.

"Yes, Will?" I said.

"Wanna buy a case of Co-Cola to help the Cub Scouts? They're a dollar and a half in the store and we're selling them for a dollar and a quarter. Save you a quarter and you don't have to tote 'em from the store."

I glanced at the car parked by the curb and saw Eustace Pilcher under the wheel. He grinned and waved. Eustace Pilcher a Cub Scout leader. My heart swelled in sympathy. Poor child.

"Why, yes, Will, I'll take a case. Just put it here on the back porch."

He didn't move. He stared at me. "Lemme see the money," he demanded.

My sympathy level dropped precipitously. The little turd was going to be just like his father. Or his mother. "Certainly, Will," I responded. "You let me see the case of Co-Cola. I'll go in the house and get your money and you put the Cokes right here on the porch where I told you."

I went in the house to the cookie jar where I threw pennies every night when I took off my pants. I counted out one hundred and thirty, put them in a sock, and returned. I handed the sock to Will, carried the Cokes inside, and locked the door.

It was fun watching him through the window count those pennies one by one, and it was even more fun to watch him carefully pocket five of them before carrying the sock to his scout master. *Poor Eustace*, I thought. Those two are prime examples of "Blood will tell" and "Water seeks its level."

In six months the Cub Scout effort in our town was abandoned for about the next fifteen years.

Chapter 15

Don't think that Toor's children were the only Cofields we had in our town to watch. Sara Belle Hipp had three girls, every one of them a real beauty. They gave us a lot of entertainment growing up and, come to think of it, as adults also. Sara Belle did not have the restrictive attitude toward her children that Mr. Johnnie and Miss Gayflowers had imposed on her, and her girls pretty well ran as wild as all the other teenagers in our town. Within certain parameters, of course; none of them ever came home pregnant or got caught smoking pot, but they were pretty well the belles of their era. I noticed that they never lacked for beaus either. (All three smoked cigarettes, but so did their mama—none of them used snuff, however; Sara Belle had her limits.)

Along came Vietnam right in the middle of our post-war prosperity and be blessed if Mr. Ed's grandson, Sport Cofield's son, didn't get called up. Our county had weathered Korea pretty well and Truman had been able to stir up patriotic fires against Communism. After all, he had saved Western Europe, including France, lest they forget, from Communist Russia, and we felt toward Truman the same way we did toward the Talmadges, as much as it was possible to identify with somebody from Missouri, of course. Lots of our boys had volunteered and joined up for Korea out of a sense of patriotic duty. Jim Harp was one I remember particularly.

Jim had been too young for WWII and had already graduated from college when he volunteered during Korea, and he was gone before you could say "Jack Robinson." We had a new preacher in our church, the smartest and most consecrated one I ever met. On top of that, his oldest daughter, Lula, was a senior in high school who was more beautiful than most movie stars. All the girls circled her like a bunch of wary tabbies with a Persian kitten set down in their midst, but she was immediately popular with every male in town who had outgrown knee pants.

And some who hadn't.

She was pretty near as smart as her daddy and took all the teachers in as completely as all the boys. She enjoyed watching as much as the old-timers, but she didn't know all the players as well as we. One night after choir practice, while I was putting up my music, she cornered me.

"Who is this Jim Harp I keep hearing about?"

"He's the only son of Mrs. Ruth Harp, who is the daughter-in-law of Mrs. Blanche Harp, who was a Perdue before she married, and therefore he is a cousin of mine. Anyhow, why do you ask?"

"I'm sure you know Mrs. Giles; I have her for homeroom. She's about a hundred and sixty years old and she prays for five minutes every morning before we break up and go to class. She's forever praying for Jim Harp, and this morning it got to the point I almost burst out laughing."

"Tell me about it. She's a good friend of Jim's mother, who teaches in the grammar school."

"I had figured that. This morning she had covered all the generalities; prayed for the school, our country, our president, the sick and afflicted. You know the routine, she's so Baptist she rattles."

"Rattles?"

"You know what I mean. Don't tell Daddy I said that. Anyway, at the end she said, still with her eyes closed, and this is exactly what she said, 'And finally, dear Lord, we pray for the safety and comfort of Mrs. Harp's son, Jimmy, who is in Korea with nothing but a gas heater to keep him warm. Excuse me, Lord, I think I made a mistake there; I believe that's a kerosene heater. At any rate, keep him safe. In Jesus' name, amen.' Can you believe she said that?"

I thought a brief moment about Mrs. Giles. "Yes."

"Well, I hope I meet that Jim Harp someday; I'll be forced to tell him we prayed for him. I'll find out if he has a sense of humor."

Well, to wind that up, Jim Harp came home from the Korean War when the preacher's daughter was finishing her freshman year at

Wesleyan, and it was like a moth seeking a flame. They got married before she had finished her second year, and if they don't have a sense of humor, I do.

I've thought about them a lot in hindsight. Because of Mrs. Giles's explicit prayer, that beautiful newcomer to our town, who managed to make only one close girlfriend in the senior class because she was so pretty and also so smart, was well aware of Jim Harp before he ever heard of her, and curious. She soon found out. He did, too, and a lot more.

He came on stage cold, but soon got hot.

I get to musing that perhaps it was all in answer to Mrs. Giles's prayer, but I have strong suspicions that she never dreamed her prayer for Jim Harp to be "safe" involved his marrying the preacher's daughter; although in my opinion, it did.

And it sure turned out they both had a sense of humor. They needed it. Jim was not nearly as good-looking as his bride, and while we're musing, I've always considered it a great blessing that the Lord makes good-looking women fall in love with homely men; I've reaped a few of those rewards myself. Jim was every bit as smart as Lula and maybe even a little smarter, for he never let on to her that he knew it.

When they prospered enough to build a house, I was drawing up some legal papers for Jim and he confided to me, "I'm not real happy about building this big; I would be just as happy living in a Jim Walters house."

I looked at him pretty straight and let him have it. "You might as well get used to the fact that you haven't married a Jim Walters woman."

He laughed, agreed with me, and they're just as happy as they can be in a three-story mansion with white columns, pink marble floors, and a living room and dining room that would make Mrs. Melrose look bourgeois. At least they still laugh a lot. Talk about the power of prayer! It's there. To my mind it's a lot like lightning; you can't direct exactly how or where it's going to strike, but when it's being called down, prudent men need to take cover.

Even in my dotage the Harps still come to see me. Jim is one of the most honest friends I've ever had. You can tell him the plain truth without any varnish on it, and believe you me, that's how he hands it to you.

The Harps have sure added a lot to this wonderful town.

Since that time long ago, they've outlawed prayer in the public schools, but I can't give Mrs. Giles or the Harps any credit for it. A heap of folks in the county still raise sand and grumble about abolishing prayer, but I tell them not to worry. As long as they teach algebra, they're going to have prayer.

I personally agree with Oscar Hosey about praying in school: "To hell with prayer. When they banned whipping butt at school is when they shit in the flax. Now they get to wear dirty linen."

Sometimes I think Oscar would have made a good president if he could just have done anything constructive besides playing checkers. Also, if he had ever deigned to bathe and shave more than once a week. Oscar was a man of his own principles, however, and was perfectly comfortable with himself just like he was. You had to like him. He had a certain presence about him which became stronger the nearer Saturday came.

Anyway, back to Vietnam. By this time we had the Kennedys, the hippies, and television. It is my personal opinion that if television and the liberal press had taken over the brain of America fifty years earlier, we would all be speaking German or Japanese, but I have evolved into what they used to call a mossback and what the *New Yorker* smartass magazine now refers to as "antediluvian."

People were not scrambling to enlist in the army during Vietnam. In fact, a lot of them were figuring out ways to avoid it. College was a refuge for many and Canada for others. We still had the draft and boys had to go whether they wanted to or not. When somebody had a low draft number and faced the likelihood of going soon, it was common practice to volunteer so that you could pick your branch of the service. The navy and Coast Guard became more popular than any time since John Paul Jones.

Sport Cofield's boy had grown up under the spotlight of village observation and had handled it better than most. His middle name was Holsonbeck and his parents had chosen to call him Holson for short. He was friendly and well liked, although he wasn't blessed with the brightest bulb in the family chandelier. He spoke with an exaggerated drawl punctuated with wagging head and an infectious grin. He had a very low draft number.

"No, suh, I'm not going to enlist just to pick my branch of service. No, suh, I know a lotta guys are doing just that, but it don't make any sense to me. They know I'm here, and if they want me they can come get me."

So they did.

The morning he left for induction at Fort McPherson, Emily Cofield got up, started to cook him some breakfast, began crying, and flew back to her bedroom behind a locked door. I am told that she pulled down all the shades, crawled between the covers, and smoked a half pack of Camels before she cried herself back to sleep. For the next two years, if she had more than two drinks, she would burst into tears and keen, "My baby, my baby," over and over. Vietnam was not popular in the Cofield household.

Holson walked across the courthouse square to the drugstore, which doubled as our bus station without the expense of anybody having to build one. Dr. Morris's widow served as station mistress. It paid little but it got her out of the house and downtown where she could keep abreast of what was going on.

Sometimes the most dedicated and diligent observers in our town never realize that they in turn are being watched. I've always tried to stay in the background myself and be as inconspicuous as possible. Mrs. Morris was very conspicuous but was completely unselfconscious, and I don't think it ever occurred to her that she might be watched with delight as an eccentric. By the time she had taken over the job as ticket master, she regarded the drugstore as a second home. She migrated every morning down the sidewalk from sleeping quarters to working station as unconcerned as if she were going from her bedroom to her kitchen. She always wore blue felt bedroom slippers and no makeup. One of her front teeth in her upper plate was rimmed in gold, and she had pierced ears from which dangled one-dollar gold pieces. That was decoration enough for Mrs. Morris. She never bothered to wear a petticoat or brassiere, which made most people stare fixedly at her face.

She was partial to loose dresses of some sheer navy blue material with tiny white polka dots. If you let your eyes slip when she moved, you could see her breasts swing to each side an unbelievable distance below her armpits. This was still fairly modest attire since her nipples were pretty well hidden at waist level. She was born and raised amongst us, and it was her privilege in her old age to appear any damned way she chose in public and still maintain respect.

When Holson came in to pick up his ticket, she had a fit, almost a hissy fit.

"Holson, you don't mean you're going to war! Not little Holson Cofield! Why, boy, I feel like I've half-raised you. I can't believe you're old enough to go in the army."

"Yes'm, Miss Lena, I'm nineteen years old now."

"You can't be, Holson-baby, somebody's made a mistake. I can't stand the idea of you going over there in those jungles with all those snakes and spiders and monkeys and God only knows what all, and none of those folks living there even speak English. I just can't believe you're going."

"Yes, ma'am, Miss Lena. I'm going." He squared his shoulders. "They've sent for me and I'm going. I'm going to serve my country."

"Well, Holson, you be careful! Those among us who pray will certainly pray for you, for all the good that will do. You be safe, you hear?"

"Yes'm. They'll train me good, I know."

About five young black males appeared for tickets. They had all worked on the Cofield farm in their adolescence and Holson knew each of them. He was the only white in the group. Miss Lena busied herself with their tickets and Holson was spared any more of her effusive wailing.

The other five inductees seemed glad to see Holson, but their eyes roamed everywhere except over the person of Mrs. Morris. They were country boys and didn't come to town often.

Just then the bus drew up outside. Its door hissed open and the driver came in to get a Coke and pick up the mail. The post office was next door to the drugstore/bus station and was ruled by Bill Pritchett, who despite having been appointed by Eisenhower had so far been overlooked by both Kennedy and Johnson. Ours was a very small post office. It didn't pay much, but it was good exposure for Bill Pritchett, who could take orders for radios and even Chevrolets and Plymouths while she worked.

I can't remember ever seeing Bill wear anything but brown. She was almost as much of a sartorial disaster as Miss Lena but with fewer body parts visible. She wore sensible brown suede shoes with knee-length tan cotton socks and brown corduroy skirts, which fortunately were usually long enough to cover the backs of her knees. She had a series of brown vests, none of which lacked holes from cigarette sparks, and at least two blouses that buttoned at the neck but strained at the breasts.

When Holson shepherded his childhood friends into the bus and had his own foot on the step, Bill burst out of the post office, threw a lighted cigarette in the gutter, and shouted, "Hold the bus!"

She abandoned her customary waddle for the determined charge of a rhinoceros and headed for Holson. Bill was certainly not an overly sentimental person, but she was a long-standing friend of Emily Cofield.

"Where's yo momma, Holson?"

"In bed with a cold rag on her head last time I saw her, Miss Bill."

"Well, Lord God, Holson, I can't stand to see you head off to the army without nobody to kiss you good-bye."

With that she flung both arms wide, jerked him into the midst of her more than ample bosom and planted a loose-lipped, slobbery kiss square on his mouth. The black boys gaped momentarily, then gazed at the ceiling of the bus.

Holson extracted himself from between the melons of Bill's breasts, scrambled into the bus, the door hissed closed, and it began slowly moving away. Mrs. Morris ran from the drugstore alongside the bus and yelled until it gathered enough speed to leave her behind in the middle of the street.

She had her hands cupped like a megaphone and screamed over and over, "Pee in the bed, Holson; pee in the bed! You hear? Pee in the bed! Harvey Brown done that and they sent him home!" Neither one of her blue felt shoes came off.

What a wonderful town. As far as I know, Holson's send-off remains unique. I've always wondered if the rigors of Vietnam didn't seem anticlimactic to him. He lived through it, came home until his parents died, and then moved to Montana and, last I heard, was raising cows, buffaloes, a considerable amount of hell, and had taken up snow skiing.

The war in Vietnam didn't decimate our county of young soldiers. A few got killed and we mourned appropriately, but it was nothing like as bad as Korea or either World War and certainly not the War Between the States. None of our boys moved to Canada, although there were probably a good many who went to college who wouldn't have under better circumstances.

The most visible effect in our whole county was not from the war itself but from the hippie movement that went along with it. It was a groundswell that damn near wrecked the United States of America and culminated, to my way of thinking, when we put two of them from Arkansas in the White House.

"If it feels good, do it" and "Make love, not war." Those two creeds sound innocuous enough on the surface, but when they're carried to fornicating and acid-dropping extremes, they're dangerous as hell and as Satan who rules over it. Timothy Leary did more harm to America than Aaron Burr or Benedict Arnold ever thought of. And while I'm at it, Jane Fonda and her ilk, and she had more ilk, come to think of it, than most, sure pitched in and did their part.

It wasn't the native-born sons who caused hippie commotion in our town. Sure, some of our boys grew their hair longer than their mammas liked, but they still had to bathe every day and wear clean clothes to school; they even had to keep saying "yes, ma'am" and "no, ma'am." Where we had trouble was with migrants and runaways.

Mr. Johnnie Cofield had been dead on the mark when he said if we paved the roads so we could get out, there was no telling what might come in on them. Progress is wonderful but it sure causes upheaval and new problems. Here they came, long, uncombed, dirty hair full of snarls and tangles all the way down to the waist; nasty blue jeans; serapes or shawls; sandals or even lots of times just plain barefooted; always grimy toenails and fingernails. On top of that, they had all discovered LSD and usually had a bountiful supply. I never discovered exactly the mechanics involved in "dropping acid," but man like you know they were all hip to it and in the groove, whatever that meant.

Their own mothers wouldn't have recognized them. They drove our sheriff and local police to distraction. They had the morals of an alley cat and no more inhibitions than a hung-up dog. When they weren't smoking something, they were urinating, defecating, or fornicating right out in public view. Our sheriff at the time had been raised Baptist by a widowed mother and, although he hadn't been inside a church in twenty years except for funerals, he had scruples. He called Dr. Hentz one morning at two o'clock.

"Doc, how 'bout coming down here to the jail and sexing a bunch of hippies for me?"

Dr. Hentz shook the receiver and came wide awake.

"Say again?"

"I've arrested twelve or thirteen of those goddam hippies and I can't tell male from female, but I'll just be damned if I'm gonna lock 'em all up together. Nothing would suit them better but I ain't turning my jail into a whorehouse for no bunch of freaks. They may be crazy as hell, but I ain't. Leastways, not yet. Get on down here, you hear? Right now." Dr. Hentz said he was almost whimpering.

After Oscar Hosey and John Pyron and Carl King teased him enough, the sheriff became a little more mellow about the situation and was even able to laugh about occasional incidents as he recalled them.

"Right after school had took in and the buses quit running one morning, I looked out the window and right there on the sidewalk in front of the courthouse this ole boy pulled out his dong and commenced to pissing into the road. Old Lady Lora Holt was puttering along in her Model-A and stalled it out in one of the boxwoods when she jumped the curb. She was screaming 'Indecent exposure!' so loud she woke my wife up and she come running in the room wanting to know what was going on. I grabbed my hat and blackjack and told her, 'Lora Holt insists it's indecent exposure, but I been looking straight at it and you might better call it "more than decent," but still it's against the law and I'll have to lock the little shit-ass up. I just hope this'll be one where I can locate the parents. This town is going to hell in a handbasket.'"

The sheriff had a good heart, but he went to great lengths to cover it up. He never got over the hippies, not even after everybody had abandoned their dress code except construction workers and painters.

Several years after most teenagers had forsaken serapes and long hair (but had, of course, hung on to free love), more crime started coming into our town than dropping acid, camping out, and streaking. The sheriff called Dr. Hentz again, this time at daylight on a winter morning.

"Doc, how 'bout coming down to Dottie-Bay's and pronouncing a hippie dead?"

Dottie-Bay's was the longest surviving restaurant in our town, mainly because all the proprietors of other eating establishments had died off and there just wasn't a tremendous demand for anything other than home cooking, except for day laborers whose wives were too indolent to pack them a lunch or boys who had dropped out of high school as soon as they turned sixteen and didn't have anybody to feed them at home.

Dottie-Bay was what anybody anywhere would call a character, at least in any part of the country that has a concept of its meaning.

He had been born Willie James Tarpley, the youngest of seven children, and his mama called him "Doll-Baby." She'd haul him around town on one hip and tell her friends, "Isn't he a little doll? He's his mama's baby doll, aren't you, Doll-Baby?" His siblings, who were not yet well formed linguistically to the point of mastering all syllables, dubbed him "Dottie-Bay," and the name stuck to him for the rest of his life.

He grew up in his family the lightning rod of as much jealousy as Joseph when he got his coat of many colors and had to fight his way through recess because of his nickname without the support of his older, stronger brothers. He always had a little staccato speech impediment just short of a lisp and stutter, but man could he fight!

He went through World War II as Willie Tarpley, served three years as an army cook, and returned to our town in triumph and to the identity of Dottie-Bay. He married a beautiful young widow who had pouty lips painted cherry red, a twelve-month-old son, and a brick house. Dottie-Bay must have saved every dollar he earned in the army, and he set himself up in business without spending a dime of his wife's money. I know because I was the lawyer for both of them and they always kept their finances separate from each other.

He bought a run-down shack of a filling station that only had one gas pump, fitted it out with a pool table, a pot-bellied stove for warmth, a refrigerator, and a big cooking surface heated by electricity. He only had one light bulb and that hung square over the pool table. His restaurant didn't have any chairs for guests, just a butt-sprung wicker rocker in the back for Dottie-Bay when he had no customers. The place was pretty dark, even in the middle of the day.

His menu was what would nowadays be called limited. Very limited. He served hamburgers or beef stew or hot dogs. With Co-Colas. Take it or leave it. The service was unique. He would take a bun, lick his thumb like my elderly aunt turning a page in her New Testament, then pry the bun open and lay a wiener in it. His specialty therefore became known as "thumb dogs." He wore a white apron which he changed every Monday. He also wore an elongated leather wallet in his hip pocket chained with a long loop to his belt.

He was the only person I ever heard of besides Herman Talmadge who had a thousand dollar bill. He carried it constantly and could show it boastfully to any of his clientele. He made a lot of money lending cash to laborers and high school dropouts by charging more interest than banks but without any background check. He was also reputed to sell beer in our dry county, but the law had never caught him.

His establishment was a favorite hangout for teenaged boys who wanted to look tough, but Dottie-Bay took a stern parental approach to them. He didn't allow them to cuss or smoke in his place and had even been known to snatch off his belt or a piece of rubber hose and put a whipping on miscreants he thought were not measuring up to his standards, which, considering everything else about him, were pretty high. One of his favorite proclamations was "What's right's right, and what's wrong's wrong," although he had his own private distinctions between the two.

Everybody in town liked Dottie-Bay, except for Emmett Pringle. Emmett had been married to Mae Ballentyne for about fifteen years, but he wasn't from around here, and she was not his first wife. She had met him her first year out of college when she was teaching school and he was one of her senior students. He was reputed to have been very good-looking, and she was too young to be teaching school a hundred miles up in North Georgia.

To hear her tell it later, it was love at first sight, at least on her part. He was the smartest kid in her English class and responded to her aversion for grammatical errors. In any event, they had some sort of romance, the juicy details of which neither of them ever divulged.

When Emmett finished high school, the owner of the biggest mill in the town gave him a job and he started flying high, drinking liquor, traveling to Europe on business, and the like of that. Before Mae realized what was happening, the boss's daughter had latched on to Emmett and married him.

Mae crawled back home to Mama, she said, with a broken heart and never taught school another day in her life. "Far as I'm concerned," she told me once, "every little bastard in North Georgia can grow up saying 'have went' or 'between you and I' and even 'we was laying in the sun.' I don't give a shit."

Mr. Johnnie Cofield got her a job at the state capitol in the tag department, and she worked hard at trying to forget Emmett. She didn't succeed. Ten years later a mutual friend came by her workplace and told her that Emmett had been divorced for five years, had lost his job, and had been lying up drunk in the Piedmont Hotel for two weeks and "Here is his room number."

Mae got her coat, left work at noon, and spent the next three days talking to Emmett in the Piedmont Hotel. "You should have seen him," she told me. "You know what a fastidious little dandy he is. Well, he hadn't shaved in two weeks and didn't smell like he'd bathed either. I got him cleaned up, filled him full of scrambled eggs and milkshakes, and we talked and talked and talked. Friday at noon we went to the courthouse and got married. I drove him out to Smyrna and put Emmett in Brawner's Sanitarium for his honeymoon and went home and told Mama I was married."

I pretty well knew the rest of their story. Each of them had promised the other not to drink any more alcohol, and by the time I met Emmett he was back on his feet and wealthy and Mae never hit a lick at a snake again for the longest day she lived. Emmett borrowed money, started a furniture business, and prospered mightily. He loved our town and enjoyed watching our characters, as long as he felt we weren't gossiping.

He had one of the most volatile temperaments I have ever witnessed. One moment he would be calm, soft-spoken, and rational; something could set him off and in a split second he would be purple in the face, the veins in his neck would be distended, and he would be yelling at the top of his lungs right in your face.

He bought the first Thunderbird put on the market, the one with a metal shell you could remove and have a convertible. He was as proud of it as a two-year-old with a big navel and made a point of taking every young 'un in town to ride in it.

One Monday afternoon he was parked in front of Ruby's grocery store on the southwest corner of the courthouse square and backed his beloved Thunderbird square into the side of an eighteen-wheeler passing through. Emmett jumped out of his car, raced around to the driver's side of the truck, gazed straight up into the face of the amazed driver, and began berating him. They were arguing over who was to blame. The noise volume was considerable.

Dottie-Bay had been coming out of McElwaney's store on the north end of the street, where he had gone to buy the hamburger meat left over from the week before to put in his stew. It was always on sale on Monday. His apron was rolled up to his waist but was already obviously spotted. He came tearing down the middle of the street, waving his arms and yelling, "Mr. Pringle, Mr. Pringle, I saw it all. I saw it all, start to finish. I saw it all!"

Emmett stopped his harangue, his color cooled, and he spoke in an indulgent, almost cooing tone. Help from a witness who was also a local was help indeed.

"Did you now, son?"

"Yessir, yessir. It saw it every bit. It was all your fault." The effect was instantaneous. Emmett jumped up and down, turned deep purple, and directed the full force of his wrath on Dottie-Bay.

"That's just your opinion, goddammit," he shrieked. "Who asked you to come down here meddling in something that's none of your goddam business? You get your sorry ass back up the street and carry it on back down to the other side of town where you belong! Go stick your pecker in that foul pot of stew of yours and keep your goddam nose out of my business!"

Emmett was a steward in our church and made a point of rarely swearing, but he made an exception for Dottie-Bay. Emmett was always a well-respected leader in the community, but we all made allowances for his temper and tried not to rile him.

A teenager passed some sort of local ritual when he was man enough to eat two thumb dogs in a row at Dottie-Bay's and go six months without getting his ass whipped. One year Dottie-Bay hung a hand-lettered pasteboard sign on his restaurant door on January 2. "Closed For Inventory." Oscar Hosey said, "Inventory at Dottie-

Bay's ought not to take more'n five minutes at most; all he got to do is stick a ruler in that fucking pot of stew."

The morning the sheriff got Dr. Hentz out before daylight was one of the most exciting times our town had since Martha Mae Phillips set a trash fire outside Roland Brown's laundry, caught the building on fire, and burned it slap to the ground. It wasn't much building, but it produced a whole lot of thick black smoke and hysterical screams out of Martha Mae that could be heard plumb to the city limits and caused several cars to pull off on the shoulder, expecting to see flashing blue lights. Martha Mae sang soprano in our church, and choir directors always had a hard time toning her down. When she soloed "His Eye Is on the Sparrow," she caused babies to cry and came close to making me miss a note or two on the piano. The laundry fire gave us something to talk about for several weeks, and we Methodists all noted that Martha Mae didn't sing a solo for six months.

When Dottie-Bay killed what the sheriff called a hippie, who turned out to be nothing but a common criminal with no background whatsoever of flower child in him, he created conversation that lasted for several years in our town, and every now and then the tale is still told to this day. Not all that accurately, of course, but close enough to make newcomers think we're lying.

I was a privileged confidant of both the sheriff and Dr. Hentz as their lawyer, and as nearly as I can piece together their accounts, it is a miracle Dottie-Bay was not killed. About five-thirty on that cold, short day of winter, he opened his door, laid his pistol on the countertop, and bent over to make a fire in the stove. This guy rushed in and whacked him over the head with a gun butt and put a stranglehold on him. Dottie-Bay hadn't been through schoolyard fights and the army to give in without a struggle, and he backed into the guy and pushed him into the counter.

By reaching desperately behind himself, he managed to get his own gun and told the sheriff, "I fired a warning shot behind him into the air and he let loose of me. I turned to run and looked over my shoulder and he had both arms reached out just like this and was lunging right at me. Wasn't nothing to do but stick my gun square in the middle of his chest and pull the trigger. Hit made a plumb mess of everything, as you can see. I'll never get it cleaned up. What's right's right and what's wrong's wrong.

"I run out the door and the only light I seen anywheres in town was in the old Ben Adams house where that lady, I don't know her name, has opened a day-care center for kids of mamas what work. I run up there and could see her in the kitchen fixing breakfast, but she didn't hear me when I knocked on the door; so I fired a coupla shots in the air to get her attention and she finally opened the door a crack. I pushed in and asked her to let me use the phone. I was bleeding like a stuck hog and she was the one what wrapped this towel around my head.

"I thanked her and told her it was all right for her to do all this for me, especially since she didn't know me from Adam but she mustn't ever do it for no stranger again; it might be dangerous. Then I called you and come on back down here to wait for you. You called the doctor? Ain't no use, the man's dead."

Dr. Hentz said the subject was lying on his back, both arms outstretched, a pistol still in his right hand, and a hole in the middle of his chest the size of your fist. "I had already checked Dottie-Bay's head and found a six-inch laceration of the scalp and asked one of the bystanders to carry him on down to my office and I would meet them there. I asked in the meantime for someone to call his wife to meet him at my office.

"When the sheriff and I turned the dead man over, I was startled to see the back of his head missing. Parts of the skull were on the stove, which fortunately had not been lit. The odor of fresh blood was enough without the addition of burning bone and brains. Dottie-Bay's warning shot into the air had gone first through the guy's occiput, and he was falling dead when Dottie-Bay potted him in the chest. Damnedest thing I ever saw.

"Damnedest thing I ever heard, though, came later. I was busy shaving Dottie-Bay's head, stanching the bleeding and putting in sutures, when in came his wife. So help me God, she had taken time

to remove her curlers and paint her face and dress up like she was
ready for church. She perched on a stool in the corner with a beaded
purse in her lap and Dottie-Bay said from under the drapes, 'Honey,
hits awful, but what's right's right, you know.' Shock was setting in
on the poor devil and he was trembling all over. Like a dog that's
passing persimmon seeds.

"His wife spoke up, 'Doc, do you think Dottie-Bay's going to be
all right?' You know how she talks with that little blossomed mouth
all puckered up and enameled red and still talking in a little girl voice
at age forty-seven. I've been dealing with her for years, although she
herself goes to a specialist downtown and regales the ladies in the
Baptist church after every visit. Told one of them last month that
'Dr. Shackleford told me I have capillaries.' She's silly as a goose but
shrewd as a snake. I thought I was prepared for anything out of her.

"'Sure, Mrs. Tarpley. Dottie-Bay's tough. This is a deep wound
but the skull's not cracked and he'll have a sore head for a coupla
weeks, but he'll be fine.'

"'But, Doctor, that's not what I meant. I mean do you think
Dottie-Bay's going to hell?'

"'Dottie-Bay winced and I nearly dropped a hemostat. 'After all,
he has kilt a man, you know. Doc, ain't you gonna answer me? Or
don't you know?'

"'The answer to both questions, Mrs. Tarpley, is "No."'

"'Well, I just worry about him all the time. He hasn't never
publicly professed Jesus Christ as his personal Lord and Savior and I
don't want him to go to Hell, at least while he's still married to me.
That might reflect on my duties as a Christian wife. I worry about
him night and day. And pray, of course.'

"She never moved off that damn stool, just sat there with that
silly pocketbook and her hands folded in her lap. And giggled a little.

"I tell you, Buster, that's the quickest I've sewed up and
bandaged a scalp wound since I got out of the bowels of Grady
Hospital. I wanted to tell her that my personal opinion was that
Dottie-Bay had probably been living in Hell ever since he got
married, but that's not covered under the Hippocratic Oath and none

of my business anyhow. I learned long ago that anybody who doesn't like being married bad enough can sure as hell get out of it."

Well, yes, I thought, *or keep from getting into one in the first place,* but I kept my mouth shut. I always thought Dr. Hentz might be on to me since he'd treated several of my pretty ladies, and women will tell a doctor about anything. Lawyers, too, for that matter. They know we won't talk. They never dream we might write.

Nobody ever told Dottie-Bay or his wife that his warning shot into the air had gone through the back of the man's head. She might have thought he had killed the same man twice, and he didn't need any more information about the horrible event or speculation about the religious fallout. People in our town can on occasion be wondrously protective. And kind. I wouldn't think of living anywhere else.

Several months later, Dottie-Bay did join the Baptist church and was immersed in his only suit. Exactly one year later, on a Sunday afternoon, he was sawing down a dead tree in his backyard and the crown fell out and broke his neck. He left double indemnity accidental death insurance and a comfortable estate. His wife raised sand with the undertaker for having to pay for a brand-new suit but caved in and paid for the funeral with Dottie-Bay's thousand dollar bill. Theologically, however, she was very secure. The Lord had struck Dottie-Bay down for violating the Sabbath but had received him with open arms and rejoicing into Heaven because he had accepted Christ and been forgiven for murder.

It soon became a tedium-driven motive for new preachers to keep her from giving personal testimony at Baptist revivals. When she was eighty she still used the same shade of lipstick. I've always thought the Baptists are more tolerant than people give them credit for, and I'm grateful to God that I've never married.

Chapter 16

All the time interesting things were happening to interesting people in our town, Toor Cofield was busy making money. It was his mission in life and was about all he could talk about, at least with any indication of good sense. Since all the rest of us didn't know enough about making money to discuss that in any depth, Toor was pretty well ignored and left to his own devices. We turned our attention to more quickly entertaining characters and their peccadillos.

When Emmett Pringle died, he left Mae with a fine house, his business, a Lincoln Continental which was blue to match her hair, a mink stole, his T-Bird, and lots and lots of pension funds and money in the bank. She stepped up to home plate and started swinging. You might say she blossomed. All her life her favorite expletive had been "shit." Under Emmett's stern tutelage, she had exchanged it for "sheesh," but we all knew what she really meant.

First off, she got her cataracts fixed. When she got her new glasses, she looked in the mirror and said, "Well, sheesh! I'm going to sue Helena Rubenstein and get my money back for all that Queen Bee sheesh I've been buying all these years."

She nearly pestered Dr. Hentz to death. He and Emmett had been good friends, although Emmett was twenty-five years the elder. Mae took the newspaper and said she read Ralph McGill's column every morning so she'd get so mad she'd stop crying about Emmett. She also read Dr. Alvarez, who presented a different disease each day with all its symptoms laid out in plain English. Dr. Hentz told me that he didn't need his alarm clock anymore. Promptly at seven o'clock Mae would call him, certain that she had the current disease of the day, and he had learned to fix his breakfast and drink his coffee while he was convincing her otherwise. Dr. Hentz said he knew it wasn't Christian but the day Dr. Alvarez died was a day of great rejoicing for him.

The two of them had sort of a running contest to see who could outdo the other. Mae liked to hang out at the Hentz home with him and his wife and she got right territorial about it. She always accepted me as a fellow guest of the Hentzes, primarily because I was usually available as an escort when she wanted to go to Atlanta for an evening or to the Elks Club in Griffin. Let it be known for posterity, however, that she was not the least bit interested in poetry, and for the life of me I could never think of any that would have been appropriate. She never did appreciate any other guest barging in on her time with me and the Hentzes and would be pretty critical of them when they left.

One night, Christmas Eve if I remember correctly and I usually do, in came Emma and Randall Huddleston with Emma, as Mae expressed it, dressed up like a sore thumb. They were already pretty tanked up and obviously full of themselves. Mae greeted them coolly and sulked in a corner.

Emma didn't notice. "Let me tell y'all the most exciting news in the world! Our only chick and child got himself engaged tonight at supper! It was so cute! They announced their engagement to us during dessert and we opened a bottle of pink champagne we had on hand for special occasions and he slipped the engagement ring in her glass without her knowing it and she almost swallowed it! Can you believe that? It was the cutest thing you ever saw!"

With this Mae leapt from her chair and hastened toward the door. As she passed Dr. Hentz, he said, "Where are you going, Mae?" She whirled and declaimed imperiously, "I am going to the bathroom! I may pee and I may puke! Sheesh!"

After the Huddlestons left, Doc tried to chide her about being rude, but he didn't get far.

"Don't lecture me, Ephraim Hentz. Who do you think you are, Emmett? I've been knowing Emma Huddleston ever since she was one of those snotty-nosed, snarly-haired little McEachern girls, and she can't put on any airs around me. I know that girl she's bragging about marrying her only chick and child, and I'll give you no more than six months before she beats the living shit out of Emma. So there! Sheesh!"

Dr. Hentz said he tried all her life to get in the last word with Mae but had never succeeded. Said one day it was close, but he got no cigar.

"Buster, you know Mae's the biggest hypochondriac in the world and also the most enthusiastic one I've ever encountered. She brings her own magazines to my office so she won't have to handle other people's germs.

"She even argued me down about her prescriptions. I'll never forget it. 'I don't care if I do need just twelve of those pills. You write it for a hundred.'

"'Mae,' I said, 'that's a waste of money. They charge by the pill.'

"'I don't care. I have the money to waste if I want to. You write it for a hundred.'

"'Why? For God's sake.'

"'Because a hundred comes in an unopened bottle with a seal and packed with cotton, and all the druggist has to do is slap a label on it. I've watched every druggist around and the best of them is either picking his nose in the choir loft or pulling at his pecker, and I don't want him counting out my pills.'

"I'm sure you've noticed in church how she'll sling that mink stole over her mouth and nose and turn around to glare at anybody who sneezes or coughs even six rows behind her. I think she's the main reason we have the name of being an unfriendly church."

I considered her rigid habit of sitting barely one space away from the center aisle and refusing to budge an inch in the pew for latecomers because "I don't want anybody sitting on Emmett" and agreed with Doc.

"She kept griping about coming to my office and having to sit in the waiting room or 'that pit of pestilence' as she expressed it. When she finally got that illness where she had to come every week or two, I afforded her what I considered a signal privilege. I told her that if she'd drive up to the side door of the office and just wait in her car,

I'd have my girls be on the lookout for her and as soon as we had a treatment room empty they'd bring her in and she wouldn't have to sit in the waiting room with all the sick and poor.

"It wasn't any trouble for the staff. They could see her creeping into the parking lot in that baby-blue Lincoln Continental, which matches her hair and which she trades every other year in as good a shape as the day she bought it. She never, to my memory, thanked me for it but acted as though it was one of the perks of royalty or something. However, she was always nice to the girls in the office, always brought them candy or lace handkerchiefs or some little something. She never let up on me, though.

"One day I was busy as a pair of jumper cables at a country funeral, the office was packed, and I was running like a hound in the Everglades. I grabbed a patient's chart and swung into a treatment room. There sat Mae. Wrong chart. Wrong room. I said, 'Excuse me, Mae, I have another patient before you. I'll be right back.'

"She didn't say good morning, kiss my foot, or smile, or anything. Just sat there glaring at me through those thick cataract lenses and snarled as I left the room, 'You wash your hands before you come back in here!'

"It didn't piss me off, but I'll admit I was a little annoyed. When I was ready to go back in, I took a deep breath, admonished myself that it didn't cost anything to be nice, and entered that room with the cheeriest smile I could manage. 'Good morning, Mae, pardon the confusion. I'm all yours now. How are you feeling?'

"She didn't smile, just glared again, and said, 'Well, did you wash your hands?'

"I decided that right then and there, Mae Pringle needed to be taught a lesson, and I was the man to do it. I walked over to the sink in the corner, flipped on the water with my elbows, squirted green soap on my fingernails and brushed and brushed, all the way from fingernails to elbow. Then I rinsed. Very carefully. And looked around at Mae. She didn't say a word, just glared and had that upper lip curled like she smelled carrion.

"So, hell, I did the whole thing over. Both hands, soap, brush, rinse. I could have been getting ready for neurosurgery. I looked at Mae. Still the same expression and silence.

"Buster, something came over me. I leaned down, took the shoe and sock off my right foot, stuck it up in the sink, squirted the toes with soap, scrubbed and rinsed. Then I looked at her and she could stand it no longer. 'Now what in the hell did you do that for?' she demanded.

"I smiled very sweetly and spoke in as gentle a tone as you've ever heard, 'Mae, I have just this minute decided that I'm going to kick your ass.'

"I had her! Right? By God, I had finally got the last word with Mae Pringle.

"Wrong. She shrugged one shoulder, smiled for the first time all morning, and said, 'Well, while you're at it, why don't you scrub your peter, too? Then we can both have a good time.'

"I tell you, Buster, there was nothing in med school that prepared me for a patient like Mae Pringle."

I wanted to ask him what he had encountered in med school that taught him to scrub his foot when dealing with an ancient widow, but I thought better of that. No telling what I might need him for sometime. I still plan to stay healthy.

Doc kept trying with Mae, though. One time he really shocked me. He forgot it was Communion day and came on to church anyhow. He decided that he'd go sit by Mae. I was watching from the piano while I played but had no idea of what was going on. He told me about it.

I wish he hadn't.

But then again, I'm glad he did. It taught me that no pianist, or preacher either, for that matter, can possibly tell from looking at all the careful faces on Sunday morning what is going on out in the congregation. Only God can see into the human heart, and when I consider some of the things I've learned just in our little old traditional church, the very fact that every church in the country doesn't explode into little bits on a Sunday morning is incontrovertible evidence to me that ours is basically a detached, probably amused God, even if He is loving.

"Buster," he said after church, "you're not going to believe this. I decided I'd sit by Mae this morning. She always looks so lonely sitting on that third pew with all that space around her. I walked down and said, 'Scoot over a little, Mae. I'm going to sit on Emmett this morning.' She gulped, but she moved her pocketbook and her Kleenex and her hymnal and slid over a little. But not enough that I couldn't still smell the mothballs from her mink stole.

"'I'm glad you came,' she whispered. 'The church is not crowded this morning. Looks like we're having Communion with the dishes of crackers and the drapes and trays of grape juice all set out. Lots of the new folks don't come if they remember it's First Sunday. Sheesh. Watch your damn foot; you cracked my shin when you sat down.'

"'Excuse me, Mae.'

"'I hate these new cushions they've spent money on; they slip and slide and try their best to dump you off the edge of the seat.'

"'*Shhh*, Mae. The music has started and the acolytes will be lighting the candles.'

"'I will not *shhh*. I've been coming here before we had acolytes or candles and I hate the damn things anyhow; they hurt my eyes.'

"I uncrossed my legs and she peered down at my feet.

"'What size shoe do you wear?'

"'Size ten, Mae. What's that got to do with anything? Church is about to start.'

"'Well, I haven't seen you to visit in weeks, and you're the one who came and sat down here. If you didn't want to talk, you shouldn't have come. Did you know that when I was a girl we all thought you could tell the size of a man's organ by how big his foot was? I very soon found that was not true.'

"Well, Buster, I decided I'd shut her up completely. If she could shock me in church before Communion, I felt like I'd be justified in shocking her into silence, so I sighed and said, 'Yeah, when I was a teenager we all said BMBP, too.'

"'Now what in the hell does that stand for?' she said.

"I whispered in her ear, 'Big mouth, big pussy. Now shut up.'

"We were sitting close to the front, so we were in the first bunch to the altar rail, and I helped her totter down and get on her knees. You were playing 'Where He Leads Me I Will Follow' and it was real peaceful and serene.

"Then when the preacher said, 'Rise and go in peace,' be blessed if that old blue-haired woman didn't nudge me and look me straight in the eye.

"She had every wrinkle in her face, the ones as big as creek beds and the little tiny ones that look like an apple beginning to dry, all bunched up into a pout and her lips poked out and clinched into a slit as tight as the buttonholes on your shirt sleeve, and she said, 'You dooon't say.'

"Then after church, when I had helped her down the front steps without falling, she turned to me again. 'For your information, Ephraim Hentz, I learned a rhyme when I was just a little girl that went,

> I love little pussy;
> She's so soft and warm;
> And if you don't hurt her,
> She'll do you no harm.

"'Notice I didn't tell you that until we got outside the church; somebody's got to manifest some manners around here. If you're not careful, God's gonna get you yet!'

"Buster, I give up."

"So do I, Doc. On both of you," I told him. While I was washing my hands before lunch, I wondered why in the world the church had relaxed so much when Baby Bunc got killed.

It wasn't just Dr. Hentz who couldn't get the last word with Mae. She was no respecter of persons. When Emmett died, one of her nephews who didn't have a job stepped forth and volunteered to run the business she had inherited. That business had given up making furniture and by now specialized in making frames and advertising displays. Under Emmett it had become exceedingly prosperous and employed about fifty or sixty workers, most of them unskilled widow women who thought Emmett Pringle hung the moon.

Which he probably would have if he could have. After all, he had risen to riches from a sodden room in the Piedmont Hotel, was a community and church leader, founded the Kiwanis Club in our town, bought his clothes at John Jarrell's, and even tamed his wife.

He was the only one I ever saw who could get the last word with Mae. It was a skill he had developed over the years, and a very effective one it was. I witnessed him use it on several occasions, most of them at Dr. Hentz's house. The Hentzes were always good to me and pretty often had me over for supper, especially after Mama died and Doc's wife thought I needed home cooking. Now, there was a woman to die for.

She was not only beautiful, she was the most intelligent woman in town and, on top of that, had the most common sense, and don't try to tell me that's not a rare combination. She was smarter than Doc but had the good sense not to rub it in. Besides which she was the kindest person I ever knew. Everybody in town adored her. I never heard anyone speak ill of Ellie Hentz, nor did I ever hear her put anyone down. Beauty, charm, wit, modesty, compassion, she had it all. Of course, I was in love with her, but I never ventured any poetry session; it would have been an insult to everything she stood for. Besides which, she had five little children underfoot all the time, and discretion would have been impossible.

I never turned down a dinner invitation from her. Her meals were better than anyone's in town and the company was without parallel anywhere. I don't think she ever had any inkling of how I felt about her.

One night at the Hentzes, right after supper, here came Emmett and Mae Pringle. They visited a while and then Emmett said, "Chillun, I've come to ask your advice about something. A group of guys came to me from East Point and College Park and talked about building a hospital. They think they can get federal funding and want it to be a tri-county affair. They asked me to be on the hospital board and I told them I'd have to think about it. What do you two think?"

Doc asked a lot of technical questions; how many beds, how many doctors on staff, proof of need, and all such as that, and then Emmett turned to Ellie.

"Little Mama, what do you think?"

"Well, Emmett, it sounds as though they're definitely going to build the hospital and the planning sounds complete and feasible. I can certainly see why they'd want you on the board and it's an honor to be asked. But," and here she paused for a moment, "let's consider the impact it might have on you. You're already involved in so many activities that I worry about you sometimes, and there'd be an awful lot of meetings involved in being on a hospital board. Where would you fit them in?"

Emmett stood up and started pacing the room. "Little Mama, you're right. I hadn't considered that. And I don't think anybody else has. Thank you for thinking about me."

He started pacing a little faster, making turns from one wall to the other. "I'm already stretched pretty thin. Let's see. I'm Sunday school superintendent, so I'm in church for two hours on Sunday morning and one hour on Sunday night. Then Monday night I have an executive meeting with Kiwanis, and on Tuesday night we have regular Kiwanis meeting. Then Wednesday night I have choir practice and prayer meeting. Thursday night there's a committee meeting with the foremen at my business. Friday night I have Boy Scouts." He was making shorter and shorter turns. "By God, I hadn't thought about it before, but Saturday night is the only night in the week I have for myself, and Mae usually has something lined up for us to do then. I'm as bad off as a field hand, working all week just for Saturday night."

He stopped across the room from her and pointed his finger at Mae who was sitting quietly on the sofa by Ellie Hentz. "I'm on the go constantly, working all day, doing civic things at night, and just look at that old woman sitting there."

Mae sat up straight. "Who, me?"

Emmett turned bright red, his neck swelled up like a lizard in heat, and he stomped his foot and yelled at the top of his lungs. "Yes, you! All the time I'm on the go, church, scouts, Kiwanis, business." His voice actually got louder. "And look at her! Just look at that old woman! By God, she don't do *nothing*!"

The lampshades quivered a little and there was as deep a silence as I've ever produced with a closing chord from Beethoven.

Doc, God bless him, defused the moment. He started laughing. He laughed so hard and so loud it was impossible not to join him, all of us. Even Mae. And finally Emmett, although he was still trembling a little.

Doc wiped his eyes, slapped Emmett on the shoulder, and said, "Well, I guess you got your answer, Emmett. You live for Saturday night. Don't mess it up."

Emmett's control over Mae was primitive but effective. She would do anything to keep from making that man mad. Even hold her tongue.

Sometimes she would slip up. She did more than slip up when she secretively bought a copy of Dr. Kinsey's report on the sex habits of the American male.

"Emmett would kill me if he knew I had it," she told me. "I mentioned it to him when I read about it in the paper, and he almost flung a fit when I bucked up to him and said I thought it might be interesting reading. Said he'd better not catch sight of such trash in his house and I ought to be reading something to improve my mind.

"Sheesh. The very idea! I got Boots to buy me a copy and I hid it on the top shelf of my closet behind my hatboxes where there's no way in hell Emmett could find it.

"Buster, let me tell you something, you need to read it." She paused. "Or maybe you don't. Hmm. Anyway, there's a lot of tables and graphs and such all through it, but if you ignore those there's some right interesting reading. A lot of references to 'outlets' and 'encounters,' but there's no doubt what he's talking about.

"Sheesh, he says the average married American male only has two encounters per week. Well, I can tell you in a hurry what's wrong. It's all the goddam little children underfoot all the time. A man comes home from work, lots of times he's too tuckered out and worried to do more than eat supper and go to sleep. And his wife is, too.

"Good God, Buster, I wish I could count the times I've stripped off every stitch of my clothes in the middle of the day. Lots of men are just not evening persons and they have to help with housework and getting the little brats put to bed and their wives don't have the time—nor the inclination, I might add—to even think about an 'outlet' or an 'encounter.' Sheesh. The book's a dud."

I made the mistake of laughing and telling Doc about the conversation. He hadn't read the book but said he didn't need to. "The problem, Buster, is primordial. All husbands think sex will make everything all right and all wives think everything has to be all right before they have sex. Somehow most folks manage to work it out."

I didn't say anything, but I thought he had a point.

Where I made the mistake was not making it perfectly clear to him that Emmett didn't know about Mae having the book.

We had supper at the Hentzes. Halfway through the meal, Doc turned to Mae and said, "I hear you have a copy of Kinsey's Report. I'd like to borrow it sometime."

Mae blinked and twitched her stomach.

Emmett spewed a mouthful of mashed potatoes and nearly choked.

"You've got *what*?" he roared.

The china and silver clanked. He turned over his glass of water as he jumped from his chair. It was like a whirlwind had hit the table.

"Get up from there this instant! I mean right now! We're going home and I'll tend to that book of yours! Get up, I say!" He jerked the back of her chair and she was anything but graceful as she struggled to her feet.

Without a word to Doc, his wife, or me, Emmett pulled Mae to the door. I'll never forget her exit line. Pulled along in Emmett's wake, she looked over her shoulder, fluttered her free hand, and said "Bye, y'all."

I dropped by their house after Kiwanis to visit once not long after that. Emmett was reading the paper but Mae was glad to see me. "Buster, I've decided to take out the azaleas by the front steps. They've been there ever since we built the house and have overgrown the steps so bad you can hardly get in the house for them. I don't want to prune them back; I want something else there. What do you suggest?"

I didn't give a rat's ass but I feigned interest. After all was said and done, you just plain had to like Mae Pringle.

"What about nandinas?" I said.

"Hmm, that's a thought. I hadn't considered nandinas. Jane Mitchell was by the other day, and she suggested an herb garden."

"An herb garden? Mae, you don't cook enough to warrant an herb garden."

"That's what I told her. Also, I don't think it gets enough sun there. Besides, I told her, that's where Emmett spits."

One moment Emmett Pringle was serenely still behind his newspaper. The next instant he had sprung into the middle of the room so violently the sheets of the paper were floating like geese in the air. Purple, trembling, eyes bulging, he screamed, "You told Jane Mitchell *what*?!"

Mae stood her ground, weakly but gamely, "Well, Emmett, you know you do."

"I do no such a goddam thing!" he yelled. "Besides, you've no business discussing things like that! You hear me?"

With that he rushed to the front door, jerked it open, hocked, and spat vehemently into the azalea bushes.

I eased on out the back door but could still hear him berating Mae as I cranked my truck. I distinctly heard "Kinsey Report" yelled out at least twice. *Poor Mae*, I thought, *we needed Doc to break that up*. I was halfway home before I thought, *Poor Emmett*. Then I chuckled and quoted aloud, "She done it to herself."

Mae had never been allowed to set foot in his plant while Emmett lived, not even to decorate his office. In addition, she was not allowed to call him on the telephone. "I've seen too many businesses ruined when wives edged themselves in," he affirmed. "I've told all my men their wives are not allowed on the premises, and I have to lead by example. If you came traipsing around down there it'd set a bad precedent. You stay home!"

When he died and Mae's nephew took over, she didn't stay out of the plant more than three days. Ostensibly it was to watch the nephew. "He's never hit a lick at a snake and I don't know whether he has any business sense or not. I can at least sit in the office and be sure he doesn't fritter everything away."

So she did.

The two of them quarreled like tomcats, but Mae had the prestige of ownership and, after surviving twenty-five years with Emmett, was not the least bit intimidated by any ordinary, walking-around male. All the foremen and widow women stayed employed and the business continued to prosper, despite the noise coming out of the office. I was frequently consulted about contracts and pension plans and such, and Mae leaned on me as a confidant.

"You and I both know Willis is not Emmett; I have to watch him like a hawk. Sometimes I think he doesn't have peacock brains, and once or twice I swear I've smelled whiskey on his breath when he's come back from Atlanta meeting with a customer. The bottom rung has got on the top, and I'll not endure it."

She fired him. Of course, her clan never wanted folks talking about family business; so it was told over town that Willis's health had broken down but nobody ever believed that. They just shrugged and accepted it like we always did when a baby came prematurely just six or so months after the wedding. Even if the baby weighed seven or eight pounds. Our town never has sweated the small stuff, even before the hippies hit us.

"Now what in the hell am I going to do?" demanded Mae. "I may have cut off my nose to spite my face. Coca-Cola is our biggest contract and we're supposed to make a presentation for a new one in just five weeks. Willis had his faults and I'm glad to be shed of him, but he could dress up and be presentable in a conference."

"Go yourself, Mae," I said.

"Are you out of your ever-loving mind? In the first place, I don't know enough about the product to present it; there's no way I could tell them how many pounds of screws or how many sheets of aluminum their signs will need. Besides, that's no place for a woman, let alone a lady. Those high-rolling, highfaluting snobs at Coca-Cola would laugh me out of the conference room."

"What about Mr. Lewis?" I asked. "He's been top foreman ever since Emmett started the business."

"Hell, no," she responded. "He's a yankee and a country yankee at that. He knows carpentry and that's all."

"Bob Russell?" I asked. "He knows the business."

"Buster, you know as well as I do, Bob Russell's tongue-tied. His job is keeping all those women happy, and he does a good job of that, but he can't talk plain."

I gave up.

Several days later she called me. "Drive me down to the Elks Club tonight, Buster. I'll pay."

She was all excited. "Buster, I'm sending William Holloway to make the presentation to the Coca-Cola people. What do you think of that?"

I almost aspirated my drink. "I'll try not to think about it," I said.

William Holloway was one of the most opinionated and outspoken guys I had grown up with. His father was a yeoman farmer whose boys grew up a little more dirt poor than some of the rest of us, but it never affected their pride or their self-image. William was highly intelligent but was a little contemptuous of book learning, and as soon as he hit sixteen, he was out of school and making a living at carpentry or bricklaying. He was not about to farm. "I've looked up a mule's ass and smelled her farts for the last time in my life," he said.

Emmett had hired him in his plant and William had not disappointed him. He could figure a job as quick as Mr. Lewis and was a much more nimble carpenter; he still had all his fingers.

He also had a dry sense of humor. He had driven Miss Walton bats in general science class. "Who says the world is round?" he asked. "It sure looks flat to me when I'm plowing in a forty-acre cotton field. A few humps here and there but round like a ball? No way." Then he had looked at me and winked.

Mae persisted. "I got to thinking real hard about who I could send to Atlanta, and William came ambling by. You know, he's not bad looking underneath all those country ways he puts on. And he knows our product from the ground up. He's shrewd with figures. I've overheard him arguing with Mr. Lewis about angles and screws and some such, and so far he's always been right.

"I called him in and told him my plans. Then I sent him to Muse's and had him fitted with a dark blue suit that had sleeves covering those knobby wrists. Got him a white shirt and a maroon tie and a new pair of shoes. Then I nagged him into getting a decent haircut and cleaning his fingernails. He kept complaining but I kept pushing.

"When the day came for him to go to the Coca-Cola Company and meet with Henry Jazwicki, their advertising manager, William came in the office for final inspection. I walked all around him, made him square his shoulders and hold his head up, and felt real proud of him—and also of myself, if I do say so. I walked around him again, tweaked the knot in his tie a little, and said, 'William, you look wonderful. I'm proud of you. Here's the briefcase with all your figures and drawings in it, and you are off to run with the big dogs. I'm sure you'll do a good job for us and represent us well.' I paused a moment, for he hadn't said a mumbling word the whole time, and I said, 'Now, just....'

"Be blessed if he didn't interrupt me, and blurted out, 'I know, I know, don't pick my nose and don't scratch my ass.'

"Well, sheesh, what was I to do? I shot back, 'Right! And don't say "have went" and "where is it at?"'"

"Then we both busted out laughing and I gave him a pat and a little peck beneath his ear and sent him on his way. He did a great job and we got a bigger order than we were expecting. Bottom rung on top's not all bad. The boy has promise."

Indeed, he did.

He recounted the same incident to me and I didn't let on that I had already heard about it. A good observer has also to be an experienced listener, and the most deflating thing you can say to someone who's confiding something to you is "I already heard about that." As Homer Greely told his mother-in-law fifty years ago, "You can't ever learn anything talking. You have to shut up and listen." Of course, Homer got hit upside the head with a fire poker, but everybody who knew his mother-in-law was proud of him.

At least he took a stand.

So when William chose to tell me about his trip to the city, I never let my eyes wander and hung on every word. "Buster, I know you and old lady Pringle are friends, but I got to tell you this. She got a bug in her bonnet that she could clean me up and send me off up to Atlanta to bamboozle them swells at Coca-Cola. Nearly run me crazy. 'Stand up straight. Look people in the eye. Don't slump when you walk. Keep your feet on the floor. Don't slouch when you're setting down.' Goddamit, she got me to feeling like I was back in the second grade and had got caught with dirt behind my ears. Then be damned if she didn't buy all them fancy clothes and dress me up like an organ-grinder's monkey. Put me out in the middle of the floor and walked around me twicet, with her finger under her chin and saying 'Hmm' now and then. Made me feel like a slave on one of them auction blocks I've heared about. Or else that Pigmail-yon woman Mrs. Cole tried to get me interested in back in tenth grade.

"Finely she drawed a deep breath and started to tell me what not to do; I could see it coming, and she'd already covered all that territory several times. My mama was a Banks and of a sudden it just come out in me. I'd heared her through the walls when she fired Willis, so I knowed she wasn't what you'd call a complete stranger to rough language, as some might call it, so I butted in and told her, 'I know, don't pick my nose and don't scratch my ass,' and you know what, Buster? She give me a couple of little grammar jabs and we both commenced to laughing.

"I figured after that I'd do all right with Mr. Jazwicki at the Coca-Cola Company, and I did. When I told him about old lady Pringle pulling me out of the woods and cleaning me up and then about our bone voyage conversation, he laughed twell he cried and invited me to lunch and tried to get me to drink what he called a Bloody Mary, but I told him no thanks, just sign the contract and I'd get on back to the plant for another grammar lesson. He told me he'd never enjoyed a presentation as much in all his life and doubled his order. Furthermore, he said he hoped I'd be the plant sales representative from now on. I ain't told old lady Pringle that. Ain't no telling what she'd undertake to improve about me next, and I done took about all the remodeling I can stand."

I didn't tell her either. Mae Pringle was no fool, but in addition to that she had a depth of heart I had not suspected. Four years later, when her workforce had increased to two hundred, only half of them widow women, and William Holloway had persuaded her to initiate a pension fund and retirement plan for all her employees, there were a lot of paperwork and legal documents involved.

She included a new will. She left her house and Lincoln Continental to an unmarried niece, the entire plant and all its assets to William Holloway, and a secondhand cut-glass cruet set to Dr. Hentz. The vinegar bottle was missing its stopper.

"Sheesh, hon," she said, "I'm leaving you nothing. You're the executor and with what all I've paid you in legal fees already, you'll do all right. As for all my kinfolks I've left out, you can tell them if they don't like it, they can ask the undertaker to flip me over in the coffin and they can all file by and kiss my ass."

When she died, her heirs found sixty-four stock bottles of pills in a drawer, each with only a few pills missing. And there was still cotton packing in every bottle.

William became an overnight millionaire but kept an even keel and level head.

Mae was buried in the traditional supine position and since the will was not probated until a week after the funeral, I saw no reason to deliver her message to her relatives. Ours is a wonderful town.

Chapter 17

Beatrice and Toor Cofield had built right next door to the Pringles, and there had always existed an unspoken distance between them. Next-door neighbors in our town are traditionally cordial to each other and available for emergencies but are only rarely close friends. That doesn't mean that they don't watch each other closely, and they are not above speculating about unusual behavior to their truly close friends who may live all the way across town. This has for generations been a pretty efficient means of rapid communication, if you think about it.

With Toor and his family, Mae had maintained a pleasant formality that forbade familiarity. In talking about them, she let her hair down.

"I had to have a talk with Beatrice and let her know that her little darlings may be precious but they don't need to be swarming over my yard or coming in my house."

She grew a little defensive. "In case you think I'm being mean and a bad neighbor, let me tell you those kids are weird. Far as I can tell, they may all wind up behind bars. That second boy that Beatrice constantly prattles about being a genius actually made what he called a minefield in their front yard, all hooked up with wires and batteries, and there were all these explosions going on while I was trying to take my nap.

"The little girl is sweet, but all three of those boys have 'took up stealing,' as Miss Phronie Cleveland calls it. C. W. caught them in his store all organized and efficient. One of them walks in and yak-yaks to the clerks while the other two wander around and fill their pockets. They've done the same thing at Putman Hardware, too. And Beatrice herself told me about opening the storage door into the carport and a dozen basketballs came bouncing out and made her fall down. Those brats had been stealing them from the high school gym and they're not even out of grade school yet."

Mae kept me posted and it was fun to watch this fourth generation of Cofields.

"Well, now they've done it. Toor has put that oldest one in the bank after school every afternoon and on Saturdays operating the penny counting machine. I'd move my account except I've got stock in the bank and you'll have to say this for Toor: he may be dumb as a plank about everything but money, and he may drink a quart of Scotch every night, Beatrice says he does, but he sure knows how to make a dollar."

Another time, "Have you seen Ephraim Hentz lately? I can't ever pry anything out of him about one of his patients, but see if you have any luck. Beatrice told me that they took the second son, the one that's just 'brilliant, brilliant, brilliant, I mean really, really, really brilliant' for a consultation with Dr. Hentz because he's not getting along well in school or with other children, and thank God she didn't mention me and every other grownup in town. Anyhow, Betsill, as she insists on calling him, and she went to Dr. Hentz's house later to talk about his opinion, and Beatrice says Ephraim recommended they put him in some fancy boarding school in Atlanta where they have one psychiatrist for every student and have one-on-one supervision by the teachers. Says the Talmadges sent their youngest son there and got splendid results.

"Everything was going well until Betsill asked how much it cost and Dr. Hentz told him ten thousand dollars a year, and Betsill swelled up like a frog and nearly choked on his cigar. 'Too much money' he said, 'ain't worth it.'

"Beatrice tried to argue for it but she has learned long since that her opinion has to be repeated 'over and over and over for months and months and months' before she can convince Toor to spend a dime on anything. Says Dr. Hentz took Betsill to task and finally said, 'Do you mean, with as much money as you have, that you'll put ten thousand dollars ahead of your son's welfare?'

"Then Beatrice said Betsill burst out like it was the most logical statement absolutely the most logical the very most logical statement in the whole wide world, 'I ain't like you, Doc; I love a dollar.'

"Beatrice said everything got very still. Said she was so embarrassed she couldn't open her mouth and say a word, not a single, solitary word; so you and I know it must have been one helluva an embarrassment. Said Doc turned real white and then real red and got up and escorted them to the door. As they went out he said, 'There is no charge for this consultation, Toor; and may the Lord richly bless you.'

"Now, see if you can get Ephraim to tell you about it. I personally can't imagine a school that would do a one of those kids any good, but then I'm not a psychiatrist. In fact, hon, the closest I ever came to any sort of counseling was after I married Emmett and had him shut up in Brawner's for his honeymoon. I decided I'd better get myself an examination; so I went to see old Dr. Noble in Atlanta who had been Mama's doctor before he left Haralson and specialized.

"I hadn't seen him since I was a teenager and he was glad to see me and 'What can I do for you today?' and all that friendly stuff.

"I told him I'd just got married and wanted a female examination to be sure everything was all right, and I'm here to tell you, Buster, he evermore gave me one.

"When I had my clothes back on and the nurse had left the room, he came back in and said, 'Now, Mae, what's bothering you? Your physical exam is perfectly normal. Why are you really here?'

"So I told him. Told him I'd been reading that premarital counseling was the going thing nowadays and that although I had done my share of necking and smooching and had learned to drink white liquor out of a fruit jar in the rumble seat of a Ford automobile and could do the Charleston and was considered to be a real flapper I didn't really know the first damn thing about sex, and I had just got married and we hadn't been yet what you might call consummated and I was, to tell the truth, a little scared.

"I've never forgotten what he said. He looked at me for a long minute and then he said, 'When everything's written and all is said about it, Mae, sex is an animal function. You just have to get down there with it.' Then he turned and walked out of the room.

"Sheesh, now that's the closest I've ever come personally to any psychiatry and I didn't have to pay but five dollars for it. For once I'm almost, not completely but almost, on Toor Cofield's side. See if you can get Dr. Hentz to talk. I don't want to gossip about my neighbors."

I never mentioned it to Ephraim Hentz nor he to me. We had pretty high standards about confidentiality. So did Mae, although some of them had shifted a bit since Emmett died.

Of course, it was no secret that Betsill Cofield drank a quart of Scotch every night. Everybody in town knew it. His wife scolded him in public about it and he grinned like a possum and acknowledged it; not the least bit sheepish, either. It didn't keep him from being at that bank every morning at nine o'clock or in church at eleven on Sundays, and he boasted about his punctuality and his alcohol tolerance almost as much as about how much money he had.

He wasn't lying about either the liquor or the money. "Dr. Hentz been treating me for ulcers. Diet, all sorts of pills, hospital twice for bleeding. Told me had to quit smoking, quit drinking, and next time I bled have to have an operation. 'Bout that time I went to a bank convention at that funny island in Lake Michigan where they don't allow no automobiles; our host said everybody had to take a five o'clock swim in the lake before cocktails every evening. Water too cold for me. I went next door to his neighbor's house 'cause I saw him sitting on his porch with a glass. Invited me in. Said he was drinking Scotch and wouldn't I have one. Told him I hadn't never drunk anything but bourbon and my doctor wanted me to stop that on account of ulcers. Told me if I'd drink a little Scotch every night and leave the bourbon alone I'd never be bothered with ulcers again. Followed his advice and it worked. That was forty years ago. Haven't even had to take a pill last twenty years. 'Course, had to increase my Scotch considerable but haven't bled nor had no operation. Did you know Scotch won't smell on your breath the next morning? And never been late to work a day in my life, neither."

This was true: that boy had worked hard on that bank. It was his life. As soon as Mr. B. M. died, he took over.

Toor looked around at his cousins, his sisters, and all the old loyal Cofield supporters in town and went to each one individually and offered to buy their stock in the bank. At a price they couldn't refuse. Everybody thought he was crazy. He yammered and jawed so persistently that eventually they all sold to him just to get rid of him. And for the money, of course. Several new mink coats and one red fox showed up at morning worship.

I didn't sell. I'd been extra nice to my old maid aunts and they'd always petted me, partly because I played the piano and had never married. I'd resisted a lot of the extravagances most veterans indulged themselves in when Eisenhower prosperity hit us, and I was regarded as a promising but struggling lawyer. Of course, the fact that I drew up all their wills and wouldn't charge them made an impression on the aunts, too. Anyhow, I wound up with several thousand shares of bank stock and didn't particularly need any money when Toor went on his buy-out campaign.

Well, sir, that bank took off like a skyrocket. This was about the time the building boom struck and land prices exploded. The great white flight from Atlanta made our little county look more attractive than it ever had, especially since we were jam up next to the airport and there were a lot of airline pilots recycling their marriages who were looking for affordable land where they could build prestigious homes. Toor was all over them. He had a shrewd eye about a person's financial potential and was making loans fast as I could draw up the papers.

First news you know, be blessed if he hadn't built a branch bank on the other side of town and the money was rolling in. He gave up trying to buy my stock when I threatened to go up on my legal fees. We had what Dr. Hentz described as a symbiotic relationship. I didn't know anything about symbiosis, but sometimes I felt like mistletoe flourishing in the crown of a healthy oak tree. I mean, I was sucking money out of that bank stock.

All this prosperity had an effect on Beatrice, of course. She got an increase in clothing allowance apparently, for she quit frequenting Bargain Brown's except when shopping for Christmas presents. She even got a full-length mink coat instead of a jacket or stole and could evermore prance when she came bursting down the aisle late at Sunday services. Jim Harp's wife was our choir director and threatened to throw Dr. Hentz out of the choir if he didn't quit humming the theme song to the Miss America contest when Beatrice came sweeping in. Toor always told how much the coat cost, which she had bought on Frohsin's going-out-of-business sale, and he was proud of her for getting a real bargain. She'd smile tolerantly because she didn't want to push Toor too far, and after all, Frohsin's label on the coat still amounted to prestige with old-money Atlanta.

After Toor had gained full control of the bank, except for my ten percent, Beatrice stepped forth and put the pressure on him to "establish a community presence." She was only able to do this after discovering the term "pre-tax dollars," and after frequent and repetitive barrages Toor fell for it. On top of that, he seemed to enjoy it immensely.

He started giving elaborate Christmas parties with pre-tax dollars. He needed deductions and was not inclined to increase his annual giving to the church, the very existence of which he attributed to Mr. B. M., and by the laws of succession was "my church" regardless of how many new members joined and contributed to its finances.

He liked pre-tax dollars. He had an in-law who belonged to the prestigious Capital City Club where Timbo Grizzelle had endured his wedding reception years before, and he used the relative's membership to arrange the fanciest parties our town had ever witnessed. The bank paid for it as a business deduction and Toor would invite a hundred or so patrons or potential patrons and write it off as a business expense.

They were true galas. Toor would have the entire third floor reserved with open bar, fancy hors-d'oeuvres, and the grandest buffet you ever saw. Capital City always had an excellent kitchen, and no one who was invited to Toor's Christmas party ever declined. If somebody pissed him off by depositing money in another bank or seeking a loan elsewhere, they were dropped from next year's guest list. The vast majority of folks in our town had never seen the like of those Capital City parties, and we dressed up to the nines and swarmed the place, beginning with the open bar, which established friendships never experienced before. It was a right convivial occasion.

Toor always included every local politician who had had enough community support to get elected, and sometimes even state politicians improved the guest list. The bank prospered. Mightily.

Toor and Beatrice would stand together at the door and greet their guests; he resplendent in a tuxedo with red cummerbund and red bow tie, she outlandishly garbed in an outfit that made every other woman there feel well-dressed by contrast. Pre-tax dollars did not apply to her wardrobe, and Toor had not forsaken his concern about money that came from his own pocket.

As soon as everybody had gotten liquored up and the latecomers accounted for, Toor would always take position at the head of the buffet table. Dr. Hentz and I took a perverse delight in joining him there, for that's when the real Toor, the old Toor we were familiar with, emerged.

"Don't fill up on all these other fancy things and not leave room for she-crab soup. It costs like gold, but Beatrice insists on having it every year because it's a specialty of the house. Says it's prestigious, whatever that means."

Doc and I would carefully avoid looking at each other.

"You see Johnny Blanchard over there? I been watching him. He's already eaten eighteen shrimp. I counted them and he's headed back for more. They're charging me a dollar apiece for those things this year."

Some things in our town never change, even when we're out of town. It gives me a certain comfort level; sort of a sense of continuity in a rapidly changing world.

I guess those parties accomplished what Beatrice wanted in the way of community presence, by which she meant, of course, community importance. Folks began taking her and Toor seriously for the first time in their lives. These were what the little remnant of us old-timers who were left referred to as newcomers or even immigrants. Oscar Hosey wanted to know how come everybody was all so upset about illegal aliens coming in from Mexico whilst we were smothered up by yankees and new-rich sonsabitches. At any rate, it seemed like all at once everybody was referring to Toor as "Betsill" or even "Mr. Cofield." He got fatter and fatter and his butt got closer and closer to the ground, but he had so many loans out that nobody ever commented on it to his face.

He had really put that "before taxes" to work, too. I kept doing his taxes for him until he got so prosperous and his returns got so complicated that I got tired of arguing with him over nickels and dimes when he was headed straight for the federal pen over tens of thousands of dollars. He even wanted to take off the cost of his clothes as business expenses. I referred him as soon as I could and felt sweet relief.

I'm here to tell you that I never intend to endure any more involuntary servitude in federal institutions of any sort for the rest of my life. Three years in the navy filled me with apprehension of another dose of that. I still remember those native women in New Guinea who didn't understand or appreciate poetry. I even, for some unknown reason, had a wet dream about one of them once. She had a bone in her nose. It took me a week to get over the experience and convince myself that it hadn't really happened and that it didn't mean I was a pervert. You have no control about what you dream, but I don't want to get any closer to the Feds than I can help.

I had been a member of Law Review at the university and had been advised several times to apply for privilege to argue before the Supreme Court. I always turned them down and have been content with my somewhat mediocre career in our town. Every time I have a flashback of New Guinea, I'm grateful for my decision. Like I said, you can't help what you have dreams about but my God in Heaven, what if I ever had one about Ruth Bader-Ginsberg? Or I might even run into Madelyn Albright if I ever went to Washington and dream about her. There's just so much one man's nervous system can stand. I bet even Slick Willie wouldn't tackle those two.

I kept on doing Toor's legal work for the bank. The children kept running into snags both in school and around town, and Beatrice had a firm grasp of the pre-tax theory by now and persuaded him to yank all four of them out of public schools and send them off to prestigious boarding schools, paying for their tuition by making a check to the school and marking it "gift." It was money well spent.

The oldest boy at age six had become the object of especial interest to the Methodist choir. We always had open Communion in our church, and little Will would go down to the altar rail after his mama had been, and when everybody's head was bowed, he'd take every little cup that had already been used and carefully lick it free of any remaining grape juice. I never would have noticed it from my piano bench if the ladies in the choir hadn't commented on it, and I swear it was true. He was the same one who had sold me the Coca-Colas when he was a Cub Scout. He never acted very friendly toward me as he grew older, and you can guess about just how much that bothered me.

Little Will did all right in the prestigious boarding school and went on to college. The second son of Toor, whose name was George, was asked to leave the school after a year and a half when too many things went missing and a bunch of them turned up under his bed. He wasn't stealing for money but apparently for some feeling of power it gave him. They were little things, like a statue or a plaque or a bundle of stationery or a book or a screwdriver from the janitor's closet and even the school seal from the president's office. I met one of the teachers from the school who asked me if I knew George Cofield and then told me that it was his understanding, when they finally expelled him, that he had a key on his person to every lock on campus. We never heard a word from Beatrice or Toor about this; all we were told was that he had transferred to a military school somewhere in Tennessee. He later went to Tech and we heard from

Beatrice that he made A's in subjects that interested him and flunked those that bored him. When I ran into him on the street several years later and asked him what his status was at Tech, he smiled and said very softly but loftily, "You might say I'm a twenty-third semester sophomore."

I never told anybody but Dr. Hentz about the keys and Tech and so far as I know it never got out on him in our town. Whenever his name comes up, people just shrug and say, "George is weird." Dr. Hentz said, "Buster, maybe his mama's right and he's a genius. Warped as hell, but then a lot of geniuses are." I miss Dr. Hentz.

The third boy, Bob, looked for a while like he was going to turn out all right. He and George had inherited the long limbs and height of Mr. B. M. and Beatrice Schwartz, while the girl and Will were exaggerations of Miss Pansy and Toor. I always thought of the Smoos in "Little Abner" when I saw them. The girl may have been built like her daddy but she talked like her mama, and I was always in a hurry to get away from her. She went on to college and did all the things expected of a Southern belle except look like one.

That boy, Bob, though, now let me tell you, he was a horse of a different color. He always carried himself so straight that he looked sway-backed and was tall enough that he looked down on most people and just generally grew up with the appearance of arrogance. On top of that, he was bug-eyed, which made his stare remind you a little bit of a billy goat. He was the closest to handsome of any of Toor's brood but it hasn't helped him much. I don't remember how many schools Toor and Beatrice put him through, but it was several.

Beatrice laughed and told about him getting kicked out of school the same time George did. "All of a sudden one morning just totally totally totally unexpected, and on the day the school was hosting a swimming meet you know a swimming meet where students come from all over just from everywhere provided they're in the same league the same standing you know what I mean. Anyhow on the day of the swimming meet the pool was full just full full full of snapping turtles swimming around just swimming around and bumping into each other and people were having hysterics and the meet the swimming meet I told you about was postponed for an hour delayed for an hour it was probably even more than an hour I should think while they got all the turtles out they even had to get a rowboat and put it in the swimming pool you know a rowboat because they couldn't reach all the turtles from the edges of the pool they had to put a rowboat in and two men with nets and it took forever at least I'm sure it seemed like forever it sure did to me because I was there because Bob was supposed to swim some event maybe the freestyle I'm not sure maybe the breaststroke he's just marvelous, simply marvelous marvelous marvelous at both of them. But anyhow it was the funniest thing you ever saw those grown men trying to catch the turtles and the turtles diving and getting away from them and all those parents from Atlanta having a fit you'd think none of them had ever seen a turtle before and Betsill's fishpond is full of them I mean just teeming teeming teeming you might say teeming with them. I couldn't help it I laughed my head off just laughed and laughed and laughed the most ridiculous thing I ever saw in my life. And then it turned out they cancelled the meet because some of the parents some of the parents who don't know anything about turtles aren't familiar with them like we in the surburbs are said they weren't about to let their children swim in that pool until the Board of Health the sanitation people you know declared it free of germs and safe. Safe to swim in and not catch some terrible disease.

"Then somebody told on Bob it turned out it was our Bob our very own Bob who had engineered the whole thing. He and a couple of friends had spent weeks just simply weeks trapping turtles and a lot of them it turned out came from our very own lake and Bob and his friends there were two of them were expelled. I was laughing so hard at those turtles and those people there must have been hundreds just hundreds of the turtles and even more maybe even a thousand people and I didn't have the heart just didn't have the drive you might say to apologize to the school or to punish Bob. The whole thing was creative and inspired just inspired you might say and Bob is going to be my creative child I just know it I already have a genius and now I've got a creative wizard. And we've found a nice school in North

Carolina for him to go to, a nice strict school smaller considerably smaller than this one and much much much stricter with more supervision and discipline. He starts next week starts on Monday morning and we'll have to leave here early on Sunday to get him there on time but we're truly lucky, truly, truly lucky to get him in at all. Betsill said be sure they don't have a swimming pool and they don't. Betsill doesn't think any of this is funny not the least bit funny but I do. I really, really, really do and it's always better to laugh than cry and Betsill did say finally grunted and admitted he was glad to have some of those turtles cleared out of his pond."

One time Beatrice had asked Dr. Hentz to call her in a prescription for cough syrup and he insisted that the druggist type the directions "one teaspoon as needed for cough, cough, cough, cough, cough, cough, cough," but she never took the hint. I was glad she didn't. Once you got used to her speech pattern, you sort of enjoyed it. It was like one of those scenes that you don't really believe existed as soon as you leave it, and then when you come back you find your memory was true. It's right comforting to realize you're not crazy; gives you a sense of stability and a definite feeling of "place."

I don't recollect how Bob got through school or college, if indeed he did, but after Toor got complete control of the bank, be blessed if he didn't start grooming Bob to take over. Will was married and working with his father-in-law in Buckhead, of all places. George was married for the third time and still going to Tech, we think. At any rate, he was working part-time repairing television sets for people. To his credit, he actually understood television from start to finish, the theory, the mechanics, you name it. He certainly wasn't interested in banking.

Toor put Bob in charge of making loans on automobiles and had him come to work all dressed out in a suit and tie like a traditional banker. He and Beatrice bragged all over town about how well he was doing and how much new business, even a lot of it from out of town, he was attracting to the bank. It seemed like he had inherited the Midas touch. Then, God bless my soul if it didn't turn out he was laundering money and selling stolen cars for a ring that stretched all the way to California.

Here came the Feds.

Then here came Toor banging on my door in the middle of the night with Scotch on his breath but the fear of God in his heart.

"You gotta do something, Buster, and do it quick. There's a federal prosecutor, a woman, who says she's got proof Bob's involved in a car theft ring and she's on fire to prosecute. You gotta do something. Anything. Ain't no Cofield ever gone to jail. And double your fee."

I knew he was desperate.

I met with the federal attorney who turned out to be a beautiful red-haired young lady named Dorothy from an old and well-established Atlanta family who had preferred law school to the life of an Atlanta pink and debutante. She had the goods on our Bob, all right. I worked my butt off, but I really enjoyed my association with the attorney. She was not only good-looking but smart as hell, and it was fun to discuss things other than auto theft with her. After about two days of intense negotiating and three nights of Millay's sonnets, beginning with "What lips my lips have kissed and where and why, I have forgotten," we struck a deal.

Bob was out of the bank forever or she'd include Toor in the injunction.

In return for personal immunity, Bob would deliver names, dates, and details of his transactions.

As a special consideration, I had to promise her she would never again have to interview Beatrice Cofield. About anything whatsoever.

As Oscar Hosey would have said had he known about it, "Such a deal."

But guess what: I had to put some considerable pressure on Bob Cofield. Toor and the investigating attorney and I met with him in the conference room at the bank. Beatrice wanted to come, but I cooked up some cockamamey excuse and then took a lesson from her and talked so fast and in such confusing circumlocution that she finally shook her head like she had water in both ears and walked off in what was sort of a daze for her. I couldn't help but throw a little Milton at her—"...thousands at his bidding speed, And post o'er land and ocean without rest; They also serve who only stand and wait." It was a close call but I couldn't afford to renege on my promise to Dorothy.

Bob was as stubborn as a mule and as sullen as an over-milked cow. He wasn't about to give up any names to anybody, no matter the blandishments or promises. He couldn't, he said, and he wouldn't betray any of his friends or business associates even if he did have to go to prison. At this, Toor winced noticeably and fumbled in his pocket for a cigarette, although he hadn't even carried one for six years. Besides, Bob continued, who was to prove that he knew those cars had been stolen? At this the lady lawyer reached for her briefcase and opened her mouth, but I stopped her.

"Come over here, Bob," I said, and carried him outside the conference room.

I looked up into his eyes and he looked over my head and out the window. His jaw was tightly set and jumping.

"Look at me, boy," I said, as commandingly as I could from my height. He shifted those billy-goat eyes of his and stared at me.

"How tight is your asshole, Bob?" I said.

"Sir?"

"You heard me. I mean it. How tight is your asshole?"

He turned red and said, "Pretty tight, Mr. Buster. That is, I guess it is. I've never thought about it."

"Well, think about it. At your age, I imagine it's pretty tight. At least it works well enough to keep you from pooping in your pants, doesn't it?"

"Well, yes, sir."

"Well, son, if you want to keep it that way, you'd better get back in that room and give that nice lady all the information she wants, including the names of all of your so-called friends. Else she's got enough on you to put you in the pen for ten years, and no amount of Cofield money could save you. If you get in the pen, let me promise you it won't be two weeks before you are gang-raped by seasoned criminals, some of them serving life terms for murder, and it'll be two months before you quit hurting and by two years you'll be enjoying it, and by the time you get out you'll be back to wearing diapers again. Are you listening to me?"

"Mr. Buster, I sure am, but for God's sake, these guys I've been working with are all in the Dixie Mafia and they'll kill me if I sing."

"By the time you've been in jail two months, Bob, you'll wish somebody had killed you. We can get you under the protected witness program in exchange for your testimony and get you a new identity somewhere else."

"What's involved in this protected witness and new identity business?"

"They get you a whole new identity. New name, new social security number, new place to live and you vanish. You'll never be able to come back to our town but they'll set you up safely somewhere else, usually far away."

"What about my parents?"

"You won't even be able to get in touch with them for at least fifteen years, nor them with you. Even they will not know where you are."

"You mean I can't even talk to my mother and father for fifteen years?"

"That's right. They won't know where you are."

I looked at my watch. "I'm going back in there and I'll give you ten minutes to think about it."

"Wait a minute, Mr. Buster. I don't need ten minutes. Thank you for explaining things to me. I'm ready. Now. Such a deal."

I swear he said it.

I've never talked to anybody that way before or since, but it sure brought Bob Cofield around. The lady lawyer was superb. The Dixie Mafia was rendered completely impotent after she got twelve convictions, and she got good publicity and a promotion. None of us has heard from Bob since, not even his parents. That's been fifteen years ago, but I still wonder where he is and how he's doing and if he ever got over being a Cofield. I don't think, from what I've observed, that is a condition from which one recovers in one generation.

I gave Toor the largest bill I could ethically render for my services to Bob, to him, and to the bank. "Ain't this pretty high, Buster?" he said.

"Betsill Cofield," I answered, "the last person I remember ratting on the Dixie Mafia was found with a broken neck and no fingernails. You don't know how fortunate you are."

He paid me but he never thanked me. About twenty years later, when we rewrote his will, he specified that he wanted Daniel D. Mookinfoos, Jr., and his children, all of whom had an address in British Columbia, to be included with a child's share. I didn't ask any questions and he didn't volunteer any information, even though it was midmorning and I could still smell Scotch on his breath.

I just hope there aren't any little Canadians running around who've been inflicted with the Pansy Cofield butt. The oldest little boy is named Robert Betsill and the only little girl is named Dorothy. The second son is named Daniel D. III, and the youngest son is named, so help me, Ephraim Holcombe Mookinfoos. Apparently Daniel D., Jr., has settled down and even looked back on his life and developed a little gratitude. To my knowledge, nobody around here has even mentioned Bob in years. I keep telling folks this is a wonderful town. And that there is a God.

Chapter 18

Beatrice kept yammering and pressuring Dr. Hentz to get Betsill to quit drinking. "I know he'll listen to you, I just know it know it know it. You got him to quit smoking and everybody just everybody that is everybody who's quit drinking *and* quit smoking says it's harder to quit smoking than drinking of course I've never had any problem myself oh I may have smoked once or twice in high school just to be naughty you know how that is but I never really really and truly smoked and of course I never drink anything nothing nothing not anything at all except maybe a glass of wine just one glass of wine when we go out to dinner with bank people well maybe once or twice a small second glass but not often. But Betsill drinks a quart of Scotch whiskey every night I mean every every every night never missed a single one not one single solitary night and he won't listen to a word I say about it. I have begged pleaded, preached just downright begged and begged and begged but he won't listen to me and I know he will to you."

Doc told me he finally tried to talk to Toor about it just to pacify Beatrice.

"It was like talking to a stone wall. 'I ain't no alkyholic,' he said. 'Everybody knows alkyholics drink before breakfast and all day long. I've known a good many of them, even loaned money to one or two. I ain't ever in my life had a drink before five or six o'clock in the afternoon. Besides, I don't ever drink anything but Scotch and that Dewar's White Label and Johnnie Walker if I can't find Dewar's. But, Doc, I ain't ever missed a morning at the bank so that proves I ain't no alkyholic.

"'And nobody else besides Beatrice ever accused me of being a alkyholic 'til you came along. And did you know Scotch won't give you a hangover and it won't smell on your breath next morning either? Nobody else in this whole town ever even hinted to me they thought I was drinking too much.'

"'Betsill,' I told him, 'calm down. They've proved alcoholism is a disease and you can't help having the disease; so it's not your fault. And while I'm at it, it would take a pretty stupid damn fool to tell his banker he thinks he drinks too much when he's set on borrowing money from him.'

"I tried my best to reason with him, but then he said, 'Ulcers are a disease, too, and I ain't had any trouble with mine since I went to Michigan twenty or thirty years ago and this fellow told me if I'd drink a little Scotch every night I wouldn't be bothered with ulcers, and I did and I haven't.'

"'Betsill Cofield, you're blocking. It hasn't been five years since you had to have two blood transfusions, and you haven't had any trouble since they discovered that a germ causes peptic ulcers and I gave you a prescription for the medicine to cure it. Don't you remember that, for God's sake?'

"Then he reared back and sort of tucked his chin down and gave that little possum grin he's got when you have him cornered and said, 'I remember years ago you told me stress caused ulcers. How come you come along and change stories on me now? I know good and well Scotch is good for stress.'

"I wanted to yell and tell him to drink 'til he busted, but I just shrugged and walked away and told Beatrice I had done my best. Come to think of it, I might do a quart of something every night myself if I was married to Beatrice. But then, on the other hand, just being around Toor makes you crave a drink. It's a wonder Beatrice herself isn't a sot. Half the folks in this town are crazy, Buster. I should have gone into psychiatry and I could die rich just from encounters at church and the grocery store and John Addison's filling station."

Dr. Hentz died right after that, about two to three weeks as I remember, of what they call a massive heart attack. In my judgment, anything that kills you is pretty damn massive, but it's become a mark of distinction to confer superlatives on victims. I never heard of anybody dying from a massive case of syphilis, but then I did have an aunt who used to threaten to have a complete nervous breakdown as opposed, I guess, to an incomplete one. It's just another example of our loose use of the language and, I guess, the importance to the family of any member's terminal event. At any rate, I do miss Ephraim Hentz more than anybody else who has died before me. We could confide things to each other in total confidence that it would never be repeated. Now, in my dotage, I'm reduced to writing.

I disagreed with him about half the people in our town being crazy. I argued that all the people in our town were crazy but only half of the time. If you weren't a little crazy now and then, you didn't get noticed and didn't amount to much. Of course, nobody had their crazy spells simultaneously; they were scattered out individually enough to keep good conversation going.

Doc himself was not immune, as I was quick to point out occasionally. He was the first one in our town to take up jogging, and he did it before it got to be popular or even accepted. Like most crazy things people do, he had a good reason for it. He was one of the first heavy smokers in our town to quit smoking when that Doctor Ochsner from New Orleans came out with figures that proved smoking caused lung cancer.

When we grew up, the only bad thing they could tell us about smoking was that it would stunt your growth, and a lot of folks learned to smoke in the army when the drill sergeant would blow his whistle and holler, "Take a break! Smoke if you got 'em; if you don't, bum one from your buddy." The different tobacco companies even started putting up little packets of three cigarettes that fit in with the C rations and the government passed them out to us. Usually they were Raleighs, which nobody liked. Occasionally there were Phillip Morrises or even Chesterfields or Camels. I never saw a Lucky Strike through the whole Pacific campaign. Lucky Strike Green may have gone to war, but it sure as hell never turned up in any of our C rations.

I personally had taken up smoking only because all the girls that liked poetry also liked cigarettes, and I very soon discovered that the only way I could stand their breaths was if I smoked myself. It was no problem for me to quit when they did.

That wasn't the way it was with Dr. Hentz, though. He was burning up two to three packs a day when he made himself stop, and he started eating like a newly penned hog. "Buster," he told me, "I can't get enough to eat! I had forgotten that grits and black-eyed peas have any flavor. And my sense of smell has come back, too; which is a good thing most of the time and not so good when Oscar Hosey comes to the office."

At any rate, within six months he had gained twenty-five pounds, none of which accumulated in his skinny legs and arms but went into a definite potbelly. He said, "I look like a pregnant stork," and it was true.

That's why he took up jogging, and you'd see him every day running all around town and even out into the country, since it was before we had all the prosperity and traffic that we have today and it was perfectly safe to run on the big road.

John McCollum, who had his own opinions about everything and never let cold facts sway any of them, told Sam Hooten, "Look at that Doctor Hentz skipping all over town half-naked in nothing but those little short breeches and tennies. Telling everybody that he cured John McCollum. And I'm here to tell you that's a damn lie; I had to *tell* him which shot to give me."

I don't think Doc was ever aware of how much attention he attracted, but he really got into that running habit. He told me, "Buster, you ought to try it. It gets to be an addiction. But a positive addiction. That first mile I always wonder why in the hell am I doing this, and then the good feeling kicks in and I feel like I could run forever. The only thing that pisses me off is when people try to stop me to ask medical questions or just to socialize. Come run with me?"

I quickly told him I would very much like not to do that, that my piano practice took up all the spare time I had. I refrained from informing him that not just John McCollum but everybody in town thought he was loony.

This was confirmed when Orvie Griggs accosted him one day when he was winding up a five-mile run and was sweating like a bull in a ginger mill and blowing like a runaway horse. Orvie was one of our less-loved characters in town. Her older sister had married Mr. Johnnie Cofield and her middle sister had turned down Mr. B. M. Orvie hadn't married till late into spinsterhood but considered herself something of a belle and a privileged character; after all, she was the baby in a trio of prominent ladies and had been spoiled and cosseted all her life. I thought she was a dreadful bore and avoided her when I could. She was a Baptist but was known to take a drink at parties, so she didn't have any real stable circle of friends.

She was in her front yard watching her older sister rake leaves for her one day when Doc went bounding by. "You always run by here without speaking," she yelled. "Why can't you stop and visit?"

Apparently Doc snapped. Without breaking stride he yelled back, "I've got up a hard and I'm trying to get home before I lose it."

Orvie had little enough sense to tell it and act like she was aggrieved and insulted, but too many people remembered her spinsterhood to give that much credence.

Oscar Hosey said, "What it would take to embarrass that woman would draw a blister on a wash pot."

We all thought she was pretty lucky to have gotten married; but then her husband sure wasn't from around here.

When I queried Doc about it, he vouched for the truthfulness of it. "I don't know what got into me, Buster, but she just rubbed me the wrong way; her sister is getting close to ninety years old and Orvie was just standing on the edge of her yard watching her rake. Believe you me, Orvie doesn't even wave when I go by there now."

It took Sam Champion to break Doc from jogging, or at least to change his habits so that he wasn't so much a public spectacle. Sam was, relatively speaking, a newcomer to our county; he had been here only about twenty-five years; moved in right after prosperity started but before we had become so prosperous that nobody but the wealthy could afford to move in here. He came from north Georgia, somewhere in Floyd or Gordon County, I don't remember which, with his wife and two chappies and settled in right away with both the old-timers and the other newcomers. He was thin and muscular, had reddish-blonde hair and a rosy complexion. His face was sharp and angular and I always thought personally that he looked like a red fox. He was forever joking and carrying on with foolishness and everybody liked him. His family and he joined the Baptist church, and I never heard the first word of scandal about him or his wife or boys.

After he'd been in town for maybe two years or so, we got our emergency medical service established with well-equipped ambulances and trained personnel to run them. Sam was one of our first volunteer emergency medical technicians, and he and Dr. Hentz got to be real close.

Doc loved the EMT service, said those ambulances were emergency rooms on wheels and carried more equipment than any doctor could pack into a black bag. They cut down on his house calls and trips to wrecks and really improved the level of medical care in our town and county.

One day when Doc was jogging about five miles north of town, Sam Champion and Randy Giordano were coming back from an emergency call. Doc was huffing and puffing up the left-hand side of the highway well on the shoulder and didn't hear them coming up behind him. On a whim, just as they got right up on him, Randy cut loose with the siren. Sam told me later that Doc jumped three feet up in the air and landed on his all fours in the ditch.

Sam turned to Randy. "Look at him; those little nylon pants and I guarantee you he ain't got a smidgen of identification on him. This is a golden opportunity."

They jumped out of the ambulance and wrestled Doc to the ground; Randy was built like that black football player they called Icebox, so it was really no contest. They penned him in a straitjacket, strapped him to the litter, and turned on lights and siren and went screaming off up the road.

"What are you damn fools up to? Where are you taking me?"

"To the hospital emergency room over in Douglas County where nobody knows you or us," said Sam. "We're obliged to look after a half-naked maniac who's running up and down the road telling everybody he's Dr. Hentz, when everybody knows the real Dr. Hentz has too much sense to do that. On top of that, Dr. Hentz has a potbelly and this guy looks like a long-legged spider. And you don't have the first bit of identification on you. Ain't that right?"

That's when Doc called him a fox-faced son of a bitch. Finally he quit begging and pleading and started threatening to sue for bodily assault and kidnapping and unlawful transportation across county lines in the EMS vehicle. And that's when Randy chickened out. They stopped a couple of miles from the hospital and let Doc ride in front while Randy sat on his butt on the floor in the back.

Sam said, "Time we got back to town, Doc had started laughing along with us. Said he'd dished it out a few times in his life and he'd be a poor sport if he couldn't take it. But if you notice, he don't run on the streets anymore; he's cut trails through his woods and runs there ever since that day. That's been years ago and I make it a point to stay on Doc's good side; take him turnip greens and collards out of my patch and such as that."

He paused, took his cap off, smoothed his hair back, and replaced the cap. With his eyes looking out from under that cap, he looked more like a fox than ever.

"But I keep waiting for the other shoe to drop, Buster. I know he's cooking up something to get even. And the hell of it is that when it happens I'm gonna be honor bound to laugh about it, and I know sure as hell I ain't gonna think it's funny."

That was fifteen years before Doc had his massive heart attack. Sam was the only one of the pallbearers who sobbed out loud at his funeral. I was glad he did; it kept me from having to blow my nose while I was playing "In the Garden." What a wonderful town.

I've already pointed out that Beatrice had a sense of humor. When she was trying to tell something she thought was funny, however, she talked so fast and giggled so hard that she reminded me of this rap

Snoopy Dog trying to gargle something that's too hot for him to swallow, but she could laugh, even at herself at times: I remember the basketballs in the garage and the snapping turtles in the swimming pool. I have often wondered, however, if she would have been able to muster a laugh about anything related to her death and funeral. It was a mixed bag in the community, but you had to laugh or cry, and most everybody chose the former.

Of course, she didn't die until years and years after Toor had become filthy rich. He had sold his bank for a huge profit and, in the process, had acquired a sizeable chunk of stock in the national bank to which he had sold. So did I.

Then that bank merged with another one and that one sold to the biggest of them all, and first thing you know, Toor was richer than my daddy had said Mrs. Melrose was. So was I, but nobody knew about me. And still doesn't. I was raised that your money and your sex life are two things you don't discuss. And to Toor's credit, I never heard him discuss his sex life. I thank God pretty often for that.

He loved to talk about his money, though. Sometimes it got pretty ludicrous. He came by my house one afternoon when I was trimming shrubbery and stopped to visit a spell. It was bank stock this and bank stock that and his cousins were all ticked off with him because they felt cheated out of fortunes. Blood may be thicker than water, but I have noted that most people lean toward their money.

"Sara Belle and her sister are right cool to me, but I gave them a fair price when I bought them out and I wasn't real sure at the time I was going to sell my bank anyhow. Both of them are married to lawyers and they saw for sure everything was legal and aboveboard. You know that, Buster.

"I won't keep you from your yard work; I saw you outdoors and just thought I'd stop and tell you that as of three-thirty this afternoon the last time I checked I'm worth seventy-five million dollars. Ain't got no idea how you've invested your bank dividends but thought I'd stop and check."

"I haven't bothered to look lately," I demurred, "but I'm doing all right. No complaints."

I meshed my hedge shears with a snap and he took the hint. He paused a moment, looked at his watch, and I'll never forget what he said. "Well, I've got to run. Beatrice wants to go out for supper. Or dinner, as she tries to make me call it. And I need to run by the store and lay in some coffee; I hear it's going up again."

I couldn't help it. I busted out laughing as I waved him goodbye and yelled, "Enjoy that seventy-five million, Betsill."

Old habits are hard to change. Some things really ain't worth a dollar. Mr. B. M. would have been proud of him.

Chapter 19

But some things are worth more than any money can buy, and I am living witness to that, although few people know it. I'm speaking now about what I suppose you could call the true passion of my life. Greater than poetry, greater than music, greater than my friendships along the way, certainly more meaningful than my law practice, which, if truth be known, has been more or less just a job, something to keep living expenses rolling in and that's about all.

What I'm talking about, of course, is my land; my woodland, my trees and ferns and wild azaleas; my trilliums and galax and rhododendrons and mountain laurel. To tell the truth, and not bragging, I have nearly every native plant indigenous to this area and a good many that are not. I've seen to that.

Everywhere else in the county all these plants have been bulldozed under, grassed over, and annihilated by progress, subdivisions, and Bradford pears, all of which in my mind are inextricably linked and equally invidious. My hobby of rescuing wild plants to safe harbor in my woods pretty soon developed into a passion. On Sundays I played for the choir, took Communion, and thought about Jesus and the Father, but all week I belonged to Mother Earth and reveled in the dirt. I was like that guy named Anteus that Hercules wrestled; he regained his strength every time he touched the earth and was defeated only when Hercules held him in the air until he weakened. I had even fantasized in previous years that a hamadryad lived in the giant beech tree on the back side of my property.

It all began gradually because of my three maiden aunts. They lived together in the house their father had built back before the war, a block and a half from the courthouse and surrounded by sixty acres of land. They were Aunt Lemma, Aunt Novella, and Aunt Palestine, the latter of whom was called Aunt Tiny, which was definitely a good thing.

I call them "maiden" despite the fact that Aunt Lemma and Aunt Novella had both been married at some time in the distant past. No one in the family ever mentioned Aunt Lemma's husband, but we all knew Aunt Novella married an old widower who died after six months from a massive stroke and left her his family plantation in the south end of the county. Both of the aunts' marriages had been such brief adventures that by the time I was old enough to know them, they were definitely maidens again, and anybody my age who was raised in the South knows what I mean. There are some conditions in the human experience that are irreversible, no matter what; being an old maid is one of them. Also, people grouped them together and, regardless of their legal married names, all the old-timers referred to them as the "Perdue Girls." That, too, is strictly Southern. I think.

I guess they had formed through the years what might be called a triumvirate. Aunt Novella was pretty much the boss; she had the spending money that most people in town thought came from the big farm she had inherited. I found out much later it came from dividends or stocks, of all things: a great deal of it Coca-Cola. She spent as little of it as she possibly could, and I will say she looked after her sisters enough for them to keep their heads up and look respectable in the community. She was what Oscar Hosey described as short-coupled, and whatever foundation garment she employed kept her breasts poked up almost under her chin so that when she walked, she reared way back and looked for all the world like a pigeon strutting and gargling in his mating efforts.

Aunt Novella approved of getting money and having money, very privately of course, but I don't think she ever approved of spending it. She had a coin purse with a snap on it tighter than a rat trap, and I noticed, even as a child, that when she had to unsnap it in the grocery store, her lips would tighten as if she had jerked them shut.

She had an automobile; a Buick back when Buick was the ultimate in luxury cars and nobody in town had yet acquired a

Cadillac. She drove it to the store, to church on Wednesday and Sunday, to the beauty parlor once a week, down to the farm every Saturday morning, and back to church on Sunday. I'll bet she put a thousand miles a year on that odometer even when gasoline went to seventy cents a gallon. When she was eighty-five and the Buick forty-five, she died and left the car to me; because, she said, she knew I'd take good care of it.

Dr. Hentz congratulated me and suggested that we collect the Widow Pringle and go to a fancy restaurant in Atlanta to celebrate, but I demurred. I told him my new ward had never been out after dark and I didn't think it was up to the shock of such a trip. Aunt Novella was known for her good works, but that reputation never got beyond the confines of the Baptist church.

On Fridays she would load her two sisters into her car and they all went to the beauty parlor, which a refined Baptist lady conducted in her house. Aunt Novella always went first, had her hair done, and then departed for grocery shopping before returning to pick up the other two. No sense in wasting gasoline, of course, but it also gave Aunt Lemma and Aunt Tiny plenty of time to pick the Hair Lady for village news that had not made the local paper. All the lady's customers were not Baptist, and the aunts were kept abreast of all current events.

Aunt Lemma was tall and statuesque and always spoke slowly in carefully selected phrases that you could diagram even as she offered them. If she had ever dangled a participle, I think the heavens would have fallen. I never saw her in a hurry and I rarely saw her laugh. Her job in the triumvirate, insofar as I was ever able to determine, was to call a male nephew when some problem arose that the three sisters couldn't handle, such as a light bulb going out, although their combined frugality about wasting electricity did not make this a frequent chore. I was always grateful that they didn't will the light bulbs to me.

Aunt Lemma was so deaf she couldn't hear well over the telephone, but she could give orders and expect them to be comprehended and obeyed. Her one luxury was her hearing aids, and so far as I know, she had the first ones in the county. They had big batteries that she carried in a sack in her bodice, and she had at least two wires running out of each ear. Long wires. As a child, I thought maybe she could get radio reception through those hearing aids, and I was sure that if she was ever caught in a thunderstorm, she would draw lightning.

Aunt Tiny was unique. Born the baby, she never quite grew up and had a childlike innocence about her that extended even to her speech. She had been overly protected by her parents because one of her legs was about the size of a broomstick and caused her to have a hopping, almost skipping gait. She saw no reason to alter her sheltered existence after her widowed sisters moved in with her. Because of her handicap, Grandpa had assumed that she would never marry and had willed her the family home and twenty acres of land for her lifetime. She did the cooking for the trio and made the best teacakes I ever tasted. When Aunt Novella suggested that she pay her share of the grocery bill, Aunt Tiny teetered up and down like a chair with uneven legs and said, "Oh, my. I don't know what to do; I guess I'll have to start charging you and Lemma rent."

Aunt Novella never brought up the subject again; she was no fiscal fool. The only thing she really splurged on without ever grumbling about the price was the beautician. She was the first one of the three to cut her hair and get a permanent wave. Aunt Lemma and Aunt Tiny quickly followed suit, not that it helped any of them noticeably. My three aunts were what the other ladies in town called "plain," which meant that no amount of makeup would ever evoke the term "pretty." Each of them did, however, have a thick head of hair and did the best they could with that. About the time they all turned gray, that bouffant style came along, and be blessed if they didn't also take to having blue coloring added.

Their hairdresser was as old as Aunt Novella and could tease their mess of hair until my aunts looked like they were carrying three giant cones of blue cotton candy on their shoulders. One on one, they were something of a sight, but to behold them together was a marvel. I'll carry to my grave the image of Aunt Lemma striding,

Aunt Novella strutting, and Aunt Tiny hopping down the sidewalk with their three blue beehives carried aloft like symbols of royalty.

The town had sure changed.

But not enough that they ever gave a thought to tipping the Hair Lady. The very idea!

I learned at an early age to flatter them, pamper them, and do little extra odd jobs for them, and I was richly rewarded. My brothers had to be forced to go over to their house to help with chores and they forever grumbled about it, but I always went with a smile on my face and stayed extra time to visit. Early on I became their favorite, their "pet," as my brothers called me, and I'm sure over time I got triple the amount of teacakes that my brothers got put together.

Grandpa had left each of the aunts a thousand shares of Farmers and Merchants Bank stock, and Aunt Novella had also inherited another thousand shares from her husband. Just before Mr. Ed Cofield died, that stock had become almost worthless, and be blessed if the aunts didn't give it all to me as a high school graduation present. That made me be even nicer and visit more often, and fortunately I put all the stock in a drawer and never thought about it or even looked at it until Toor took over the bank. The brothers had all received a shirt and tie when they graduated, and they teased me about getting "worthless paper." They were always teasing me about something, so I just shrugged and kept on cozying up to the aunts.

Then I got the land. I began by asking Aunt Novella to sell me her share that Grandpa had left her; it was adjacent to the tract that had the home place on it. She hemmed and hawed and found a thousand reasons not to sell. I listened and agreed with everything she said, complimented her on her hair, and pointed out that if I built a house back up in her woods, it would be really easy for me to look in on them when they got old. If Aunt Novella gave any hint of feeling like she was old, she never manifested it to me. Price had never been mentioned, but finally after about six months of my persistence, she said, "Well, Aloysius, if that land were yours, what would you take for it?"

"Aunt Novella, if that land were mine, to tell you the honest-to-God truth, nobody in the world could buy it from me. I wouldn't consider selling it to anybody. At any price. That's family land, and if I weren't family, I wouldn't even mention it to you, but I want to build on it and live there."

"But if you *were* going to sell it, what would you take for it?"

I knew that she had sold fifty acres out in the county two years earlier for twenty dollars an acre. I also knew that I had paid five dollars an acre for my thirty where I built the little house in which I was currently living. I drew a deep breath and paused a moment, a device I have found to be most conducive of the illusion that I am not only in deep thought but also very sincere.

"Aunt Novella, if that land were mine and my own brother wanted to buy it, I wouldn't even consider taking less than two hundred dollars an acre for it."

She didn't bat an eye, but her bosom threatened to tilt her chin a little more upward.

"Hmmm," she said. "I declare. I see." She cleared her throat. "Is that a firm offer?"

"Yes, ma'am," I replied. "And if I could afford it, I'd pay even more. I've been all over that property ever since I could walk, and I love every inch of it."

I saw no need to tell her that the first time I ever jerked off had been while hidden in the leafy crown of the great beech tree near the western end of her property. My aunts had a Victorian innocence about them that I was not about to breach. All three of them used the words *gay* and *queer* in their original meanings until the day they died, and no one ever enlightened them.

"Come back tomorrow, Aloysius, and let me study on this overnight. After all, you *are* family, the closest I have, if the truth be told."

I slept soundly. I had used good bait, had been patient, and I was sure I had set the hook.

So had Aunt Novella.

"Aloysius, I have decided to sell you the acreage you want."

My heart speeded up. I am sure my face reddened.

"For the price you recommended. There are certain stipulations, however. First, you must promise me never to sell it while I am alive; it is, as you say, family land. Second, you must build your house on it right away and move in, say within the next twelve months."

"No problem there, Aunt Novella."

"Wait a moment. I also require that you build a chicken yard for your Aunt Palestine, complete with a secure henhouse. It must be finished before you build your own house."

"I don't understand. A henhouse and a chicken yard?"

"You need to learn more about family, Aloysius. You don't know how difficult it is at times for three sisters to live under one roof, especially when it belongs solely to just one of them. Palestine doesn't want me to sell my share of Papa's land; says she can't bear the thought of stepping out the back door and realizing that those woods don't belong to her anymore."

"But Aunt Novella, those woods don't belong to her. And never have."

"That's beside the point, Aloysius. Palestine is the baby of the family and also has that deformity, of which we never speak, of course; and sometimes she can be most childishly stubborn about her opinions whether they have any root in reality or not."

"I still don't understand."

"Aloysius, the only way I could stop her threats to charge me and Lemma rent was to promise that I'd get you to build her a chicken house so that she could have fresh eggs for her cooking. Also, by the way, that would cut down a little on my grocery bill each month."

I think my mouth was hanging open.

"Now are you beginning to understand about family, Aloysius?"

"I'm getting a little glimmer here and there, Aunt Novella."

I decided I didn't want her to think that I was a fiscal fool, since we did share the same bloodline, and I sure didn't want her to put me down as a thoughtless spendthrift.

"The cost of the henhouse and chicken yard is to be deducted from the purchase price, Aunt Novella?"

Her reply flashed back. "Most certainly not." She drew herself up straighter, if that was possible. I'd never noticed before how small her eyes were. "You pay it all. Out of your pocket, not mine. Regard it as a guilt tax to Palestine."

"Closing costs, Aunt Novella?"

"There will be none. You're a lawyer. You draw up the deed and you pay to have it recorded."

"That will be probably five or ten dollars, Aunt Novella."

"Don't pinch pennies with me, Aloysius."

"I wouldn't dream of it, Aunt Novella. I'll get the deed prepared and bring you a check."

"And don't forget the chicken house. Palestine needs something else and something new to keep her busy."

I mean, I had sure learned a lot about family and in a hurry.

A week after I filed the deed to my new property, be blessed if Aunt Lemma didn't approach me. I think she must have been real good at lip-reading, for I had found that if you got right in her face and managed not to get in the way of all those wires, you didn't have to yell nearly so loudly and she could understand you. Even then it was an ordeal to converse with her. I braced myself.

"Aloysius," she proclaimed in that measured diction of hers, "you may know that Papa left me an equal tract of land next to Novella's, and I was wondering if you might be interested in purchasing it also, since it is adjacent to you now and also comprises family acres. It would make a nice square parcel."

"Why, Aunt Lemma, that had never occurred to me," I lied. "How much would you want for it?"

"What a question, Aloysius: the same sum you paid Novella. Of course."

"Aunt Lemma, have you ever walked that property of yours?"

"Of course not, Aloysius. Such a question. There are too many briars and too much undergrowth and more than likely snakes."

"Aunt Lemma, that's the point. A good two-thirds of your property is pure swamp, covered with alder bushes and ankle-deep in water most of the year. It's just plain not worth as much as Aunt

Novella's. Or, for that matter, Aunt Tiny's. There's no way I could see my way to giving you two hundred dollars an acre for it. No property in this county has ever before sold for more than fifty dollars an acre."

"I see. Well, it was just a thought, Aloysius. I have decided to sell it since Novella sold hers, and quite frankly I need the money. You are not aware of the financial arrangements between me and my sisters, nor should you be. Prices keep going up and the small amount I get from my husband's estate barely pays for my personal needs. I shall keep up my tithe to the church, of course, but I may be forced to give up the beautician."

I looked at her teased blue hair with the sunlight picking out separate glistening strands and felt urged to help her. "Aunt Lemma, I keep reminding you that most of your land is an alder swamp, but I might go to one hundred dollars an acre, which is five times what it's worth."

"Well, Aloysius, I'm disappointed. I asked your brother Harold about it and he said the land should be worth more to you than to anyone else, since it joins you now, and if I sell to someone else, there is no telling what they might use it for. He said it was worth a great deal to you just for protection. He said you could afford it and it would do you good to spend a little. Besides, I would hate to face Novella if I got any less for my property that Papa left me than she did for hers. You're young, Aloysius, and you just don't understand about family."

I swallowed hard. My own brother. My own aunt. Tell me I don't understand about family. The whole world should have learned about family if they'd bothered to read the book of Genesis as a factual account of human beings, rather than as the myth of creation.

My word! Cain and Abel for starters; then Abraham and what he let Sarah nag him into doing to Hagar and Ishmael; then what he nearly did himself to Isaac; and then Rebecca fooling poor old blind, hen-pecked Isaac into giving Esau's blessing to Jacob. All that wasn't anything but sibling rivalry that later grew into hatred and war, with the Ishmaelites and Esau's descendants hating the Jews and all of them eventually leading to Mohammed, who conquered more of the civilized world than any pharaoh or Alexander or Caesar ever imagined in their wildest dreams. Of course, man hadn't discovered petroleum back then. It's obvious as the nose on a McElwaney face that they're all kin and that Islam is out to reform the world again.

Chesterton put it pretty plain in "Lepanto":

It is he that saith not 'Kismet'; it is he that knows not Fate;
It is Raymond, it is Richard, it is Godfrey at the gate!
It is he whose loss is laughter when he counts the wager worth,
Put down your feet upon him, that our peace be on the earth.

Tell me I don't comprehend family. All those Semites are kinfolks, and the feelings have spread all through humanity. I know family and I'm convinced it was no coincidence that Sigmund Freud was a Jew. He had been raised orthodox, teethed on the Torah and the Talmud, and I've considered that his approach to psychiatry was probably teenaged rebellion on his part, but he sure as hell learned about family from Genesis and Judges. He got into our culture soon enough that my aunts didn't use poison or knives on their kin. Regardless of what the Muslims are doing now, I learned long ago that kinfolks can screw you just as soundly as a stranger, and as for old maids, they are definitely not financial virgins, say what you will about their hymens.

I bought the property.

I built the damn chicken house.

Then I got a machete and an axe and began cutting paths through my new domain. It was only then I fully realized how beautiful it was. I hired an architect, which had not heretofore been done in our town, not even by the Cofields. My kitchen was almost as big as the house I had moved from. I began to enjoy cooking. I for sure and certain always had plenty of fresh eggs, for I had struck a deal with Aunt Tiny. In return for my cleaning out the henhouse, I got a dozen eggs a week and half of the chicken manure, which was great fertilizer for my flowerbeds.

I had some rural clients who owed me legal fees they couldn't pay and were glad to settle their bills by cleaning the alders out of Aunt Lemma's swamp. Then I dredged the creek bed and, lo and behold, I had a perfect place for all sorts of moisture-loving plants. Somebody brought me cypress trees from Florida and fever trees and spider lilies, and from north Georgia traveling friends brought me galax and grass of Parnassus and all sorts of trilliums. All this became the glory of my life, and I had such privacy that behind rhododendrons and laurel thickets I placed benches where visiting ladies were well content to rest and listen to poetry recited in their ear and sip a little wine before they straightened up their clothes and went home. I had sense enough in the beginning to place my driveway on the far side of the property, so that the aunts could not sit on their porch and see that I was having visitors.

At least I knew that much about family.

Don't think that in the midst of all this wonderful horticultural activity I didn't continue to pay for it dearly. It seemed that every crisis next door always centered around Aunt Tiny. Be blessed if all unexpectedly and explosively, at the age of seventy, she didn't up and get herself engaged to be married. Aunt Novella had persuaded a family friend to give Aunt Tiny a part-time job in a gift shop she had opened on the courthouse square because she thought Aunt Tiny needed something else to occupy her time besides cooking and feeding chickens. Thought, she said, that it might be good for Palestine to get out from underfoot and become a little more independent of her and Lemma. She never dreamed, she told me, that at her advanced age Palestine would behave like a teenager and come home with a diamond ring on her finger and start giving herself airs.

Aunt Novella consulted me in tears. "Aloysius, it's just terrible, terrible. We've lived together, the three of us, for years, and everything has gone smoothly. All the time. Well, most of the time; you know how families are. I never dreamed of anything like this happening. I just don't know what's got into Palestine, or come over her, or however you want to express it, but there's no reasoning with her. She's talking about marrying this man and has come home with a diamond that's even bigger than mine, a solitaire it is and looks plumb gaudy on anybody as old as Palestine. Now she's talking about him moving into *her* house and them living in *her* house, and I think she's planning to kick me and Lemma out, and we'll be left in our old age without a roof over our heads, and I can't bear the thought of ever moving, let alone living anywhere else.

"As Papa would have said, 'She's stepped over the traces, got the bit between her teeth, her tail over the dashboard, and is running over Fool's Hill in the buggy.'"

Her nose was red and her eyes swollen, and I swear that it even looked like her bosom had drooped. I know her shoulders were slumped. Aunt Novella was in misery and she was a miserable sight. It never occurred to me to hug her, but I did pat her on one of her drooping shoulders and offer her my handkerchief. She blew hard and vigorously and, I must add, copiously, then tried to return my handkerchief, which I gently refused.

"Oh, Aloysius, try to talk some sense into her; maybe she'll listen to you. After all, you are a lawyer and maybe you can think of something to say that will bring her to her senses. I know she has been spoiled all her life, but I never realized she was this selfish."

I thought for a moment about a couple of houses Aunt Novella rented out which could make quite a comfortable home for her, and my heart warmed toward a seventy-year-old maiden who finally had an opportunity to have a life of her own and experience it fully.

Then I encountered Aunt Tiny, and my attitude shifted as fast as a barometer in a tornado.

I had overlooked some of her mannerisms. She persistently addressed any male to whom she was talking as "Mister." It was a slovenly device to keep her from remembering names and perhaps embarrass herself by calling Mr. Bazemore Mr. Cofield. Also, I had forgotten how long her teeth were and how carelessly attended and how her prolonged and whistling use of sibilants resulted in a slightly malodorous mist that was visible in the air. As a little boy, I had sat by her once at prayer meeting, and when we got through reciting the

Lord's Prayer, my hair was wet on the side next to Aunt Tiny. I usually remember her when we get to the trespasses.

She approached me one afternoon at the henhouse. She habitually used the phrase, "Oh my, I just don't know what to do," not as a valid excuse for indecision but as an impregnable defense of her own will. She fluttered with the "Oh my" and then used "just" as an atomizer. I had long since learned that my Aunt Palestine was not as vague and helpless as she affected.

"Oh, Mister, I hate to interrupt you while you're so busy with that shovel and wheelbarrow, but I need somebody to talk to, and Sister and Lemma won't even listen to me for crying and yelling. Oh my, I just don't know what to do."

"It's okay, Aunt Tiny, I'm about through here anyhow. Let me get my wheelbarrow outside the fence and close the gate so the hens won't get out. What's on your mind?"

"Mister, I'm sure you know I'm engaged; everybody in town is talking about it, and Mr. Holt gave me this lovely ring when he proposed, and Sister keeps telling me I should give it back and that I'm not qualified to make a man a good wife and keep house for him. Oh my, I just don't know what to do. What do you think, Mister?"

"I think that's a lovely ring, Aunt Tiny, and I congratulate you. I'm glad you've found happiness."

"But, Mister, I haven't. Sister and Lemma have seen to that and they've even got all the nephews but you trying to talk me out of it. Your brother Harold even got real red in the face and told me there's no fool like an old fool just because I'm ten years older than Mr. Holt. Oh my, I just don't know what to do."

"Aunt Tiny," I interposed, "stop a minute. Think. Think about what you want and quit worrying about your sisters and the neighbors. Do you love this man?"

"Well, I think so. Oh my, I just don't know what to do."

"Do you want to marry him?"

"Yes. Yes, I do. Even if Novella says I couldn't make a good wife, I think I would. I could cook for him. I could keep house for him. I could do his laundry for him. I could make him happy. What do you think, Aloysius?"

I took a deep breath. "Aunt Tiny, quit fluttering and look at me. Could you share his bed with him? And all that that entails?"

"Oh my. Oh my goodness. What are you talking about, Aloysius?"

I let her have it. "Sex, Aunt Tiny. Sex. The act of procreation upon which all marriages are based. By my calculations from what you've told me, Mr. Holt will still expect to be sexually active. Haven't you two lovebirds discussed this?"

"Oh my goodness, no. We've talked about how lonely we both are and where we'll live and we've decided on my house, of course, which is what Novella keeps bawling about, but Papa did leave it to me, after all. But," she paused a moment, "he did kiss me once. I liked it tolerably well, but he hasn't done it since. Oh my, I just don't know what to do."

"Well, Aunt Tiny, you're the only one who can figure that out, and you'll have to do it for yourself. There's a lot more to sex than kissing and most of it happens below the waist. Think about it." For meanness, I added, "Long and hard."

I grabbed the handles of the wheelbarrow. "I have to go. Got to get this chicken fertilizer scattered before dark; it's supposed to rain tonight, according to the radio. Lots of luck, Aunt Tiny."

I didn't look back.

Two days later, Aunt Novella actually walked through the woods to see me while I was eating supper. Luckily I was alone.

She was her usual puffed-up, sway-backed self. Mae Pringle always said Aunt Novella was "pussel-gutted," but I never saw the reason. I'm sure Mae knew a lot more about foundation garments than I, so I never challenged the assertion.

"Aloysius, I don't know what you said to Palestine day before yesterday, but I am here to thank you. Lemma and I were watching through the kitchen curtains and saw you talking to her most earnestly. By the time she got back to the house, we had just enough time to move to the front room and pretend to be listening to the news on the radio. Tiny never said a word to us but went to her room and slammed the door.

"Yesterday she came home from work and I asked her where her ring was, and she snapped, 'I gave it back to Mr. Holt and broke the engagement. I hope you're satisfied.' She didn't cook anything but grits and a little sausage for our supper and then left me and Lemma to wash up. Today she's happy as a lark, acting like her old self, and when I left she was in the kitchen making teacakes. What in the world did you say to her, Aloysius? I'll never tell."

I looked Aunt Novella straight in the eye and said, "Neither will I, Aunt Novella."

She pulled her shoulders back, tucked her chin a little downward, and I thought for a minute she might even let out a pigeon gurgle. "Well, I'll just declare," she said. "You've always been a close-mouthed little boy, but if you won't talk about that, you won't talk about anything."

For some reason, Baby Bunc and the goat peckers flashed through my mind, and I was grateful that he and Aunt Novella had never had any social exchange. The town does tend to protect its own. On occasion.

"I guess it's all that lawyer training," she said. "But be that as it may, I want to express my gratitude to you."

"You don't have to do that, Aunt Novella. It's family, you know." I couldn't resist the little dig.

"Yes, I know. The point is that I have two thousand shares of Coca-Cola stock that I intend to give to you."

"Thanks, Aunt Novella, but I hope it will be a long time before I receive them; I think you have many happy years ahead of you."

"Listen to me, Aloysius Holcombe. I shall be at your office tomorrow with the shares; you just have the necessary paperwork ready. At two o'clock. I'll also expect a revision of my will to omit any reference to Coca-Cola."

As I sat speechless, she rose and said, "Also, I think it would be wise for you to have a check made out to me for five thousand dollars. So that if any of my other nephews and nieces ever question the transaction, it will all be open and aboveboard. Understand?"

"Indeed I do, Aunt Novella; I understand perfectly." Some things never change. "It's all family. Thank you."

"You're quite welcome, Aloysius."

Two months later, Mr. Holt gave Aunt Tiny's ring to a fifty-five-year-old widow woman who blinked an awful lot but was very cheerful. His grown children seemed relieved. After their honeymoon, John McCollum at the board of stewards meeting clapped Mr. Holt on the thigh and blurted out, "How's your new marriage coming, Bob?"

Mr. Holt turned red and blustered, "Just fine. That's the easiest thing to get behind on and the quickest to get caught up on I've ever seen. But you wouldn't know about that, would you, John?"

I'm told they both made it a point from then on not to sit together at board meetings.

To my knowledge, Mr. Holt's name was never mentioned again in the Perdue house and not even in the beautician's shop if either of my aunts was present.

Our town can be pretty perceptive on occasion.

Years and years later, after Aunt Lemma and Aunt Novella had both died and Aunt Tiny was living all alone in the family home, becoming more eccentric and doddering with every year, I was walking to work, as Robert Service said, "one pearly day in early May" and encountered her sweeping the sidewalk in front of her house. Full of the joy of springtime and the flowering in my woods, I greeted her more heartily than usual.

"Good morning, Aunt Tiny! How are you this morning?"

"Well, I declare, if it isn't Aloysius. You're out mighty bright and early this morning."

She stopped her sweeping, gave a little skip with her bad leg, and rested on the broom handle.

"Tell me, Mister, have you heard from our neighbor across the road this morning?"

She was referring to Miss Arizona Cunningham, who in her nineties was living proof of my axiom that it takes a sweet young woman to evolve into a sweet old lady and that a mean woman just gets meaner with age. No one had ever referred to Miss Arizona as "sweet." Ten years before, her widowed daughter had moved in to "look after Mama" when the doctors had said she couldn't possibly live more than three months. Over the ensuing decade, the daughter had lost a little of her own sweetness and acquired a few characteristics of her mother.

"I saw Mary Martha on their front porch getting the milk when I came out on the sidewalk a while ago and called over to ask how her mother was doing, and do you know what she said to me? She said, 'I don't know about Mama; she yelled and hollered all night; but I feel like I'd slept with every man in this town all night.' Now, what in the world did she mean by that?"

"Beats me, Aunt Tiny. I have no idea."

I turned to go, but she grabbed my arm to stop me. "Well, tell me this, Mister; does she feel *good* or *bad*?"

Her grip tightened and she gave me a little shake.

"Aunt Tiny, I've never slept with a man in my life and neither have you; so I guess neither of us will ever know, will we?" Ten feet away from her, I turned and said, "If you really want to know, ask Miss Mary Martha, but either way, be prepared for a shock."

I'll never forget how she looked, propped on that broom handle to support that little bitty leg and the early sun shining blue and silver through her hair. It's the last time I ever saw her upright. She fell going back up her front steps and snapped the long bone in her thigh, plus her hip socket. Miss Mary Martha heard her calling for help and called Sport Cofield, who hauled her to Georgia Baptist Hospital in Atlanta, but she died ten days later. Intestate.

What a scramble. What a lesson in family. Brother Harold said he wasn't surprised Aunt Tiny hadn't left a will, that he'd been suspecting for years that she had plans to take all her land and the house with her and that he was grateful there wasn't a big hole square in the middle of town where her twenty acres had been.

After about a year and a half of dickering and bickering and a lot of things being said that should never have produced sound waves, I wound up with the twenty acres and a distant cousin from out West bought the house and moved in. It's all still in the family, so to speak. I paid forty thousand dollars for the land. Family isn't everything and seldom cuts anybody any slack.

Several years after Aunt Novella died, I had bid on a beautiful four-foot white marble statue of St. Francis of Assisi at an estate auction on West Paces Ferry Road in Atlanta. I had to sell two shares of Coca-Cola stock to swing it, but it was worth it. I had it in my woods near a bird feeder and loved to sit in my swing and look at it. Until the day Steven Stinchcomb came through my woods, pointed his finger at St. Francis, and said very cryptically, "Don't talk to him. He won't fuck."

I had never realized before how confirmed a protestant Steven was, but yet put the saint in a whole new light for me. Two weeks later I had him moved to the edge of my property facing the henhouse, and I only see him from the back now, with his bald head gleaming like a beacon.

Whenever I walk by him, I think of Aunt Palestine Perdue.

And Aunt Lemma.

And Aunt Novella.

And Steven Stinchcomb.

And Mary Martha Cunningham.

What a town!

If Geoffrey Chaucer had known these folks, *Canterbury Tales* might have been longer. And possibly even richer. What a town!

Chapter 20

Now, don't think for a minute that Beatrice Cofield didn't ride Betsill's millions like Queen Elizabeth on her favorite mare. Of course, she had to ride within Betsill's guidelines; for instance, they never drove anything but Ford automobiles and Beatrice was known to have done some of her Christmas shopping at Jordan's Salvage Yard. But, give her credit, when "pre-tax dollars" wore out, she discovered "charitable deductions," and before she died she had got herself on the board of the Atlanta Symphony Orchestra and made Betsill buy tails and a white tie, which made him look more like a penguin than ever. When you saw them together all dressed up, you couldn't help but compare Strut to Waddle.

On top of that, Betsill managed to be on the board of every bank as it sold, and Beatrice discovered that they could take tax-exempt trips all over the world as a business expense, long as they were with a bunch of other drunk bankers. I mean, they rode high. They had to get a fancier lawyer than me to draw up a trust to shelter all their money, but Betsill always wanted me to review the documents. Free of charge, of course, which was a favor I was glad to grant since it was a wonderful inside track to watching, and I often mused on what the old Major or Mr. Johnnie would have thought of the present leader of the Cofield clan. Not to mention the prosperity and changes that had overtaken our town and county.

Betsill really got his back up with Dr. Hentz when he and Beatrice applied for million-dollar life insurance policies and had to produce their past medical records. Beatrice had no problem, but every time Betsill had them send in a new form, Dr. Hentz filled it out accurately about peptic ulcers and alcohol consumption. It finally wound up that Betsill's premium was three times higher than that of Beatrice. She gloated and he grumbled. "Looks like long as he's known me, Doc could shade all that stuff down at least a little bit. I ain't never had a drink before five o'clock in the afternoon and he knows it. He's got this hang-up about falsifying medical records and says he ain't going to no federal pen if every Cofield in the county winds up in a pauper's grave. Right insulting, I thought he was, but I can't budge him."

I wanted to ask about the price of coffee but restrained myself.

When Dr. Hentz died and everybody had to pick a new doctor from the pile that had swarmed in on the heels of our prosperity, the Cofields, like everybody else, soon learned the difference between a family doctor and a family physician. The latter has a computer that he totes around the office with him, a paging service, a physician's assistant that handles overflow for him, and he would as soon be caught getting a blow job as to make a house call. The very idea.

The tighter the Feds get, the more medical care looks like it's merging with the postal service. And Hillary has yet to do a damn thing about it. What a waste of ovaries.

At any rate, be that as it may, when Beatrice took sick, Betsill was in a quandary. They lived all alone in their big house, the kids were scattered to the winds with families of their own, Betsill's insurance called for a one-hundred-dollar co-pay for an emergency room visit, and he didn't know what to do. Finally he got through all the recorded directions and defensive linebackers protecting his new doctor from phone calls.

"Doc, I know y'all don't make house calls anymore, but I live right on your way home, and I'd appreciate it if you'd drop by here when you leave your office."

"What's your problem, Mr. Cofield? I'm pretty busy."

"It's my wife, Doc."

"I've been knowing that. But what's the immediate problem?"

"Well, Doc, her brother called her on the telephone at twelve o'clock. Telling her about a new will her mama has made. Upset her bad. Heard her yelling at her brother. Hung up the phone and has just been sitting there ever since. Staring at the phone. Won't say a word. Not a word. And that's been four and a half hours ago.

'Preciate it can you drop by. Don't know what to do. Ain't like her not to speak to me."

The new doctor had succumbed to electronics and federal guidelines like all the rest of the new doctors, but his daddy was a real country doctor in rural south Alabama, and Young Doc had not forgotten all his raising. He had accepted Beatrice Cofield as his patient, had experienced probably six encounters with her. He swore that even his computer groaned whenever she came in the office. He hadn't seen her for three months, but by God he recognized an emergency when he saw one.

"I'll be right there, Mr. Cofield," he said and told his secretary to reschedule his last two patients.

There is hope for the younger generation and we're still the best town around.

Well, to make a long story short, or at least a little shorter, for believe me it's sure going to get a heap longer, it turned out Beatrice Schultz Cofield had a brain tumor. Some sort of –oma, I can't ever remember all those medical terms, but it was cancer for sure and certain, and the whole community was shocked. Oscar Hosey said he had knowed it ever since the first time he laid eyes on her, or rather had his ears bent, but only a very few thought Oscar was funny this time.

It didn't bother me. Oscar was Oscar and you could take him or leave him but you sure weren't going to change him. Everybody stumbles now and then.

Young Doc called the ambulance and shipped Beatrice off to a big fancy hospital in Atlanta. The one where they had something called the gamma knife which was some new-fangled way of operating with laser rays on brain tissue. Betsill tried to explain it to me, but I don't think it had been explained too clearly to him, for I couldn't make heads or tails of it. It sounded like something out of Star Wars to me, and that got my mind to wandering and I wondered why I'd never before considered that R2D2 was built like Betsill but talked sort of like Beatrice once you got him activated.

At any rate, the town was relieved to discover that Beatrice had responded to some medicine to cut down the swelling around her tumor and that she could talk again. There are some norms in this world that should not be shaken. The preacher was allowed to visit her and reported that she made pretty good sense. I thought of "Pippa Passes" but was not invited to go to the hospital.

Betsill kept me well informed. "They're going to use this gamma knife on her and then she'll get radiation for two, three weeks; the doctors will decide later. Say she can do that as an outpatient, which will be considerably cheaper. Glad I got insurance. Costing over three hundred dollars a day just for the room, plus X-rays and medicine, and what they charge for use of that gamma knife is more'n what I used to be able to buy a new car for, and I'm talking about a Crown Victoria. On top of that, they say ain't no cure for this particular tumor, just temporary relief. Wasn't for insurance I guess I'd just have to let her go. Now."

"Yes, thank God for insurance," I responded. "I'm going to the store. Can I bring you anything? Need any bread or eggs? Got plenty of coffee?"

You couldn't change Betsill Cofield any more than you could change Oscar Hosey, but the same applies to Aloysius Holcombe, I guess. Fortunately there's room for all of us. The town gathered in around Betsill and Beatrice and everybody was concerned.

That didn't stop anybody from watching, however. Or talking.

Brother Richard came bursting into my office. "If I didn't know better, I'd swear that at sunup this morning I saw Beatrice Cofield standing on the sidewalk with a bloody bandage wrapped around her head. Wasn't she operated on just yesterday?"

"Right," I replied. ""You're not hallucinating. Betsill explained it to me yesterday. Seems that they've discharged her last night since she's herself again and she's starting radiation today. The hospital has so many patients in this area that they're running a bus service to pick them all up and bring them into the hospital's X-ray department."

"That's a kind and magnanimous thing for the hospital to do," said Brother Richard. "I know that's a comfort to the families."

"Richard!" I said. "Wake up and smell the coffee. All the hospitals in Atlanta are in cutthroat competition with each other; they've even started advertising in the newspapers, on television, and on billboards. All that hospital is doing is guarding its market share. Betsill and Beatrice were told there are ten or twelve patients to be picked up five days a week, and they're scattered from here to Jonesboro, Fairburn, McDonough, and Riverdale. It'll take at least an hour and a half to collect all of them and the same amount of time to bring them home. The bus comes through our town at six-thirty and it'll be at least two-thirty in the afternoon before it gets back."

"Why doesn't Betsill take her in for her appointment? Or one of those children?"

"I asked the same thing, but Betsill hasn't been getting much sleep lately and he doesn't like to drive in Atlanta anymore, and on top of that he likes to sleep 'til at least eight or eight-thirty since he sold the bank. This is a convenience and it is a freebie from the hospital and saves him a lot of gas money. Did you know regular is almost seventy cents a gallon now and his Crown Victoria takes ethyl? Poor, poor, poor, poor Betsill."

"Oh, shut up, Buster. Poor Beatrice! She doesn't deserve to be treated this way. I'm going to see Betsill and talk some sense into him."

"Lots of luck," I said. "I hope you don't have anything else planned for the rest of the day. And don't forget, Beatrice will be getting back at two-thirty."

"I'm not forgetting that she was operated on just yesterday morning and that she'll be on that bus or on her feet for a total of eight hours today. This is inhumane! I'm going to go talk to Betsill. Right now."

"After that, why don't you drop by and get Oscar Hosey to bathe and shave and change clothes, even if it is just Thursday?" I wanted to tell Brother Richard why didn't he just spit in the wind or go piss up a rope, but I saved my breath. The world is not as it is but as it seems to Richard. He, to paraphrase Housman, will be forever one and twenty, no use to talk to him. I had no desire to go with him to see Betsill.

The town buzzed for awhile about Beatrice, but it takes too long to die with a brain tumor to hold the attention of TV-oriented America. Also, Jimmy Carter was running for president, of all things, and there were other distractions along the way. He went on to win the presidency, and our newspaper editor's wife told him he was going to have to do something about that smile, that she wasn't going to be able to stand looking at all those teeth for four years. But she did, of course, and still does. Talk about the Cheshire Cat! We had plenty to divert our attention, at least briefly, from Beatrice.

Betsill had become uncommonly reticent about discussing her condition. I think myself this was about the time he increased his Scotch intake to a quart and a half, but never before five p.m. That boy did have his principles.

Scotch costs a lot more than coffee, but I was not inclined to discuss this with him. It has been said that one man's genealogy is another man's ennui, and that's about the way I've come to feel about another man's principles. For God's sake, the older I get the harder it is for me to hang on to my own. Our town has always had somewhat of a live-and-let-live policy, at least as long as you could watch and discuss.

Beatrice for several weeks obviously improved. She didn't get out around town by herself but sure spent a good deal of time on the telephone. She knew her diagnosis and her prognosis and she used what time she had left on this earth to call people and say goodbye to them, usually accompanied by an expression of thanks for kindnesses she remembered from the past. This pulled the town solidly in behind her, and it was her finest hour.

She abandoned none of her speech patterns. She called me once and thanked me thanked me thanked me for what my music had meant to her and had really really really truly meant to her and she was most sincere most most most truly sincere in what she was saying. She knew my fingers were too old and stiff just naturally too old and stiff and everybody's fingers get that way with age just too

stiff to play at her funeral but she was sure just as sure as she knew
she was sitting there that I'd find somebody to serve in my place
maybe Jim Harp's wife wouldn't mind and she knew she was dying at
least that's what the doctors in Atlanta had told Betsill and she wasn't
enough of a ninny to think otherwise even if Betsill hadn't blurted it
out and after all when all's said and done and everything everybody is
going to die sometime and she had the blessing that's the only way to
look at it was a blessing for she had time to call her dear, dear, dear
friends and thank them for what they had meant to her.

It was real sweet and real meaningful, and since she was on the
telephone, I could lay it down very quietly and go ahead and make
my toast and oatmeal and get breakfast ready without her breaking
stride or losing wind.

Then, be blessed if she didn't say all she'd wanted about dying at
least all of her adult life—you know, after she'd grown up and seen a
lot of people just a tremendous number of people really up and
die—all she wanted was to die with dignity. Dignity, dignity, dignity
is what's important more important than anything else about dying
and she did hope and trust really trust and really really hope that
she'd be able to do that.

My oatmeal was getting cold; so I interrupted to thank her for
calling and to say that I really, really, really appreciated it. I couldn't
help that triple *really*, it just popped out; her speech pattern had
become infectious.

I told her I wished I had a recording of that conversation and
that I would never forget it, both of which statements were true.

I did not tell her that standing on the sidewalk at daylight every
morning waiting to catch a bus to the hospital while her husband
slept off his Scotch wasn't very dignified, especially since the first
time she'd had her head swathed in a bloody bandage.

I suspect Carlotta would have mentioned it but she'd been long
gone. Our preacher, one of the good ones, once quoted Alice B.
Toklas in a sermon, something I'd never dreamed of occurring in a
Methodist church. He said that Toklas, in describing her lifelong
companion, had said, "What made Gertrude Stein great was not what

she gave to people, but what she didn't take away from them." That didn't have much impact on our town but it made a big impression on me. So did that bloody bandage.

When she finally went back in the hospital and then into its hospice on a separate floor, we all waited for the inevitable. Miss Mae had been dead for ten years or more, but we still had dedicated telephone monitors, and there were frequent bulletins about the decline and resurgence and decline and resurgence of Beatrice Cofield. Today she was talking and eating, yesterday she didn't know the children and wouldn't take nourishment. Up and down, on and on it went. "Sink and rise and sink and rise and sink again." I began to be concerned about dignity.

Then it all blew up. Betsill had busied himself making preparations for the inevitable. He had gone to see P.L. Arnall, the undertaker who had replaced Sport Cofield in town, and told him that he wanted him personally to embalm Beatrice and supervise her funeral. "I've told them at the hospital that when she dies you'll be the one to pick her up. And I don't want any of your interns or helpers or whatever you call them to see her naked body. I want you and you alone to do all the embalming."

Betsill told me that himself, which opened up a whole new vista of concerns and principles I had never even considered before. I was very glad it was Betsill who had them and not I. I don't care what Jesus said about the Pharisees, I can't help occasionally praying like one of them. Not out loud, mind you, but down deep inside where secret thoughts will pop up no matter how hard you try to control them.

Gussie Bell came rapping on my back door just as I was cleaning up after breakfast. She had been Beatrice and Betsill's maid for twenty or thirty years and seemed always to me a stereotype of Prissy.

"When I come to work awhile ago, Mr. Betsill come out in his bathrobe and it wa'nt fasten too good all the way up the front neither and tole me Miss Beatrice done died. Say Mr. P.L. Arnall done come by and awoken him 'bout two o'clock this morning and say the hospital call him. Mr. Betsill tole him to go on up there and fetch her home and tole me to come over and tell you 'bout it and also axe you to tell yo nephew cause he want him to sing at the funeral. Mr. Betsill done pissed his bed again, and I come over soon as I changed his sheets."

I thanked Gussie Bell and considered Betsill's new set of principles that would allow someone else to send for the undertaker to fetch your wife while you went blissfully back to sleep until the maid came. It also seemed like a little out of the ordinary behavior for P.L., who was a very dedicated professional in his field. But then I considered that this was still our town, despite all the progress and new people with their ideas, and shrugged.

I went to the piano and played "The Old Rugged Cross" and "Those Golden Bells" and "Sunrise Tomorrow." Just in case I was invited. But I discovered Beatrice was right; the fingers really have become too stiff to perform to my standards. I called Jim Harp's wife and put her on notice.

It's been years since I've even attempted "Flight of the Bumblebee."

The entire funeral machinery of the old-time village cranked into action. People called Betsill repeatedly to ask if there was anything they could do. Word of the demise of one of our most prominent citizens spread rapidly; some people take pride in being the one to announce major events.

"You heard about Beatrice Cofield, didn't you?"

"No, what about her? Is she worse?"

"She's dead."

"Oh, my God! I didn't think it would be this quick. Let me call Tootsie." (Or Mary or Jane or Jennifer or whoever else was on her list.) "Did she go peaceful?"

With that one visit by Gussie Bell, Betsill had sure created a lot of activity, and he vigorously accepted and organized all volunteers and well-wishers.

"Yeah, it's sad. Come on over and help rearrange furniture. P.L. said it'd be about three o'clock this afternoon before he'd be done embalming her, and I want her brought home in her casket.

"Yeah, it sure is. She loved you, too, Lizzie. How about calling the preacher and reserving the church? For Friday afternoon about two o'clock. And while you're at it, how about ordering flowers? You know, a blanket for the casket. I sure appreciate it. Call Alvin; he always gave Beatrice a discount on flowers. Remind him of it.

"Yeah, we all hate to see her go. Come to think of it, Sara Belle, there is something you can do. You're a member of the family and know all the dates and such; how 'bout you calling the Atlanta paper and writing up the story for them."

A reporter from the local paper called Betsill, who affirmed the demise, and then his editor called the new doctor to inquire about the hour of death. By now it was ten o'clock in the morning and the news was all over town and spreading like a prairie fire. New Doctor told the editor that he hadn't heard anything about it and was surprised that the specialist in Atlanta hadn't called him. Told the editor he'd check and call him back.

The specialist told New Doctor that Beatrice was indeed somewhat improved, had eaten a good breakfast, and responded to some of his questions when he had rounded that morning.

That's when the walls came crashing down. The editor was a newcomer over in Magnoliadale who was determined to establish a daily newspaper and took himself more seriously than any of the rest of us did. He already had his front page and headlines laid out for an impressive scoop.

New Doc told us, "I called him back and said, 'This is something I've been wanting the opportunity to say for years—Hold the press!'

"That man said, 'Whatta you mean?'

"I said, 'She ain't dead. In fact, she's somewhat improved.'

"There was a long moment of silence. And then he sort of half-yelled, half-whispered, 'Oh, my God!' Then I could hear him take a deep breath and he said, 'I owe you, Doc. I owe you big time. Thank you, thank you, thank you. I've got to run. Thank you, thank you, thank you.'"

I had to laugh; I couldn't help it. When New Doc told me about the editor triple-thanking him, I wondered if that editor might not be some distant kin to Beatrice. Also, I thought he was a man of limited vision and no daring whatsoever. If he had really wanted a scoop for his daily paper, he should have put out a special edition with four-inch headlines that said, "She ain't dead yet!" It would have attracted wide attention, sold out every copy, made him some money, and who knows? Maybe even gotten him a Pulitzer Prize, as screwed up as that process has become lately.

About eleven-thirty, Sara Belle Hipp called me. "Buster, Betsill awakened me early this morning and told me the sad news about Beatrice. He asked me to write up the obituary for the Atlanta paper. I hate to bother him, but do you remember the date they were married?" Her voice was as sultry and controlled as ever, and I couldn't help wishing for a moment I'd had the opportunity along the way to quote a little Millay to her. Too late, now; so I replied.

"She ain't dead yet. It's all a mistake."

All sultriness vanished. She sounded like a fishwife. "What?!" she screamed.

I told her about New Doc calling the specialist and everything, and she said, "Let me call Sister Liz real quick. She's already reserved the church, scheduled the preacher, and ordered the blanket. I can't believe this. Betsill told me himself that P.L. Arnall came by his house at two o'clock and told him the hospital had called him to come and get her body. I just can't believe this."

"Sara Belle," I said, "calm down and think about it. You know Betsill as well as I do. I strongly suspect that it was Johnnie Walker who spoke to him at two a.m."

With that she and I both busted out laughing and she said, "Let me call Liz real quick. I know she's going to say she'll never be able to hold her head up in this town again."

With that her husband grabbed the phone and said, "Buster, call that specialist back and tell him to go ahead and let her die; we've got everything ready." Then he laughed.

I hung up the phone and said out loud, "Well, there goes dignity out the door."

I rapidly discovered that it's a lot easier in our town to start a funeral ritual than it is to stop one after it's been cranked up. People got in their kitchens and cooked; a cornucopia of food overflowed Betsill's kitchen. Olivia Ramspeck, who had grown up in the house next to Mr. Johnnie Cofield and was now in her early eighties, appeared at Arnall's Funeral Home at four o'clock and royally announced, "I have come to view the corpse."

"What corpse?" the bewildered attendant asked. "We don't have a corpse."

"You most certainly do," asserted Miss Olivia. "Mr. Cofield, himself, did me the courtesy of calling me. I wish to view Mrs. Cofield's body; we've been close friends and neighbors with the Cofields all my life."

"Ma'am, I don't know what you're talking about. I don't think Mrs. Cofield is dead."

"Well, I know she is, for I've already baked a cake. Let me speak to Mr. Arnall, young man."

"P.L.'s not here, lady. He's been in Savannah for two days on a convention."

"Well, I never heard of such. You'll certainly hear more from me about this, young man. It's my special coconut cake."

Miss Olivia had always been a lady of such impeccable manners and strong opinions that she had never married.

After the third telephone call from prospective visitors, the intern called P.L. in Savannah. P.L. in turn immediately called me. "I don't know what's going on up there, Buster, but I've been in Savannah for two days. Betsill Cofield came to see me about a month ago and laid out his plans for his wife's funeral and all sorts of instructions about who was to embalm her that were sort of embarrassing, if you want to know the truth."

I assured him that I didn't and that I was currently assimilating all the truth I could accommodate; so he continued, "Well, I don't know who woke him up at two o'clock this morning, but it sure wasn't me. I don't want to lose a client or a customer or you know what I mean, but I sure don't want my name dragged into this on false charges, you know what I mean; so you get the word out that I didn't wake Betsill up."

I told him about Calhoun Hipp's premise and P.L. finally broke down and chuckled. He is a very dedicated undertaker and takes a dim view of any evidence of frivolity about his profession, but this was shaking even his dignity.

People, as Baby Buncum said, will let you talk about most anything, and there's been a lot said and written about *coitus interruptus*. Well, our town went through about two weeks of *funeralis interruptus*, and I couldn't help making comparisons. Roasts dried up, salads wilted and rotted, cakes dried and molded, pies shrank to the consistency of flannel cakes, and people were totally frustrated. Nobody felt comfortable about eating food that had been prepared to honor the dead and comfort the bereaved; except for Agnes Walker, who lived alone and was notorious for secreting food from church suppers and carrying it home in her big handbag. She froze her string-bean casserole against the day when Beatrice eventually would die and called Miss Olivia to tell her that if she wasn't going to eat her coconut cake, she'd be glad to take it off her hands.

The funeral home for three days refused delivery of any floral offerings for Beatrice Cofield. It was total mayhem for a little under a week.

Through it all, Betsill stoutly maintained that P.L. Arnall had been the harbinger of all of it, and the town universally believed P.L. but shrugged off any confrontation with Betsill. It wasn't worth it.

Then the *interruptus* reaction set in. I thought of Service's introduction to "The Ballad of Touch the Button Nell": "...the Klondike simmered 'neath the moon and gossiped o'er its bars," except, of course, our town didn't have any bars, and still doesn't for that matter. We did, however, simmer and we for sure and certain gossiped. Those of us who couldn't laugh actually got depressed and had sort of a hangdog look. Not everyone is born with a sense of the ridiculous.

Calhoun Hipp was. Three weeks later he called me. "Toor told Sara Belle that Beatrice finally died last night about midnight. I thought you'd like to know, but I'm waiting myself 'til I see the death certificate. She's been in a coma for the last three days, and that bell-bottomed daughter of theirs has been sitting by the bed reading out loud from some goddam book about the art of dying and telling her mama over and over that it's all right to turn loose and go. Which is true, of course, because she sure didn't have anything to look forward to unless she could recover enough to slap the shit out of Toor."

"Reading to her for three days? And her in a coma? I can't believe it."

"Yep. You and I know she must have been in a coma because she wasn't talking. If it wasn't a coma, she died of boredom from listening to all that reading. Beatrice always said she wanted to die with dignity, and if that's dignity, I'm a sumo wrestler. I told Sara Belle she sure has some weird kinfolks."

"Calhoun!" I remonstrated. "That's what makes our town so wonderful. Jesus told us to *rejoice*." He hung up the phone laughing.

I'm not sure with how much dignity Beatrice left this earth, but Betsill sure set out to have a grand and dignified funeral, and I guess he succeeded to the best of his ability. I have always suspected that he let himself be influenced too much by the three of his children who could still show their faces in town. Whoever said, "For God so loved the world that he didn't send a committee" was a pretty astute observer, and so was the one who coined the proverb "Too many cooks spoil the broth."

I think Betsill truly tried to accommodate the wishes of each child, no matter how disparate those wishes might be, but he sure didn't let P.L. Arnall fulfill the function of funeral director. He treated him as a technician who could embalm and as a chauffeur who could drive a hearse and direct traffic. Any discreet suggestion on P.L.'s part about propriety, local tradition, or consideration of the mourners met with the same impervious wall as Beatrice's imprecations for him to quit drinking. Betsill Cofield could no more change his personality than Stone Mountain could move to Cobb County, no matter who had died or what a community expected.

He called me. "P.L. is embalming Beatrice this morning. He's doing it himself. Personally. I told him I didn't want any of his interns seeing—"

"I know, I know," I interrupted hastily, "you've told me that before. I'm sorry about her death, Betsill. She was a good woman."

"Yep. It was time, though. The doctors told me three months ago what to expect, and I got her the finest doctors money can buy and even offered to send her to Mayo Clinic if they thought it would do any good. She didn't suffer, though. The doctors saw to that. She was in a coma for three days. I didn't go up there. Wouldn't have done any good. She wouldn't have known me. The doctor called me once a day and the children were in and out. In fact, my daughter sat by her bed every day for three days and held her hand and read to her."

"I'm sure that's a comfort to you, Betsill," I volunteered.

"Yep. I wanted to tell you about our plan. P.L. is going to bring her to the house this afternoon about four o'clock and we'll have a private viewing—nobody but immediate family and a very few close friends. Very few. You can drop by if you want to. Then P.L.'s going to take her back to the funeral home till morning, but we're not going to open the casket for the public. Just a sort of reception from two to four and six to eight. If you decide you want to come for a private viewing this afternoon, no need for you to bother with the reception.

"Then the following morning we'll open the casket at the funeral home for nobody but the immediate family. Her mama's ninety-two years old and is coming down from Chattanooga. She's going to spend the night in Atlanta with friends and come to T. J.'s the morning of the funeral but not going to stay for the ceremony itself. Did I tell you she's ninety-two years old? Her mind's still sharp but she has bad arthritis. The casket's going to be open for an hour at P.L.'s the morning of the funeral just for the immediate family, like I said, and Mrs. Schultz will leave right after that. We've got everything all planned. Come by this afternoon, that is, if you want to."

At this point I decided that Betsill was the one who wanted me to come by the house, and I assured him that I would and hung up.

I've never been one to appreciate the embalmer's art. I go to viewings and hear mourners standing before the casket saying, "Doesn't she look natural?" or "He looks like he's just a-laying there sleeping," but I studiously avoid close scrutiny whenever I possibly can, and I usually can.

Writer Olive Ann Burns was at one of Faith Brunson's soirees long ago with her husband, whom we all knew had terminal cancer, and she regaled us all with her account of a cousin's funeral.

"I hadn't been to a country funeral in years and I had forgotten how they carry on. I was standing near the casket and everybody who came by said he looked like he was sleeping. On the way home it occurred to me that it had been years since I saw anybody sleeping; so that night I waited up after Andy had gone to bed and tiptoed in and looked at him; but to me he didn't look like he was sleeping; he looked like he was dead."

After a second of startled assimilation, we all had laughed, including Andy. I've always wondered what he thought was funny, but he so adored Olive Ann he thought anything she said was cute. Which was true, for the most part.

In the presence of death I can't help recalling the poem,

These be three still things:
New fallen snow,
The hour before the dawn,
And the mouth of one just dead.

And that's it. I've never been able to recite it in any consoling fashion to a family, of course, so I just say, "I'm so sorry" and move the line along. Too damn many people linger forever and yak their heads off. Nobody remembers what you say on these occasions, but they always remember your presence. Our town is pretty rigid about the protocol of departure from this world. One picture is truly worth a thousand words; so don't wear brown shoes to a funeral. If you don't have a dark suit, stay home, or at least sit in the back and away from the aisle. And for God's sake, don't chew gum if you're a pallbearer.

I was not prepared for my call at Betsill's house. In the first place there was only one car in the driveway and I wondered where the close friends and immediate family were. When I got inside, the lone visitor was Miss Olivia, who sat erect with rigid spine on the edge of a sofa with both hands clasped on the purse in her lap, her legs crossed primly at the ankles. As soon as I came in and we had greeted each other, she arose and said, "Betsill, I must run. I didn't realize you were here all alone or I'd not have stayed so long. I have a cake in the oven." She paused. "The second one I've cooked this month. I'll drop it by tomorrow. I'm so sorry about your loss. Beatrice was a wonderful woman and she looks so natural, like she's lying there sleeping."

Which was a lie, but I said nothing. One does not challenge Miss Olivia over trivia, and I murmured some inconsequential farewell as Betsill lumbered her to the door, oblivious to her little jab about the cake. Nobody was in that room but the corpse and me. Beatrice Schultz Cofield did not look like she was sleeping and she certainly did not look natural. The sides of the casket had been let down and she lay in full-length exposure like one of the popes at Avignon, her hands folded traditionally on her breast. She wore a dark brown dress that did nothing for her skin and I thought perhaps P.L. had over-rouged her cheeks a bit; the pink did nothing to complement the particular dark brown of that dress.

The dress was knee-length and the most startling thing to my eyes was that her long, stocking-clad legs ended so abruptly in upturned feet. Those feet dominated. They were long and narrow and I thought briefly of Carlotta Melrose. The startling thing, however, was that she had on no shoes and the feet stuck straight up in the air. Also they were a good two feet apart. Before I could summon any reason why a dead person should need shoes, Betsill joined me.

"She's real pretty, isn't she? P.L. did a good job. Did I tell you that he was going to personally do the embalming? I want you to notice this casket, though. It's special order and it's really one casket inside the other; gives an extra layer of air between the coffin and the vault." He tapped it. "Notice how thick it is. It was pretty expensive, but I felt like she deserved the best."

He paused expectantly, but I would have bitten my tongue until it bled before I asked what it cost.

"Look over here on the table at the blanket. I know you like flowers and you'll appreciate it more than I do. She got all her flowers from Alvin because he always gave her a discount and he fixed these special for her. Both of them stayed Democrats after all the rest of the county had turned Republican. The flowers go on top of the coffin when it's closed, but we laid them over here on the table so people could see them before the funeral. The children wanted the sides of the coffin left down while she lies in state so it wouldn't look like she was down in a box. Myself, I never saw it done like that before."

"It's very effective, Betsill," I replied. "I'm terribly sorry about your loss. Wouldn't you like to sit down?"

"No, I'm fine. P.L.'s going to take her back to the funeral home tonight, but we won't open the casket again until the next morning for about an hour just for the family and then the funeral is at eleven. We've got three preachers lined up. I invited the bishop but he's tied up, but the district superintendent is coming and our regular preacher and then the one who was here two or three preachers back that she always liked so much."

"I'm sure it will be a wonderful service, Betsill," I soothed. "And you're right, she deserves it." About this time his two older sons came in. Neither of them did more than glance at their parents but stood in the middle of the room after greeting me.

George spoke up, the one who keeps on going to Georgia Tech. "Mister Buster, perhaps you can settle the argument Will and I are having." His tone was as soft and silky as I remembered.

"About what?" I inquired dubiously.

"About whether to seal the coffin with nitrogen or not."

"To what purpose?" I asked.

"To delay decomposition."

"To what purpose?" I insisted.

He ignored my question. "It's a well-proven fact that things decompose much more slowly in pure nitrogen than they do in oxygen."

I borrowed a phrase from Mae Pringle. "Do tell," I said.

Will began arguing with George and they began talking at the same time, right in each other's faces, and right there in front of those upturned feet of their mother; so I murmured further condolences to Betsill and escaped.

Outdoors I borrowed a phrase from Bill Pritchett. "Now, if'n that don't beat a hawg flying sideways," I said aloud.

The next two days I heard folks commenting on the hegira from the house to the funeral home back to the house and then back to the funeral home. People in our town were somewhat confused, I am here to tell you, and P.L. commenced to chewing Maalox tablets and telling people, "I'm not sure."

They finally got her in the ground after a three-preacher funeral, which included tributes from six different people to the beautiful character of Beatrice Cofield. It lasted an hour and a half and John McCollum, who had prostate trouble, dribbled in his pants, but for the most part it was pretty dignified and formal. Gussie Bell, who had been invited to sit with the family, had never attended a white funeral before and, at what she judged the appropriate moment, let out a mourning wail, threw her arms in the air, and attempted to fall out. Bubble Butt restrained her and comforted her and the preacher didn't even bobble. I heard from several people that nobody cried but Gussie Bell.

I myself did not attend. I had been invited to give a five-minute tribute but had declined at the last moment because of intractable diarrhea. To keep from being caught in a lie, I had taken a large dose of Epsom salts, but no one ever knew that my affliction was self-induced. There is a limit to what I will do for a friend, a neighbor, or a client, and speaking at funerals heads the list.

About a week later, Myrtle Hibbel was in the office to get a deed drawn. Myrtle was an outsider who had lived here for only thirty or thirty-five years but had fit in real well and everybody liked her. When we grew so much that the post office expanded, she had worked there with Bill Pritchett and was just as stocky but very feminine. She wore her long white hair in a flattened bun that always reminded me of a dried cow patty, but she used lipstick and eye shadow appropriately and was all in all an attractive female.

"Buster, did you go by the funeral home to see Beatrice?"

"No. I went by the house three days before and was told by Betsill it was to be closed casket until the morning of the funeral and then it was going to be opened only for the immediate family."

"That's right. That's when I saw her. I had missed all the hullabaloo when she died the first time; so I cooked up a bowl of beans and carried it by the house on Thursday. Would you believe not a living soul was there but Betsill?

"I asked him where he wanted me to put the beans and he said in the refrigerator, and I've never been so surprised in my life. You know how this town is about bringing in food when somebody dies, but I'm here to tell you there wasn't anything in that refrigerator but a carton of milk and a box of eggs. I felt right sorry for him, and since he was all alone, I felt compelled to visit a while. I heard all about the final days and P.L. waking him up in the middle of the night on a false alarm and how fine the casket was and the blanket that Alvin had supplied on a discount. He told me about six times that the casket was going to be opened the next morning just for the family but that if I wanted to come I'd be welcome. He said it so many times I decided he was trying to tell me he wanted me to come."

"I know the feeling," I interjected.

"Well, I took him up on it and went by the next day. Buster, I've never been so shocked. There lay Beatrice all stretched out full length with both sides of the coffin down. She had on this horrible brown dress and her feet were sticking straight up with these little white slides on them. They just glared at you.

"Betsill saw me come in and came over to me at the side of the corpse. I guess he saw me keep staring at those white cotton slides, for he said to me, 'Beatrice's mama is here. She came down from Chattanooga to tell Beatrice goodbye but she's not staying for the funeral; got real bad arthritis and is ninety-three years old. She's always been a little bossy and the minute she came in the door and saw Beatrice, she yelled at me to get some shoes on her daughter. So I gave my daughter ten dollars and sent her down to Wal-Mart and she brought these slippers back. That still didn't satisfy Mrs. Schultz—Beatrice was a Schultz from Chattanooga before we married—and as she went out the door, that old lady pointed her walking stick straight at me and yelled out, 'Furthermore, you tell that undertaker to get my daughter's legs closer together!'"

"Best thing I could do was get out of there quick as I could. I know you're not supposed to laugh at anybody's death, but I couldn't help it. Soon as I was in my car and out of sight I busted out laughing until I cried. I can still see those white feet sticking up in the air. What a fashion statement! And ten dollars at Wal-Mart! I guess they were top of the line. Isn't old Betsill worth several million dollars?"

"A little over seventy," I told her. "At least that's what he told me several years ago when he said he had to go by the grocery store and lay in some coffee because he'd heard it was about to go up again."

"Poor, poor, poor, poor Betsill," Myrtle said. "He owns all that money and he gets eight-dollar slides at Wal-Mart for his dead wife's funeral and worries about the price of coffee. Furthermore I'll bet his daughter didn't give him his change."

"You're wrong, Myrtle," I remonstrated. "The money owns him. Lock, stock, and barrel. He's created a monster, and I suspect it's already got its claws in his children. 'Where a man's treasure is, there is his heart also.' But it's better to laugh than to cry and we do enjoy watching, don't we, Myrtle?"

"You got that right, Buster. This place is full of weirdos but it's still a wonderful town."

I couldn't have said it better.

But I did feel moved to recite,

> Three strange men came to an inn.
> One was a black man, pocked and thin.
> One was brown with a silver knife,
> And one brought with him a wonderful wife.
>
> That beautiful woman had hair as pale
> As French champagne or finest ale....

Myrtle looked at me sort of funny and responded, "Say which?" Then she laughed and said, "We're sure some pair to be talking about weirdos, Buster Holcombe."

Several years later, when it came Betsill's time to die, and the longer I live the more I tend to agree with the mostly black euphemism that you don't die until "your time," which is mysteriously linked to "God's will," it temporarily shook our town. People were about evenly divided between "He brought it on himself" and "I guess it was his time." I just listened and kept my mouth shut.

One night about one a.m., after he had finished his usual quart of Johnnie Walker, he discovered that his toilet was running. He called a friend who had done maintenance work for him at the bank after Mr. Big Buncombe Braswell passed and asked him to come and fix it. The friend, who always did piddling repairs for Betsill free of charge, advised him to turn the tap at the base of the toilet to cut off the water and he would be glad to come by the next morning. Betsill remonstrated that if he left the toilet running all night it might run his water bill over the minimum he was accustomed to paying and he didn't know a tap from a hole in the ground.

The friend held his position and told him that he no longer drove at night, on orders from his doctor and his wife and his four children. Betsill apparently did some quick comparison between the price of water and that of gasoline (he was always good at figures) and told the man he'd be over to his house in a few minutes to pick him up.

The friend told the coroner's jury he went back to sleep and that the next thing he heard was a great commotion and discovered that Betsill had run off the street by his house, hit an ancient oak tree, and been thrown some thirty feet from his car. The friend was given to more than occasional stammering and summed up his testimony with, "He-he-he was ju-ju-ju-just a-laying there d-d-d-d-dead as a hammer."

When New Doctor testified that Betsill had a broken neck, the coroner ruled it was death by accident and that was that. Nobody even mentioned the question of a blood alcohol test, which proved that the Cofield name still amounted to something in our town and was somewhat of a comfort to me. P.L. Arnall was also the coroner, and I've always suspected that he didn't want any dealings with those Cofield kids about an autopsy or anything else that he could avoid. He signed that death certificate with a flourish. We really do look after our own.

At Betsill's funeral, one of the preachers expounded on what a full life he had led. He mentioned that Betsill had been born after the airplane but before radio and television. During his lifetime he had seen the development of the jet engine, space flight, a man walking on the moon, computer technology, and the Internet and that in his astute financial dealings had at least peripherally benefited from each of them. He didn't mention that he had witnessed and objected strenuously to the price of coffee rising for some brands to eight dollars a pound.

Chapter 21

Our schools all over the county had been segregated since there were any schools here, and there was no arguing the fact that the black schools were glaringly inferior to the white ones. There was also no need denying that there was a great deal of bitter rhetoric about mingling of the races and the dire results that were sure to follow. Well, let me tell you, I've never been prouder of our town and county than when racial integration occurred in our schools.

I've always been ashamed that it took a bunch of yankees to prove to us how wrong we had been about segregation; it had for a long time been a little prickle in my consciousness, but I was a creature of my time and place and I had drifted along, never having any inclination to be a local leader, let alone any sort of activist.

Well, I am here to tell you, our little county was held up in Washington as a model of how integration should occur. We did it abruptly, from kindergarten through high school, all in one day and without a single untoward incident. I give a lot of credit to our sheriff. He was a WWII veteran with hands as big as pork shoulders and his own shoulders as wide and heavily muscled as a side of beef.

He had grown up with as much race prejudice as any of the rest of us, but he had never let it interfere with his law enforcement: he would knock a white miscreant to the ground just as quick as he would a black one and nobody thought anything about it. He had even turned Miss Lottie Ashmore's twenty-year-old son over his knee when he arrested him the third time for being drunk in public and spanked him 'til his butt was blue. Then he told him that wasn't a circumstance to what he'd do to him if he ever heard of him taking another drink of liquor.

That was before we had an AA chapter in our town, but Lamar Ashmore never needed one. He went back to college and wound up in later years being principal of one of our high schools. Gloer Ballard was a very influential and dedicated public servant and stayed sheriff 'til he died.

On integration day, Gloer made it a point to be at the schoolhouse where the protestors had gathered. The Klan had experienced a resurgence since *Brown v. Board of Education* but didn't amount to much. Nobody took them seriously but themselves.

They, however, took themselves very seriously and I've never heard any nastier talk before or since than I did in the weeks before our schools were integrated. The Klan was supposed to be a secret organization, but everybody in town knew who they were. There weren't very many of them, but not a one of them had clean fingernails. Oscar Hosey, to his credit, did not belong. In fact, further to his credit, he described the last Klan parade our town ever saw.

"Here come three carloads of jackasses wrapped up in bed sheets with pillowcases for caps down the street in colored town with a cross in the lead truck with red light bulbs shining. All the little black children run out to the side of the road and commenced to laughing and pointing their fingers. It was a hoot. I don't 'spect to see no more night riding in this town; not if any of 'em got bat shit for brains. One little pickaninny even waved at the leader and hollered out, 'How you doing, Mr. Fred?' They going to carry on any more that foolishness they need to get masks declared legal again."

Gloer Ballard was not amused. He let it be known that if the Klan showed up anywhere around the schoolhouse or if he heard any person yell out any insult, he'd slap them flat to the ground and then lock their asses up. What Gloer referred to as slapping was comparable to being round-housed with a twenty-pound ham and, when successfully administered, produced a definite concussion. There was not a citizen in our town who would not choose jail over a slap.

It was a very peaceful integration.

I don't give all the credit to Gloer Ballard, although it came pretty close to being his finest hour. We were still, at that time, a small enough town that everybody, black and white, knew everybody else. The children of maids and of their employers had been playing ball together for years and I don't believe there was a mama in town, black or white, who hadn't issued the dictum which I've come to believe is strictly Southern, and maybe even local: "You just be nice, you hear me?"

I also don't believe that on that distant day when parents had not become afraid of their children and the term "child abuse" had not yet reared its Medusa-like head that there was a single child, black or white, who had not responded, "Yes, ma'am." Courtesy titles were still *de rigueur*.

No ifs, ands, or buts about it, we were integrated and nobody picked up an axe handle and nobody peed in a coffee urn or crapped on a countertop. I keep telling you it's a wonderful town.

On top of that, within two months I don't believe there was an athletic director in any high school in Georgia who wanted segregation back.

I still attribute, however, the major portion of credit for our local tranquility to the families of our town. As small as our town was, the families, black and white, had known each other for generations and had managed to get along for the most part with mutual consideration and courtesy, even through racial oppression and occasional heinous injustices.

I didn't hear much about how integration affected the children, but the white teachers were as apprehensive as a horse crossing a wooden bridge. One of the ladies from an old family hereabouts who had no rural background and had consequently never had any close association with Negroes, told me, "Aloysius, I know it was foolish of me and realized it at the time, but I had this deep-seated fear that if I touched one, the black might come off on my hands."

In those days the women, white or black, were ladies. If they weren't born that way, becoming a teacher conferred it upon them, and we all respected them. The vast majority of them taught because of inner passion and not just for a paycheck.

As far as I could tell, the teachers rapidly became comfortable in their newly integrated classrooms and saw each child as an individual with individual needs and abilities. We now have five high schools in our county and last year one of our black graduates went to Harvard as a National Merit Scholar. I think he'll be all right, though.

The county next to us hasn't been so fortunate in maintaining academic excellence in its schools. They have a much higher percentage of dropouts than the state average, and the majority of their students, I am sorry to say, are black and from broken families and apparently ride that condition like it was a horse of privilege.

I had a fascinating encounter at a local establishment with one of the teachers from there. It turned out she is an immigrant some twenty years ago from Germany, a widow, an accomplished musician who teaches in an all-black school; highly intelligent but also mirthful. She is full of the joy of living, proud to be an American, and if I were twenty years younger I'd be quoting Browning and Millay to her and moving in for conquest.

"I have for ten years been teaching music in that school, but our new principal is, I am convinced, trying to get rid of every white teacher in her school. Discipline is deplorable since she took over. Last week one of my classes got completely out of control despite all I could do, yelling, laughing, singing, swearing, throwing things at each other. To the principal I went and asked her help, and you know what she said to me? 'You don't understand. It's their culture. You must learn to deal with it.'

"I could not believe my ears. I looked at her for a minute and then got right in her face and screamed as loud as I could. She stepped back and said, 'This is unforgivable. Control yourself.' And I said, 'You don't understand. I'm Jewish and this is my culture. Deal with it.' I have my application in to teach in your county next year."

I'm interested to see if she gets a position and recommended that before she developed what some people around here call an attitude, she go by our library and get acquainted with the head of our library services. This lady is a Mississippi native who is very beautifully black and as full of intelligence and joy as my new friend. They'll get along well together and I anticipate a lot of laughter. I'll bet they learn a lot from each other, and I fully expect this Jewess to be playing some instrument on next year's Blended Heritage Night at our library. That librarian is a wizard.

Early in my law career, not long after Harry Truman had integrated the armed forces, I had my first black client. Willie Hugh Swanson was the middle son in a very respectable black family in our town. He hired me to represent him in a bastardy trial, a most unusual event given the mores of the times.

The reason he hired me was convoluted. His girlfriend, also a member of a very respectable family, had a baby. She was tall and willowy, and had finished high school, possessed a lovely voice, and sang in the choir. Their romance had been a rocky one. Willie Hugh had dropped out as soon as he hit sixteen and had a good job as a truck driver. He was a few years older than Ruthie Mae Hunnicutt and apparently had been a little too domineering for her taste and they had frequent arguments, but no fights.

"I ain't never hit her the first lick, Mr. Buster," he assured me. "We just holler and yell at each other when we have a disagreement, and she usually win; she got the highest voice you ever heard, and when she mad and crank it up, hit'll make your eardrums rattle. So she usually win. Arguing just ain't worth it."

I felt immediate affinity for him.

"Willie Hugh, I need some facts here. Are you sure the baby is not yours? Have you not had sex with Ruthie Mae? If I'm going to be your lawyer, you must tell me the complete truth."

"Oh yes, sir, Mr. Buster. We had sex, the best in the world. You know Ruthie Mae; she the purtiest gal in town, and when she ain't mad, she the sweetest and most loving. Smart as a whip, too. I ain't denying I had sex with her and that at just about the right time for her to cotch. I ain't disputing the baby might be mine, but it done got to be a sticking point between us that he might not be mine."

"You mean she had another lover, Willie Hugh?"

"No, sir. I mean, she had two other mens. Both on the same night. Hit was a Saridy and two soldiers had come in here from Fort Benning and she took on both of 'em in they automobile and then brag to me about it. We got back together and the baby come and she mad 'cause I won't pay her no child support. She hurt my feelings bad and she vow she go take me to court and 'We'll just see 'bout that, Mr. High-and-Mighty-Big-Dick Willie Hugh Swanson,' she say."

"Willie Hugh, are you sure this baby isn't yours?"

"No, sir, Mr. Buster. I'm reasonable sure he bound to be mine. My brothers say he look like he been dug out my ass with a toothpick, and ain't no denying he my baby."

"Then, Willie Hugh, what's the problem?"

"Mr. Buster, Miss Ruby Blisssit taught me civics before I drop out of school and go to work. Say this country founded on justice for all and that a man innocent twell he prove guilty. Ruthie Mae done yell and scream at me so much I just had to call her hand when she say she go sue, else I never will be able to get along with her. She gotta prove it."

This was eons before DNA, and I responded, "You better be sure she doesn't bring the baby to court, Willie Hugh. The case will be heard before the probate judge and there won't be a jury. You sure you want to go through with this?"

"Yes, sir, Mr. Buster, my manhood on the line now. How much you go charge me?"

I looked at him steadily and his gaze never faltered. I have never had my choice of bachelorhood more pointedly confirmed.

I tapped my teeth with a pencil while I pondered. Finally, I said, "Willie Hugh, I'll charge you fifty dollars if we win and not one red cent if we lose."

If he hadn't brought Miss Ruby Blissit and her civics class into it, I'd have turned him down flat and referred him to Bill Hardwick.

That trial remains a vivid experience in my memory, although by now I think everyone else has forgotten it. We went through the ritual of the bailiff reading the accusation and the judge asking the plaintiff to stand. You could tell the judge was nursing a hangover. He had been pretty testy all morning and was wearing dark glasses to conceal reddened eyes. He raised the glasses a little while he read the indictment.

"Miss Ruthie Mae Hunnicutt, is that correct?"

"Yes it is, your Honor."

"And who is your counsel?"

"Say which?"

"Your counsel. You know, your lawyer. Do you have a lawyer to represent you?"

"No, sir."

"You are aware that the defendant has employed a very able attorney, aren't you?"

"It make no difference to me what Mr. Willie Hugh Swanson do, Judge, long as he pay me child support for my baby."

"Miss Hunnicutt, that is not what this trial is about. The complaint before this court is proof of parenthood. Any other consideration follows after the presentation of evidence and final decision. If the defendant has a lawyer and you have none, you might be at some disadvantage. Do you wish me to appoint you an attorney?"

"No, sir, Judge. I will represent myself."

"Have you had any experience, Miss Hunnicutt?"

"Yes, your Honor, nearly 'bout all of it with Willie Hugh Swanson."

There were a few titters in the courtroom which the judge silenced by raising his glasses and glaring. I knew he wasn't about to endure the sharp sound of his gavel. He continued.

"Miss Hunnicutt, I am speaking of legal experience in a court of law. I feel that you need someone to represent you."

"I will represent myself, Your Honor. I don't need any lawyer; the truth is on my side."

"What a novel concept, Miss Hunnicutt. You may proceed."

Ruthie Mae was most impressive. Her syntax may have been weak but her appearance made up for it. Tall and very black, long-necked and unconsciously regal, lips painted bright red beneath an aquiline nose, there was not a male in the courtroom who was not more than a little envious of Willie Hugh Swanson.

"I am black, but comely, o ye daughters of Jerusalem, as the cedars of Lebanon, as the tents of Kedar" kept rising in my mind, but I had a job to do. This was no time for poetry and also no time to muse on Solomon and Sheba.

When she finished her recital and plea, the judge inquired if she had any witnesses to call.

"No, Your Honor, nobody else know anything about all this but that sorry, low-down Willie Hugh Swanson, and he'd be bound to lie."

I arose and said, "Your Honor, I object. In representing my client, I have only one witness to call, and that is the plaintiff herself. If you would, please have her sworn in."

She shouldn't have said that about Willie Hugh. I had bonded with him, and in contrast to Ruthie Mae's affect of serene authority, he was as nervous as a hen on a hot hoe and was sweating like an eleven o'clock mule. Also, I could hear him sucking his teeth.

I rose to earn my fifty dollars.

"Miss Hunnicutt, can you give me the length of the human gestation period?"

"I be glad to, Mr. Buster, do you esplain your querstion."

Dammit, she was going to be cordial and even familiar with me from the years she had come with her mama to help clean my mama's house. This was not going to be easy. She was absolutely at ease on that witness stand.

"Ruthie Mae, how long does it take to make a baby?"

"Well, Mr. Buster, it all depend. Some time 'bout haffa nour; sometimes seem like no more'n ten-fifteen seconds."

I maintained my composure while the judge winced and brought his gavel into play. I felt my face flushing; it's that damned blonde hair. When the courtroom had quieted, I continued.

"Ruthie Mae, how long after one makes the baby, as you have so revealingly testified, before the baby is born?"

"Oh," she said. "'Bout nine months, give or take a week or two. Mr. Buster, you know *that*."

I coughed and continued.

"And now, Ruthie Mae, you are asserting that approximately nine months before the birth of your child you had sexual congress with my client, Mr. Willie Hugh Swanson?"

"Mr. Buster, I swear on God's holy book to tell the truth; the answer is ''nen some.'"

This girl was taking too much control of the situation and was beginning to get under my skin. I looked at Willie Hugh. His head was bowed, he was trembling like a leaf in a brisk breeze, and drops of sweat were dripping from his nose and chin. He kept mopping the tabletop with his coat sleeve. I spoke with as much intimidating formality as I could muster.

"Miss Hunnicutt, I admire your dedication to the truth. It is an admirable virtue, and continuing on that path, did you also have sex with any other man besides Mr. Swanson approximately nine months before your baby was born?"

She didn't flinch or bat an eye. "Yes, I did."

"Did you, by any chance, have sex with more than one other man during the same period of time?"

With royal dignity came the reply, "I know Willie Hugh has already told you, Mr. Buster. They was two of them."

"Could you give this court their names, Miss Hunnicutt?"

"No, I couldn't."

"And why not, Miss Hunnicutt?"

"Because I disremember them. One called hisself Paul and said he from Alabama; the other one say his name Lionel or something like that and he from off somewhere because he talk funny. I don't think they even introduce they last names. To the best of my memory, that is."

"I see. And now, Miss Hunnicutt, could you recount for the court how you met these two men and why you granted them your favor? At that particular time?"

That young woman sat with hands folded calmly in her lap, spine straight and not touching the chair, chin uptilted, and began. I thought briefly of Sheba addressing her subjects or of Marie

Antoinette suggesting that hers eat cake. She was definitely queenly; I was impressed.

"Well, Willie Hugh and me had a date on Friday night and he made me so mad I decided if I had the chance, I'd just show him he wasn't the only man I could please. And on Saridy evening just about dusk dark I was walking down Church Street and this big Cadillac stopped. They was two soldier mens in it and one of them say to me, 'Gal, where the action in this town?' And I say, 'What kind action you talking about? We just finished choir practice and the church empty by now.'

"And the one call hisself Lionel, I find out later (he was the one driving the car), say, 'Ain't they some place we can buy a beer?' And I say, 'Well, not official; we dry in this county. Mr. Bubba Eason done close up by now and he don't sell it to nobody he don't know real well anyhow. You might try Head Durham's House of Shine if he ain't done sold out by now.'

"And the one who turned out to be Paul say, 'How 'bout hopping in and show us where this place is.' And with that he got out the car and hold the door open for me to sit in the middle. Then he say how come a good-looking gal like me all alone on Saridy night, and I say I was just axing myself the same querstion, and I got in the car with them."

She paused and looked at Willie Hugh. He never raised his head. A loud sniffle as he used his coat sleeve on his nose was the only sound to break the silence.

"And then one thing just sort of natural led to another. They got theyselves a six-pack at Head's and found a place to park. They try to get me to drink a beer and I told them real quick that I don't drink any kind of alcohol. It's against my principles.

"And then they commenced to hugging on me and talking 'bout how lonely a soldier's life is and how they need a woman and we all got out the car and I climb in the back seat with one, Lionel I think it was, whilst the other one stand outside and smoke a cigarette. And then they change places and then they carry me home. That's it. I have never seen them since."

I moved in. "And this encounter with those two soldiers occurred one night after you had sex with my client."

"Yes it did, Mr. Buster."

"Within twenty-four hours you had sex with three different virile young men and you are accusing Willie Hugh Swanson of being the one who got you pregnant?"

"Yes I am. I'm absolutely sure of it."

"And how, Miss Hunnicutt, can you be sure?"

She lowered her eyes and manifested the first sound of embarrassment in her voice.

"I know, Mr. Buster, I know it was Willie Hugh. I'm sure of it."

"And how can you be so sure, may I ask?"

"Just because."

I waited.

"Because both of the soldier boys used, you know, *protection*, and Willie Hugh never did."

"And what do you mean by protection, Miss Hunnicutt?"

"You know. You know, they put them rubber things on theyselves."

"You mean condoms, Miss Hunnicutt?"

"That's right."

"Both of them?"

"Both of them. I'm sure of it."

"How can you be so sure?"

"Because I axed and they said they did, that's how."

I bore in.

"And you believed them? Come now, Miss Hunnicutt."

She lost it. With eyes blazing, she rose from the witness chair and shrieked so loudly that the judge dropped his gavel and dislodged his glasses when he fumbled for it. I saw instantly what Willie Hugh meant. "Well! Mr. Buster Holcombe. I didn't just git right down there and look! That wouldn't have been decent or lady-like."

As she resumed her seat and the judge pounded the courtroom to silence, I had recall of Mrs. Sport Cofield and her interaction with

Brother Harold. I turned to Willie Hugh and murmured, "The Colonel's Lady and Judy O'Grady are sisters under the skin."

"Say which, Mr. Buster?" He raised his head.

"Put your pride in your pocket, get your ass off your shoulder, you fool, and marry that girl before somebody beats you to it. If you don't, you'll be sorry the rest of your life."

Of course, I didn't add that the same might be true if he did.

And don't think for a second that I refunded his fifty dollars; I had worked too hard for it. I have some principles myself.

Willie Hugh did follow my advice, however. He and Ruthie Mae had three more children, all of whom have college degrees. The oldest one is now a superior court judge in Fulton County. The name on his birth certificate is Willie Hugh Junior Swanson, but when he went to college it became William Hugh Swanson, Jr. Sometimes progress just inches up on us.

Ruthie Mae strained her vocal cords during her second delivery and now sings alto in the senior choir. Willie Hugh is a happy man.

She was the first black president of our PTA and graduated from Clayton State College with her youngest daughter. She has just been appointed principal of our newest elementary school.

I have always admired Ruthie Mae and appreciated what she has accomplished, not only for herself but for her race and our town.

Chapter 22

The only other legal case I ever had that stands out as a real turning point in my life came about while I was serving a couple of years as attorney for the city. That was after we got big enough to need a lawyer occasionally but not so big yet that we required one full-time. It was after a good many of the roads were paved and some shortsighted city council had allowed a few apartments to be built in the city, purely in defiance, I always thought, of Mr. Big Buncombe Braswell and his rigid restrictions about apartments in the county outside of the city limits.

I still praise Mr. Big Bunc's name whenever I get the opportunity.

Also, it was after we were so big that we had to have a full-time police force of about four policemen and a chief and not a one of them hauled garbage or read water meters, either. I mean, progress had come upon us.

The council had selected a member of one of the pioneer families out in the county to serve as chief of police of our city, and he had the uniform and badge and cap to prove it. He was tall and lean with strap-like muscles, and his speech was heavily accented by our region; at age forty-five he had resisted succumbing to the progress most of our natives had made in grammar and diction. He was who he was and what he was, and he had definite principles and opinions about law enforcement.

Even though he had spent his time in the army and had made sergeant in the MPs and brought home a Japanese war bride who spoke good enough English, he never saw any reason to ape anyone else. She never mastered "y'all" and he forever teased her about it. He never ate sushi.

His family had subsisted for generations on a fifty-acre farm, the soil of which they had pretty well leached out with repetitive cotton farming, but they were a proud clan and always married respectable women who never put on airs or bobbed their hair.

His mama had escaped the farm and married an outsider when the price of cotton bottomed out. Her husband set up a barbershop, and they prospered for a while, until the barber manifested a propensity for diddling little boys under the drape while cutting their hair.

The parents were enraged but enraged quietly; in those days we didn't put private laundry on the front page of the newspaper, and there were still some things people just did not discuss, not even Carlotta Melrose and certainly not Beatrice. Beatrice just started sending her boys to the barber on the other side of town and never mentioned why. This was probably a tremendous exercise in restraint on her part, but as I have said, there were still some things we just did not discuss.

None of the fathers of the considerable number of boys involved had seen it coming, although one of them later said, "I wondered how come that damn barber asked me why I didn't have my boy circumcised." That's always seemed to me like a good enough backwoods example of *naivete*.

I think the other fathers involved would have settled for beating the man to a pulp and running him out of town, but there was a salty old maid from the next county who, under considerable stress, was raising two great-nephews, and be blessed if she didn't go to the sheriff and take out a warrant, and the barber wound up spending three years in jail and we never heard from him again.

His wife went back to the family farm, got little jobs sewing or anything that was ultra respectable, and raised her son with the help of her daddy and her brothers, of which she had a whole gaggle. If homosexuality is genetic, it has to be on a recessive gene, for that boy grew up a wizard with the women, and Oscar Hosey said, "He'll frig anything what squats to pee."

On top of that, he was a star football player when our school got big enough to have a football program. He was long-legged and bow-legged and he loped instead of running, but nobody could ever catch him, and every now and then he'd jump plumb over somebody who tried to tackle him and tear on off down the field for a touchdown. The fans got where they'd expect it from him, and that's how he got the nickname of "Jump"; not from his sexual prowess. Oscar Hosey suggested "Hump" as a substitute, but it never caught on.

At any rate, when he got to be chief of police in our town, he had settled down and did a great job. He wasn't as rough or explosive as Sheriff Ballard had been, and he never raised his voice nor lost his good-ole-boy drawl, but he evermore enforced the law and tolerated no foolishness.

One night at city council meeting the mayor noted that one of the agenda concerned a citizen's complaint about the police department, and he had asked Chief Jump Henson to be present. Word had leaked out that the complainant was an airline pilot who was renting an apartment and had become involved in a fracas with a neighbor, who had called the police. Everybody in our town was a little wary around airline pilots and a little dubious about whether they were real flesh-and-blood, sweat-and-salt human beings who could do anything except play golf and brag and marry more than once, so we had a large turnout at council meeting.

When the mayor called for citizen input, he dropped all the joviality and bonhomie that he usually affected and that had kept him in office for upwards of fifteen years and adopted his grave and judicial manner. I mean, in a flash he quit grinning and the corners of his eyes and jowls drooped and he was evermore serious. It always fascinated me. In a split second, right before your eyes, it was like watching a jack-o-lantern morph into a bloodhound, and it always created its own atmosphere. I don't recall our mayor having to use his gavel before that night.

"Will you step forward and state your name, please?"

The pilot obliged. The mayor carefully and slowly wrote it down.

"And your address, please?"

"101 Stonewall Jackson Court, Apartment 2A." He sort of snapped it out and didn't say "Your Honor."

Mistake number one, I thought.

If it annoyed the mayor, there was no evidence of it; if anything, it only slowed down his penmanship.

"Is that your permanent address, Mr. Tomlinson?"

"Certainly not. Just as soon as our house in Magnoliadale is finished, my wife and I are moving. Probably within two months. I sure hope so."

"I see," said the mayor. There was just a hint of smugness in his voice and several in the audience sat noticeably straighter. "I believe, sir, that you have requested a public audience to voice a complaint against our law enforcement body; is that true?"

"Correct," came the sharp reply.

"Well, here is the council, here is the public, and here is the police chief. Proceed, sir. And," he added, "we are all ears."

The man consulted a little notebook. "On the night of October 12, my wife and I were grilling dinner on our patio. We had a radio playing. The tenants in the next apartment, who have been very rude ever since we moved in, complained about the noise and even used profanity. One thing led to another and someone called the police. I had gone inside and brought my pistol out and had it lying on the table, just in case the neighbors in the other patio became more aggressive.

"When Chief Henson arrived, he threatened me with bodily harm. In fact, he also insulted me and used opprobrious language in front of my wife, and I am here to demand a personal apology from him in public. If that is not forthcoming at this meeting tonight, I am prepared to sue the city."

"Well, now, Mr. Tomlinson," our mayor said very calmly but very seriously, "that in itself sounds almost like a threat to me, as head of the city government. How did Chief Henson insult and threaten you with bodily harm? Will you please elaborate and be more specific?"

The mayor wouldn't have used those big words if that pilot had not pulled "opprobrious" on him.

"He walked out on my patio all swelled up and belligerent and talking like a hick, except real loud. He started walking pretty rapidly toward me. I felt intimidated and cautioned him that I had a pistol and, if I needed it in self-defense, I was prepared to use it.

"That's when he insulted me and my wife and used vile language and threatened me. And I am here for an apology."

That's when the mayor said, "Be specific, sir. Exactly what did Chief Henson say to you?"

The man drew a deep breath and responded with a note of both defiance and belligerence. "He said, and I quote directly, 'If you point that gun at me, I'll cram it up your goddam ass.' Now, that's exactly what he said, and I'm not leaving here without an apology. Else, I'll sue."

He sat down. He was red-faced, breathing hard and trembling, but at least he sat down. The room was unnaturally quiet. It felt like every person in there was holding his breath.

"Chief Henson, could you respond?"

Jump was among home folks, some of them kin, and you could tell he wasn't flustered. He strolled over from his seat in the corner. "Your Honor," he began, and you could see the mayor's jowls tighten, not that he smiled, but his lips formed a little straighter line.

"Lemme give you'n the council a little background on this Mr. Tomlinson. Seems like ever time he's home from a flight, there's a ruckus down there in them apartments, en he's allus at the center of it. He cain't git along with nobody.

"My men been called down there to quiet him down a total of seven times, en I got they reports to show effen you need them. He's right about me being a little what you might call impatient when I answered the call that evening, but I never threatened him. I said something like, 'Whatcha been up to this time, Mr. Tomlinson, to stir up a ruckus?' as I was walkin' toward him.

"His gun was laying there on the patio table..." (I wanted to interrupt and say "lying" but figured if Mrs. Jimmie Kate Cole hadn't been able to change him, I sure couldn't; so I kept my mouth shut.)

"I seen it a-laying there but he didn't have it in hand or nothing and then he pops out with that business about he was prepared to use it on me."

I couldn't help but admire Jump Henson. He was maintaining his laconic drawl without rancor or raising his voice, and his grammar, if anything, was ever so slightly improved. Jump was his own man and was buckling to no one.

"That's when I became what you might call threatened my own self. And I did tell him what I'd do with that gun effen he drawed it on me. As I recollect, Your Honor, I never used God's name in that conversation; I just very plainly told him where I'd place that gun effen he did draw it; and I would have, too, but it would have been not in my nature to use the Lord's name in vain. I was raised better'n that."

"Chief Henson, Mr. Tomlinson is demanding an apology from you. How do you feel about that?"

So help me, Jump paused a long moment during which he scratched his head. Andy Griffith in his heyday couldn't have done it better.

"Your Honor, considering everthing and being plumb honest about it, I still and yet feel exactly the same way. Effen he was to draw a gun on me, that's exactly what I'd do with it, and I cain't in all honesty offer no apology for it."

Mr. Tomlinson sprang to his feet. "Mr. Mayor," he yelled, "I did not draw my gun on him! His conduct was and is deplorable, and as a citizen I absolutely demand a resolution of this. I will accept his apology and nothing less. You can force him to apologize; you are the mayor."

Jump's response was immediate, but his speech remained unhurried. "Your Honor, effen you or anybody else tries to make me apologize, then I reckon you can have my badge right now."

There was a loud murmur swelling from the crowd, and the mayor raised his gavel. Before he could bring it down, I spoke up. I couldn't bear to see the mayor's record ruined.

"Mr. Mayor, Your Honor," I said.

He let the gavel down slowly. The murmur ceased. "Yes, Mr. Holcombe? You wish to speak?"

"Yes, Your Honor, as your counsel I feel impelled to do so."

I rose from my chair behind the council and came to the center of the room. I felt just like Perry Mason.

"Mr. Tomlinson, you assert that you did *not* point your gun at the chief of police; is that correct?"

"It most certainly is! I never made a move to touch it."

"Then this so-called threat is founded on an unfulfilled supposition, namely the word *if*. In other words, it is implied that if you did not point your gun at Chief Henson, he would not cram it up your ass, correct?"

I quit feeling like Perry Mason but was glad my mama couldn't hear me talking like that.

Tomlinson looked a little confused. Good.

"Well, yes, I suppose."

"Well, sir, if Chief Henson tells you in public, tonight, in the presence of the mayor and council, that 'If you don't point that gun at me, I will not cram it up your ass,' would that appease you?"

Be blessed if he didn't scratch his head.

"Well, I suppose so. Yes."

I turned to Jump. His jaw was hanging open a little.

"Chief Henson, would you be willing to tell Mr. Tomlinson that if he doesn't draw his gun on you, you will not cram it up his ass?"

He swallowed. Hard. "Say that again?"

I repeated it.

Chief Henson drew himself up straight and tall and proud.

"Mr. Tomlinson, effen you don't never draw a gun on me, I promise you in front of all these folks I will not cram it up your ass."

I was just about to feel relieved when Mr. Tomlinson jumped to his feet.

"Mr. Holcombe!" he yelled.

"Yes?"

"He was not accurate. I will not accept that apology unless he quotes himself exactly. Otherwise, it makes me out to be a liar."

I turned. "Chief?"

He turned red, took a deep breath, and finally drawled, "Effen you don't never draw a gun on me, I won't never cram it up your goddam ass. That's a promise." He surveyed the crowd. "And effen anybody here ever tells my mama about this, they ain't no telling what I'll do to you."

"Mr. Tomlinson?" I said.

"I think Chief Henson just proved my point, and as far as I am concerned, the incident is closed."

The mayor had to bang his gavel three times, but no record was ever broken for a better cause.

I felt like Henry Clay.

For days I basked in some degree of self-adulation and considered that I had uncovered in myself a heretofore unsuspected gift for diplomacy. I even fantasized about expanding my horizons to a national level; perhaps even the United Nations. God knows, they could use some diplomacy and good old horse-trading up there. Then I thought, *No way in hell a Georgia boy could get in there.*

I remembered my dream in New Guinea, considered that Bella Abzug was still active in New York, and settled unobtrusively back into writing wills and recording deeds.

I did bill the city for fifty dollars and received a brief thank-you note from the mayor. I framed it and hung it on my bedroom wall. Sometimes I lie in bed and look at it and reminisce. That airplane pilot proved himself to be a man of some pretty high principles after all, and I've always felt like he could have eventually settled into our town, been accepted, and amounted to something if he just hadn't moved to Magnoliadale. Look at Ruthie Mae.

Then I think about Chief Jump Henson who wound up running for sheriff and has been in office now for more than twenty years, and I suspect he'll stay there until he dies. We always knew he was a person of high principles, but that night in council meeting he proved he had enough flexibility to accommodate common sense when the public weal was at stake.

Be that as it may, I'll guarantee no one ever told his mama a mumbling word about that meeting. At her funeral, I was the only pallbearer who had on a dark suit and black shoes, and she had as serene a look on her face as any corpse I've ever viewed. That P.L. Arnall is a wizard with worry lines above the nose and wrinkles, but I've always felt that part of her serenity was that she had never learned that her only son had taken the Lord's name in vain in a public meeting.

As I have said before, this is a marvelous town, and we sure tend to look after our own.

Chapter 23

Most people have no idea how wonderful our town truly is. That's because of all this new prosperity we've had. So many new people have moved in that you hardly know anybody on the streets anymore. Instead of Mize's Grocery and Ingram's, we now have Kroger and Ingles and Big Lots and Winn-Dixie and Publix and also such an influx of pharmacies that we have a drugstore on nearly every corner, and be blessed if they don't all sell groceries, too. Even Wal-Marts.

That place has about five acres under one roof, and you've had a workout if you walk across it about twice in a row. All these places are swarming with people and nobody knows anybody anymore.

We're getting a bad attitude also. More like New York City every day, what with all the traffic and everybody being in such a hurry. Somebody even honked their horn at Lee Hugh Crews a few years ago because he was a little slow moving off when the light changed. Lee Hugh's family has been here for five generations and he is hard to impress. He turned off his motor and went back to the car behind him and politely inquired, "Did you want me for something, fellow?"

"Hell, no," the man answered, "I just want you to move that truck. I have an appointment in Atlanta I can't be late for."

"You're not from around here, are you, mister?" Lee Hugh asked and shifted his cud of Red Man from his left cheek to his right. Anybody who knew Lee Hugh would have recognized this as a danger signal.

"What in the hell has that got to do with it?" snarled the man.

"Just about ever thing, I reckon," said Lee Hugh. Then he reached in the back of his truck, grabbed a tire tool, and smashed both the man's headlights and bumped his own back fenders enough to dent them.

"Let me tell you something, mister. The longest day you live don't you honk your horn behind a car in this town ever again. Now then, do you want to move on around me and go about your business and never say a word about this, or do you want to call the police? If you do it'll take three light changes before he can get here, and in the meantime I will have hauled your yankee ass out of that fancy Lexus and stomped the living shit out of you.

"The policeman is my first cousin and I'll swear you rammed me while I was at a dead stop. He'll see those two new dents in my fenders and believe me, not you. If you'll notice, ain't nobody stopped and offered to be a witness. You don't know about kinfolks, do you? It's your call. Speak up, goddammit."

The newcomer very wisely chose the first option. Kin may fight among themselves around here but they form a solid phalanx before outsiders. And most all of us old-timers are kin in one way or another, some of it not mentioned openly.

Lee Hugh became something of a local hero. We natives thought of him as a modern-day Leonidas defending our culture at Thermopylae. When he died, I sent a tire tool smothered in orchids. A bunch of us passed out some bumper stickers we had printed up that said, "Just be nice." A lot of cars still wear the stickers and you hardly ever hear an automobile horn in our town anymore.

You still run into a considerable amount of honking in Magnoliadale, but a great majority of their folks are not from around here and it takes a while for them to adjust to a different culture. You do see a few more of the bumper stickers out there every year, though, and hope does spring eternal in the human breast. If our town has it, Magnoliadale can get it, although it may take several generations.

We may owe Lee Hugh Crews for changing some attitudes and we certainly owe a lot to Gloer Ballard for peaceful racial integration, but don't leave out Mr. Big Bunc Braswell. He's the one who got such stringent zoning passed in our county that it takes prosperous people to buy a house and lot around here.

That, in turn, has led to superior schools, and that has had the domino effect of attracting more upper-level income families who are concerned about the education of their children. Black and white. I find as many black families as white who want to get their children out of the high-crime areas of Fulton and Clayton counties.

Also, I give kudos to our local law enforcement. We don't tolerate drug trafficking of any sort in this county. We have a diligent sheriff and policemen who work with stern judges, and the whole community is behind them. Our town has a reputation for breaking up meth labs, and Magnoliadale has a reputation for apprehending child molesters on the Internet. I guess everybody has to have a specialty of some sort these days.

One of my clients said just before he left for a ten-year sentence resulting from dealing in cocaine, "God hoss, you ain't safe nowhere." That was just his outlook. Most of us feel pretty safe around here, although I have noticed that some years ago people started locking their houses at night and almost everybody nowadays locks the car when they get out of it.

Progress will do that to you, and Mr. Johnnie Cofield was right about paving the roads.

I also need to brag on Oscar Hosey a little bit for putting some things in proper perspective. About six months before he died, he was playing checkers with old man Mance Turner and somebody came up and grumbled about our black, educated, and prosperous newcomers and said they had an "attitude." Oscar said, "Whatcha mean by attitude? Crown that king, Mance."

"Well, a lot of them are arrogant and snappish when dealing with store clerks and such."

"Oh," said Oscar, "you mean they got they ass on they shoulder. I know what you mean; I've seen it all my life, but it shor ain't a racial thing for some folks to get in that predicament. I just didn't know you called it 'attitude.'" He paused and spit snuff in his Coke bottle.

"You know why them kind of folks wear they ass up on they shoulder, don't you? It's the most convenient location for them to get they heads up it. And first news you know, they begin to like the view and, for all I know, the smell. That's all the checkers I want today, Mance."

Oscar tried to get somebody to print up a bumper sticker that said, "Just get your head out your ass," but he wasn't successful.

I sure miss Oscar; he added a lot to the flavor of our town and he sure had his own principles.

When I walked away from Oscar's casket, I thought back to my early teens when I had a meaningful encounter with him. I was on my way to a piano lesson with Miss Gayflowers and he was reared back on a bench by the courthouse, whittling on a stick. The newest Baptist preacher was talking to him most earnestly and I couldn't help stopping to listen. I had heard Papa say that every preacher that came to the Baptist church always set out to save Oscar Hosey's soul, and I was curious to see how it was done.

I got in at the tail end of it. All I heard was Oscar say, "Preacher, I tell you what I'll do. Effen you'll sign a affydavit that there's a sign over the Pearly Gates with big gold letters that says, 'Fucking don't count,' I'll be in your church next Sunday soon as the doors open."

Well, sir, that preacher sucked in his little potbelly, held his head high, and said, "Mr. Hosey, you are doomed, but I will pray for you."

With that, Oscar said, "And I'll pray for you, too, Preacher, for I don't think you're getting much."

That preacher left with the straightest spine and the fastest walk you ever saw. I thought about what Mrs. Melrose had said about Mr. Bazemore when Mr. Ed Cofield shot off her pecan limb.

Oscar looked at me. "Whatcha turning so red for, Boy? With them blue eyes and white hair you look like the American flag. It ain't natural for folks to preach *against* nature. And if you think them Baptists is prudes, I hear tell the Catholic preachers ain't allowed to git any at all. Not even oncet. Not here and for sure and certain not in the hereafter.

"And whilst I'm at it, that Pope fellow would be a heap closer to God doing the big nasty in a hayloft somewheres than he is setting on a throne in a white dress and letting folks kiss his finger ring."

He paused and cut a long curl out of his stick. "Now, that's just my opinion, but it's very true.

"And I tell you one other thing: effen you ever want to git a Baptist preacher off your back, just mash his pussy button. Don't ever fergit that, Boy. Hit'll work ever time."

I scampered off late to Miss Gayflowers and made such a hash out of Mozart's "Turkish Rondo" that she asked me if I'd been practicing like she told me. I told her I was just a little distracted and promised to do better next week. And I did. That was when she told me I was about ready to tackle "The Flight of the Bumblebee."

After I grew up, Oscar and I got to be good friends, despite the difference in our ages. About two months before he died he told me, "All this whooping and hollering about life after death and many mansions in our Father's house jest don't hack it with me. When I die I hope whoever speaks at my funeral will git up and say, 'He's dead!', and set down; don't say another mumbling word.

"And I'm leaving instructions that whoever gits up to pray is allowed jest one word and shuts up. That one word, Buster Holcombe, is 'Jesus'! And for anybody with bat brains that covers about everything you need to think about."

He spit and wiped his mouth on his coat sleeve.

"All these religions, seems to me, is hung up on after-life and sex anyhow. You take these Mooselooms that has lately come to everbody's attention for instance; God knows they ain't thinking straight. Going around blowing themselves up all over Israel cause they think it gives them a fast ticket to Paradise where seventy-two virgins is waiting for them. They don't even consider that they git seventy-two mothers-in-law with that package, and at least two to three hundred brothers-in-law what ain't got no job and wanta borrow money.

"And here lately be blessed if they ain't got a few women doing the same thing. All in the name of Allah, for Pete's sake. Effen them women git seventy-two male virgins, me'n you both know hit ain't gonna take but ten seconds apiece to knock the first bloom off them fellows and for all the rest of eternity that pore woman's gonna have all them mothers-in-law and no telling how many sisters-in-law criticizing ever move she makes.

"They'n call it Paradise effen they wanta, hit's still a free country, but it sounds like pure old Hell before breakfast to me. They just ain't much excuse for all these rules these religions swear by, anyhow."

I felt bold enough to interpose, "I guess they all have faith, Mr. Oscar. You know what faith is, don't you?"

With this he filled his lower lip again and sputtered, "There you go. In addition to sex and heaven they all gotta drag faith into it. You mighty right I know what faith is; hit's believing something you know goddam well ain't so."

After I'd become so addicted to poetry and what I could accomplish with it, I felt guilty about going to church and taking Communion because I frankly had no intention of abandoning my evil ways and henceforth leading a better life. For Pete's sake, how better a life could you get?

Then when I got in college and the navy and completely away from Mama, I quit going to church altogether, but I'd be the first to admit that I truly missed it.

When I went to law school and watched how young law students could twist things around in moot court while the professors beamed in approbation, I got to considering that maybe I wasn't so bad after all and that there was a lot more in the Bible than Number Seven. Adultery is defined as sex outside of marriage and since I wasn't married, and had no intention of ever being, there was no way I could be an adulterer. I was just a plain old everyday, walking-around, put-your-pants-on-one-leg-at-the-time, enthusiastic fornicator, and the Big Ten doesn't say a word about fornication. It sure felt good to get back home and into the church, and since the preachers wanted soft music all through the Communion service, they always came to the piano and served me my grape juice and crackers first of all. Such a deal.

On first Sunday every month, I always make a little prayer for Oscar Hosey and thank the Lord for his insight, but I never mention that stupid Baptist preacher, nor yet the Muslims or Catholics. This may be very puerile religious philosophy, but it has served me well and been a great comfort.

Oscar's wife asked me to speak at his funeral; said I was the only one in town he thought had a lick of sense. When they'd been married about thirty years, the Hoseys had more or less separated. They still were married, but Mrs. Hosey had been deviling him to get their three-room house wired for electricity and put a pump in the well so they could have a refrigerator and indoor plumbing.

Oscar resisted and they quit being nice to each other.

It was reported and widely quoted that he said, "Effen a man's too lazy to go outdoors to shit, he's too lazy to live."

Me? Stand up in church and say, "He's dead"?

Me? Called on to pray and I stand up and say, "Jesus"?

P.L. had cleaned Oscar up so that nobody recognized him or said he looked natural. His nails were clean and there was no snuff around his lips.

I wasn't about to speak at his funeral; I still had a lick of sense.

But I sure do miss him.

I never saw a Catholic until I went off to college; I thought they would look different. Now we have three Catholic churches, two Catholic schools, a synagogue, a mosque and what passes for a Buddhist temple. I'm sorry Oscar died before I heard him comment on that. He took a dim view of organized religion all the way round. I'm glad I knuckled under to him and didn't quote Tennyson to him.

> Strong Son of God, immortal Love,
> Whom we, that have not seen thy face,
> By faith, and faith alone, embrace,
> Believing where we cannot prove....

I think it was Milton who said, "There lives more faith in honest doubt than in a thousand creeds," but all in all I think Oscar pretty well had a grip on things. I wish he could see our town now; it's just about gone.

We have fancy homes you wouldn't believe, a few of them costing a million dollars or more. Of course, we don't hold a candle to Buckhead or Cobb, but it's getting pretty commonplace to see a bunch of them thrown up for three hundred to five hundred thousands of dollars, and I mean to tell you, they sell, too.

We have industry out the wazoo, most of it over in Magnoliadale, and we have shopping centers—Wal-Mart, Belks, Talbot, Joseph A. Bank; you name it, we have it. And, of course, for those folks who have attitudes, there sits Atlanta with Nieman Marcus, Parisian, and Macy's. Rich's is a thing of the past and there's no place for old-time, middle-of-the-road quality to go.

We started off being Democrats and now we're so Republican that it's been twenty years since the last Democrat was elected to a public office here. An interesting twist to me is that most blacks used to be Republicans and whites solid Democrats and now it's completely reversed. As Mae Pringle would have opined, "Sheesh, bottom rung done got on top." This after she'd had "three drinks, hon, and my limit only two." Gene Talmadge is now a distant memory, unmourned and forgotten. As Major Summerfield once said, "Things are better now."

We have lots of racial diversity. Hispanics are about to outnumber the blacks, and we have lots of Caribbean, Nigerian, Haitian, Cambodian, and Vietnamese immigrants. We even have a couple of Japanese industries out in Magnoliadale, and I get amused listening to our locals grumble about the severity of their work ethic. Nobody remembers picking cotton and pulling fodder from daylight to dark, and I'd be very much surprised if there's a single person in the county who can remember a complete verse of "Just remember Pearl Harbor as we did the Alamo." I confess that, despite my tour in the Pacific, I don't; but then as often as I've played it in the past, I also have trouble remembering the notes of "Dixie." You never hear it anymore. We're all so obsessed with the present that we've buried the past and we're scared to death of the future.

Not me. I can remember when Social Security in this town didn't mean a monthly paycheck but denoted that your womenfolk were members of the UDC. There are still some constants in a few human breasts around here.

I'm no fool. I know the numbers are catching up with me and that sooner rather than later I will join the majority of my old friends in the graveyard. But be damned if I'll be like Prufrock:

> ...I grow old.
> I shall wear the bottoms of my trousers rolled.
> I have measured out my life in coffee spoons.

I'm more like Mae Pringle, "I aim to perk 'til I poop." Or Gibran:

> For what is there to dying but to hang naked in the wind?
> Or to melt into the sun?
> Or to breathing but that the breath ceases its rhythmic labor
> To rise and meet God unencumbered?

At every funeral I've ever attended, either the preacher or some other well-intentioned idiot says, "They're in a better place." Well, that's a bunch of horse hockey; I'm convinced there is no better place than our town. I tend to agree with the philosopher who said, "This is the best of all possible worlds. If it were not, God would not have made it thus." I don't give a hoot about Voltaire and Candide and those fifty strokes on the soles of your feet with a bull pizzle or getting raped by one thousand Barbary pirates. What an imagination but what a warped perspective. You can ride that atheistic BS just so far. I intend to enjoy every minute I have left. I love the seventeen-year-old Millay:

> ...spring silver, autumn gold
> That I shall never more behold,
> Sleeping your myriad magics through
> Close-sepulchered away from you....

Or the older Millay:

"Thou famished grave, I will not fill thee yet;
Roar though thou dost. I am too happy here.
Gnaw thine own sides, fast on.
I will not come anear thy dismal jaws
For many a splendid year."

For God's sake, let's get on with living. Who wants to spend their latter years stooling and drooling in a wheelchair?

All this ruminating on death was instigated by a visit I made to the nursing home. I went by the other day to check on Sara Belle Hipp, who's been there now for six months. She is definitely not with it nor ever again will be. Her girls see to it that she's dressed becomingly and has on her usual makeup. She still has her smile and her social graces up to a point, but I could tell she didn't know me from Adam's housecat; she had a vacant look in her eyes and kept picking at the safety belt they had put on her wheelchair and never called my name. She told me four times, "I never intended to get like this," and twice, "Calhoun's around here somewhere, and he'll want to see you." Calhoun, of course, has been dead ten years.

I stayed maybe five minutes and told her goodbye. I hadn't gone ten feet down the hall before she let out a scream. "I need somebody to help me!"

I stopped dead in my tracks.

"Lord, send somebody to help me! Please, Lord, send somebody to help me! Now, Lord; right now! Please, please, please! Send somebody to help me."

A slight pause and then, without lowering her voice, she yelled, "But not that bitch you sent last time!"

I had never heard her use a bad word in her life.

There was only one nurse on duty in her hall on that shift, the same one and only one who attended her. She came up and soothingly said, "Misris Hipp, honey, you goan be all right. Let me get you some juice. I won't let that ole bad girl get close to you again." She saw me staring and winked broadly while she comforted Sara Belle.

That nurse is fat as a hog and black as tar, and she has a heart, as Oscar Hosey would have said, "as big as her behind and as soft as summer butter." Now, try to tell me this isn't a marvelous town, as old Shakespeare said, "to have such creatures in it."

I still cannot envision a better place to have grown up and watched human nature than our town, but this is as good a stopping place as I can contrive for the journal I promised you. I don't have much more time to write, and you don't have much more time to read.

I think of Mr. B. M. and the Rev. Cleveland Jones, and I don't want to go past 11:40.

Therefore, young Ephraim Holcombe, a.k.a. Bo, the Benediction follows. With heartfelt love and admiration from James Aloysius Holcombe, providentially known as Buster...the only language I can think of in which to say this, without sounding sanctimonious, maudlin, or even ominous, is Spanish: *vaya con dios*.

Benediction

The most exciting thing in ten years happened in our town, and nobody knew about it except me. That's all right, because there isn't anybody else in all this mob who lives here now who would have realized the significance of it; nor relished it properly; nor even have given a rat's ass. Sara Belle Hipp is the last person left in our town who was born a Cofield, and she would have enjoyed it as much as I if she still had all her marbles, but no need to grieve over that.

I was in my office. Reared back in my chair with my feet on the desk. I was trying to memorize Chesterton's "Lepanto," which is not a sexy poem, but I've outlived that anyhow, and it's a marvelous depiction of the age-old struggle between Christianity and those fanatic Muslims. I'm not busy with law anymore, but everybody needs a place to get away from home when they're my age; anything that makes them get up early, bathe, and put on clean clothes and move around, for God's sake. I've been around too many old folks, men and women, in my day who smell nasty or like urine, pure and simply because they've reverted to thinking they only need to bathe once a week. Most of them are also wearing souvenirs of their last several meals, which comes from a combination of trembling hands and drooling. I spend more money on laundry in a week than Betsill Cofield spent in five years on coffee. It's worth it. Mama taught us that cleanliness is next to godliness.

My secretary I've had for fifty years was in what they call rehab recovering from a broken hip, and I was alone in the office when there came a knock on the door.

"Come in!" I yelled, took my feet off the desk and tightened my tie, checking it for spots.

I'm vain about my ties. I keep enough on hand to wear a fresh one every day for six weeks; the minute one gets gravy or a grease spot on it, I give it to one of my lady friends who has rediscovered quilting and buy a new one. I have a few principles of my own. It's fun to have women say, "I love that tie" and to look at them real steady and say, "I like you, too." It leaves most of them flustered or at least a little quizzical. Then, if the person is appreciative, you can say,

> ...I am thy prey and thou shalt have me,
> I cannot starve thee out but I dare say
> That I can stave thee off and I dare defend
> I'll be but bones and jewels on that day
> And leave thee hungry even in the end.

Edna St. Vincent Millay has sure served me well.

There came a second knock, so I got up and opened the door. I knew right off that I was supposed to know the young man standing there, for he sure looked familiar, but for the life of me I couldn't place him.

"Good morning, sir. Are you Mr. Aloysius Holcombe?" He had a funny accent, and anybody from around here of his age would have called me "Mr. Buster Holcombe," so I figured he was probably an attorney wanting to discuss a client with me.

"Yes, I am. And your name, young man?"

"Ephraim Holcombe Mookinfoos, sir, from Vancouver, British Columbia."

I've never fainted in my life, but if I'd been the type, that sure as hell would have been the moment I'd have done it; the whole world seemed to be spinning. I knew, of course, exactly who he was. He was as tall as Bob Cofield and had his carriage, but his hair was straight and jet black, as were his eyes. His skin was dark brown but he definitely had his father's aquiline features. He was what the young folks today would call a hunk or else a stud, and if I were younger I'd have been envious.

"Come in, come in, young man! I'm delighted to see you. Your father, no doubt, is Daniel D. Mookinfoos, Jr."

He had a great deal of assurance about him, and if he was the least bit nervous, it was not manifest. This was my territory; so I adopted the same affect and invited him to a seat.

Then I sat and studied him, making no inquiries or small talk. I learned long ago in my brief encounter with psychotherapy after the Pacific War that total silence is a compelling stimulus to conversation. Also, many years ago I had heard Comer Kelley say of his garrulous mother-in-law, "She don't know nothing; you have to listen to learn something; you'll never learn nothing talking and she ain't never quit."

I sat and I waited. So did he. I never saw a black-eyed billy goat but Ephraim Mookinfoos's gaze sure reminded me of his father.

He answered my question without my ever asking it. "You are wondering about my coloring, Mr. Holcombe. When my father moved to British Columbia, he got in the construction business and, I am told, began immediately to prosper. One afternoon he got an injury to one of his hands, went to the hospital emergency room, and there he met my mother, who was a young and beautiful nurse working with the surgeon."

I waited.

"My mother, Mr. Holcombe, is an Inuit, an Eskimo, if you will."

I never let my gaze move from his nor did I bat an eye. In fact, I was a little relieved.

"He always said that she turned his life around. They had four children, of whom I am the youngest. By the time I came along, he was one of the most prominent men in all of British Columbia. He owned a huge construction company with lots of government contracts. He had purchased a local bank in Vancouver, which prospered so that he built branches in Victoria, Calgary, Banff, and Jasper. In addition to this, he was CEO of the largest timber company in all of northwest Canada; he was president of the regional Boy Scout Council and worked with my brothers and me until we all became Eagle Scouts; and he seemed to have his finger in every pie in B.C."

I thought about Betsill selling puncheons to the black folks in town and about the Cofields in the banking business and pondered on genetics, but like Brer Rabbit, I lay low and say nothing.

"My two older brothers, both of whom have made extremely successful careers for themselves, financially at least, look like me. Both of them are married and have children."

I wondered if old Major Cofield had any idea how far his influence, and his genes, might possibly spread when he came home from the war. Then I thought about Mr. B. M. and quit thinking.

"Our only sister was very short and quite fat." Visions of Miss Pansy resurfaced. I hadn't thought of her in years.

"She had Down Syndrome, Mr. Holcombe. You are familiar with that condition?"

I shifted in my chair and refocused. "Indeed, I am. We have a small school in this community which specializes in teaching and caring for those children."

"I am well aware of that, Mr. Holcombe. It is on the Internet with a Web site that is quite comprehensive. They have a vision of expanding their program to domiciliary care in adulthood when necessary. In other words, from birth to the grave."

I'd never cared for Henry Wallace and his philosophy. I tented my fingers under my chin and waited.

"That is why I am here, at least one of the two reasons. My father spent his childhood here, under a different name, and he always spoke of this as a wonderful town filled with wonderful people. In fact, he said he named me for two of them. I've always wanted to come here and meet any relatives who might still be around and learn more of my father's history; he was always evasive about specifics. When I inquired about my name, he told me it was for two men who had saved his life, one for a doctor who had treated him for meningitis and the other for an attorney who had more or less forced him to look at himself and thereby to turn his life around. Are you that attorney, Mr. Aloysius Holcombe?"

Enough was enough.

"You bet your sweet ass I am, boy, but my friends call me Buster. Keep on talking."

For the first time, he grinned. It must have been pure Eskimo; I never saw that smile on any Cofield face. His eyes slanted almost shut and his cheeks puffed out. I was beginning to feel like I might cry, but not from sadness.

"Before he got Alzheimer's, Father used to tell me this was a wonderful town, but when I would try to pin him down to any details, he'd shut up like a clam and change the subject; tell me I'd have to go and see for myself someday; that he couldn't ever come back here himself; that, anyhow, it would have changed by now."

He paused but I did not rise to the bait. I just kept looking at him.

"Mr. Buster, and I call you that only by your express permission, do you know why my father left this town in the first place?"

"Ephraim," I began, but he interrupted me.

"If I'm to call you Mr. Buster, I need to let you know that my friends have called me Bo all my life; I'd like for you to reciprocate."

I was beginning to like this young man, but I was still a little wary. Some of the Cofields I had known saw the world only as it seemed to them and not as it truly was.

"All right, Bo; to answer your question, I surely do, and I guess I'm the last living person who knows all the details. But before *I* talk, *you*'ve got to do a lot more talking. Let's go back to your first reason for coming here; the school, I believe you said it was."

"Yes, sir. While my parents were both alive, they had grave concerns about the welfare of my sister should she survive both of them."

I nodded my head; I had written several wills addressing exactly the same concern, most of them much more magnanimous and unselfish than the majority of wills I've written.

"Mr. Buster, you need to understand the position of Sister in our family. She was the favorite of all of us; she taught us how to love, how to love each other, if you will, and thereby how to love the rest of mankind in tolerance of all handicaps. She taught us how to laugh;

not just at jokes but in true glee over little things. She kept happiness alive in all of us.

"I was always the closest to her. Mama said it was because she was older than I and had felt like she needed to look after me; had been delighted to help raise a baby."

"Have you ever read a book called *Clowns of God*?" I inquired.

"No, sir."

"You might find a copy and tackle it; I think it would speak to you."

"Anyway, when Mama got breast cancer and before Father got Alzheimer's, they went to court and had me declared the legal guardian of Sister; person and property. Then some man named Betsill Cofield died in this very town and Father got a check for eighty million dollars from his estate."

I couldn't help a little whistle. "I had no idea it had grown that much," I said. "That means he was sitting on three hundred and twenty million dollars over there in that lonesome house."

"Mr. Buster, was Betsill Cofield my grandfather?"

"Yes."

"I thought he had to be, but when I asked, Father would only say that he was a dollar-worshipping old skin-flint who would strain at a gnat and swallow a camel. When I asked him what he meant by that, he said he'd spend a fortune sending his kids to private schools but made them buy their clothes at J. C. Penney's and grudgingly paid a maid fifteen dollars for a seven-day week. Was that true?"

"I have no idea what he paid that maid," I evaded.

"Father laughed and laughed when he saw that check and said he was surprised the old sot hadn't figured out a way to take it with him."

I was feeling very uncomfortable and interrupted, "You were talking of your sister, Bo?"

"That's what I'm getting around to: Father said he'd spent a lifetime proving he didn't need anything from Betsill Cofield, and he divided that check between the four of us. Said it needed to stay in the family."

I did some quick math, sat up straight on my chair, and uncrossed my legs. "I'll just be damned," I blurted out. "You're controlling forty million dollars at your age, young man?"

"Nearer one hundred, Mr. Buster; it's been growing steadily. I've seen to that. Being guardian is a terrific and not always pleasant responsibility."

He paused, which gave me a moment to muse that some genes are so strong they are generation-proof.

"And that is the main reason I have come to this town," he resumed. "I intend to give it all away. Every cent."

Because of years of learned restraint, I managed not to poot, but believe you me I came out of that chair. "Have you lost your fucking mind?"

I couldn't believe I'd said that until I heard it hanging in the air, but at least it beat pooting.

Bo Mookinfoos laughed out loud. "Sit down, Mr. Buster, and relax. My mind is all right; so is my soul, and that's what this is all about. Please, sir, hear me out."

"I'm hanging on every word, Bo, but you're turning my world topsy-turvy. Get on with it and I'll try not to interrupt again, at least not so colloquially."

"Don't fret about that, Mr. Buster. And, to digress a bit, I've heard that question often from Daniel D. Mookinfoos, Jr., and so have my two brothers. After we were all in our teens, of course, and out of earshot of my mother. Or the preacher or the scoutmaster. It's quite an effective tool in encouraging maturity, jerks one up and lays it all out there, you know. Quite challenging question, don't you think?"

I just stared at him.

"I hate to get so personal, Mr. Buster, but there's no way around it. Mama died with breast cancer and I moved in with Father and Sister; I had promised Mama I'd look after Sister and that was the most comfortable way for her, familiar surroundings, stability, and all that stuff. We did all right for a few years; then Father's Alzheimer's got so bad we had to put him in a specialized facility; he doesn't know night from day and recognizes no one.

"My oldest brother is his guardian and executor, but I had the sole care of little Dorothy, or Sister, as we have always called her. When we moved Father out of the house, she went into an abrupt decline, lost her memory and began having seizures. It was awful, but I won't go into detail about that. Suffice it to say that a year and a half ago she died with a seizure the doctors could not reverse.

"I had lived through losing my mama and in reality my father, but I was not prepared for the devastation I endured when Sister died. Mr. Buster, I discovered that the greatest stimulus in my case for working, for living, for being happy, if you will, is to be needed, and all of a sudden not a living soul in the world really and truly needed me.

"I moped so long that my fiancée returned my ring. I needed her but she didn't need me. Erich Fromm said childish love is 'I love you because I need you' and mature love is 'I need you because I love you.' I tried to explain the difference to her, but in six months she married the president of one of Father's banks. Have you ever read Swinburne?

'From too much love of living, from hope and fear set free,
I thank with brief thanksgiving whatever gods may be,
That no man lives forever, that dead men rise up never,
That even the loneliest river winds somewhere safe to sea.'

"My mama was proud of her Eskimo heritage and had told us that when her grandfather got so old he couldn't hunt whales or kill seals, he got in his kayak in the middle of the winter and paddled into the Arctic Ocean without food or water, and that was it."

I marveled at this young man of Anglo-Saxon and Eskimo heritage who had managed to blend both his backgrounds so positively.

Swinburne, indeed. I made a mental note to introduce him to some more poetry about dying if I got the chance. After all, I was a lot closer to it than he was. At the time, however, I said nothing.

"My mother had been reared in a mission school and claimed she'd never even seen an igloo, let alone been inside one. When she left Alaska for nursing school, she never went back. She was a very devout Catholic until she fell in love with my father and he persuaded her to become a Methodist. They used to laugh about it. He had apparently been very adamant about 'tom-fool Popery,' as he called it, and she would giggle and say, 'If you don't like a Pope, why do you keep acting like one?'"

I couldn't help butting in. I laughed and said, "Point well taken, Bo. Believe me, it's genetic."

We were getting pretty relaxed with each other, and I was liking Bo Mookinfoos better by the minute. Nothing like a little crossbreeding to produce exceptional creatures. A Cofield with insight, sensitivity, perception, and compassion? *Come on!* I thought, and then a little verse surfaced in my mind:

> In men whom men condemn as ill
> I find so much of goodness still.
> In men whom men pronounce divine
> I see so much of stain and blot.
> I do not dare to draw a line
> Between the two when God has not.

Point well taken, Buster, I thought to myself.

It turned out I hadn't heard the half of it yet.

"To return to the subject, Mr. Buster, I did more than my share of grieving and it kept recurring to me that if there had ever been anyone I needed because I loved them, it was my sister. And her love for me was so unconditional and absolute and untainted by self. I sure had no need of the money I'd inherited from her, and I resolved to do something exceptional with it in her memory and to her honor.

"I did some research. The University of Washington in Seattle has been a pioneer in research on Down Syndrome and education, and I learned from them that some twenty-five years ago they worked with a trio of mothers in this town to establish an early-learning school here, with accreditation from the University of Washington. That's all the way across the continent! I was impressed.

"From there I went to the Internet and this little school's Web site, and I was even more impressed with their progress, their support from the community, and their vision of establishing a larger campus to provide lifelong support for what they call 'children with special needs,' not just Down Syndrome but autism, fragile-X syndrome, and other rare genetic aberrations. This vision is superhuman and will require more financing than I believe can be acquired even in this open-hearted community."

"I agree with you, Bo. This is a wonderful town, just as your father has told you, but it will be a formidable task to accomplish their goal. An almost impossible one, in fact."

"Hear me out, Mr. Buster. I've done a lot of research and I flew into Atlanta last night, rented a car, and drove down here this morning. I have visited the school and was received most warmly when I explained that my late sister had Down Syndrome. Those people are angels with the children and when I left I felt like I'd been to church. A real church. I don't know about the Pope and Jesus, but I felt like that school was full of the Holy Spirit."

I felt my jaw drop. A Cofield with spirituality. What is this world coming to?

"And now, Mr. Buster, let's get down to brass tacks, the meat of this meeting, if you will. Do you happen to know an eccentric old attorney, one who has never married but has managed to accumulate fifty acres of his family land right next to the courthouse and the library and hold on to it as untouched woodland all through this boom of prosperity that has expanded this village into a thriving small city? Do you know anyone like that, Mr. Aloysius Holcombe?"

That did it. I pooted. I couldn't help it; it just popped out. I'm sure he heard it, but his expression didn't change, although his eyes crinkled in merriment. He knew he had me.

"Where did you learn all that, Smart Alec?" I retorted. "Don't tell me you found it on the Internet, and that property was not easily acquired, let me tell you. I got it by spending my teenage years and a good part of my adulthood kissing up to old maid aunts and buying property from them. I guess you'd say they loved me because they needed me, but you're right about being needed as a great stimulus to living, and they sure needed me. I have an idea you're going to add to that stimulus for me. Get on with it."

"Forgive me, Mr. Buster, for initiating the responses in you that I did, but I had to be sure I have your undivided attention. You know where I'm going with this, don't you?"

"Maybe I have a glimmer. Keep talking."

"To answer your question, I learned 'all that,' as you call it, right here in your town, on the ground. When I made my plans, I had to move quickly, and I'll get to that a little later. I flew down here two weeks ago, posed as a real estate developer, and looked at every map and most of the deeds in your courthouse, checked land-use plans and zoning requirements, considered every option, and flew back to Vancouver."

"And?"

"I consulted a planner, a landscape architect, and I am dedicated to seeing this little school attain its visions. With your help, we can attain it very soon."

"My help?"

"Yes, Mr. Buster. You own almost a city block of pure forest right here in the center of town, and I understand you have refused more than several lucrative offers for the property. Right?"

"So?"

"Mr. Buster, I am absolutely dedicated to expanding this school in tribute to the person in my life who has loved me the most sweetly and the most acceptingly. That way Dorothy Mookinfoos's life will be an inspiration for generations to come."

I waited. What sort of ego trip was I beholding?

"I propose to donate all of Dorothy's estate to this school, Mr. Buster."

"What's your hurry? You say she died two years ago, and all of a sudden you're flying back and forth, spying on people, and getting premature plans drawn up. I'm a little bewildered."

"Mr. Buster, three weeks ago I was told by the finest team of doctors I could find that I have pancreatic cancer, inoperable, untreatable, and with a probable lifespan left me of no more than three months. You can understand my haste."

"My God, son," I stammered, "I am so sorry." I started to rise.

He held up his hand to stop me. "No problem. We Esquimaux have more sang-froid than you Anglos. I watched my mother die with cancer and I watched Sister die with seizures. They were not defiant nor were they afraid. I am emulating them. We believe in fate."

I did not, at that moment, feel inclined to go there.

"You want to buy my property?"

"I intend to buy yours first, provided you agree to sell it. The fifty acres adjoining you is already for sale and will be easy. Also, there are several adjacent houses, the procurement of which should be no problem. At least, not to an attorney of your ability and your standing in the community. You are the key to the fulfillment of several dreams here."

"Some of the neighbors may raise a ruckus about this type of school next door to them, Bo. Presently the property is zoned residential, and the people in this town can turn a zoning hearing into a storming of the Bastille if they feel their turf is threatened."

He didn't move a hair.

"That's where you come in, Mr. Buster. Buy the houses before we announce the plans. You have a reputation for being eccentric and people will assume that, to quote a local I heard in the courthouse, 'He don't want all the land in the world, just that what joins him.'"

I smiled. "I know who he was talking about, and I can assure you it wasn't I. This can get pretty pricey, Bo, before it even gets off the ground. Some of those folks can really squawk."

"To quote Andrew Beven when opponents to socialized medicine asked him how he proposed to bring the doctors on board, 'We shall stuff their mouths with gold.'"

"And I presume that applies to me and my property?"

"To quote a character in one of your more graphic American movies, 'I'm going to make you an offer you can't refuse.'"

"And that is?"

"You've been listening to it. Think about a school and a domiciliary facility for this particular population located on a one-hundred-acre campus right squarely in the middle of town. It will change the entire perception of this town, which has apparently been so developed and exploited by progress and developers that it is rapidly becoming another small monument to materialism and greed."

I responded,

> Generations have trod, have trod, have trod;
> And all is seared with trade; bleared, smeared with toil;
> And wears man's smudge and shares man's smell—the soil
> Is bare now, nor can foot feel, being shod.

I had felt a little poetry might help this young man. Then be blessed if he didn't trump me.

"You know Hopkins, Mr. Buster?"

> But despite all this, Nature is never spent;
> There lives the dearest freshness deep down things;
> …Because the Holy Ghost over the bent
> World broods with warm breast, and ah! bright wings.

I mean, this young man had trumped every ace I held.

"Think about it, Mr. Buster. Just think about what your town would become a symbol for, all over the nation. 'Faith, hope, and charity, but the greatest of these is charity.' I don't have any heirs who need my money; so I'm writing a new will leaving all I have accrued to the school."

He hushed and I shut my eyes.

For God's sake, here I am in the twilight of a rather mediocre career and settling into the routine of a dull but comfortable dotage, and here comes a Cofield Eskimo to rattle my cage. The very idea!

I've worked my ass off for sixty years to get my woods fixed just like I want them: indeed, they have been the one enduring passion of my life, and he proposes opening them up to a bunch of feeble-minded kids. I'll never forget the advent of those children in this town. Every one of the first six students had little bitty heads, slanted eyes, and a tongue so thick they couldn't contain it behind their teeth. In the fall, winter, and early spring, every little snub nose was red as a cherry, and there were interlocking snail trails across chapped cheeks. It was not a pleasant sight, and I had considered going before the city council and requesting they not rezone that building right across the road from me as a school for a bunch of Mongolian idiots.

I remembered, however, that when I had built my house, that clapboard house had already been present for forty or fifty years and that a middle-aged idiot lived in a streetcar, of all things, right jamb up by the main house, where his parents lived. He drove his father's lawnmower all around town and some bleeding hearts actually paid him a quarter to cut their lawns. Agnes Walker, of course, paid him only fifteen cents.

Furthermore, he went into some sort of self-mutilating fit one day and crept to the back of my property and cut out one of his testicles. When it got infected and Dr. Hentz prescribed penicillin and hot tub baths, be blessed if they didn't treat him on their front porch, which faced my driveway. It took me ten days to get my driveway rerouted; I was not about to view that grossness every time I drove in and out of my woods. Since I had lived with that, I decided I didn't have a leg to stand on before the city council about the little school.

After about six months of grumbling, I decided to call the school's supervisor—pleasantly, of course, but very plainly and positively—to establish some actual rules of conduct. Aunt Palestine was still living, and I cajoled her into making a basket of teacakes for the kids.

What a shock, I remember. There was at least one teacher per child, plus the full-time administrative staff, and the kids were as quiet as any advanced class settling into a geometry examination; but these children were being taught how to eat, how to walk, how to pull their tongues back in, and how to say "thank you." They even had speech therapists working on the alphabet and phonics, and they had physiologists teaching them to walk with hands outstretched at arm's length, and every time a kid was successful in a task they carried on like he'd won an Olympic gold medal.

The teachers made me sit at a little table with the cookies while each child filed by, took one ("Only one, Joe, only one.") and then thanked me. Three of them insisted on hugging me, and I blocked out about the snail trails and thanked God I'd already taken my flu shot. One little girl pulled my head down and planted a loudly smacking kiss on my cheek, which as nearly as I can remember is the only time in my life that a child has kissed me.

When I left they all stood on the porch and waved, and be blessed if I didn't hear the teacher say, "Now, children, that is Mr. Holcombe and you must all remember that we do not go into his woods or on his property."

Bo is right—you feel like you've been to church and felt the Holy Spirit. He's also right about another thing—I've turned down some pretty extravagant offers for my land. But then I've never needed any money and never really spent much, except on my woods and pretty neckties. People would be astonished if they knew how much money I have in the bank and in stocks.

Now Bo Mookinfoos has come along and challenged me. I have enjoyed my cynicism and ability to see ulterior motives, but I've not been able to discover a single one in this young man's vision. Who does he think he is? Jesus? Or a Jesuit? I'd never run into more than two people in my life who had even heard of Gerard Manley Hopkins, and they weren't from around here.

That, of course, made me think of "Suffer little children to come unto me, and forbid them not; for of such is the Kingdom of Heaven," and that led to "the Kingdom of Heaven is within you," and "Sell all that you have and give to the poor." All of a sudden it seemed like a pleasant thing to provide a setting in nature for these afflicted children, and I could imagine some of them even being taught a little botany, ornithology, and horticulture, all of which had enriched my life; more than music, to tell you the truth; even-steven with poetry. Of course, New Doctor would have to be on call to treat poison ivy and insect stings, but that would be his problem, not mine. And for that I thanked God ahead of time.

All this time I kept my eyes shut, and Bo was perfectly immobile; I'd have heard the rustle of clothes if he had crossed his legs or shifted in his chair. Not many people his age are that sensitive and perceptive. He knew as much about silence as I did, and I wondered briefly if he had ever had psychotherapy.

Then here came John of Patmos into my mind, and I envisioned our transformed town, a new Jerusalem, let down from Heaven, so to speak, with a one-hundred-acre campus next to the courthouse and Main Street, all full of little children with grown-ups helping them, all of it right in my woods. Being of a practical bent, I even saw a security fence all the way around the property, both to keep the kids in and the deer out. I'd been intending to do that for years, just to protect my plants and flowers, but to tell the truth, I'd been too penurious to pay for it. A line from Millay popped up:

> ...Lord, I do fear
> Thou'st made the world too beautiful this year;
> My soul is all but out of me,—let fall
> No burning leaf; prithee, let no bird call.

That did it.

I opened my eyes and grunted. Be blessed if Bo hadn't been sitting with his eyes closed, too.

"Young Mookinfoos, let me get this straight. Provided you can secure the real estate, you propose to put forty million of Dorothy's money and forty million of your own into this project?"

"That is correct; but it's more like a hundred million total by now."

I whistled a little ditty. "For that, you cannot only build the facility but endow it in perpetuity."

"That is my hope, Mr. Buster."

I drew a deep breath. "Well, I'll be damned to eternal hell through the kitchen door and back again if I let a Cofield Eskimo get completely ahead of me. I can't match your contribution, but I'll give the school a quitclaim deed to my woods; I'd been wondering what to do with them anyhow. The Conservancy, Audubon Society, and Sierra Club have all been up front with me that they'd accept the property but sooner or later they'd sell it. You're on. And so am I."

Before he could say a word, I added, "And I'm changing my will like you. I've a few nieces and nephews to whom I need to leave a token pittance, but the rest of it goes into your trust fund for the school. It will surprise you how much it is."

"No, it won't, Mr. Buster."

"Well, it sure surprises the hell out of me," I retorted. "What do you propose to name the school, Bo? The current school is named after one of the charter members who died at age fourteen after having been mainstreamed into public schools successfully at age seven; the community is accustomed to that name and very supportive, and as you have demonstrated, it has international recognition through its Web site. I hesitate to change the name of the school itself."

"What about 'Cofield, Mookinfoos, Holcombe Annex'?"

"Over my dead body," I shot back, "and not even then, even if I have to write a paragraph to that effect in the contract."

"What's the problem?"

"Well, number one is that this is going to be at least ten times as large as the original in size and even larger in capability, so the term *annex* is deceptive. Secondly, one side of the property already faces on Cofield Street which was named that because it went to your great-great-grandfather's homestead and not in recognition of any philanthropy on the part of your ancestors, particularly not your grandfather. Your dad had him pegged pretty accurately.

"Third, I don't want my name singled out for recognition, and from what I've seen of you, I don't think you do either. Yours is the most unselfish and therefore unegotistical magnanimity I have ever witnessed or even heard of, and it must have come from your mother's side."

"You're right about the names, Mr. Buster, and also my mama, but it seems to me that you, yourself, are being as magnanimous as anyone I've ever heard of. What do you suggest?"

I shut my eyes again and he became very still once more. I peeped out of one eye and both of his eyes were closed.

Could this boy possibly be praying?

In my office?

To my knowledge, it had never happened before. Perhaps it should have. I thought of Betty Talmadge who had said, "Just don't do it out loud."

After some intensive concentration, I sat bolt upright. "Bo, I've got it! See what you think. Over the entrance arch we'll put in very small letters the name of the school as it is. Then underneath, dominating the sign in big letters, we'll have 'Down Town Campus.' What do you think of that?"

It didn't take him a minute. That boy is quick. "I like it. It proclaims the location, the continuity, and best of all the purpose. It is primarily for Down Syndrome students. Every time anyone says it, he'll become more conscious of the condition, and it is truthfully right in the center of town.

"Down Town. I really, really like it."

"Don't throw a third *really* in there, boy, or you'll topple one of my impressions about you."

"Pardon?"

"Never mind. We'll talk about that later. But, Bo, this entire little city may become known as 'Down Town.' I've always thought this was a very special place to live and to observe. It would be a real thrill if outsiders started calling the whole place 'Down Town.' Think about it!"

"I did. That's why I said I really like it. Why did you tell me not to use 'really' three in a row?"

"It goes back a long way, Bo. To your grandmother, in fact, who had a very distinctive and peculiar speech pattern."

"Tell me about it."

"We don't have time. Both of us have to get terribly busy if we're going to accomplish all you're planning before that cancer gets you."

"Is it important?"

"Boy, what isn't important? In a small town? Where everybody knows everybody else? And where every living soul is an individual character? No matter what is happening in the outside world that is horrible and terrible, the people in our town, and I suspect all other towns, find what is going on here day to day more gripping and amusing. It anchors one's sense of place in the universe."

"But I want to know."

"I tell you what I'll do. You go back to Canada and get all your end of this mountain of paperwork done, and I'll do the same on this end. In the meantime, I'll write a journal for you about this town and the people in it. I'll write in it every night before I go to bed and I promise I'll have it before you die."

"Will you confide about the Cofields?"

"Will I? I'll start the journal with, 'Whenever Major Cofield went down town, we people on the pavement stood and looked at him.' How's that for openers?"

"That's from 'Richard Cory' by Robinson, isn't it? I like it, and right off it mentions 'down town.' You're a wizard, Mr. Buster."

"I don't think so, but I've sure had a good life in this town. It's a wonderful place, and I've seen a lot I've never mentioned."

"The last line says, 'Richard Cory one calm summer night went home and put a bullet through his head.' You're not trying to tell me my great-great-grandfather killed himself, are you?"

"Not to worry. Some of the Cofields may have come close to being victims of homicide, but never suicide."

"Could you answer me just one question about my family before you write the journal, Mr. Buster?"

"Ask it before I give you an answer."

"The last time I was here, I took a lunch break from the courthouse and found the cemetery."

"Yes?" My head started whirling.

"On my grandfather's grave there was a Maxwell House coffee can with plastic flowers in it. It seemed inappropriate."

I hesitated. "Bo, let me tell you it is very appropriate."

"Why is it there?"

"Because not a single one of his children has been back to this town since they buried him and got their inheritance. And they had hardly showed their faces for ten years before he died. The oldest one, I hear, has bought a vineyard in France and moved there. It produces a wine of very creditable repute among connoisseurs called 'Le Vin de l'Enfant Jesus'; getting its name, I am told, from the archbishop who tasted the first bottle a century and a half ago and said, 'It's so smooth it goes down like velvet breeches on the Baby Jesus.' I tried a bottle once, although it's terribly expensive, and thought it an apt analysis. His inheritance will probably keep Will in style for his lifetime.

"George took his inheritance and invested it, I understand, in four successive wives, all of whom he persuaded to sign air-tight prenuptial agreements; so he should be fixed for life.

"Your aunt is the truly greedy one of the siblings. She invested all her eighty million in stocks, divorced her husband, has an apartment in New York on Park Avenue, and spends all her interest on diamonds. I'll tell you straight out, she'll never get enough money to cover herself in them; her weight could bankrupt the Aga Khan."

"What's that got to do with the coffee can?"

"Well, Bo, someone who gives a rat's ass ought to decorate your grandfather's grave."

"Mr. Buster, is that you?"

"Yes, Bo, I cannot lie to you. I change the flowers every month."

"Why are they plastic?"

"Given your grandfather's tastes, they are appropriate, and Alvin supplies them at a discount, which would truly please your grandfather. Now, we had both better get to work. This is the most exciting venture I've had in sixty years."

"Me, too."

"It's got all that Swinburne crap out of your head, hasn't it?"

"Right. But one more thing, Mr. Buster. Why the coffee can?"

I sighed. Writing him a journal was going to be easier than facing him while I recalled facts. "Because, Bo, the only other container which would have been appropriate would have been a leaking commode, and the cemetery committee wouldn't tolerate that. Even in our town." I paused. "And certainly not in Down Town. Wait for the journal, Bo."

I sat down and closed my eyes again. Bo was standing, but if he moved a muscle, I could not detect it. I began considering the strange confluence of events that had resulted in this moment. I wanted to tell Bo that the coffee can was a test of the verity of resurrection of the body, for if Betsill Cofield came out of that grave intact and touched that coffee can, it would turn to solid gold and King Midas would know he'd made it into heaven.

Then, of course, I had to face the fact that if Betsill Cofield had not dedicated his life to accumulating money, Ephraim Mookinfoos would not have been able to endorse this vision. Nor, to be perfectly honest, would I have been able to participate. After all, it was Betsill's bank stock that had been the foundation of my not inconsiderable fortune.

And all these years I had been judging him, even sneering at him. Of a sudden, Oscar Hosey's proposed bumper sticker came to mind. I was forced to apply it personally: *Get your head out of your ass, Aloysius!* I thought. I began to look at myself.

If my brothers had nicknamed me Al instead of Buster, would I have been different?

If I hadn't learned the piano?

If I hadn't loved poetry?

If I had played baseball as a child?

Why have I always held a jar of mayonnaise against Toor?

What if I had married Beatrice? How much liquor would I have drunk?

In the space of one morning, I had changed from being an observer of life into being an enthusiastic participant. All because of a spiritual young millionaire who would be dead in three months. And him full of Cofield genes and money.

I swear to this day that I heard a distant voice intone, "My ways are not your ways." Without realizing it, I muttered aloud, "*Mea culpa*. Forgive me, Lord."

Bo brought me back to the present. "Did you say something, Mr. Buster?"

I felt tears swelling in my eyes, spilling over from a full heart.

"Damn right I did," I said. "*Domino Gloria!* Now, I'll tell you this: 'Daylight's burning and the field is white unto the harvest.' We've both got work to do. Get out of here, boy, and I'll see you in three weeks."

"Thank you for everything, Mr. Buster. I'll be back loaded for bear." He paused. "You really are eccentric, sir. You know that, don't you? Do you think I will ever be able to understand you?"

*   *   *

Now do you understand me?

*   *   *

Sometimes I don't understand myself.

*   *   *

Am I a sounding gong and a tinkling cymbal? Not on your life.

*   *   *

Be as proud of your Cofield heritage, Bo, as you are of the Inuit side. Stick with Milton and Tennyson; forget about Swinburne; don't judge Oscar Hosey too harshly. I'm convinced that he and I both know that God is Love.

And so do you, Bo Mookinfoos. Obviously.

These are two great mysteries in the Life Experience: why *not* lump them together.

This is the best town in a wonderful world.

I promised you I'd concentrate on the Cofields for you; but there are hundreds more people who have made the town what it is.

*   *   *

Again, *vaya con dios*.

*   *   *

Down Town!

*   *   *

AMEN.